MIRIAM'S QUILT
APPLE LAKE AMISH
BOOK THREE

JENNIFER BECKSTRAND

SIX ROSES PUBLISHING

Published by Six Roses Publishing, an imprint of Jennifer Beckstrand Publishing

Centerville, UT 84014

jenniferbeckstrand.com

Miriam's Quilt

Copyright © 2013 by Jennifer Beckstrand

ISBN 978-1-964246-01-7

All rights reserved. No part of this publication may be reproduced in any form, except for brief quotations in printed reviews, without prior written permission of the publisher.

All scripture quotations are taken from the King James Version of the Bible.

This is a work of fiction. Any resemblances to actual people or events are purely coincidental.

To my sisters Allison Sharp, Andrea Gappmayer, Juliet Sanders, Melinda Boyack, and Alesha Thompson, all incredibly talented and accomplished women who make me laugh and know how to play a mean game of Nertz.

CHAPTER ONE

Seth Lambright couldn't stand the sight of Miriam Bontrager. It didn't matter that her eyes were the shade of lavender spring crocuses or that her skin was surely soft as silk. He still felt that familiar twinge of irritation when he saw her at the auction.

Miriam didn't even acknowledge Seth when she came to the stable with her *dat*, John. Oblivious to the unkind feelings Seth harbored for his daughter, John was his usual amiable self, smiling and complimenting Seth generously on his horses.

"The chestnut is a beauty, ain't not, Miriam?" John said.

Miriam simply nodded while looking about.

Seth followed her lead and attempted to ignore her as she stood a few steps apart with her boyfriend, Ephraim. A stranger would never guess that Miriam and Seth attended *gmayna* or church services in the same district and had ever since they were babies. Nor would anyone ever believe that they'd gone to the same primary school. Even though he was four years older, she knew him well enough, but she still treated him as if he were invisible.

For one irrational second, Seth was tempted to insist that Miriam actually make eye contact with him instead of offering the indifferent pride that always got his hackles up. But ultimately he wanted to make a sale, not a point, so he patted his horse on the neck and said, "She's a pretty one. Strong and gentle. A perfect riding horse." Then he couldn't resist. "You like to ride, don't you, Miriam?"

She shrugged and rubbed her hand tenderly along the grain of the mare's coat. Seth was surprised when she nuzzled her face against the mare's nose.

"She is a *gute* rider when she has the time," said Ephraim, her self-appointed mouthpiece and probably soon-to-be fiancé.

It seemed Seth would not be privileged to hear Miriam's voice today.

John examined the mare with the careful eye of a husbandman, running his fingers along the muscles in her legs and knees, lifting her feet and checking the hooves, prying open her mouth and inspecting the teeth. "Superior horse," John finally said, folding his arms and standing back to take a look at the animal as a whole.

John looked at his daughter. "This is the one I want. She don't move when you saddle her, and me and Seth took her out this morning. Smooth gait."

Miriam narrowed her eyes and suddenly paid closer attention. "Are you sure, Dat? Seth is just a beginning trainer." She walked around the horse and performed the same inspection John had just completed.

While trying not to be offended by her lack of faith in his abilities, Seth couldn't help but be impressed at the same time. She knew what to look for, how to properly assess the value of a horse. She examined the mare head-on, looking to see if it favored a lead and studying the ears and eyes for illness.

"How old?" she said.

"Two years," said Seth. "One of the first I bred."

"I will admit...," John said, "three years ago I thought your horse-breeding idea far-fetched, considering how young you were and how you only had that old stable. But I've heard good reports of you, and the quality of these animals speaks for itself. You have a gift."

"*Denki*," Seth said, bursting with pride but keeping his satisfaction contained in a proper show of humility by lowering his eyes and lacing his fingers together.

"May I take her out?" Miriam said.

Ephraim took off his hat and swished his fingers through his hair. "We don't have the time to spare today."

Miriam knit her brows together. "Oh. Very well. If you think we are short on time, never mind."

"You've got to ride a horse before you even think of buying it, Ephraim," John said. "*Cum*, Miriam. Try her out."

Miriam looked doubtfully at Ephraim and then at her father. Seth had the mare saddled before the boyfriend said another word.

The mare didn't move a muscle as Miriam deftly mounted and situated herself. She raised an eyebrow in appreciation.

"This one ain't bothered by the noise," John said.

Miriam nodded.

"She doesn't spook," Seth said. "Real calm." He walked the mare out of the stable and into the sunlight.

"Good eyesight," Miriam said.

Seth released the reins and Miriam directed the horse to the corral used for staging livestock during the auction. He rested his hands on top of the barrier fence that ran the perimeter of the corral and watched as Miriam walked the horse around the yard. When Miriam prodded the mare into a trot and then a canter, the animal had no problem switching gaits. Seth couldn't keep a smile from his face. He had trained her well.

Miriam began turning the horse around imaginary obstacles. She'd have no trouble there. The mare obeyed the slightest pressure from the reins and legs.

Miriam proved herself a superior rider. Just one more thing she did better than anyone else in the community. She must be so proud of herself.

After about ten minutes, Miriam rode the horse back toward Seth and the stable. She leaned over and patted the mare's neck, cooing words that Seth could not decipher.

He relaxed his shoulders and released his grip on the fence. He hadn't realized he'd been clinging to it so tightly.

Once she reached the gate, Miriam dismounted, strode to Seth, and handed him the reins without raising her eyes to his face. "I hardly had to touch the reins to slow her down. Very light in the mouth. For a beginner, you've done a nice job with the training. Good for you."

Seth clenched his teeth. Wonderful. She had gone from standoffish to condescending in a matter of seconds.

"I will tell Dat I like her. Matthew Eicher has some gute horses too, but I know you need the money."

Seth tried to keep a straight face. This was what she thought of him—poor Seth Lambright, the motherless boy who depended on the kindness of his neighbors to make a living?

Give me strength.

Miriam smiled. "Dat says it is gute to invest in a boy like you, just starting out in your own business."

"Don't do me any favors."

Miriam probably wouldn't have paid heed to his reply except that he couldn't keep the bitter edge out of his voice. She stopped short and frowned. "What do you mean by that?"

"If you think you're too good to own a horse trained by me, please feel free to buy elsewhere."

Miriam's mouth gaped and her eyes went wide with indignation. "I do not think that."

Seth clamped his mouth shut and marched for the safety of the stable. He should have held his tongue. Wasn't any skin off his teeth if Miriam Bontrager was stuck-up. He shouldn't have let her get to him like that. But today was a milestone, his first auction as a seller, a day of accomplishment for all those months of hard work of getting his horses ready. And Miriam Bontrager had to dampen his mood. He wished she'd never stuck her lightly freckled nose into the stable.

When he neglected to reply, Miriam pulled his arm and stopped him up short. "I don't think I'm better than you."

Why had he opened his big mouth? "I am joking," he said. "I'm a little tense today yet."

She trained her eyes on him. "*Nae*, you are not joking. Why do you assume you know what I am thinking?"

"I don't."

" 'If you think you're too good to own a horse trained by me, please feel free to buy elsewhere,' " she repeated to him, with the same irritated emphasis he'd used. "What have I done to offend you, that you judge me so harshly?"

With no desire to be cornered by Miriam Bontrager, he gripped the mare's reins, lengthened his stride, and scowled in any direction but hers.

She stepped in front of him and stared until he wanted to turn to dust. "Tell me."

He paused, ran his hand across his forehead, and looked for an escape route.

She didn't budge. "You don't like me." This realization seemed to take her by surprise. She lifted an eyebrow in disbelief. "Why don't you like me?"

Her arrogance and maddening self-assurance goaded him past endurance. "You are a snob, Miriam Bontrager," he said.

Whatever she expected him to say, it wasn't that. With her mouth open wide enough to catch flies, she turned to stone, and Seth led the horse around her and back to the stable.

She didn't follow.

Who does Seth Lambright think he is?

Miriam cocked her arm back, grunted, and threw another rock as hard as she could into the field behind the stable. She'd always had the best arm of all the girls. She looked down at her feet. There were plenty more rocks to throw to express her utter frustration.

Why did that boy have to go and ruin a perfectly wonderful day? Ephraim had bought her a frozen lemonade, Macie Glick had told her she liked the color of her dress, and her quilt had sold for three hundred dollars at the auction.

Three hundred dollars! She'd need less than half of that to buy more fabric, and the rest she could send off to the Haiti Mission Fund. Surely no other girl in Apple Lake had ever donated so much. *Mamm* would be pleased.

And then Seth Lambright had to go and wreck her entire day. At times like this, Miriam hated that she put so much stock in what other people thought about her—even someone like Seth, whom she shouldn't care a snit about.

She raised her hand to heave another rock in the direction of the cornfield but thought better of it. The tiny cornstalks, barely six inches tall, didn't deserve her abuse.

"Miri, what are you doing?"

Ephraim leaned against the outside wall of the stable with his arms folded, smiling in amusement. Ephraim stood an average height with a shock of curly golden hair and a smile that always sent a warm sensation tingling into her fingers. When he smiled, he showed all his teeth, and Miriam loved the little gap between his bottom front ones. "Getting some baseball practice in? Or throwing a tantrum?" he said, still laughing at her with his eyes.

Miriam threw down the three rocks in her other hand and brushed her hands on her apron. "Throwing a tantrum."

"Better here than in the stable where everybody can see you, I guess."

He came closer but didn't touch her. Even though they were madly in love, Ephraim thought it best that there be no touching until after the wedding. Miriam rejoiced to have such a careful boyfriend.

"What are you throwing a tantrum about?"

"Do you know what Seth Lambright said to me?"

"I have no idea."

"He said I am a snob."

Ephraim raised his eyebrows then threw back his head and laughed.

"It's not funny, Ephraim."

"Yes, it is. Seth Lambright doesn't know anything about anything."

"Why would he say that about me?"

Ephraim waved his hand as if swatting a fly. "Don't worry about it. He's jealous."

"You think so?"

"He had a crazy mother who took her own life. His dat makes almost nothing at the plant and misses services all the time. Not to mention, his sister is jumping the fence and going to college next year. His family is a mess. You, on the other hand, have a perfect family that everyone looks up to. Your dat is a minister and owns all that property. You're well-off, as far as Amish people go."

Miriam looked away. "We give a lot to charity and the church."

"Of course you do. Seth Lambright is jealous, plain and simple." Ephraim tucked a lock of his hair behind his ear. "Why does it bother you? Instead, you should count your blessings that you aren't one of them. I thank the good Lord every day that I was born into my family, not an unfortunate one like Seth Lambright's."

"He says I think I'm too good for him."

"Don't let him make you feel ashamed about that. Some families *are* better than others. His dat will never be bishop or even minister, sure as you're born."

Miriam wasn't quite as pleased with Ephraim's reasoning as she wanted to be. She almost contradicted him. Weren't all people equal in the sight of *Gotte*? Surely Seth Lambright, who kept to himself and had lost his poor mother five years ago, was as good as Ephraim Neuenschwander, a minister's son. Wasn't he?

"I don't want to talk about Seth Lambright," Ephraim said. "I want to talk about my plans for a blissful future. Two and a half years from now in November sounds like a wonderful time for a wedding, don't you think?"

Miriam tried to hide her disappointment behind a wan smile. "But you said we would marry next year. I'm almost nineteen years old."

"I overheard Bishop Schwartz and my dat speaking of it yesterday. Young people rush into marriage, letting their eagerness overtake their self-control. The bishop specifically mentioned your cousin Rebecca, who married only two weeks after getting engaged."

"Some would say they are so much in love, they just

couldn't wait to be together." In fact, it was Miriam's dream of an ideal love story. She'd stayed up until midnight for two weeks straight to make Rebecca's wedding quilt.

"You wouldn't believe how many tongues waggled because of it," Ephraim said. "The bishop said that young people should carefully plan and prepare before taking such a big step."

Miriam hesitated. Rebecca and Levi's sudden decision had started gossip in Apple Lake by people who were appalled that they had broken with long-standing traditions. Miriam would hate to have her marriage cast in a bad light from the beginning. "I would not want to go against the bishop's counsel. If you think waiting is best—"

"I do. And so does my dat. It will give us more time to earn money for a house. Bishop Schwartz says a couple should be financially stable."

"That is sound advice. I will make more quilts to sell."

The extra time would also allow her to make the most beautiful quilt of all for her almost-fiancé. They wouldn't be officially engaged for more than two years. Miriam let a sigh escape her lips.

"We could make thousands of dollars from your quilts."

Miriam thought of the Haiti Mission Fund. Maybe she could set aside a little of that money for her marriage. As the bishop had said, she and Ephraim must carefully plan and prepare for their life together. A life of bliss and love and financial stability.

CHAPTER TWO

"Mamm?"

Miriam came through the door after a long but pleasant day of work and hung her black bonnet on the hook. Next to the crisp spring air outdoors, the warmth of the house felt like suddenly being wrapped in a blanket.

Surely no one in the world had a better job than she did. Four days a week, she sold and fussed over quilts at Martha Mullet's quilt shop in Apple Lake. Martha's shop was a tourist mecca with over two thousand square feet of rows upon rows of quilts—and not just average, ordinary, assembly-line quilts either. Martha's shop featured the finest one-of-a-kind designs and meticulously hand-stitched items the Amish had to offer. The most expensive quilt, hanging on the back wall in all its king-sized glory, cost over two thousand dollars.

On the front of that quilt grew a three-dimensional garden with flowers of every shape and color. Vines twined up a pole to a little birdhouse with a cardinal perched on the roof, and Miriam could almost hear the melody of his cheery tune. The quilt maker, Miriam Raber of Holmes County, Ohio, had signed her name on a small patch of fabric on the back of the quilt. Miriam loved that she shared a name with a woman who crafted a two-thousand-dollar quilt. Someday she dreamed of making such a quilt. Ephraim would burst his buttons.

"Is that you, Miriam?" she heard Mamm call from upstairs.

Miriam skipped up the stairs and found her mamm in the little boys' room, making up beds with her brothers Callie and Isaac.

"Pull it out, Callie," Mamm said. "Make a square corner. Miriam, how was work?"

"Wonderful-gute. We sold seven quilts," Miriam said, helping Isaac with his pillowcase.

Callie pulled the edge of the sheet from under the mattress and fanned it up and down. "I can't do the corners right."

"I'll help," Miriam said. "Tuck it under the end of the bed first. Good. Now pull out the corner. Make a little fold. *Jah*, like that. And under."

Mamm examined Callie's perfectly mitered sheet corner. "Very good, Callie."

Miriam mussed Callie's hair and pulled him in for a kiss on the cheek. He dodged her lips and giggled.

"Do you want me to start supper?" Miriam said.

"There is meat loaf in the icebox and potatoes," Mamm said. "I was about to stick them in the stove. But will you check on your sister? She looked out of sorts when she came in from work today."

Miriam seized Callie around the shoulders and gave him a big kiss on the cheek.

"Hey!" he protested.

Miriam simply smiled and waltzed out the door. At nearly nine years old, soon Callie wouldn't allow kisses at all. She had to steal them while she could.

Miriam was the oldest child left at home. Her two older brothers, Marvin and David, were married and both lived in Ohio. Marvin had two children, and David had married in January. An eight-year gap fell between twins Yost and Susie and little brothers Callie, Isaac, and Raymond. "You take them as they come," Mamm had always said.

Miriam knocked softly on Susie's bedroom door.

"Who is it?" said her sister.

"Are you alright?"

"*Cum reu.*"

A pair of twin beds sat in the small bedroom Miriam shared with Susie. Burgundy-and-navy Log Cabin quilts covered each bed. Miriam and Susie had made the quilts together four years ago. Miriam still loved to walk into the room and let the rich colors saturate her senses.

Susie must have just washed her hair. She sat on the edge of the bed clutching a towel and letting her hair drip onto her clothes and the bed. Her eyes were red and swollen, and she sniffled at regular five-second intervals while staring at the opposite wall.

Miriam sat next to her on the bed and put her arm around Susie's damp shoulder. "You are ice cold, Susie," she said.

Susie tightened her fist around her towel and kept staring at the same spot on the wall.

Miriam put her hand up to Susie's forehead. No fever, but she did look a little green around the gills. "Are you feeling chilled?"

Susie's answer came out like a groan. "I wanted to feel clean," she said. Tears flowed anew down her face.

"Cum," Miriam said, taking her hand. "Dry off your hair and get into your nightgown. I am sending you right to bed."

Miriam's decisive tone shook Susie out of her foggy mood. She stood and wrapped the towel around her hair. Miriam went to the bureau and pulled out Susie's flannel nightgown she wore during the cold winter months. Susie mechanically raised her arms, and Miriam helped her pull the nightgown over her head While Susie stood motionless, Miriam took the towel from her head and pressed strands of Susie's hair between folds of the towel until it was sufficiently dry.

She directed Susie to sit on the bed and began to comb through her sister's long golden tresses. Susie sat speechless with her spine rigid, her shoulders pulled back. She made no acknowledgment of Miriam's presence except a light hand on Miriam's knee.

"Do you remember when Callie got gum in his hair and we had to shave most of his hair off?"

Susie nodded.

"*Mamm* almost cried when all those beautiful blond curls fell to the floor. Your hair is like his—the color of sunshine." Miriam deftly fashioned Susie's hair into a braid. "Now," she said, "lie back and try to rest. I will make you some chicken soup."

Susie squeezed Miriam's hand before she could pull away. "Miriam." An idea seemed to flicker in her eyes but died. "Denki."

"You are welcome. I want you to feel better."

With urgency, Susie pulled Miriam toward her. "Miriam, have you ever done something really, really bad?"

Miriam went cold, and her mind began to race. Would could Susie have done that she seemed to regret this deeply?

"We all do things we wish we hadn't," she finally said.

"Not you, Miriam. You are perfect." The sincerity in her voice made Miriam want to blush.

"*Ach*, no. None is perfect but God. You should have heard my thoughts on Saturday for a certain ill-mannered young man at the auction."

"You are perfect, Miriam." Susie turned her head away and looked out the window. "I wish I were you."

"Why would you ever wish to have my stick-out ears? Or my freckles? You are the prettiest girl in our family."

Susie shook her head and started to cry again. "I wish I were you."

Miriam rubbed her hand up and down Susie's arm. "What is wrong?"

"I—I—I cannot say."

"Susie, tell me." Susie's idea of wickedness was taking more than her share of butterscotch pie at supper. She was probably feeling ashamed for having an unkind thought toward one of her brothers.

A tear fell to Susie's lap. "I am so tired."

"Rest. Chicken soup will take a half hour."

"Will you put paprika in it?"

"Of course."

In the kitchen, Mamm popped the meat loaf into the belly of the wood cookstove. Miriam pulled a saucepan from the cupboard. "Susie is not feeling well," she said. "I put her right to bed."

Mamm furrowed her brow. "Three days in a row now. I told her she should have stayed home from work." Mamm wrapped the potatoes in foil, stuck them into the stove with the meat loaf, and went upstairs to check on Susie.

Miriam chopped carrots and celery and set them to boiling. Then she picked last night's leftover chicken from the bones and set the meat ready to plop into the water when the vegetables cooked soft.

Hearing a soft knock at the front door, she left Susie's soup to simmer and headed to the great room.

Miriam opened the door to a stone-faced Seth Lambright

standing on the narrow porch. He seemed as uncomfortable about seeing her as she was him.

The corners of his lips turned down slightly. "Your dat said he would leave money for me."

No "Nice to see you today, Miriam," or "How are you?" The boy's conversation skills were seriously lacking. Of course, he'd made it very clear on Saturday that he'd rather converse with anybody but her.

"You're a snob, Miriam Bontrager."

Why would he scold her, when they'd hardly ever spoken?

A small envelope lay beside the mail on the small table in the great room with Seth Lambright written across it.

Miriam snatched it from the table and shoved it into Seth's hand.

"Denki," he said, stuffing the envelope into his pocket. Before she could shut the door on him, he said, "Your dat wants to buy you a horse as a wedding present. The money is a down payment. I have two mares about to deliver. Do you want to come over sometime and pick a foal?"

The horse wasn't even born yet? How did Dat know she wouldn't need a horse for another two years? Ephraim and Dat must have talked behind her back. The thought irritated her like an itchy collar. Her marriage plans were personal. How could Ephraim reveal something that important to her dat without consulting her first?

Seth waited for her to answer, and the corners of his mouth dropped farther. "You don't have to make an excuse for my benefit. If you don't want to come, don't come. I can choose the foal for you. And in spite of what you think, I know enough about horses to pick a gute one." Indignation smoldered in his coal-gray eyes, and he turned on his heels and marched down the steps.

"I wasn't going to make an excuse," she said, chasing him down the steps. "I wasn't even thinking such a thing."

"Don't bother smoothing things over. I already know how you feel about me."

"Stop right there," she said, raising her voice to a level she seldom used except to call her brothers from the pasture for supper.

Still frowning, he squared his broad shoulders and faced her. He stood tall, considerably taller than Ephraim, so he towered over Miriam like a sycamore.

His height did not impress her. "Tell me what I have done to deserve your dislike."

"Why do you care?"

"Because...I'm a person who... I try to be nice to everybody." She blurted out exactly what she thought. "Everybody likes me."

"And you are astounded that I don't."

She knit her brows together. "I—I suppose so."

"It is unfair to blame you for my own weakness. I know I shouldn't, but I get riled up when you look down your nose at me."

Miriam lifted her chin. "Maybe you are bitter because everybody else has it so much better than you do."

He shook his head. "That is exactly what I mean. I do not think everybody has it better than I do. *You* are the one who thinks everyone has it better than I do."

"I didn't mean—"

"Yes, you did." He folded his arms across his chest. "You watch my family from a distance, feeling sorry for our misfortunes but staying far enough away that our bad influence doesn't rub off on you. You don't even dare sit by my sister at *gmay*. It is primary school all over again."

Miriam pursed her lips. "I have never shown anything but compassion for your family."

"Oh, jah, you look down from your high-and-mighty perch—as if you are doing me the biggest favor in the world just by acknowledging me."

Miriam remembered her conversation with Ephraim and felt her face get hot. "It sounds like you do not need my compassion. You have plenty of self-pity."

"I hope I am past my own pity, but I cannot abide yours."

Again he tried to escape, and she darted into his path, determined to talk him out of his dislike. "When your mamm felt poorly, our family brought supper to your house every Wednesday night for two months."

"Then why did you never set foot in our house?"

Miriam clenched her fists. "I came every Wednesday."

"You stood at the front door and handed food to my sister."

Miriam wanted to deny it, but she stopped short, unable to recall ever seeing the inside of the Lambrights' home.

"Why didn't you come into our house?"

"I don't remember." Miriam stepped closer and narrowed her eyes. "You are holding bad feelings for something that happened five years ago?"

"Last month your cousin Rebecca had you and me coupled up for her wedding."

Miriam's heart thumped in embarrassment. "How did you know that?"

"Levi let me look at the list the day before. But then you must have seen the list too, because the next day we weren't coupled up anymore."

"I asked her to put me with Adam Yoder because he is so shy. I wanted to help him out of his shell a bit."

"Your brother Yost and my sister Laura were coupled on Rebecca's list. But that changed by the time of the wedding too. It seems you don't want any of the Lambrights associating with your family."

Shame rendered Miriam speechless. There was no way to defend herself. She *had* asked Rebecca to change the couples for the wedding. And she hadn't done it because of Adam Yoder's shyness. She'd worried what people would think of her if she were coupled with Seth. And Yost? She had wanted him to be coupled with JoAnn Kiem, the deacon's daughter.

She had to go on the offensive before he saw the truth of his words in her eyes. "If all you want to do is insult me, don't come here again."

Seth studied her face and slumped his shoulders in surrender. "I am sorry," he said, shaking his head. "You are right. I have held this grudge when I should have forgiven. I can't control your actions. I can only control my own, and I should know better. Forgive me for offending you." He kicked the dirt at his feet and turned away from her. "You can still come see the foal, if you like."

She watched him ride away on his beautiful chestnut horse, outrage warring with embarrassment inside her.

"I can't control your actions. I can only control my own, and I should know better."

The disrespect! Talking as if he were a martyr made to suffer at Miriam Bontrager's hands—*"Oh, surely I must forgive Miriam. Her nature makes it impossible for her to ever change. She doesn't know any better."*

She seriously considered staying home from the gathering tonight. She didn't want Ephraim to see her so angry.

But the sting of Seth's accusations overshadowed her anger. Was she the proud girl Seth accused her of being? Her conscience weighed upon her like a full bucket of milk; there was no denying that she'd regarded Seth Lambright and his family with a sense of superiority.

Did other people think her as prideful as well?

The very thought sent her marching to the house. The screen door slammed behind her as she rolled up her sleeves, pulled a bag of noodles from the cupboard, and poured its contents into the soup. While the noodles cooked, she opened a can of pumpkin and whipped up three loaves of pumpkin bread to put into the stove when the meat loaf finished cooking.

While dinner baked, Miriam ladled the soup with extra paprika into a bowl and took it to Susie's room. Susie lay back on her pillow with her eyes open. She sat up when Miriam came in.

"Denki, Miriam. You are so kind."

Miriam laid the tray over Susie's lap. "I am not kind. I just told Seth Lambright to never come to our house again."

"The horse boy?"

"He said I am a snob. It made me so mad, I almost closed the door on him."

Susie caught her breath, and her mouth fell open. "A snob? How could anyone say that about you? I never would have thought that Seth Lambright could be so mean."

Susie's indignation cheered Miriam considerably.

"Next time he comes over," said Susie, "I will give him a stern talking to."

"You'll do no such thing."

"Remember in grade school when Davie Shirk stole my lunch and threw it in the mud?"

"Jah."

"Yost and his friends helped me attack him with snowballs after school."

"I chastised you both," Miriam said.

"Jah," Susie said. "If Miriam won't do it, then I know I

shouldn't do it either. Seth Lambright is safe from me. Even if he deserves a few snowballs."

CHAPTER
THREE

Miriam's steps echoed through the quiet house as she tiptoed into the kitchen after returning home from the gathering. Despite her determination not to go, Ephraim had showed up at the door at exactly six fifteen and wouldn't hear of her staying home.

Yost sat at the table eating a piece of pumpkin bread.

"Gute bread," he said, motioning to her with his butter-covered slice.

"I got angry today," Miriam said. After Seth riled her up this afternoon, Miriam had made three loaves in her indignation. She took one loaf to the Dennings, her *Englisch* neighbors across the road, and Mrs. Denning told her she was the nicest young lady in the neighborhood.

The nicest young lady. Take that, Seth Lambright.

"You cook when you're angry?"

"And when I'm not." Miriam cut herself a slice of bread, poured two glasses of milk, and sat at the table with Yost. Yost was Susie's twin brother and, at seventeen, had grown to almost six feet.

"I thought you said you would come to the gathering tonight," Miriam said.

Yost ran his thumb up and down his glass. "I had other stuff I had to do."

"Like what? Clipping your toenails?"

The corners of Yost's mouth turned up. "Plucking nose hairs." He took a swig of milk. "How was the gathering?"

"Abner Yutzy conked Lizzie Zook on the head in volleyball."

"He's such a show-off," said Yost, "just because he is tall. I never like to be on his team. He is a ball hog, plain and simple. Thinks he is the only one who can get the ball over the net."

"He spiked it so hard that Lizzie didn't have time to duck. She had to sit out the rest of the game."

"Did you tell him to take it gentle?"

"We tried. But during the third game, little Sue Lyn Sensenig hit the ball harder than I've ever seen a girl hit it. I think she surprised herself. It flew straight up into Abner's face and whacked him squarely in the nose."

Yost laughed. "Did he cry?"

"Like a calf stuck in a fence. He might have broke it. It bled something crazy."

"Serves him right," Yost said, finishing his last bite. "That boy would spike the ball at his own *mammi* to win."

"Don't say such things, Yost. It's uncharitable." Miriam sighed and arched her back to stretch the tight muscles. She had rocked the Weavers' new grandson for practically half the gathering. He was cutting teeth and as fussy as a grumpy bear. Miriam had taken the baby so his mamm could pass out lemonade, and then she cuddled and bounced and entertained him while everybody sang. Ephraim wasn't happy having to share Miriam's attentions with a baby, but Miriam was determined. Keeping the baby happy proved to be exhausting, but a less thoughtful girl would have given up after a few minutes.

"*Inasmuch as ye have done it unto one of the least of these my brethren, ye have done it unto me.*"

To top off her display of humility after the gathering, Miriam did dishes and swept the floor while the Weavers took down chairs. Anyone noticing would see what a helpful, modest girl she was.

If he saw her behavior, a certain young man would have to eat his words.

Miriam growled inwardly. What did she care of Seth Lambright? Just as Ephraim said, he didn't know anything about anything.

"I wonder how Susie is feeling."

Yost took a last drink and glanced at Miriam. "What would you think if I bought a car?"

"A car? You cannot afford a car."

"What if I could?"

Miriam curled her lips into the funny little expression she gave her brother when he said something ridiculous. "You can't, so forget it. Everybody knows that boys who buy cars are trouble, looking to jump the fence. Don't even suggest it."

"I could drive you places so you wouldn't have to walk or ride Daisy everywhere. Then I could sell it when I got baptized." He drummed his fingers on the table. "Joe Bieler bought a car last year."

"He wrecked it, and his parents had to pay two thousand dollars for the fence. You are a Bontrager. The Bontragers don't do such things."

Yost frowned. "Sometimes I wish I were a Bieler."

"You do not."

"I do. Because then my parents and my righteous sister wouldn't expect me to be perfect all the time."

Miriam didn't think she deserved his tone or his scornful

words, but she ignored them and jumped up and cleared their empty glasses. "You could buy a bike."

"Yeah, a bike. Loads of fun."

Miriam let his sarcasm slide right off her. So he wanted a car. The desire would pass.

She glided up the stairs, skipping the fourth one that creaked like a rusty gate, and stepped into her dimly-lit room. Susie sat on her bed in almost the same spot from this afternoon, staring at the far wall without seeing it.

Susie's unusual behavior triggered the alarms in Miriam's head. She must be very ill indeed.

"How do you feel?" Miriam asked.

"It's very bad," Susie said.

"I'll get Mamm."

"No." There was no mistaking the desperation contained in that single word. "Shut the door."

Miriam did as Susie asked and then sat next to Susie, placing her hand on the back of Susie's neck. Still no fever. "What's wrong? Tell me how you are feeling."

To Miriam's surprise, Susie burst into tears and rocked back and forth with her arms wrapped around her stomach.

"I'm getting Mamm," Miriam said as she rose from the bed.

Susie grabbed Miriam's hand and pulled her back. "Miriam. Swear to me you won't tell Mamm or Dat."

"That you're sick?"

"Swear."

Miriam put her arm protectively around her sister. This behavior was the strangest of all. "I promise. What is the matter?"

"Do not leave me alone. Promise you won't."

"Susie, what are you talking about?"

"I am so, so wicked, and you are so perfect. You won't want me to be your sister."

"Don't talk like that."

Susie lowered her voice as if she were afraid the walls were listening. Miriam could barely hear what came out of her mouth.

"I'm going to have a baby."

The words knocked the wind right out of Miriam. A baby? She found it impossible to wade through the dense fog of emotions and doubts that came with such a revelation.

Susie threw her arms around Miriam's neck and sobbed into her shoulder. "Don't leave me," she said.

Stunned and reeling, Miriam haltingly wrapped her arms around Susie and squeezed tight so Susie knew she planned on hanging around. What else could she do?

"Are you sure?" Miriam said.

"I went to the drugstore yesterday for a pregnancy test. I was too ashamed to pay for it, so I hid it under my apron and took it into the bathroom right there at the store. Three positives."

They sat for an eternity, sharing the weight of the world.

"How did this happen? Who is the father?" Miriam almost choked on the questions.

"He doesn't know."

Miriam thought of the boys Susie associated with. She could think of two or three Susie seemed to show a preference for, but none so close as to get her pregnant. Had she been too wrapped up in Ephraim to pay heed to her sister's fall into sin?

Miriam pressed her fingers to her forehead. "I think the boy has to be told."

"No, that is the last thing I want. I don't want him to feel like he has to marry me."

"He should do his duty."

"I don't ever want anyone to be forced to marry me."

Miriam couldn't argue with that. Every girl deserved a man

who adored her and wanted to marry her because he couldn't stand being apart. The bile rose in Miriam's throat. Susie should have thought of that before trading away her virtue.

"What are we going to do?" Susie said.

We. Susie's problem was now Miriam's. She had always been her sister's protector, the one to shield her from pain and heartache. But this situation would not go away with a wave of Miriam's hand. And what would the community think when the truth became obvious?

What would Ephraim say?

Miriam had few answers, but she did know one thing. Ephraim must never know. His opinion of Miriam and her family must never be damaged. The truth about Susie would devastate him.

"I am so wicked," Susie said, clutching Miriam's hand for reassurance.

For a split second, Miriam wanted to lash out at her sister. *Yes, you are. How could you do this to our family?*

She bit her tongue. Susie craved her compassion, not her censure. No matter how she or Ephraim despised what Susie had done, Miriam would be kind. The Lord Jesus said, "Neither do I condemn thee: go, and sin no more." Who knew the strength of the temptation Susie had faced?

Miriam smoothed an errant lock of hair behind Susie's ear. "You have done something very bad with serious consequences. But I know your heart, and you are not wicked. You are an angel to your brothers. You make pillowcases and hangings for the Haiti Mission Fund. I don't remember a time when I have seen you angry. I know you are not wicked."

Susie let out another gut-wrenching sob. "I'm afraid, Miriam."

"What about Mamm and Dat?"

Susie grabbed Miriam's wrist like a lifeline. "Don't tell them. They will hate me."

Miriam almost breathed a sigh of relief. The fewer people who knew, the better—even Mamm and Dat. Then there would be fewer ways for the awful truth to reach Ephraim's ears. "Everything is going to be all right. We will put our heads together and come up with a solution. And pray. We need to pray."

"I haven't stopped praying for a week. In the bathroom at the drugstore, I begged the Lord for a negative test. I promised to do anything, *anything* for Him, if I wasn't pregnant. He didn't listen."

"He listened," Miriam said. "But He does not restrain our free will. Or the consequences."

"I wish He did."

With resolve, Miriam stood and propped her hands on her hips. "First things first. How is the morning sickness?"

"I wish it were only in the morning."

"Can you get through work tomorrow? Then it will be the Sabbath."

"Jah. I feel better knowing you will help me."

"Tomorrow on my lunch break I will buy some ginger pills. And maybe peppermint tea."

Susie flashed a cautious smile. "Oh, Miriam, I love you. You are my only friend."

Miriam sighed in resignation. Seth Lambright might despise her, but she would always have Susie's loyalty.

CHAPTER
FOUR

Seth walked to his house with a lighter heart than he usually felt with his face toward home. All three of his horses had sold at the auction last week and brought more money than even he anticipated in his most liberal estimates. He determined that his profit would be enough, with his carefully accrued savings, to buy a prime stud horse he'd had his eye on.

He tried hard not to be carried away with optimism. For as carefully as he managed his resources, it seemed something always went wrong to derail his plans. The last time he came into some money, his dat's roof had needed repair and his stepmother Ellie insisted that Seth help pay for it.

"You live here; you eat our food; we support you. The least you can do is pay for the roof that shelters you and your brothers and sisters."

Work at the mill paid well enough, but Seth looked forward to the day when he could breed horses full-time. But with Ellie dipping her hand into the savings with regularity, that goal seemed further and further away.

With a pencil tucked behind her ear and a you've-got-to-do-something expression on her face, Laura met him at the front door. Ellie's yippy little dog, Pookie, barked incessantly, as if Seth were an intruder instead of a person he saw every day after work. Maybe Pookie could smell Seth's intense dislike.

Seth raised an eyebrow to Laura. "Problem?"

"Scilla has been standing in the corner for almost half an hour."

Seth nearly growled out loud as he took a deep breath and marched into the house. Nothing made his blood boil like the mistreatment of his little sister, Priscilla.

Even Laura, with her modern ideas and superior education, didn't dare confront their stepmother. Only Seth could make Ellie back down, and only then because he paid for groceries. He tried, heaven knew he tried, to show Dat's wife the respect and honor due her, but no amount of honor would constrain him to stand by and watch one human being mistreat another.

He walked through the kitchen with its sparkly clean floor, past Ellie as if she weren't even there, and into the washroom where Scilla stood in the corner, facing the wall.

"Cum, Scilla," he said kneeling and taking her hand. "Your punishment is over."

Scilla turned her tear-streaked face to Seth and threw her arms around his neck. "I didn't mean to. I wanted to see the lady dance. Pookie barked at me."

No wonder she'd been standing there for half an hour. Priscilla had broken the weightiest commandment of all. She had dared to set foot in the "no-no room," also known as the front sitting room, and Ellie's six-inch guard dog had tattled on her.

Almost from the day she moved in, Ellie had designated the sitting room her sanctuary and did not allow anyone under the age of twenty to set a foot over its threshold. Actually, no one but Dat, Ellie, and that dog were welcome in the room containing two new sofas and a chest with Ellie's prized music box.

The music box was a gross piece of vanity, but Ellie justified keeping it because it had belonged to her favorite mammi. When Ellie sat in the room by herself, she pulled the small box out of the chest, wound it up, and hummed along with the tune.

The music box fascinated Scilla, because when it opened, a tiny dancer in a fluffy skirt popped out and twirled in circles to the music. Even with the threat of severe punishment hanging over her head, Scilla couldn't resist the temptation of the music box.

"She spanked me," Scilla said.

Seth lifted Scilla into his arms and held her tight. "Come outside with me, and we will feed the chickens," he said.

"Did Mamm say okay?" Scilla said.

Seth frowned. He still had to smooth things over with Ellie so she wouldn't take her irritation out on the little ones when Seth was not home. And she was the "mother." He had to at least try to show respect to her wishes, even if groveling was not in his nature.

With Scilla tightly in his arms, he emerged from the washroom into the kitchen. Ellie stood with her arms folded, a spatula clutched in one hand, glaring at Seth as if he were the angel of death.

Ellie stood nearly six feet tall with a square jaw and a thin, beak-like nose. Before she met Dat, she had been an old maid living as an only child with her parents in Ohio. One thing was certain: with her upbringing, she was accustomed to getting her own way.

Ellie waved her spatula in the direction of the washroom. "Get her back in there. The hour is not over yet."

"How long has she been standing there?" Seth said, gritting his teeth. He mustn't lose his temper before supper.

"Twenty-seven minutes. She is not getting off a minute earlier than I say."

"You have every right to be mad." Seth tried his best to sound sympathetic. "Scilla should never have gone in there. But if she has learned her lesson, do you think you could give her thirty-three minutes of mercy?"

"She has gone into the no-no room three times in the last month. I won't stand for it."

Seth nudged Scilla, who had her face buried in Seth's neck. "Scilla, tell Ellie you are—"

Ellie cleared her throat and bit her upper lip.

"Tell Mamm you are sorry."

"I am sorry," Scilla said, the regret evident in her pathetic little voice.

Seth jostled his sister. "And promise to not go in there unless you are invited."

"Yes."

Ellie stood like a statue, considering her options. Seth knew of her reluctance to concede anything to him, but she showed him grudging courtesy for the support he gave the family.

She shrugged her shoulders. "I'll let you out thirty-three minutes early. But let this be a lesson to you."

Seth swallowed his pride. "Thank you."

Ellie leveled her spatula at Scilla. "Go outside so you aren't underfoot before supper. And take care on my clean floor."

Seth set Scilla down, and she scampered through the door like a convict out of prison.

Ellie turned her attention to the chicken frying in the pan. "She will turn into a rotten child if you keep spoiling her. I try to teach her discipline and responsibility, but you block me at every turn. That is Laura's problem. No one kept her behavior in check, and look how she turned out. Spare the rod, spoil the child."

"In the Bible, the rod is a stick used to guide the sheep, not hit them."

She scowled as if he had said something offensive. "You are just like Laura, thinking you are so smart. But I'll tell you something, young man. I've been reading the Bible for thirty-nine years. I know the Bible. Don't think you can lecture me on what the Bible says. You'll lose that contest every time."

Seth longed to point out that if she had been reading the Bible for thirty-nine years, she must have learned to read directly out of the womb. Instead, he shut his mouth, stirred the corn, and set the table. Scilla had been delivered from bondage. That was all that mattered.

"My two sisters and their husbands are going on a Florida cruise in November," Ellie said. "I know your dat would like to go."

Seth didn't reply. He knew what Ellie wanted, but he refused to sacrifice his hard-earned money so that Ellie and Dat could sail around the peninsula. But there was no use in getting Ellie's hackles up again. Let her interpret his silence any way she wanted.

Ellie glanced at the clock that chimed a different birdcall for each hour. "Your *fater* is late again. He assured me that he would be home by five o'clock without fail." She put her hands on her hips. "If he insists on being late, I suppose we will simply eat without him. Call the children, Seth."

Seth stuck his head out the back door, where his little brothers, Joshua and Jacob, knelt weeding the garden. "Supper," he said. "Bring Scilla."

Both brothers leaped from the ground, and eight-year-old

Jacob threw himself into Seth's arms. "I caught a salamander. A great big one."

"Show me." Seth set Jacob on his feet, snatched the hat from Joshua's head, and threw it like a Frisbee.

"Hey!" Joshua giggled as he sprinted to the forsythia bush to retrieve his hat.

Jacob's eyes twinkled. "It's in the barn. I will show you after supper."

"You should have seen Jakey's face," Joshua called as he ran back to Seth with his hat firmly in place. "We was weeding the garden and his fingers touched it before he even saw it. It was all slimy, and he jumped forty feet in the air."

"I did not."

"Can I come to help with the horses tonight?" Joshua asked.

"Of course," Seth said. "If Ellie gives permission."

Jacob jumped up and down. "Me too?"

"Jah, you too. Now go fetch Scilla from the swings and come to supper."

Seth smiled as his brothers practically danced their way to the swing set and helped Scilla down from the slide. He ducked back into the house and trudged up the two flights of stairs to Laura's bedroom in the attic. Laura sat in her usual place by the A-shaped window, reading *Elements of Psychology* with a highlighter in her hand.

Laura loved books as much as Seth loved horses. Even as a small girl she had resisted the Amish traditions, but when Mamm died five years ago, Laura, who was twelve at the time, made her mind up that she would not join the church. A shocking decision for a young Amish girl.

After primary school, she enrolled at the public high school and studied persistently to catch up with the other students. She had always been exceptionally bright. Now at the end of her senior year, she had been accepted to the University of Wisconsin with a full year's scholarship. One more reason Miriam Bontrager and her boyfriend thought of the Lambrights as an unfortunate family. Dat hadn't been happy about Laura's decision, but he dealt with his disappointment as he did every other problem. He ignored it.

"I thought you took the AP test last week," Seth said.

"That was biology. This week is psychology and calculus."

"I don't even know how to spell those words, let alone take a test on them."

"Psychology will be easy. Calculus might kill me." Laura shut her book. "I don't remember a word I just read. I was so upset about Scilla. Did you work it out with Ellie?"

"Jah, but I wish I'd come home sooner."

"I never know what to do when she gets like that. I even tried to quote psychology to her about appropriate punishments for children, and she said, 'It's a good thing you are smart, because you ain't pretty.' I got my feelings hurt and gave up. I am such a coward."

"Do not be hard on yourself. It is easy to make things worse with Ellie."

"*You* never do."

Seth shook his head.

Laura laid her book on the window seat. "I want to go to college mighty bad, Seth, but what will the boys and Scilla do when I leave and you move out to your farm? I cannot leave them with her."

"I sold three horses at the auction."

"Three! That is wonderful-gute. Did you get a gute price?"

"This fall I will have enough to build a small house on the farm and move the boys and Scilla in with me."

Laura stared at Seth in astonishment. "What will Dat say?"

"Do you honestly think he will care?"

"Of course he will care, Seth. Why are you so hard on him?"

"Maybe because he's never done anything to prove me wrong. If he would stick up for his own *kinna*, I wouldn't have to."

"But to take his children?"

"Ellie and Dat haven't had much time alone since they married three years ago," Seth said. "I will plant the idea in her head and she will convince Dat in no time. She always does."

"But how will you support yourself?"

Seth shrugged. "We will get by. I may not know how to do calculus, but I can add numbers. I will work extra shifts at the mill. Joshua and Jacob can help with the horses and farming. I already pay for most of the food that comes into this house."

Laura smiled with restrained gladness. "If we had our own house, I wouldn't have to put up with Ellie during Christmas break. I could send money home every month from my job."

"Nae, keep your money. College is expensive. I will manage."

Someone stepped lightly up the stairs to the attic. "Seth," they heard Scilla say as she knocked softly on the door, "Mamm says come down for dinner or we will eat without you and if you think you can eat later you got another think coming. And Laura too. And wash your hands."

Seth opened the door and invited Scilla into the room. He sat down on the bed and pulled Scilla onto his lap. Pointing to Laura, he said, "Look at your sister, Scilla. She's pretty, ain't not?"

"Jah," agreed Scilla, "she is the prettiest."

Seth smoothed the hair sticking out of Scilla's bob. "I hope you grow up as pretty as her."

"Ach, stop with the flattery," Laura said, but she smiled and blushed bright red.

"You are very pretty, Laura. Don't ever let Ellie tell you otherwise, either of you."

They heard Pookie from two flights down, yapping his annoyance at Dat's arrival. Seth scooped Scilla in his arms and hopped down the stairs. Although Ellie was an excellent cook, Seth seldom looked forward to supper with the family. Ellie's company proved irksome.

Seth sighed. *"Honour thy father and thy mother: that thy days may be long upon the land."* He recited that verse to himself several times a day.

Ach, if only he could root this knot of resentment from his heart—resentment for his dat's indifference, his stepmother's selfishness, and his mother's death. Seth resolved to pray harder to show more kindness to those who trespassed against him.

Trespassed against him.

As soon as the thought formed in his mind, he cringed at his own arrogance. How could he justify holding onto supposed wrongs when his own behavior was so imperfect? Who was he to criticize a mote in someone's eye with a beam in his own?

A stab of guilt caught him between the shoulder blades as he thought of his behavior toward Miriam Bontrager. He shouldn't have let his irritation take control of his nobler instincts. No amount of bad treatment justified hurting her feelings. What a hypocrite he was!

Seth placed Scilla on her stool and sat in his place next to Joshua. The moment Laura plopped into her chair, Dat bowed his head and the rest of the family followed in silent grace. Seth breathed in the mouthwatering aromas—mashed sweet potatoes with cinnamon, fried chicken, and corn.

The actual serving of the food went slowly, because Ellie insisted on dishing up the food for everyone. Each family member waited patiently—and quietly—for Ellie to serve Dat first, then Scilla, and on up to Seth.

And no one thought about wasting even one bite. They ate what Ellie spooned for them. No more, no less.

Once Ellie served herself, she sat across the table from Dat and declared that the eating could begin.

Ellie had impeccable table manners and ate as delicately as a bird. "Jacob, elbows," she said. "And Joshua, quit yapping like a magpie. Close your mouth and eat." Ellie put down her fork a mere minute after she had picked it up and gazed over everyone at the table. "Next Sunday, gmay will be at our house for the first time since your father and I married. Everything must be perfect. We are doing extra cleaning to prepare. Seth, you will have to spend less time with your horses until then. This place is to be scrubbed from floor to ceiling."

Dat smiled at his new wife. "Ellie, you keep this house spic and span. Since we married, I have not seen so much as a crumb on the floor."

Ellie lifted her eyebrows. "I should say not. My standards are very high. Gmay at Rosie Neuenschwander's was a disgrace. She may be the minister's wife, but that is no excuse for the rust ring in her sink." She picked up her fork and shook it in Laura's direction. "There won't be so much as a smudgy fingerprint in this house come Sunday."

Laura kicked Seth under the table then grinned at him. He skewered a piece of chicken with his fork and kept right on eating.

"We will be packed to the rafters as it is," Ellie said. "Thirty-three families and four widows. Our district is big enough to be divided in half, but it seems the men aren't interested because they don't have the hassle of preparing food and trying to squirm their way through a crowd to get one-hundred and eighty-three people fed. When the room gets stuffy, the men open the windows and the women and children sit there shivering."

"We could bring the extension on the back yet," Dat said.

"And put people on the grass, Abbie? Not at my gmay."

Ellie took a bite and chewed slowly while Seth enjoyed the silence.

"Laura," Ellie said, "you will need to scrub ceilings and walls. With Pine-Sol. Orange-scented."

"I will be happy to help redd up," Laura said. "My last AP test is on Thursday, and then I am all yours."

Ellie pursed her lips. "Fine. If you are too important to take time out to help me, then I am too busy to fix your meals. Don't expect to eat anything in this house until Thursday. Your dat doesn't seem to care if you jump the fence, but I won't be a willing party to it. Either pull your weight, or go hungry. It's your choice."

Dat ate his sweet potatoes with a serene look on his face, as if Ellie were discussing the minister's latest sermon. Seth hadn't expected anything different. To Dat, a problem didn't exist if he ignored it.

Seth silently debated with himself. Should he protest Ellie's plan to starve Laura, or let it go? Ellie meant what she said. If Laura didn't lend a hand because she needed to study, Ellie would see that she didn't put a crumb of food in his sister's mouth.

Laura wouldn't actually starve. She could eat breakfast and lunch at school and go to her Englisch friend Britny's for supper. Seth could even pick something up from the grocery store and Laura could eat in his stable.

But if Seth stayed quiet, would Ellie think she could get away with bullying his siblings? And if he said something, would Ellie dig in her heels and insist that Laura starve all summer until she left for college?

"I will help extra if you let Laura eat," he finally said, hoping Ellie would recognize how ridiculous her ultimatum sounded. "I am tall. I can scrub the ceilings without a ladder. Laura needs all her strength to take those tests. If she passes, she gets college credit. Saves a lot of money."

"What do I care about that? It is not my money," Ellie said.

"But it might be mine," Seth said slowly, letting the meaning of his words sink in.

Ellie had never cared to know anything of Laura's college plans, had almost considered it a sin to talk of them, but Seth and Laura had been able to work out the financial details with the help of Laura's counselor at school. With a good job, a scholarship, and something called the Amish Education grant —from some well-intentioned people who thought the Amish needed rescuing—Laura would be able to afford school without any family help. But Ellie didn't know that, and Seth could use her ignorance to his advantage.

Ellie turned up her nose. Seth could see her debating with herself. She couldn't stand to back down, especially in front of the other children.

Seth forced humility into his voice. "Please, Ellie. We will all help extra."

"I will give Pookie a bath," said Joshua.

What a good boy. Joshua hated Pookie.

Ellie shook her head. "No one bathes Pookie but me. You have to rub his fur just so or he develops a skin condition."

"I will oil the cabinets," Seth said.

Ellie relaxed the lines of her frown. She couldn't resist a well-oiled cabinet. "Very well. If you all work doubly hard to make up for Laura's vanity, I will agree to let her eat."

Seth clenched his jaw and bit his tongue and focused squarely on the beam in his own eye. Ellie couldn't help herself. She refused to be wrong about anything. Seth's greatest challenge was to convince her to change her mind while she still believed she was right. It was exhausting. And humbling.

"Joshua," Ellie scolded, "quit talking and eat. I declare, you could talk a goat to death."

With a few more horses sold at auction, Seth could eke out enough to start work on his own house. Then his siblings would be safe from Ellie.

That day couldn't come soon enough.

CHAPTER
FIVE

Miriam glanced around her and ducked into the drugstore, reluctant to be caught anywhere near the scene of the crime. Oppressive, accusing silence attacked her senses as soon as the glass door swished closed behind her. A fluorescent light above her head buzzed and flickered as her gaze darted around shelves piled high with sterile white boxes and jars of antiseptic cream. She covered her nose for fear that her lungs would be scorched by the smell of alcohol and orthopedic shoes.

A young woman with three different colors of hair and ears full of earrings stood at the cash register. "Can I help you?" she said, popping her gum.

The force of Miriam's heartbeat surprised her. It took a minute for her to form words on her tongue. "My...a friend of mine came in here a few days ago and took something from your store. She forgot to pay."

The clerk looked at Miriam suspiciously and paused her gum-chewing. "What did she take?"

Miriam forged ahead with her rehearsed speech. "It cost fifteen dollars. Here is twenty. Will that be enough?"

"I have to know what it was so I can key in the right code," said the clerk. "Otherwise my count is off by the end of the night."

"Won't you just take the money?"

The young woman folded her arms and shook her head. "Show me the item she took so I can ring it up."

Miriam felt as if her lungs were stuffed with cotton as she stood at the counter with the twenty-dollar bill wadded in her fist. What could she do now? She refused to even go down the row with the pregnancy tests, let alone touch one. The thought of such humiliation made her ill.

"Can I help?"

Already completely mortified, Miriam turned to see Seth Lambright standing behind her. Her throat constricted, effectively cutting off any air she might have taken into her tight lungs. Had he heard her entire embarrassing conversation? The possibility left her lightheaded.

"Hello," Seth said, with a no-nonsense, stiff line to his lips.

Until she actually formed the words, Miriam thought it would be impossible to speak. "Nae. No, thank you." She felt the heat travel up her neck and overspread her cheeks.

He studied her face as if she were a criminal with a horrible secret.

She couldn't bear his piercing eyes. Who was he to judge her? "I—I was just leaving," she stuttered.

Seth shook his head slightly, nudged his way past Miriam, and leaned over the counter to the clerk. The young woman backed away, but Seth motioned for her to lean closer. She inched slightly nearer and allowed him to whisper into her ear, as Miriam watched in stunned humiliation.

He pulled away from the clerk. "Thanks," he said. He gave

Miriam a half smile and marched out of the drugstore as if he had only come in to deliver a message.

The clerk turned to Miriam and waved her hand dismissively. "Okay, give me the money and I'll take care of it."

Miriam smoothed the creases of the bill and laid it on the countertop. As soon as the money fell from her hand, she made a beeline for the door and burst through it. She risked a look around. As far as she could tell, Seth had completely disappeared. Releasing the stagnant air in her lungs, she raced to her buggy and never looked back.

"Hullo, Miriam." David Herschberger leaned on the counter of the combination fruit and pretzel stand and grinned at her. Flour dusted his shirt and trousers. Susie said he didn't make the pretzels but still managed to make a mess of himself by the end of each day. David's parents owned the stand, and not only did Susie work here, but she was a close friend of their daughter Esther Rose. Being May, it was still too early in the season for much in the way of local produce, but pretzels were in demand all year round. The stand offered plenty of dried fruit and jams, as well.

David, the same age as Miriam, was skinny as a flagpole. Ever since he'd started in as a teenager, he'd grown to the sky, but his weight stayed the same, so he got taller and taller and skinnier and skinnier. They all teased him for having a bottomless stomach and a hollow leg. One of his friends had started calling him "Hollow Davey," and the name stuck.

"Hollow," Miriam said, "could I take Susie for a few minutes?"

Susie and Esther stood with their backs to the booth's opening, rolling out and shaping pretzels with quick, precise movements. Susie made dozens, hundreds, of pretzels every day. She could form a perfect twist with her eyes closed.

She glanced at Miriam and furrowed her brow.

"Oh, sure," Hollow said. "Supper rush ain't for another hour yet."

Susie rinsed her hands and dried them on her apron.

"Take these." Hollow grabbed two pretzels from the basket and wrapped them in a napkin. "And the honey mustard," he said, pointing to the small containers on the counter.

"Denki."

"Anything for the Bontragers," Hollow replied.

Susie wasted no time leaving her booth. She scooped the food from the counter, grabbed Miriam's hand, and led her to one of three red-stained picnic tables sitting in the middle of the grass a hundred feet from the pretzel stand.

Susie had always seemed so delicate to Miriam, like the exotic orchid that her cousin Rebecca kept in her kitchen. Her skin looked as white and smooth as fresh cream, with eyes like a doe's set against her thin face. Today her eyes looked even bigger, in contrast with her hollow cheeks and lips pulled tight with worry.

"You have something to tell me?" she said. "You look like you have something to tell me."

"How are you feeling?" Miriam said.

"Not bad today. Hollow gives me an extra pretzel now and then. They help." She laced her fingers together. "Do you have something to tell me?"

Miriam unfolded the letter in her hand and took the flowered stationery from the envelope. "This is from cousin Hannah."

"Hannah? Did you tell her?"

"Of course not. I told her it is a friend of mine."

Susie pursed her lips. "She will know it is me."

"We can't worry about that. Hannah has no reason to think that it is you, and even if she did, Hannah is no gossip. I asked her to keep quiet about it. We will have to trust her." Miriam patted her sister's ice-cold hand. "She keeps in contact with Mamm's cousin, Katie Martins in Ontario. Katie's children have grown, and she is willing to take you in. They say they can find a gute Amish home for the baby and then you can come home and no one here would ever have to know about the pregnancy. We can tell folks you went to Canada to work for a few months."

Susie turned pale, and for the hundredth time, Miriam wondered if Mamm and Dat might be wiser in this than she.

But how could she ask them for help? Not only had Susie sworn her to secrecy, but Miriam feared that the more people who knew, the more likely the secret would get out.

No one would ever have to know. Not Mamm and Dat, not Ephraim. Susie's reputation would be safe.

Susie slumped her shoulders and lowered her eyes. "I would be away from Apple Lake until January. Away from the family."

"It is only eight months, Susie. It will be a great adventure."

Tears pooled in Susie's eyes. "You won't be there. What if I am frightened? What if the people don't like me? We don't even know if they are good Amish folk."

"Don't think about that. Think about the people who love you. The ones, Lord willing, who will never discover the secret. Don't you think eight months is worth your reputation? Once you come home, you can start your life anew without fear that people will judge you. Or think cruel things about you."

"I will be lonely. What if they don't like me?"

"Hannah knows them, and she says they are happy to take you in. They will love you."

Susie wiped her eyes and sniffed. "When would I have to leave?"

"We must make the travel arrangements and explain to Mamm and Dat without bearing false witness. I have money to pay for the bus fare." She thought of the quilt she'd sold at the auction. The Haitian Fund would have to wait. "We need to come up with a good reason for your departure. With all the letters that have to travel back and forth, it might be four or five weeks yet before you can leave."

"Four or five weeks?" Susie burst into tears and buried her face in the crook of her elbow on the table. "I don't want to go."

Miriam pulled a handkerchief from her apron and reached over the table to nudge Susie's chin up. "Don't cry. It is silly to worry about such things. I don't know what else to do."

"Do you really want me to go?"

"What other choice do we have? Like as not, you will have a wonderful-gute time and want to stay forever."

Susie searched Miriam's face. "Do you want me to stay forever?"

"Nae, of course not."

Susie wiped leftover tears from her face and grabbed Miriam's hand. "If you think I should go, I will go. I don't want to hurt our family."

"It is for the best."

"Can you help me buy a bus ticket?"

"Don't you worry. I will take care of everything. Your job is to stay healthy and happy for the trip."

Susie didn't shake her despondent air. "Jah, okay. You know what is best." She stood, gave Miriam a terse hug, and practically ran back to the pretzel booth. She pressed the hem of her apron to her eyes before opening the small door and disappearing inside.

A twinge of guilt nagged at Miriam like a fly buzzing in the corner of a room.

It is for the best.

Surely it would be better for Susie if no one in Apple Lake knew about this. She could return home after the baby's birth and no one would be the wiser that she had fallen. Still, the tortured look on Susie's face forced Miriam to second-guess herself and her motives.

If this was the right thing, why did she feel so uneasy about it?

"It's time. Now," Miriam whispered to Susie.

Mamm sat in the great room crocheting an edge on a blanket for baby Rudy, her second grandchild, born four months ago. Miriam's oldest brother, Marvin, and his wife Ruth now had two little ones.

Dat propped his stocking feet on the footrest while he read the newspaper. The three little boys had been tucked into bed and Yost was with Joe Bieler, probably riding around in Joe's car and wishing he had one of his own.

The propane lantern standing between Mamm and Dat hissed softly as it bathed the great room in bright light and cast shadows over the adjoining kitchen. Arm in arm, Miriam and Susie walked into the room and stood facing their parents in a show of unity. Susie shook with anxiety. Miriam was only slightly calmer. What if their parents would not give their permission? What other plan could they possibly come up with?

Mamm and Dat looked up simultaneously. Dat lowered his paper, and Mamm glanced curiously at Dat.

Miriam knew that the longer she waited, the more tongue-tied she would be. "Mamm, do you remember your cousin Katie Martins?"

Mamm raised an eyebrow. "Do you mean my cousin Katie Martins Stutzman or second cousin Katie Ann Martins?"

"Katie Ann in Ontario."

"She is a bit older than me. Lost three babies but had six that lived. Why do you ask? Do you remember her?"

"She and cousin Hannah Weaver keep in touch," Miriam said.

"Okay," Mamm prompted, looking from Miriam to Susie.

Miriam took a deep breath. "Their children have grown and are tending farms of their own, and Hannah said Katie and her husband need help this summer and fall with the gardening. And the canning."

"I want to go stay with them in Canada," Susie blurted out—not exactly as they had planned, but she sounded sincere.

The declaration rendered Mamm momentarily speechless. She looked at her daughter as if they had dragged a dead horse into the house. "Why would you want to do a thing like that?" she finally said.

"They need help, and I want to go somewhere new and exciting," Susie said.

Mamm shook her head. "This doesn't sound like you at all, Suz. You don't even like to sleep over at the cousins'."

Susie's voice cracked. "I know. That is why I need to go to Canada. To get away. To learn to be strong. I can't be a proper wife always longing for home. What would my husband think?"

"You can cross that bridge when you come to it," Mamm said. "A trip to Canada is *deerich*, foolish. You'd be homesick within a week and they would have to put you on the first bus back to Apple Lake."

"Nae, Mamm," Miriam said. "She really wants to go. It will be so much fun."

Mamm dropped her crochet in her lap. "I won't allow it. You are only seventeen."

Dat motioned for Miriam and Susie to sit on the sofa across from him. "Cum, let us talk about it." He laced his fingers together and looked over his glasses at Susie. "How long have you been considering a trip to Canada?"

"A...awhile."

"What inspired this idea? Canada is very far away."

"Hollow Davey Herschberger apprenticed in Ohio last year. And Esther Rose stayed with her aunt in Tennessee all winter. Hollow says it is good to see the world, to have new experiences."

"But that is Hollow's opinion. You have never liked change. Help me understand why you want to go."

Susie started to cry—a common occurrence these days. Miriam hoped her parents hadn't noticed the frequency. "I'm not brave. Miriam is always brave for me. I want to do something on my own. Without anyone's help."

Miriam put her arm around her sister. They hadn't rehearsed that. She sensed that Susie had revealed her deepest fear and her deepest desire at the same time.

"Come here, little one." Dat held out his hand.

Susie went to him and sat on his lap, and he wrapped her in his arms as he had when she was a very little girl. She put her arms around him and buried her face in his neck. "There, there," he said, patting her on the head and pulling her closer.

"I really want to go, Dat."

Dat reached over and took Mamm's hand. "Can we spare her until winter, Lisa?"

Mamm sighed and shook her head. "I can never spare my Susie, but you decide what is best."

"I'll not give my permission if you do not approve." Dat and Mamm exchanged a look that did not escape Miriam's notice. "But maybe it is what our Susie needs."

"We have noticed the change." Mamm gave Susie a weak smile. "Maybe you are restless. A trip to Canada might help you realize how much you love Apple Lake."

"The very thing," Dat said. "Although wintertime would be a better season for that. Ontario is colder than a block of ice in January."

Mamm clicked her tongue. "And Wisconsin ain't? Summer will be hot enough to convince Susie that she doesn't want to live there. The air is so wet, you can stick a cup out the window and catch a drink of water. Perhaps you should take Yost with you. He seems as restless as you do."

"So she can go?" Miriam asked.

They all looked at Mamm.

"I don't feel perfectly right about it, but if she is determined to go, I will trust her decision. She is seventeen, after all."

Miriam leaped up and hugged her mother tightly. Susie stayed put in the rocking chair, nestled in her father's arms.

She wouldn't be able to stay there forever.

CHAPTER
SIX

Miriam pulled a bolt of green-and-blue fabric from the shelf at Glick's Fabric Shop and ran her hand along the muted watercolor design surely made just for her. The midnight blues were interrupted by lighter shades of cobalt and gray mingled with greens the color of crisp Wisconsin lakes and tall maples. The most beautiful colors of nature in one piece of fabric.

This was the perfect material for her engagement quilt. If she started on it now, she would finish well before she and Ephraim were published and she could give it to him on the day he proposed. By that time, Susie would be back from Canada, all would go back to normal, and Miriam would not have this constant hollow feeling in the pit of her stomach.

The haunted look on Susie's face kept Miriam away from home as much as possible these days. She worked late at Martha's quilt shop and visited Aunt Emma Weaver and Aunt Erla Miller often. And Miriam was always the first to volunteer to run errands for her mother. She didn't want to be reminded of the pain, and she didn't want to second-guess the decision to send Susie away.

Everything would be fine if they could both get through the next eight months without being discovered. Susie would recover, their family would return to normal, and Ephraim would never have to know.

Glick's specialized in fabrics for Amish clothing but also had a good selection of material for quilts and other handicrafts. Miriam laid her fabric on the cutting table and thumbed through a basket of dress patterns. Frustration bubbled inside her. She had an awfully long time to sew a dress for her wedding. She could make twenty dresses before she and Ephraim were even published.

Suddenly, Miriam's almost-fiancé walked into the fabric shop. Ephraim sometimes delivered packages for his dat, and today he carried two big boxes into the store along with a clipboard and invoice.

Miriam didn't want him to see the fabric. She quickly picked it up and hid it behind her back. A silly thing to do, really, but she hadn't time to come up with a better plan.

Ephraim's eyes lit up when he saw her standing there. He laid the boxes on the counter, ran his fingers through his hair, and in three long strides was at her side.

"This is a wonderful surprise," he said, flashing his bright teeth. "Although, where else would a person expect to find Miriam Bontrager than at the fabric store? They probably let you sleep overnight."

His joy at seeing her overflowed into laughter. She would have been overjoyed as well if she hadn't been caught in the act of picking out fabric for his engagement quilt. She would hate it if the surprise were spoiled.

"Delivering for your dat?" she said, backing away slightly.

If she could manage to slip the bolt onto the nearest shelf, Ephraim wouldn't be any the wiser.

Ephraim grew serious. "You've got a secret, Miri."

Her heart did a somersault. Did he know about the baby?

"A secret? What—what are you talking about?"

His face bloomed into a grin. "What are you hiding behind your back? Is it a present for me?"

Relief washed over Miriam like a spring rainstorm. Of course he was talking about the fabric. What else? These days she jumped at her own shadow.

She shook a finger at him. "Oh no, you don't, Ephraim Neuenschwander. You are not allowed to see behind my back. Turn around and march right out that door."

"I want to see. You know I'll die of curiosity if you don't show me." He bobbed his head right then left, trying to discover what Miriam held out of sight. She turned her body to block his view.

"I don't want you to see." My, but he was persistent.

In a swift movement, he reached over her shoulder and snatched the bolt from her hand. She tried to grab it back, but he opened his eyes wide and waved the fabric over his head like a flag.

When she gave up trying to retrieve it, he lowered the bolt and examined the pattern. "This is what all the trouble is about? Material?" He tucked the bolt under his arm and rubbed his chin. "You are making a quilt?"

Miriam nodded.

"For me?"

"Jah, if you must know."

Ephraim hooted and did a little two-step shuffle with his feet. "For a certain event coming up in a couple of years?"

Miriam frowned and furrowed her brow. "Now you've ruined the surprise."

"Don't be cross. I *am* surprised. The surprise isn't ruined at all."

Miriam took a deep breath and swallowed her irritation. Ephraim didn't deserve her displeasure. He was just having fun with her. "I suppose you'll be surprised when you see the finished product." She plucked the bolt from his grasp. "Get a good look, because this is the last time you will see the fabric until it is made into a quilt."

Ephraim stuck his hands into his pockets. "I like it, Miri. I mean, I really do, but what would you think about picking out a nice brown instead?"

"Why?"

"I love brown. You are making the quilt for me, and I would like it better if it were brown."

Miriam repressed a twinge of disappointment. "Oh, okay. If that is what you would like better." She marched down the aisle to the browns. Ephraim followed. "What kind do you like?"

He studied the chocolate browns, chestnuts, and beiges until he pointed out a perfectly horrid tan, good for men's underwear or curtains in a blind man's sitting room.

"This is gute," he said. "The quilt you make me should be simple, to keep us warm. That is what a quilt is for, after all."

"I never thought about it that way," Miriam said in concern. "Do you think my quilts are too fancy? I do not want to seem proud."

"Quilts you make to sell can be fancy. They bring more money. But you and me are going to be an ideal Amish couple —pious and humble."

A pot of trouble stirred Miriam's insides, but she couldn't put her finger on the reason. Was it sinful to surround herself with beauty? Surely the Ordnung did not discourage the people from keeping their homes as clean and as comely as possible. If so, no one would plant flowers or paint their barns. The quilt on Mamm's bed had a double wedding ring design that sent a thrill through Miriam whenever she laid eyes on it. Was it gross vanity? Miriam's head swam with questions.

"My mamm says Susie is going to Canada," Ephraim said, running his hand over the bolts of brown fabric. "It wonders me why you didn't tell me."

"We made the arrangements only a few days ago. She will be leaving in four weeks."

"Why is she going?"

"We have relatives up there. They need help on their farm, and she wants to get away for the summer...have an adventure, meet some new boys." Miriam forced a playful smile onto her lips.

Ephraim raised an eyebrow. "An adventure? She's not thinking of jumping the fence, is she?"

"Nae, she plans on being baptized when she comes home in the winter, Lord willing."

Ephraim furrowed his brow and went so far as to put a hand on her shoulder. "I must tell you, Miriam, I don't think this is a gute idea. You have never mentioned these relatives before. Are they trustworthy? Will they be careful to not let Susie fall into temptation? She is prone to it, you know."

Miriam bit her bottom lip. Had Ephraim already sensed the truth? "It is an older couple with six grown children. They will take gute care of her. And I hear the Ontario Amish are more conservative than Pennsylvania."

"I have heard that." He pondered the information and folded his arms. "I suppose she will be okay. You should write her often."

"I will."

From behind the counter, a small, plump Amish woman called to Ephraim. He winked playfully at Miriam and went to get the woman's signature on his invoice.

Miriam couldn't stifle a grin. She loved it when he winked.

Once all the papers were signed, Ephraim set the boxes behind the counter and waved across the store to Miriam before disappearing through the door. The string of bells on the handle tinkled as the door swung closed, and Miriam marveled for the thousandth time just how blessed she was to have Ephraim's affection.

Ephraim, so handsome and clever, could have had any girl he wanted. Miriam remembered sitting on Lizzie Herschberger's porch after school with Lizzie and Frieda, waiting to catch a glimpse of Ephraim Neuenschwander as he walked home from school. Their ten-year-old dreams consisted of planning a wedding day with the best-looking boy in the district.

He took notice of Miriam when she was in the sixth grade, much to the envy of her friends, and asked her to walk home from school with him. The attention of an eighth grader became the high point of every day. As a young teenager, he had singled Miriam out as the girl he wanted to marry. "You are the prettiest girl in town," he'd told her. "And not bossy like Lizzie Herschberger." Every other girl in the district had swooned at Miriam's blessed circumstances.

Miriam stared at the tan broadcloth for a good five minutes before she pulled it from between two potato-brown bolts and carried it to the cutting table. If she made a Nine-Patch design, she could dress up the tan with yellows and reds—give it some country charm. Surely Ephraim wouldn't object to a Nine-Patch. The bishop's wife had made a Nine-Patch quilt for her granddaughter's wedding last winter. If it was good enough for the bishop, it would be good enough for Ephraim.

Feeling more encouraged, Miriam found a beautiful burgundy and a sunshine yellow to accent the tan fabric. It might be a beautiful quilt after all.

Only the best for Ephraim.

Only the best for their marriage.

CHAPTER SEVEN

"Whoa there, Daisy."

Miriam reined in her horse at the top of the lane, where a small hand-painted sign stood at the entrance to Seth Lambright's property. It looked lonely and insignificant, standing by itself under the shade of three tall maples. "LAMBRIGHT RANCH" it read in black lettering that could only have been painted by a man. No well-formed letters, no neat, straight lines. It might as well have said "No trespassing," for all the charm it conveyed.

Daisy had been Miriam's companion for as long as she could remember. She was technically Dat's riding horse, but Miriam rode her more than anyone else in the family did. It would have been fitting for Dat to give Daisy to Miriam as a wedding present, except that Daisy was a little long in the teeth. At almost twenty-six years old, Daisy was ready to be put out to pasture, literally. Dat knew that Miriam would love a horse she could ride for years to come.

Miriam patted Daisy on the neck and spurred her forward. Dread and eagerness warred inside her head. She dreaded seeing Seth Lambright again after all the hurtful things he'd said to her. Would he admonish her once more? Or treat her to the cold silence he so often gave her?

But those questions only motivated her to win Seth over, if she could, and convince him that she wasn't a bad person, to show him that she bore him no ill will—even though she'd never seen the inside of his house.

Her desire to see her new horse overshadowed every misgiving she had about the visit. A new foal frolicking around the pasture was about the most adorable thing Miriam had ever seen. Her excitement at picking her very own horse provided all the motivation she needed.

She rode through the thick stand of maples that stood at the edge of Seth's property. Once past the trees, Miriam slowed Daisy to a walk as the vibrant green of Seth's alfalfa fields took her breath away. Set against the bright white of the fences and the brilliant blue sky, the pastures looked invitingly lush.

Almost a quarter mile down the hard dirt lane stood the old stable. Seth had come into the land when his old *dawdi* passed away and had no sons to sell the property to. He gave it to Seth for ten dollars an acre. At least that was the rumor. Miriam didn't take a keen interest in Seth Lambright's affairs.

The stable looked ancient. Rust from the hinges streaked down the edges of the large doors. Four long windows along the side were bare of glass, and the wood siding had long ago lost any hint of paint.

Miriam headed to the small door at the far side of the stable, where she would begin her search for Seth.

Before she got close, the door opened and Mary Shetler walked out of the stable with her baby balanced on her hip and her little daughter Annie holding tightly to her free hand. Miriam waved. Mary glanced around furtively, caught sight of Miriam, and walked quickly and resolutely in the opposite direction. Miriam was far enough away that Mary could pretend not to have seen her. But why did she? Mary Shetler and Mamm were good friends.

Miriam rode up to the door, dismounted, and secured Daisy to a shiny hook bolted to the side of the stable. It looked out of place against the weathered wood. She straightened her *kapp* and regarded the gray sweatpants peeking out from under her dress. Ephraim didn't like the look of Miriam's riding outfit, but surely Seth Lambright wouldn't pay notice. His sister probably rode all the time.

She tapped on the door before deciding that knocking on a stable door looked a little silly. She cracked open the door, which squealed like an angry cat, and stepped hesitantly into the dim space. To her left was a small room with a desk and a cot that could in no way be ample for Seth's long legs. A loft, stacked to the ceiling with bales of hay and bags of feed, loomed above the little room.

To her right, ten stalls ran the length of the stable, the stall doors as old and decrepit as the outside walls. The sun shone through the glassless windows like beams of solid light, illuminating the particles of hay and dust that hovered in every barn ever built.

Miriam strained her ears. "Hello?"

No sound. Venturing farther into the stable, she heard water dripping into one of the troughs but couldn't see a single horse. Probably all out to pasture.

"Hello," she said again and listened to her voice echo off the rafters.

Light flooded the space as Seth opened the door across from her and marched inside. He stopped short as he caught sight of her. The surprise was evident on his face before he replaced the expression with a slight downward curl of his lips and a look of—what was it—concern? Like as not, he didn't welcome her presence in his stable.

"You came after all," he said.

She smiled as best she could—wanted to make sure he knew that she harbored no hard feelings. "I just saw Mary Shetler."

"Did you now?"

She puzzled over his cryptic response and decided not to pry further. "Is—is this a gute time? I am sure you are busy."

"The foals are out running with their mothers. Cum, I will show you."

Seth motioned for her to lead the way and followed as she ambled out the door, and then he took up the lead to an adjoining pasture where two mares grazed while their foals jumped and ran around, testing their legs like two mischievous toddlers.

Miriam didn't try to contain her enthusiasm. She clapped her hands in delight. "Oh, they are adorable! Cuter than kittens." She giggled as one of the foals leaped into the air and kicked up his back legs as if he were showing off for her.

Seth seemed pleased with her enthusiasm. "The one with the white patch on his nose is a colt. The other is a filly. Both thoroughbreds."

Miriam climbed one rung of the fence, wrapped her arms around the top slat, and watched the foals in silence. The short hair of their coats shone in the sunlight, and their long legs seemed disproportionate to their bodies. Miriam loved to see their developing leg and hind muscles flex and stretch. The colt was a chestnut brown while the filly's coat was lighter, much like the tan Ephraim had picked out for his quilt—a beautiful color on a horse.

"Have you named them?" she asked.

"Nae. I thought you would want to name your own. Which one do you want?"

Miriam propped her chin on her hands. "They are both so beautiful. I feel like a mother forced to choose between her two children. Which would you choose?"

"Me?" He rubbed his chin. "That one might be something of a handful," he said, pointing to the colt. It danced around the pasture.

"I can handle it."

"I know you can," he said, turning his face to the pasture. "You handle a horse like you were born in the saddle."

Miriam suddenly felt shy and lowered her eyes. "Thank you."

"Neither of these foals will ever throw a rider. I will train them well."

"I know you will. I've ridden a horse you trained."

The corners of Seth's lips turned down slightly.

Miriam cleared her throat. "The pastures look very pretty. I love the golden Alexanders up against the fence. Did you plant them, or do they grow wild?"

"They're volunteers," Seth said.

"Your stable is nice and big. Lots of space and light. You must be very proud of all the work you've done here. The horses are very high quality, and the property is well-maintained."

"This old stable is more than sixty years old. The only things well-maintained are my horses."

"Nae, truly. The stable floor is clean and the stalls are gute size."

Seth shook his head and cracked an uncharacteristic smile.

Miriam frowned and jumped down from the fence. "What's so funny?"

"You don't have to try so hard."

"Try so hard at what?"

"At getting me to like you."

Miriam planted her hands on her hips. "Maybe you should try harder at getting me to like you."

"I don't care if you like me."

"Oh, really?" Miriam arched an eyebrow. "Well, maybe I don't care if you like me."

"It's too late to try to pull that one, Miriam Bontrager. I can read you like a book."

"There you go again, thinking you can read my mind. If you are so smart, what am I thinking right now?"

Seth furrowed his brows and pointed to a bucket near the corner of the stable. "You are thinking you would like to pour that water all over my head."

Miriam looked away. "Hmm. You really can read my mind."

His eyes sparkled like a five-year-old with a frog in his pocket. She hadn't expected that.

Her heartbeat quickened.

He wasn't cross with her after all.

His momentary amusement gave way to that look of concern she saw earlier, and he took her by the elbow and led her to a short, rustic bench sitting against the side of the stable. The unexpected touch sent a warm sensation up Miriam's arm. Ephraim wouldn't have dreamed of taking such a liberty, but when Seth did it, the gesture didn't seem improper at all.

He motioned for her to sit and then sat next to her. "Miriam, I need to apologize for what I said at the auction and then at your house. I hurt your feelings, and I wish I could unsay every word."

"But you meant what you said, didn't you?"

"I never should have said any of it."

"But isn't it how you feel?"

He fixed his gaze beyond her left shoulder. "I want to take it back."

A short burst of laughter escaped her lips.

"What?"

"I like watching you try to dance around this," Miriam said. "You meant every word."

Seth laced his fingers together and rested his elbows on his knees. "But I still shouldn't have said it."

"I am sorry for behaving in a way that upset you. I have thought about what you said, but I am at a loss to know what I can do differently. I sincerely want to be better."

He stared into her eyes for an eternity, as if he really were trying to read her mind. "You really do?"

"Of course. The last thing I want to do is turn a blind eye to my own weaknesses."

He stood up and put some distance between them. "Most people do a good job of pretending they don't have weaknesses. I am a good example of that. I should never have criticized you."

She nodded in satisfaction. "At least you admit you are partly to blame for the fact that we hate each other."

"Hate each other?" He looked troubled. "I hope not."

Miriam gave him a teasing grin. "Oh, so you do care what I think about you?"

He relaxed his stiff posture—as much as she could expect from someone as somber as Seth Lambright. "You will never know. You cannot read minds."

Miriam wished she could read Seth's mind. She was dying to know what Seth had told the clerk the other day at the drugstore to persuade her to take Miriam's money. But that question would take them too close to Susie's difficulty. She could not bring herself to ask, even to express her gratitude for what he had done.

She stood up. "Can I come back next week to look at my horse?"

"Jah, but you have not told me yet which one you want."

"When they are a little older, I want to come play with them. Then I will decide."

"Play with them? Like puppies?"

"Jah, like puppies."

Seth walked with her around the stable to Daisy. "I will take gute care of both of them until you return."

Miriam turned to see two girls walking up the lane. Seth's sisters. Laura, the older one, was about Yost's age, and Priscilla was probably six. Priscilla's feet were bare, and she cuddled a plastic doll in her arms.

Miriam's face warmed when she remembered that her last heated exchange with Seth was when Laura's name had been mentioned.

"Seth!" Still grasping her doll, Priscilla ran into her brother's arms.

Miriam's heart swelled when Seth gathered Priscilla into a hug, swung her around, and planted a big kiss on her cheek.

He brought her back to earth and turned his face to Miriam. "You know my sisters, jah?"

Laura didn't smile but nodded in Miriam's direction. Miriam tried to swallow her guilt and nodded back. She barely knew either of Seth's sisters even though they were in her district. Laura attended gmay, but Miriam realized in dismay that she usually avoided the Lambright family at church. And Laura never came to gatherings. She had her own Englisch friends from the high school.

"I lost a tooth in school today," Priscilla said as she transferred her doll to one hand and fished inside her apron pocket. She produced the tooth then smiled wide to display the small gap in front.

"Very nice," Seth said. "Lose a few more, and you won't be able to chew."

"Tomorrow is the last day of school," Priscilla said. "I am supposed to bring twenty cookies, and Laura said she would help me make them tonight. And you are coming to my program, okay?"

"I would not dream of missing your program. Let me hear what you are going to recite," Seth said.

"Nae, it is a surprise."

Miriam felt a bit ashamed at how little she knew about Seth's sisters. Had she disregarded them as easily as Seth said she had? The thought would not quit nagging at her. She could start remedying that situation right now. "Are you still going to the high school, Laura?"

Laura put an arm around Priscilla and studied Miriam with unguarded suspicion. "Yes, I graduate next week."

"Oh, that is nice," Miriam said.

Poor family, to have a daughter jump the fence. Thank goodness Miriam's family was firmly planted in the community and wouldn't dream of embracing the Englisch ways.

The train of Miriam's thoughts ran merrily down the path they always had until she stopped and examined where her notions were taking her.

Seth was right.

She had always felt superior to the Lambrights.

She, who had a sister with a horrible secret, found it easy to judge Seth for his very public misfortunes.

"Laura is going to the University of Wisconsin this fall, Lord willing." Seth obviously didn't view Laura's choices as shameful or wrong. He put an arm around his sister. "She got a scholarship."

Miriam found her voice and tried not to force her sincerity. "That is wonderful-gute. What subject will you be studying?"

A smile bloomed on Laura's face. Miriam wondered if anyone besides Seth ever cared to ask. "I am thinking about being a history teacher."

"I think I would be scared out of my wits to leave home like that. Are you excited?"

"Oh, yes. And a little scared. But one of my friends is going with me, and I hear they are very nice at the school."

"I'm sure you will do well," Miriam said.

Laura nodded gratefully. So did Seth.

"Laura is going to help me make a blanket for Lady Dancing before she goes away to the unisity," Priscilla said.

Seth looked at Miriam. "Scilla calls her doll 'Lady Dancing.'"

"We will just cut a square out of a piece of fabric," Laura said. "I do not know how to make a proper quilt."

Miriam held out her hand and Priscilla placed her doll into Miriam's care. "What kind of a blanket do you want for Lady Dancing?"

"Like a patch quilt," Priscilla said. "I have fabric of my mamm's."

"I can help you make one," Miriam said.

Seth raised an eyebrow.

Laura did too. "Oh, you don't have to do that. It is only a doll blanket."

"But I want to help. That is, if you'd like me to. I can see that Lady Dancing is a special doll. She deserves a special blanket."

"Okay," Laura said. "You make beautiful quilts. It will probably be the fanciest doll blanket in the world."

Fancy. Ephraim didn't like fancy.

Miriam cleared her throat. "Not too fancy, of course. Tomorrow is the school program and Saturday is full of chores. Would you like to come to my house on Tuesday next?" She glanced at Seth. "Or, better yet, I could come to your house. Do you have a sewing machine?"

Priscilla nodded and showed all the teeth that were still in her mouth. "Can it be pink? Lady Dancing loves pink."

"You and Laura find the fabric you want to use."

"Okay," Priscilla said.

Laura took Priscilla's hand. "We want to say hello to the horses."

Laura and Priscilla walked behind the stable and left Seth staring at Miriam with an unreadable expression on his face. He frowned slightly but his gray eyes glowed with an unexplained warmth.

He loosened her rope from the hook and handed it to her. "Denki," he said. "If you are kind to my sisters, I am your friend for life."

"Does that mean you might decide you like me after all?"

He rubbed his chin. "Jah, I might decide I like you."

Miriam swung her leg over the horse and perched squarely in the saddle. "Too bad, because I don't care if you like me or not."

As she turned Daisy down the lane toward the green pastures and cheerful yellow wildflowers, she heard Seth Lambright chuckle for the first time ever.

CHAPTER
EIGHT

"Denki, Yost. When will you be back to get me?" Miriam jumped from the buggy with her sewing basket in hand.

Yost fingered the reins impatiently. "Can you walk home? I have places I need to be."

Miriam frowned and squinted in Yost's direction. "Where do you have to go that is so important? You don't work today. Being with your friends does not count."

"Maybe I'm earning some extra money for a car," Yost said. "What do you think about that, Miss High-and-Mighty?"

She shook her finger at him. "That a silly idea has crawled into that empty head of yours and taken up residence. Come fetch me at two o'clock."

Yost jiggled the buggy reins and the horse started forward. "Walk home. I won't be back to get you."

"But..."

Yost snapped the reins and the buggy was a hundred feet down the road before Miriam could argue. She huffed in exasperation and hoped that brother of hers would come to his senses before two o'clock.

Not likely.

In front of the Lambrights' house, young grapevines grew up a trellis that formed a fence at the edge of the grass. Later in the summer it would be heavy with grapes.

Fourteen flagstones dotted the grass leading up to the Lambrights' front door. Miriam remembered them well. When she and Susie and Mamm brought meals five years ago, Miriam would count the stones as she stepped on them. At the time, she found it fascinating that there were fourteen stones and she was fourteen years old.

Her heart raced as she stepped onto the porch and knocked on the door. It surprised her how badly she wanted Seth and his sisters to like her, to think she was a good person. And when she was this anxious about pleasing someone, she usually messed up terribly, like at the stable when Seth told her she was trying too hard.

But he'd smiled when he said it.

A dog yipped incessantly inside the house as Miriam heard the patter of little feet. Priscilla opened the door, and a miniature white ball of wire and porcupine quills darted out of the house and barked around Miriam's ankles.

"Pookie, be quiet," scolded Priscilla. "Pookie...be nice."

Pookie ignored the chastisement and kept up the noise until Seth appeared, grabbed the dog by the collar, and pulled it back into the house. Pookie gave Seth one yap of displeasure and trotted away without a second look at Miriam.

"Sorry about the dog," Seth said. "He's been kicked out of three obedience schools."

Miriam willed her racing heart to slow down. "He's cute."

Seth grimaced. "Only if you are fond of nails and pokey things. Please, come in."

Miriam walked into the Lambright house for the first time in her life. Neither she nor Seth thought it necessary to comment on the occasion.

"I chose the fabric I want," Priscilla said, taking Miriam's hand and leading her into the kitchen. "It's pink and purple. And with flowers."

Seth's stepmother, Ellie, sat on her haunches, scrubbing a table leg. Ellie had come from Ohio to marry Seth's fater a few years ago, but Miriam knew almost nothing else about her. Miriam scolded herself again. She hadn't taken interest in any of the Lambrights.

Ellie popped up the minute she saw Miriam. "Why, Miriam Bontrager, how nice to see you. You were not here at church two weeks ago. Was everything all right?"

"Callie came down with a fever, and I stayed home to care for him." She glanced at Seth. "I most surely would have come if I could have. Mamm told me the sermon lifted her heart, and she said you made delicious cookies for the dinner afterward."

Ellie beamed. "Oh my, I never had so many people in my house. I wish you could have seen. I scrubbed and waxed this floor 'til it shown like a mirror, and then the men tramped the dirt in on their boots. But my walls shone clean and the whole room smelled of Pine-Sol."

Miriam nodded. "I'm sure it was a wonder to behold."

"Trying to keep this house clean with five messy children can send anyone to an early grave. It's a task, I'll tell you that."

Miriam smiled to herself. She wasn't the only one trying too hard. "You do a fine job. This home is cleanliness itself."

Ellie wiped her hands on a dish towel. "I'm glad you've come for a visit. Sit down and have a cup of coffee. Special blend."

Miriam motioned to Priscilla, who stood patiently waiting

for Ellie to stop talking. "That would be lovely, but we should get started."

"On what?"

"I've come to help Priscilla make a quilt for her doll."

Ellie's smile faded. "Oh. Well, I would have helped her myself, but keeping house is a constant job."

"I know it is," Miriam said. "My mamm barely has time to breathe most days."

"Priscilla," Ellie said, turning on her stepdaughter, "it was very rude of you to ask Miriam to make you a quilt when she has so many other things to do. That old burp rag works fine for a blanket."

Out of the corners of her eye, Miriam saw Seth tighten his jaw muscles.

"I asked Priscilla if I could help her make a quilt," Miriam said. "I've always wanted to make a doll blanket. It is no trouble at all."

Seth unclenched his fists and fixed his eyes on Miriam.

"Where is the sewing machine, Priscilla?"

"Upstairs in Laura's room."

Ellie waved her hand in dismissal. "That old thing? It is very slow. I told Abbie we need a new one, but he doesn't listen to me. The men don't have to make school clothes for the children, so they don't care what we go through to sew a decent stitch."

"An old machine is fun. They are built so sturdy." Miriam hoped Ellie didn't mind being contradicted. She bent over to Priscilla. "I thought we could do a Nine-Patch."

"What is a Nine-Patch?" Priscilla asked.

"I will draw you a picture. Ellie, would you like to come up with us? We can visit while we sew."

Priscilla shook her head slightly and stared at Miriam with

pursed lips. Miriam returned her gaze. Had she said something wrong?

"I'd like to, but I must get these scuff marks off the table legs where certain people keep scraping their shoes even though I tell them not to."

Priscilla's smile returned. "I will show you Laura's room."

Ellie sighed. "Don't blame me if it's a mess up there. Laura's room is a pigsty, and I refuse to be her maid."

Seth took the sewing basket from Miriam. "Cum, I will show you."

As soon as they started up the steep steps, the dog came out of nowhere, stood at the bottom of the stairs, and resumed barking.

Seth furrowed his brow. "The good news is that Pookie does not climb stairs except in extreme emergencies."

At the top of the stairs, they turned down a hall where a set of ladder stairs with a rope handrail led to the attic door. Priscilla went in front of Miriam.

Seth followed her. "Careful. I'm right behind you if you slip."

Priscilla threw open the door and revealed a light-filled room with a large window shaped like an upside-down V. A small coal stove stood in the corner atop four cinder blocks, and a sewing machine sat next to it. The walls were bright white and bare except for a certificate tacked at the head of the bed. "CASHTON HIGH SCHOOL, 4.0 GPA," it read.

Laura stood by her bed sorting through fabric in a box. She looked up and smiled tentatively. "Hi."

"Hi," Miriam said.

Laura motioned to the sewing machine. "Seth carried it up. By himself. Without dropping it."

Seth put Miriam's sewing basket on the bed. "I'll be going now. Have a gute time."

Laura looked as uncomfortable as Miriam felt. Seth was the one person who could keep them from sinking into an awkward silence.

"Stay and keep us company," Laura said. "Why do you have to run off so soon?"

Seth's eyes danced in amusement. "Because I've got to get to my horses, and a quilting bee is no place for a man."

"Oh, posh," Laura said.

Seth reached out and cupped his hand around Miriam's elbow. "Thank you for coming here. You'll never know how grateful I am."

"No thanks necessary," Miriam said.

"You'll never know."

He bounded down the stairs, leaving Miriam to make conversation with someone she hadn't ever made an effort to know. Her discomfort stuck in her throat like a dry piece of bread.

Miriam looked from one sister to the next then pointed to the pile of fabric on Laura's bed. "Is all this your fabric?"

Laura waved in the direction of two other boxes sitting in the corner. "And that. My mamm loved to quilt. She collected scraps and bought some at auctions."

"These is what I want for mine," Priscilla said, holding up a pink piece and a purple piece and a floral print that incorporated both colors.

Miriam opened her sewing basket and pulled out a small notebook and a pen. She drew a big square on the page and filled it in with three rows and three columns of smaller squares. Nine squares altogether.

"This is what a Nine-Patch square looks like," she said, showing Priscilla her drawing. "A big Nine-Patch quilt would be several of these smaller Nine-Patches sewn together. I am making one like this for a friend. But for your quilt, I think we should do nine squares. It will be just the right size for Lady Dancing."

Priscilla jumped up and down and clapped her hands. "Jah, that is esactly what I want."

Miriam pulled out her tape measure, and Priscilla decided how big she wanted the quilt. Then the three of them marked the fabric and cut out squares.

"Now cum, Priscilla, and I will show you how to use the machine," Miriam said.

Priscilla cheerfully hopped into the chair, too young to be intimidated by something new. Miriam regarded the machine, which looked old enough to be considered an authentic antique. Most of the gold paint on the letters on the front of the machine had worn off, and there was even a large scratch through the last letter, but Miriam could still read the word "Damascus," regardless.

Miriam pointed to the pedal. "Put both feet there." Priscilla had to sit on the edge of her seat and stretch her legs, but she could reach the pedal.

"First, put the presser foot down and turn the handwheel, like this. Now slowly press down with your toes and relax and then press down with your heels."

Priscilla giggled as the machine clicked and the needle moved in rhythm with her feet.

"A little slower. There you go. You want to go slow enough that your stitches will be straight."

Once Priscilla got the hang of the movement, Miriam threaded the machine and then took a scrap of fabric and placed it under the presser foot. "Practice on this."

She showed Priscilla how to turn the wheel to move the needle into the fabric. "Now move your feet up and down like I showed you."

Priscilla worked the pedal, and the needle bobbed up and

down through the fabric, leaving a crooked line of tiny stitches behind it.

"Gute, Priscilla. Now practice guiding the fabric through the machine to make a straight line. Use the line on the plate under the fabric to help you. And be careful of your fingers. I sewed right through mine once."

"That must have hurt," Laura said.

"Jah, my mamm made me get a tetanus shot."

Laura groaned. "I can sympathize. I had to have about seven shots to get into school."

Once Priscilla had sewn through her scrap, Miriam gave her a longer strip to practice on. Straight lines were the key.

Laura ran her hand over the pile of fabric on her bed. "Thank you for coming today. My mamm loved to quilt but never felt well enough to teach me. Not that I blame her. I could have learned if I hadn't been so lazy."

"You are going to college," Miriam said. "I doubt you have a lazy bone in your body."

Laura sat on her bed and pulled Miriam to sit by her. "You are uncomfortable around me, aren't you?"

"What do you mean?"

"Please don't mind my frankness. I say what I think too often. But everybody acts nervous now that they know I'm jumping the fence." She held up her hands as if to stop traffic. "Keep your children away from Laura Lambright. She will corrupt them."

Priscilla giggled without taking her eyes from her sewing. "You are silly, Laura."

Miriam looked at her hands. "I don't know what you want me to say."

"I want to be friends," Laura said. "And I want you to know that I am a normal girl and you don't have to be afraid of me."

Miriam lifted her feet onto the bed and tucked her knees under her chin. "You think I'm afraid of you?"

"Maybe 'uneasy' is a better word—that you'd rather not associate with me. But it's not just you. Most Amish behave that way toward me."

"Seth says I act that way all the time."

Laura howled with laughter. "Oh, my brother! His mouth gets him into trouble sometimes. Like me."

Miriam took a deep breath. "I suppose I am uncomfortable around you because I don't understand you. It wonders me why you want to leave us."

"Most of the great religious wars were fought because people didn't understand each other. They didn't want to understand each other."

"I want to understand."

"I am done practicing," Priscilla said, scooting back in her chair and swinging her legs.

Miriam inspected Priscilla's stitches. Then she pinned two squares together and handed them to her. "Sew these together, making the seam this wide. Be careful with the pins. Do you think you can do that?"

Priscilla nodded. "I will go slow."

Miriam watched over Priscilla's shoulder while she sewed the pieces of fabric together. Priscilla sewed to the end, cut her thread, and held up the two squares now attached with a nice curvy seam. "It's crooked."

Miriam handed Priscilla two more squares. "Try again on these while I unpick." Turning to Laura, she said, "I spend more time taking stitches out than I do putting them in." She sat on the bed and pulled the seam ripper from her sewing kit. "Tell me about your decision to go to college. I want to understand."

"My mother got sick—depressed, Seth says." Laura leaned in and whispered, "After the baby."

Miriam glanced at Priscilla. Laura was wise. Priscilla need never carry guilt for what happened to her mother.

"I spent a lot of time at Britny Engle's house while Mamm lay in bed. Britny is Englisch. I first considered leaving the community because I loved television. It helped me to forget how bad things were at home." Laura leaned back on her hands. "I don't mean to offend you when I say this, but when Mamm died, I realized how isolated and insignificant her life had been. That's what made her so unhappy in the first place. I didn't want to end up like that."

"But most Amish are very happy."

"I know," Laura said. "I've seen the studies. Happier than the general population. But I'm not happy in this way of life. And I knew five years ago that I wouldn't be."

"Was your mamm...was she unhappy with your dat?"

"Nae. Dat is easy to get along with. He is perfectly content with himself and everybody else. He couldn't understand what was happening to Mamm, so he pretended nothing was wrong. Seth begged him more than once to get Mamm some help. Dat simply did not know what to do. The uncertainty paralyzed him."

"It must have been terrible to lose your mother."

Laura's eyes grew moist. "It made everything worse. To know that she wanted to leave us—that was the deepest cut of all." She looked away. "It took me a long time to forgive her for that."

"I'm sorry."

"Seth disappeared for three days after she died and then didn't say a word, not a word, to anyone for a month. He spent hours at the stable brushing the horses."

"I don't know what I would do without my mother."

Laura gazed at Miriam. "Everyone treated us like lepers because of how she died."

"Maybe they didn't know what to say."

"To be sure. Most people meant no harm," Laura said. "But some still hold it against us. The looks and whispers behind the hands still sting, but we've endured worse, so we try to pay no never mind."

Miriam felt her face get hot.

"I'm done with this one," Priscilla said.

Miriam slid off the bed to the sewing machine, to examine Priscilla's latest attempt. "Better. Here, let me show you. Put your hands flat like this and guide the fabric along this line. As slow as you can go. Try one more time while I unpick."

"Believe me," Laura whispered, "it would be worse if I were trying to work that machine."

"You should try it," Miriam said.

"I'd be useless."

"What about a quilt for your room at college? We could whip something up using your mamm's fabric."

The shadow of a grin played at Laura's lips. "You'd be unpicking for days."

"It would be fun."

Laura's face bloomed into a full smile. "It would be nice to have something of my mamm's at college. But I would need a lot of help."

"Please, let me help. Quilting is my favorite thing to do."

The machine fell silent. "Miriam," said Priscilla, "I'm done. Is this good?"

Miriam went back to the sewing machine and examined Priscilla's quilt blocks. Not a perfectly straight line, but definitely good enough.

"Jah, jah, wonderful-gute, Priscilla. Here is the next one."

Priscilla sewed with determination while Laura ironed and

Miriam unpicked seams. They soon had a beautiful square made up of nine smaller squares. And if all the corners didn't match up exactly right, only Miriam noticed.

Miriam cut a piece of batting to fit the square and then chose a matching purple for the back. She showed Priscilla and Laura how to baste the top, the batting, and the bottom together, and then she stretched the small quilt into an embroidery hoop.

"Let me show you how to do the stitches," Miriam said. She threaded a needle with quilter's thread, showed Priscilla how to secure a knot, and made a stitch. "Go down and up, like this." She moved slowly, making sure Priscilla saw how she worked the needle to make tiny stitches, and then handed the hoop and quilt to Priscilla. "You try."

Priscilla concentrated with all the energy of a five-year-old while she tried to copy Miriam's technique.

When Miriam was satisfied that Scilla could do it on her own, she said, "You can work on your quilt any time of the day. Then I will come back and show you how to bind it."

"When will it be done?" asked Priscilla, her eyes glued to the work of her hands.

"As quickly as you can stitch it."

Holding firmly to the embroidery hoop, Priscilla jumped up and down. "I will go fast."

Miriam gathered her supplies in her sewing basket. "Laura, decide what kind of quilt you want to make, and when I come back to help Priscilla with her binding, we can get started on yours."

"I will."

Miriam took hold of Laura's arm. "Just so you know, I am not uneasy around you anymore."

"And I'm not scared of you. But"—the corners of Laura's mouth twitched upward—"I think Seth is."

CHAPTER NINE

Before suppertime, Miriam finished cutting the fabric for Ephraim's Nine-Patch quilt. She stacked the three colors and neatly folded the scraps in her basket. Ephraim had better taste in colors than Miriam thought. The tan fabric he'd chosen grounded the bright red and yellow and would give the quilt a charming country look. Aunt Emma had recently taught her a new way to sew a Nine Patch together, and Miriam looked forward to using it on Ephraim's engagement quilt.

She arched her back and looked out the window. Susie was hanging the last of the day's laundry on the line.

Miriam walked outside to help and put her arm around her sister. "Three more weeks, and you won't have to do so much laundry."

Susie didn't even look at Miriam as she bent over and retrieved another pair of trousers from the basket. "They don't have any children. I'll be all alone with them in their big house."

"But you can meet people at gmay and gatherings. You will have double the friends by the time you leave."

"Oh, jah, surely they will want to befriend the unwed pregnant girl who plans to give up her baby."

There was no mistaking the bitterness in her voice. Susie was understandably frightened, but why did she have to be so ungrateful? Miriam had bent over backward to make this work out for them.

"I just wanted someone to love me, Miriam. Is that so wicked?"

Miriam tried to ignore the stab of indignation that Susie's declaration gave her. What Susie had done was wrong because she sought for love outside of the arms of Jesus. "You are loved."

"I am ignored."

Miriam pulled a dress out of the basket. "Here, I will help you."

Susie didn't reply, but a tear slipped down her cheek. Miriam's irritation won out, and she couldn't muster any sympathy for her sister just now. She'd gotten herself into this mess. Miriam was trying to help her out of it.

They worked alongside each other in silence, fastening the clothes to the line and then sliding the rope so the laundry rose higher and higher into the air. With not even a hint of a breeze, the clothes hung limply on the line, waiting for the sun to dry them.

Miriam heard the crackle of tires on gravel and turned as a police car slowly made its way up the driveway. She held her breath. There was almost nothing more frightening than the sight of a police car. It could only mean that something terrible had happened to someone they loved.

Miriam dropped the wet apron in her hand and sprinted

for the house. Could Aunt Erla have taken a turn for the worse? Or had there been a buggy accident with one of the neighbors? Miriam's heart raced with the possibilities. "Mamm, Dat, come outside quick."

Mamm was coating chicken to fry for supper. Concern bloomed on her face when she looked at Miriam. "Is there an accident?"

"Where's Dat?"

"In the barn."

"Come outside."

Miriam bolted out the back door and found her dat pitching hay. "There's a police car come up the lane."

Dat frowned, stabbed his pitchfork into a bale of hay, and followed Miriam.

The policeman turned off his engine and got out of his car just as Dat and Miriam reached it. Mamm emerged from the house wiping her hands on a dish towel.

"I'm looking for Mr. John Bontrager," said the policeman.

Dat removed his hat. "I am John Bontrager."

By this time, Susie and the three little boys had gathered near the police car with eyes wide, as they stared at the shiny badge and gun holstered at the officer's side. Miriam had never seen anyone quite so intimidating.

"Your son, Yost, has been arrested and is being held at the Sun Pines Juvenile Detention Center."

Miriam's stomach lurched as if she were falling down a flight of stairs. *There must be some mistake.*

Mamm put a hand to her throat. "Arrested? Why?"

"I do not understand," Dat said.

The officer kept any emotion from his voice. "We caught him selling drugs in the city park."

Miriam swept the floor for the third time that day. She didn't have the heart to do anything useful while she waited for Mamm and Dat to come home. They had been gone since eight o'clock that morning, and it now was long past suppertime. Miriam and Susie had fed the three little boys and told them to go play. Instead of bolting outside at the first opportunity, they moped around the great room as they kept their eyes on the front window for any sign of Mamm, Dat, or Yost.

Susie knelt in the corner, scrubbing the seams in the wood floor with an old toothbrush. She sniffed periodically as she swished the toothbrush back and forth.

Miriam let out a sigh and put her hand on her hip. "You don't have to do that, Suz."

Susie turned her head and looked at Miriam out of the corner of her eye. "I want it to be as clean as the day we got it."

"It will never be that clean again."

Susie stubbornly stuck to her futile task. In another hour, she'd have three or four square inches of floor sparkling clean.

More than anything, Miriam wanted to believe the entire affair as some sort of misunderstanding. The policeman had told Mamm and Dat that they weren't allowed to see Yost until this morning, when they could meet with a caseworker to evaluate Yost's situation. Miriam had prayed more than once today that they would bring Yost home with them. What if he had to stay in detention? The thought sent panic surging through Miriam's veins. Lord willing, Yost would be allowed to come home.

Isaac and Raymond, standing at the front window, both yelled at the same time. "They're here. They are back."

Miriam bolted out the door with her little brothers and stood at the front gate while a white car ambled up the driveway. Yost, looking as pale as a sheet, slid out of the backseat, followed by Mamm and Dat. He kept his eyes to the ground as

Dat paid the driver then shuffled to the house while his family followed close behind. Six-year-old Raymond tried to grab Yost's hand, but Yost pulled away and quickened his pace to the door.

As they entered the great room, Yost turned to the stairs to ascend to the safety of his room.

"Nae, nae, Yost John," Dat said, pointing to the sofa. "You will sit here, and we will talk."

Yost slouched his shoulders and plopped himself onto the sofa. When Dat used that tone of voice, no one dared disobey him.

Miriam grabbed Raymond's hand and pushed Callie and Isaac toward the kitchen.

"Let them stay, Miriam. They will want to hear what I have to say in case they think of being so foolish in the future."

Miriam hesitated, but Dat motioned for the little boys to sit on the floor next to Mamm in the rocker. Miriam backed away to the wall, unwilling to bring herself any closer to the conflict between father and son. She wanted to run to the far pasture.

Dat wasted no time. His first words were loud and harsh. "Shame on you. What were you thinking?"

"Dat, I'm sorry—"

"The answer is, you weren't thinking!" Dat yelled, not caring what Yost had to say for himself. He scowled and pinned Yost with a look that could have frozen the sun. "Do you know the evil you have brought into the world with your actions? How many people have taken that poison into their bodies because of you? How many children are addicted because of you?"

Miriam had never seen her fater so angry. In truth, she had never seen him lose his temper in her entire life. His usual calm, loving manner had completely disappeared.

Dat paced up and down the room and yelled even louder.

"People die every day because of drugs. There are evil men who kill people for drugs. They *kill* people. You have blood on your hands!"

Yost buried his face in his hands. "I didn't mean—"

"Look at me," Dat said. "Look me in the eyes so I know that you understand what you have done."

By this time, Susie had tiptoed into the room. She stood beside Miriam with her eyes wide and her fingers clamped around Miriam's wrist. All three little boys were now crying. Isaac dug his fists into his eyes. Raymond clamped his hands over his ears to shut out the yelling. Mamm held on to the arms of the rocker as if by sheer will she could make Dat stop.

Yost glared at Dat through his tears. "I wanted to buy a car," he said, his voice barely audible.

Dat's face turned red. "Our family is shamed because you wanted to buy a car? Our community is shamed because you wanted to buy a car? You greedy, selfish boy. I raised you better."

Yost sprang to his feet and stood toe-to-toe with Dat. "If you had loaned me the money to buy a car, this wouldn't have happened."

Dat lowered his voice to a growl. "You are responsible for your own actions. Until you learn that, you will continue to wallow in wickedness. Shame on you. Go to your room and think upon your sins instead of who you can blame for them."

Yost didn't have to be excused twice. He turned his back on Dat, stomped up the stairs, and slammed the door to his room so hard that it rattled the rafters.

Mamm, with tears trailing down her cheeks, gathered the three little boys in her arms and hugged them tightly.

"Does he have to go to jail?" Miriam said.

A soft knock at the door sent Mamm and Susie and the

boys fleeing for the safety of the kitchen. "I don't want to see anybody," Mamm said. "Just make them go away."

Dat opened the door. Bishop Schwartz stood on the doorstep holding a small book in his hand. "How is Yost?"

"You heard?" Dat said.

"Martha Kae saw the commotion at the park, and then the Bielers came to the house last night."

"Jah," Dat said, "they were at the detention center this morning with Joe. He and Yost were selling drugs together."

Joe Bieler—the one Yost envied because he had a car.

The bishop nodded, a mixture of sympathy and resignation on his face. This was not news to him. "Is Yost still at the jail?"

"Nae, he has been released to us," Dat said. "The judge says he must be under house arrest for three weeks and then, if he behaves, probation for six months and a fine."

Miriam felt a tiny bit better. At least Yost would not be locked up like an animal. She couldn't bear the thought.

"Would you like me to talk to him?" the bishop asked.

Dat glanced at Miriam. "I think another day would be better."

Bishop Schwartz laid a hand on Dat's shoulder. "Of course. I am sure it has been a bad day for all of you. I brought him a prayer book he might find comforting."

Dat took the small book and handed it to Miriam. "Take this to your brother, would you?"

"What can we do to help?" Miriam heard the bishop say as she numbly dragged herself up the stairs to Yost's room.

What can we do to help?

Miriam felt dizzy. Martha Kae had seen the arrest and the bishop had already visited with the Bielers. No doubt the news had spread to every Amish home in the community. There would be no hiding this latest family tragedy from Ephraim.

Holding back a flood of tears, Miriam knocked on Yost's door and entered without waiting to be invited. Yost paced back and forth in the small room he shared with Raymond like a caged animal. "What do you want?" he snapped.

"The bishop brought this for you." She held out the book to him, but he didn't take it.

Instead, he threw up his hands. "The bishop? Why did he come?" He turned his back on her, raised his fist, and pounded the wall.

Miriam set the book on his bed and ignored what felt like a gaping hole in her chest. "Are you okay?"

"Would you be okay after getting arrested and then having Dat yell at you like that?"

"He is very angry."

"I didn't mean no harm to anyone. I want a car, a little freedom. Is that too much to ask? But Dat doesn't care how I feel. All he cares about is the shame I brought to the family."

"You got arrested by the police, Yost. What do you expect from us?"

Yost growled in frustration, sat on the bed, and clenched his fists. "I feel like I'm going to explode, like if I sit still I will break into a million pieces. I hate it." He dug his hands into his thighs. "I want to be left alone. Can't people see I want them to leave me alone?"

He looked so pathetic, sitting there like a naughty schoolboy who'd been severely disciplined by the teacher. Even though he acted unreasonably, Miriam felt sorry for him. She softened her tone. "Can't you see how you brought this on yourself?"

His eyes flashed with fresh pain as he snatched the prayer book from the bed and hurled it across the room.

Miriam flinched.

"Save your sermon for someone who cares," he said.

Scowling, Miriam put her hands on her hips. "I'll leave you to wallow in your self-pity. I've heard how badly you want to be left alone." She turned on her heels and marched down the stairs. Only when she got to the bottom did she realize how much she was shaking.

Everyone but Dat had congregated in the kitchen, hoping to find comfort in each other. Susie stirred the stew and whimpered softly. Raymond had his arms clamped securely around Mamm's waist as she leaned motionless against the counter. Callie and Isaac set the table in silence.

Miriam took the stack of paper napkins from Callie. "Let's fold these to look like little flowers. I will show you."

"We are going to be all right. It will be alright, Lord willing," Mamm said. She smoothed Raymond's hair. "We must all pray very hard for Yost."

"Will the police come again?" Callie asked.

"They will come to check on Yost sometimes," Mamm said. "That is one of the rules."

"I don't like their guns," Callie said.

"Does he have to go back to jail?" Raymond asked next.

Mamm shook her head slowly. "Not if he obeys all the rules."

Raymond wiped tears from his face. "Dat must make him obey all the rules."

Miriam concentrated on folding the flimsy paper napkins. Napkin design was so much safer than real life.

Someone else knocked at the front door. Susie pretended not to hear, and Mamm stood as if listening to a distant train whistle. Miriam found herself sharing Yost's sentiments. Why couldn't everybody leave them alone in their shame?

She left her napkins and dragged herself to the front room.

There certainly wouldn't be happiness on the other side of that door.

Ephraim, with hat in hand, stood on her doorstep. He narrowed his gaze, and Miriam could see a vein pulsing in his neck. Her tongue suddenly seemed to swell, as if she had a mouthful of cotton.

"Can we talk?" he said.

Miriam nodded, stepped outside, and closed the door behind her.

"Oh, Miri, such a tragedy. I came to see how you are doing."

"Terrible. We feel terrible."

"How could Yost have fallen into this gross wickedness? I can't hardly believe it. Selling drugs. I have never been so shocked as when I heard."

Miriam could only incline her head. The lump in her throat made it impossible to speak.

"The only thing for your dat to do is to cast him from the house so he does not influence the little boys to follow in his footsteps."

"Throw him out?"

"Your whole family is tainted with his sin as long as he stays, especially since your dat is one of the ministers. My dat said so."

"But how can Dat throw him out? He has no place to go."

"Yost should have thought of that before getting himself into trouble. When I think of the wickedness, I am almost sick."

Miriam felt long-delayed tears stinging her eyes. "What he did was very wrong."

"And selfish. Think of how his crime has affected your family. It makes you look weak in the eyes of the community. People wonder if your parents have neglected their duty to train up their child in the way he should go."

"They do?"

"Where else should the blame be placed when a child goes astray?"

Miriam's head began to throb. She massaged a spot above her right eye.

"We know what will become of him if he stiffens his neck and refuses to get off the path to hell. Remind him daily of his wickedness, Miri. Do not let him forget what he has done to you."

Miriam didn't respond. The last thing she wanted to do was give Yost another lecture. She'd seen how far that had taken her.

Ephraim swished his hair with his fingers. "I am so, so sorry for you. Yost must repent quickly of this great wickedness. I don't want anything to delay our wedding."

"Delay our wedding?" It is two and a half years away.

"I must go now. I only wanted to see how you are doing. I will pray for you every day, dear Miriam."

"Denki," Miriam said, forcing the air through her tight throat. "We will see you tomorrow at the singeon?"

He raised an eyebrow. "Do you think it would be wise for you to come? It is better that you should attend to matters at home."

"Oh...I didn't think of that. I will stay home if you think it best."

"I do."

She forced a smile. "Then I will see you sometime next week?"

"Jah, Lord willing. Good night." He turned his back on her and sauntered down her sidewalk as if he were going to a picnic.

Miriam sighed and wiped away a lone tear. Seeing Ephraim usually sent her soaring to the sky with elation, but his visit had only succeeded in making her feel worse than ever. She felt selfish, wishing for Ephraim's comfort at a time when the whole community reeled from the arrest, but loneliness still encompassed her as she watched him disappear into the darkness.

CHAPTER
TEN

"Anything I should know about before I look in these drawers?"

Yost stood in the doorway with his hands balled into fists, his eyes on the floor. He shook his head. Miriam waited beside him, fixing her eyes on the caseworker or parole officer or whoever he was as he opened one drawer after another and stirred Yost's few clothes around, looking for drugs or something else illegal.

Mamm, Susie, and the three little boys had shut themselves in Mamm's room while this Englischer invaded their privacy. One of the conditions of Yost's release was that an officer of the court could appear at the home any time of the day to check on Yost and search his things for drugs. Only a week and a half after Yost's release, the Englischer had already made three visits.

There wasn't much to search. Yost and Raymond's room consisted of two beds, a small chest of drawers, and a rag rug on the floor. The Englischer still managed to make a mess of the room as he checked under the mattresses and pulled clothes out of the drawers.

Leaving both mattresses askew, the chubby, balding man picked up his clipboard and jotted down a few notes.

He spoke to Yost, but Yost wouldn't look at him. "Be at the justice center on Wednesday at three to meet with your parole officer. You're doing good, but don't forget that one of your parents must be with you at all times. If they both have to go out, you gotta go with them."

Yost nodded, his eyes still glued to the floor. He had already experienced the humiliating consequences of that rule. Last Thursday, Miriam and Mamm had dragged Yost to a quilting bee. He sat in the corner of the kitchen at Mary Hoover's house enduring the pitiful looks of the women and the curious eyes of the little girls. He had come home and barricaded himself in his room. From below, Miriam heard him pacing the floor and pounding on walls.

Now, she followed the Englischer to the front door. He didn't smile, and she didn't smile. They simply nodded to each other before she closed the door and shut him out. Yost endured the humiliation because he had no other choice, but Miriam found it nearly unbearable.

Upstairs, Yost stood in the spot where she had left him, carved from stone and sand.

"Cum," Miriam said. "I will help you tidy the room."

"I can't stand this," Yost muttered. "I can't stand this."

Miriam didn't know how to respond except with anger, so she chose to ignore his turmoil. "Tuck the sheet on that side."

Yost didn't move. "I felt like I was on fire, like the flames would jump out of my hands and burn me up. I hate him for coming."

Miriam's pulse raced with the urge to lash out at her brother. *You brought this on yourself, you know. Mamm hides in her room in shame because you let greed overtake your virtue. My Ephraim hasn't set foot on our property for ten days because your behavior has spread a stain of sin over our entire family. Our perfect, exemplary family.*

Get out! she wanted to scream. *Go away and never come home again!*

Instead, she turned her back on him, adjusted the mattress on Raymond's bed, and tucked the sheet into place. She smoothed the quilts on each bed—red, white, and blue pinwheel patterns. She had made them last year right before her baptism.

Yost slumped his shoulders and leaned against the doorjamb. "I'm sorry, Miriam."

Miriam stood up straight and looked at her brother. The pain she saw in his eyes almost cracked the wall of her anger. "Straighten the drawers. And refold Raymond's clothes too. You owe him that much."

She marched out of the room and downstairs to the kitchen to make breakfast for the family. Holding back self-indulgent tears, she pulled bacon from the icebox and arranged it in the skillet. Then she whipped up pancake batter and poured four perfect circles into the second skillet. When the batter began to bubble, she tried to turn the pancakes...only to discover that they were stuck like glue. She had forgotten the oil.

Gripping her spatula with white knuckles, she scraped the pan vigorously until the first pancake surrendered its hold on the skillet and folded into a doughy heap. With the half-cooked pancake balanced on her spatula, she walked to the garbage can and flipped the pancake in. Of course, the ruined pancake wouldn't go quietly. Dough splattered on the wall behind the garbage can and on the floor in front of it.

Miriam slammed the spatula onto the counter, unrolled seven or eight sections of paper towel, and wiped up her mess.

About the time she got rid of all the little drops of pancake batter, she smelled burning dough. Jumping to her feet, she snatched the skillet off the cookstove and burned her thumb. She hissed in pain and frustration as she looked at her cooking efforts thus far. Raw bacon and pancakes...doughy on one side, charred to a crisp on the other.

She couldn't help herself. She burst into tears and cried like a newborn *buplie*. Tears sizzled on the skillet as she scraped out the rest of the blackened pancakes and tossed them into the garbage.

Mamm must have heard the screeching of metal against metal. She appeared at Miriam's side, put her arm around her, and gently took the spatula from her hand. "Oh, *leibe*. You carry everyone's sorrow in your apron pocket."

"Everything is all wrong," Miriam said. "How can everything be so wrong?"

Mamm held Miriam's chin in her hand "You need to get out of the house, away from our problems. Go. Go take a walk."

Miriam didn't argue. She longed for a break from the depressing atmosphere of the house. Because of their troubles, Martha had given her some time off from the quilt shop, but that only served to make Miriam feel isolated and trapped.

"Go. I will see if I can rescue breakfast." Mamm gave Miriam a half smile and nudged her out of the kitchen.

Miriam retrieved her black bonnet from the hook and practically sprinted out the door. She knew exactly how she wanted to spend the morning.

The walk to Seth Lambright's ranch took almost a half hour. In her solitude, she found it impossible to think of anything but the dreadful circumstances of her family. Her mind jumped from Susie to Yost and back again, and the closer she got to Seth's place, the heavier her steps became. By the time she turned into the lane, she felt as if she had an anvil in her chest instead of a heart.

Even though she wanted to see the foals, Miriam dreaded the reception she would get from Seth. Would he lecture her as Ephraim had done? Or gloat over the stuck-up girl's misfortunes?

What did it matter? She deserved every unsympathetic look or cross word she got.

This time she didn't knock. She pushed open the stable door and took a tentative step into the dim space.

Seth stood with his thumbs hooked around his suspenders, talking to an Englischer who wore jeans and a green button-down shirt. Seth looked up and flashed a genuine, if tentative, smile. The expression took her breath away. The comfort of a friendly face almost brought forth a fresh bout of tears.

"Miriam, this is my friend, Doug Matthews."

Doug, the Englischer, stepped forward as if he would run her over and took Miriam's hand firmly in his. "Nice to meet you."

"I am sorry if I am interrupting," Miriam said.

Doug shook his head. "Not at all. I was just leaving. We'll see you next Tuesday night, Seth."

"You got it," Seth responded, as he watched Doug walk out the door.

"I thought you might be at the mill this morning yet," Miriam said.

Seth hung a harness on a hook on the stable wall. "I work the afternoon shift. Come to see the horses?"

Miriam nodded.

"They are in the pasture. Cum."

With measured steps, she followed him behind the stable as she had before to where the foals played in the pasture with their mothers.

"They have grown since last time."

"Jah, they grow so fast you can almost watch it before your eyes."

Miriam clicked her tongue and held her hand between the slats in the fence. The foals paid her no heed.

Seth tapped the top of the fence. "I will fetch some apples."

He jogged back to the stable and reappeared shortly with some apple slices, which he handed to Miriam.

She stuck her hand between the slats again and called to the horses. The bait worked. All four horses trotted her way. She spread her fingers and let the colt take the piece of apple out of her hand. She fed each horse one slice of apple and then rubbed the colt's nose while he nudged her arm looking for more.

Yost loved apples. Miriam had made him a half dozen fancy caramel apples for his birthday last winter. He had been so excited that he practically danced around the kitchen. That was the last time she saw him so happy.

Miriam took a deep breath and tried to cleanse the dark feeling from her soul, but she couldn't find a speck of hope.

Not even the foals could lift her spirits today.

"Does Ephraim like horses?" Seth asked. "Maybe you should get two horses so both of you can ride."

The mention of Ephraim brought to mind their last encounter.

"Yost must repent quickly of this great wickedness. I don't want anything to delay our wedding."

Did he truly see Yost's sins as a stumbling block to their wedding? Was her happiness in jeopardy because of her brother's wickedness?

Anxiety overwhelmed her, and the tears began to flow despite all her efforts to stifle them.

"Miriam, what is wrong? Did I say something to upset you?"

Miriam dragged the back of her hand over her eyes, but new tears took the place of the old ones faster than she could wipe them off. "I'm sorry...I didn't mean to..." Her attempt at speech made the crying worse. A sob escaped her lips, and she couldn't stop her limbs from trembling.

The look of concern in Seth's gray eyes turned to alarm. He put an arm around her and took her by the elbow. "Cum inside. It is too hot out here."

She let him lead her into the cool stable, where he pulled a folding chair out of his tiny sleeping room and bid her to sit. She sank to the chair and wiped her eyes again.

Seth handed her a handkerchief.

She nodded her thanks, buried her face in the white fabric, and wept as if no one were watching. Let Seth think what he wanted. She was too distraught to care.

The pain, the humiliation, rushed at her like a swollen river. What if Yost did not mend his ways and had to spend his life in prison? What if he got addicted to drugs? Was he a wicked boy beyond help? And Susie, Susie, who always seemed like a delicate, beautiful flower, had fallen onto forbidden paths. Now she faced exile and the pain of giving up her baby to the care of strangers. Where had their family gone wrong?

Where had she gone wrong?

With every emotion spent, Miriam blew her nose in a very unladylike manner and looked up to see Seth sitting next to her on another folding chair with his brows furrowed and a worried frown on his lips. He leaned toward her with his elbows propped on his knees and studied her face.

"I'm sorry," she said, her voice cracking in an effort to stifle the sobs.

He held up his hand. "No need to apologize."

He fell silent, and she refused to speak until she could do so with composure. Her sniffles echoed off the high ceiling of the stable as she felt his gaze upon her.

He cleared his throat. "Do you want to be alone? I can step outside."

She shook her head. "I am sorry. I did not mean to disturb you like this."

"There is nothing to be sorry for."

"If I had known I was going to bawl like a baby, I would have been sure to go to the market and let everyone stare at me."

Seth gave her a half smile. "Everyone stares at you anyway."

"They do?"

"Because you are so pretty."

Miriam felt her face flush hotter than it already was. "I am not."

Seth looked suddenly uncomfortable, averted his intense gaze, and leaned back in his chair.

"I should not go out in public until I can think about Yost without crying," she said.

"What's wrong with Yost?"

"You know. His arrest."

Seth's eyes went wide. "He was arrested? For what?"

"You haven't heard?"

"I had two shifts off at the mill this week, and I've been sleeping here for three days," Seth said. "And I try not to listen to gossip."

The shame almost choked her. "The police arrested Yost ten days ago for selling drugs."

Seth rubbed the back of his neck. "I can't believe it."

"They locked him up in detention Wednesday night and then they let him come home. Dat was very angry."

Miriam half expected Seth to make some sort of excuse to leave her presence. Instead, he pulled his chair closer. She felt the warmth spread through her as he put his hand over hers. "Oh, Miriam. I am so very sorry. You must feel terrible."

"I do. Yost has disgraced the entire family."

"Is that what you think?" He stiffened and withdrew his hand. "Or is it what Ephraim told you?"

"It is what everybody thinks."

"I don't think that." Seth leaned his elbows on his knees once more and laced his fingers together. "Is Yost okay?"

"I don't know."

"I am sure he is suffering. I can't imagine being taken away by the police and put in that awful place."

"Don't you think he deserves the punishment?"

Seth rested his chin in his palm. "It is not mine to judge what Yost deserves. His own conscience is punishment enough, I'm sure. I am more concerned for his well-being. People are always more important than what they have done."

Miriam thought of Yost's grief-stricken face and mournful moaning on the night of his release. She had been so preoccupied with her own embarrassment that she hadn't cared about Yost's. Thinking of his pain took her breath away. Why hadn't she shown more sympathy for her brother?

"I have worked alongside Yost at frolics and barn raisings," Seth said. "He is a hard worker and a gute boy. Never has a cross word for anyone. It wonders me why he did this. Is he using drugs?"

"They did a drug test when they arrested him. Nothing was in his system, praise the Lord. That is why they let him go. He wanted the money to buy a car."

"A car? Is he planning to jump the fence?"

"I do not think so, although after this week, who knows?

He told me he is angry at the whole world. Like he is going to explode if he doesn't get more freedom."

"He must be miserable."

His tone melted Miriam's heart and made her feel ashamed of her own reaction to Yost. Seth offered sympathy instead of condemnation.

"My friend Doug—the man who was here when you came—is a counselor. A social worker. He helps people with problems like this. Would you like me to ask him what he thinks?"

"About Yost?"

"I don't have to tell him your brother's name. If Yost is living with so much anger bottled up, maybe Doug can tell us how to help him."

For some reason, Miriam felt a profound sense of relief. "I would..." She let the emotion wash over her before she continued. "I would appreciate that."

He studied her with those slate-gray eyes that looked almost blue in the dim light of the stable. How could she have ever have thought he had an icy stare? They sat there without saying a word until he broke the connection with a reassuring grin and a quick pat of her hand.

"I am certain you did not come here to inspect the dirt on my stable floor. The filly has learned a new trick. I will show you."

He stood up and, with one quick flick of his wrist, collapsed the folding chair. She grabbed the back of her chair to do the same, but he quickly took it from her hands.

"It is my job to take down the chairs," he said. "It is your job to enjoy the horses. Cum."

CHAPTER
ELEVEN

"Why won't they stop fighting? I just want them to stop," Susie said.

Miriam had found Susie sitting on her bed, covering her ears with her palms and crying.

After a morning spent with Seth's horses, Miriam felt as if she were ready to face anything...until she opened the door to the sound of Dat and Yost yelling at each other in the kitchen. She sighed and slumped her shoulders. Until ten days ago, she had never heard Dat raise his voice in anger.

And lately, Susie couldn't go for more than a few hours a day without bursting into tears over the most trivial matters, like what shoes to pack for her trip or the fact that Raymond refused to eat his brussels sprouts. Would her family ever be back to normal?

Miriam gazed at her sister and longed for the other Susie— young and innocent, eager for love and happy to be alive. But that wish was impossible. Susie had lost her innocence, and there was no getting it back.

Miriam sat next to Susie on the bed and put her arm

around her. Susie rested her head on Miriam's shoulder. "Things will get better with time," Miriam said, taking Susie's hand. "It's only been a week and a half. In two weeks Yost will be able to leave the house and go back to work."

"I won't be here in two weeks."

Miriam tried to smile even as she heard the despair in Susie's voice. "Aren't you glad you'll miss the worst of it?"

"I should be here to help Yost."

"I will be here for the both of us."

Susie lifted her head and slid a few inches away from Miriam. "Of course. You don't even need me."

Miriam took a deep breath and smothered her temper. "We will always need you, Susie. But what else is to be done?"

"Nothing. You have taken care of it."

Miriam didn't think she deserved the bitterness. It always crept into Susie's voice now when they talked of her going away.

Someone knocked forcefully on the front door. Miriam listened to hear if anyone downstairs would answer it. A few seconds later, another knock came. Miriam sighed. It seemed she was the only one willing to risk opening the front door these days.

She ran down the stairs and flung open the door just as Hollow Davey Herschberger walked down the porch steps. He turned back when he heard the door open. He carried a box wrapped in cheerful yellow paper and tied with an orange ribbon.

"I thought no one was home," he said with a big smile on his face.

His expression seemed foreign. How long had it been since anyone had smiled in this house? Miriam smiled weakly, grateful for a little uplift. "Come in."

He stomped the dust off his boots. "I hope I'm not bothering you. After all the trouble with Yost, you probably don't want to see nobody." He stared at Miriam as if he didn't know what else to say on the subject. Miriam hoped he'd drop it.

Clearing his throat, he resumed smiling. "Is Susie here? I wanted to bring her a going-away gift before she leaves next week."

"Jah. I will fetch her."

Miriam tripped up the stairs and found Susie right where she'd left her.

"The door is for you," she said.

"For me? Who is it?"

"Hollow Herschberger."

Susie's eyes widened and the ghost of a grin played at the corners of her lips—the most sparkle she had shown for weeks. She bounced from the bed, straightened her kapp, and smoothed out her dress. "Do I look like I've been crying?"

"Yes."

Susie raced into the washroom and examined her reflection in the small mirror before pressing a damp washrag to her face.

"That's better," said Miriam.

Susie squinted at her reflection and pursed her lips. "It will have to do."

Although she was tempted to follow Susie down the stairs, Miriam knew instinctively that she wasn't wanted in the conversation. She sat on the bed and listened to the soft hum of their voices but couldn't hear well enough to distinguish words.

Hollow and Susie worked together every day at that pretzel stand. They seemed to be good friends. What other boy was Susie so close to?

Miriam covered her eyes and massaged her forehead. Was she blind to what stood right in front of her? She had assumed that Hollow gravitated to Susie at gatherings and singeons because Susie and Hollow's sister, Esther Rose, were friends. With her heart beating against her rib cage, Miriam clasped the bedspread in her fists to keep herself from jumping up and running downstairs to confront Hollow.

How could he have done such a thing to her sweet sister?

Taking deep breaths, Miriam willed herself to stay calm. Hollow didn't seem to be remorseful. Maybe he didn't know that Susie was three months pregnant. Miriam bit her lip. She wouldn't be the one to tell him. Yet. But she saved that thought for another time in case she changed her mind.

She heard the front door close. A few seconds later Susie appeared, holding the yellow gift. Miriam wasn't surprised when she burst into tears.

"He brought me a present. He said he doesn't want me to forget Apple Lake." Susie sat on the bed next to Miriam and fingered the curly orange ribbon on the top of the box. "I will never forget Apple Lake, but you will forget me."

Miriam thought she would explode with indignation. "Susie, you've got to tell him. He's got to do right by this child."

Susie's eyes could have popped out of her head. "You think Hollow is the father?" She stopped sniffling. "Hollow would never—"

"Are you telling me the truth?"

"Don't ask me about the father. Hollow is ten times a better man than he is." Susie wrapped her arms around the box and held it as if it were a baby. "I was so stupid, Miriam. He said no one would ever know what we did and that it wasn't a sin when two people loved each other so much. He said we were two souls who shared one heart."

"You didn't know any better."

"Yes, I did. I knew what he said was wrong, but I thought I loved him the way you love Ephraim. I wanted to believe him with all my heart."

Miriam grasped Susie's arm. "Maybe he still loves you. It's not too late to marry and make things right."

A bitter laugh escaped Susie's lips. "He has not said a word to me since that night. He won't even look at me when we pass on the street. I wouldn't marry him now even if he asked."

"But if he knew about the baby—"

Susie lifted her chin in stubborn determination. "He would reject both of us. I will never be taken in by him again."

Miriam looked at her sister in surprise. Susie had never displayed such backbone.

Susie slid the ribbon from the present and tore back the paper to reveal a wooden plaque with a house and trees painted on it. Letters set against the blue of the sky said East or West, Home Is Best.

"That's our house," Miriam said.

"Hollow painted it. He does scenes on milk cans and plaques for his mamm." Susie ran her fingers over the letters and started crying again. "I don't want to go to Canada. What if I throw up on the bus? What if the Martins are mean? What if they don't like me? I don't want to go."

The weight pressing on Miriam's heart grew heavier and heavier. Susie was slowly sinking to a place from which Miriam could not pull her back.

Dear Lord, what would you have me do?

Susie soon cried herself out. She laid her head on her pillow and fell asleep. Leaving Susie napping, Miriam made her way downstairs. The yelling had stopped almost a half hour ago, so it felt safe to enter the kitchen.

Yost sat at the table eating a piece of bread with some sort of white spread on it. He didn't acknowledge her when she entered the room, simply frowning and staring at his lunch instead.

"Is that mayonnaise?" Miriam said.

"There is nothing to eat."

Miriam opened a cupboard. "Would you like a tuna fish sandwich?"

"Okay."

First retrieving Yost's bread with one bite out of it, she then opened a can of tuna and mixed it with mayonnaise and pickle juice. She smoothed the tuna spread over the slice of bread, stacked pickles on top, and handed it to her brother. Next she pulled three hard-boiled eggs from the icebox, peeled them, cut them in half, and scooped the yolk from each one. To the yolks she added mayonnaise, salt, garlic, and chili oil before scooping the yellow paste back into the whites.

After artfully arranging the six halves on a plate, she set them in front of her brother.

He looked at them as if they'd been poisoned. "What do you want, Miriam?"

"I want you to put some meat on those bones."

He didn't touch the eggs. "You don't have to try to be nice. I know what everyone thinks of me."

"That you are too skinny?"

"That I am a terrible person. That I've brought shame to the family and don't deserve to be called a Bontrager. That you wish I wasn't your brother."

"Last week you helped me wash all the windows in this house. You got up on that ladder and knocked down the wasp nests. And you carry coal to the basement because it's too heavy for Mamm. Remember when Callie broke his arm and you carved that little frog out of wood to cheer him up? Or how you used to give me a hug every day and tell Susie she's beautiful?"

Yost turned his face from Miriam.

"I never wish you weren't my brother."

"Only when I behave the way you want me to. But as soon as I slip up, all that love flies out the window. What if I do buy a car or jump the fence? I won't be so lovable after that."

Miriam sat beside Yost and laid her hand on his arm. "I don't want to shoulder the responsibility for your past and future choices, and I am not going to try to drag you back to the straight and narrow. I love you no matter what you do or how bad you think you are."

Yost pulled his arm out from under Miriam's hand. His expression didn't change, but he picked up an egg and popped it into his mouth. "I like them spicy."

"I want to understand you, little brother. Talk to me."

"About what?"

"Tell me about the drugs."

Yost frowned. "Nothing to tell."

"Then tell me why you want a car."

Yost stared at his plate. "Joe and I were at the movies once and there was a boy with a really nice red Mustang convertible. The top was down, and he was laughing and having fun with his friends. How can something that makes someone so happy be bad? He can go wherever he wants. He's free."

"Do you feel trapped?"

"I have all these rules that I must follow, but they don't make me happy, only angry. No one understands how it is except Joe. Joe met a man who told him he could make lots of money selling marijuana and no one would ever suspect two Amish kids. I didn't do it to hurt anybody or get anybody hooked on drugs, Miriam. I wanted the money for a car."

"I know. You wouldn't hurt a soul."

"I thought my life was over when they took us to that

detention center." He buried his face in his hands. "I never, never want to go there again."

Seth was right. Yost's own conscience would punish him far better than anything anyone could say. Miriam scooted close and put her arm around Yost. "I'm sure it was terrible."

Yost wiped his eyes. "Dat hates me. I see it in his eyes whenever he looks at me. Like he wishes I had never been born. I wish that sometimes too."

"Dat is afraid of losing you. He feels helpless, and so he gets angry because he doesn't know what to do. He wouldn't be this upset if he loved you less."

"I used to believe he loved me, but that was when I was younger and didn't do anything wrong."

"Nothing like this has ever happened to us or to anyone we know in the community. Our family, including you, is trying to do our best when we don't have any idea what to do. Do you think you can forgive Dat's mistakes and my mistakes while we try to figure it out?"

Yost ran his finger around the edge of his plate. "I can't be perfect like you, Miriam."

"That is a ridiculous notion. None is perfect but God." She snatched the last egg and stuffed it into her mouth.

"Hey!"

"That's what you get for tempting my humility." Suddenly her eyes teared up, and she coughed until she was forced to jump up and pour herself a glass of milk. "Hot, hot!"

"That's what you get for stealing one of my eggs."

Miriam fanned her face with her hand and stuck out her tongue. "I can't believe I made these."

"They'll clear out your sinuses."

She took another swig of milk. "I hope you enjoyed those, because we are almost out of chili oil. I bought that bottle in La

Crosse, and I don't know where I can find anything like it in Apple Lake."

"If I had a car, I could drive you to La Crosse for shopping every week."

Icy fingers of disappointment curled around Miriam's heart. "You are never going to have a car, Yost."

With a flick of his wrist, Yost slid his plate across the table to Miriam. She caught it before it fell to the floor. He stood up, scowled, and pinned her with a fiery glare. "I'm not perfect like you, Miriam. I never will be."

A hopeless, sinking ache filled Miriam.

Yost kept insisting that she was perfect, and for the first time, Miriam realized that he meant it, not as a flippant insult, but as a condemnation of himself. She had admonished him harshly, and now every time she lectured or scolded him or even tried to influence his behavior, she made him feel smaller.

She was completely helpless to make things better. For anybody.

CHAPTER
TWELVE

Miriam's heart pounded as soon as she saw Ephraim walk through the Yoders' door for Sunday services. Her eyes followed his every move as he shook hands with Gabe Yoder, said something to his brother, and waved to the bishop. His eyes, however, did not stray to her side of the room.

She already sat in her place on one of the benches with Susie so she couldn't very well leap from her seat to greet him, but she felt jealous of everyone Ephraim talked to or smiled at. She wished he would send one of his smiles her way. Although they hadn't been cross or disagreed with each other on the night Yost came home from detention, she felt they had not parted on good terms. She hadn't seen him since that night over two weeks ago and she ached to talk with him, to get his comfort for the tragedy that had befallen her family.

Yost had his elbows propped on his knees with his face buried in his hands. Even though Dat had insisted, Miriam admired Yost's courage for coming to church. Despite his angry denials, she knew how embarrassed he felt about his arrest. If it had been her, she would have crawled under her bed and never come out again.

Ephraim and his brother always, always sat beside Yost at gmay. There were no assigned seats, but many boys and girls had the habit of sitting in the same place week after week. Yet today, something changed. Ephraim looked directly at Yost, patted his brother Freeman on the shoulder, and guided him to the row behind Yost. Miriam caught her breath and quickly averted her eyes. What had just happened?

She took a deep breath and tried to relax her tense shoulders. The change in seating arrangements was out of the ordinary, but surely it wasn't a cause for alarm. With all that had happened in the last two weeks, she was overly sensitive.

Even though the room felt cramped, no one else filled the row after the Neuenschwanders abandoned it—mainly because they were all in the habit of sitting somewhere else. Miriam glanced at Yost in concern, but he sat with his head in his hands and didn't seem to notice his surroundings.

Halfway through the first hymn, the Lambright children slipped through the front door. Seth nodded sheepishly to the minister and mouthed "Sorry" to the congregation in general. Priscilla and Laura tiptoed to the back row of benches behind the women, and Seth and his little brothers filled in next to Yost. Out of the corner of her eye, Miriam saw Seth grab Yost firmly by the shoulder and hold out his hand to him. Yost took the proffered hand, and Seth pumped it vigorously as if the whole congregation weren't right in the middle of a hymn.

Miriam smoothed an imaginary lock of hair from her face and studiously kept her nose in the *Ausbund* as warmth spread through her body. Seth would have her undying gratitude for that small gesture of friendship.

She didn't listen to much of the sermon given by the visiting minister. She sat with her heart in her toes, wishing she could steal into Ephraim's thoughts simply by staring at him. No matter what else happened today, she determined to talk to him, to assure him that she stood strong and loved him beyond expression. The final hymn couldn't be over soon enough.

As the service ended, women separated to the kitchen to prepare the afternoon meal and men stacked benches to use as tables. Miriam kept her gaze glued to Ephraim as she left Susie with Mamm and weaved her way through the men and benches. Ephraim walked out the front door with his fater and brother before she could reach him.

When she finally made it to the door, he was halfway across the yard.

"Ephraim, where are you going?" she called.

He looked back at her but kept walking. "We are going to visit the shut-ins."

"You can't even stay for dinner?"

"Nae, I will see you later. I need to go."

He hopped into his buggy without so much as a reassuring smile and rode away. Miriam wrapped her arms around her waist and watched his buggy travel down the lane until she could not see it anymore.

She knew Ephraim had a gute heart—always thinking of others before himself—but she wanted to be with him.

She trudged to the kitchen and helped spread peanut butter on bread for dinner. When it was her turn to sit down, she ate a small pickle and a red beet but couldn't muster an appetite for anything else. How could she think about food?

So many ladies helped with clean-up that there was hardly any room left in the kitchen to stand. Miriam wiped a counter then stood in the middle of the room looking for something to do.

"Miriam," Mamm said, "take this basket to our buggy, will you?"

Glad to be occupied, Miriam grabbed the basket of empty pint jars and walked it to the buggy, enjoying the beautiful summer day. The fleecy white clouds hung high in the sky, and the apricot tree in the Yoders' front yard sagged with bright orange fruit. Miriam breathed the fresh air and said a prayer of gratitude for her many blessings. The troubles would pass, Lord willing, but His mercy remained constant.

Seth sat on the lawn under a willow tree while Mary Shetler stood a few feet away. They seemed to be having a conversation, but Miriam couldn't be sure.

After delivering her basket to the buggy, Miriam walked back to the house. She stopped before she opened the screen door and watched the younger children play in the backyard. Seth still sat under the tree, but Mary was nowhere to be seen. He caught sight of Miriam staring and waved. She smiled and waved back.

"Joe Bieler and Yost Bontrager? I hadn't thought it possible."

Miriam froze as she heard her brother's name uttered by her neighbor, Treva Kanagy, on the other side of the screen door.

"They say Yost has been selling drugs for months."

"It wonders me that John and Lisa did not know about it," Treva said.

"John is busy working and managing his farms."

"He should be more mindful of what is going on at home."

"To be sure. I work my sons so hard, they don't have no time to fritter away. Some parents are not careful. I am sorry for them."

Miriam could not move her legs even though she wanted

nothing more than to be a hundred miles away from this conversation.

"We reap what we sow, Ruth. 'A child left to himself bringeth his mother to shame.'"

"They used to be one of our strongest families."

Miriam slowly backed away from the door and somehow stumbled down the steps without falling flat on her face. Her hands shook uncontrollably, and sweat beaded on her forehead. She wanted to run as far away as possible, but it would soon be time to go and Mamm mustn't be forced to come searching.

How could her family have sunk so low? Why was God punishing them like this? They had gone from being the most highly regarded people in the community to a family of troublemakers. Was this what it felt like to be a leper?

In long, purposeful strides, she made her way across the yard to Seth's tree. She sat down next to him so that her back faced the yard and the children.

Seth arched an eyebrow. "Do you find that trunk interesting?"

"Okay...," she began. "Okay, I need to tell you..." Her voice cracked, wavered, and shook, and before she could control it, she once again found herself bawling like a newborn buplie in Seth's presence.

Sincere concern covered his features and he leaned toward her. "Are you okay? Do you want me to fetch your mamm?"

Miriam shook her head and went right on crying while Seth watched her. She had already made a fool of herself in front of him once. No need to hold anything back now. "Will you...will you pretend we are having a conversation so this doesn't look strange to anyone watching?"

A ghost of a smile flitted across Seth's face. "Do you want me to move my lips as if I am talking to you, or would you prefer that I actually say something, like I'm doing now? If I just move my lips, you won't actually have to listen to any boring speeches, but I don't know if I am skilled enough to move my lips and make it look like I am actually talking. Simply moving my lips might appear more peculiar than you and I sitting here in silence. I don't want to trouble you, but the strangest part of all this is that you are sitting next to me and staring at the trunk of a willow tree while I talk to the side of your head."

Miriam couldn't help giggling through her tears. "I think I can pull myself together now." She wiped her eyes with the hanky Susie had embroidered for her and blew her nose as discreetly as possible.

"Gute," Seth said. "I was running out of things to say."

"I am sorry about the blubbering."

"Every time we meet, you cry. I am starting to wonder if there is something wrong with me."

"Nae, there is something wrong with me."

"Not likely."

"Okay," she said, her voice shaking like a leaf in the wind. "Okay, I want to apologize for being a snob."

"That is out of the blue."

"It has been too long in coming."

He sprouted a sheepish grin. "Why in the world would you think you are a snob?"

"A wise young man told me."

Seth looked down at his hands. "He sounds like a rude young man to me."

"I am grateful to him for showing me the truth."

"Miriam, I never should have said that to you. It was in a moment of anger, and I wish every day I could take it back."

"Will you forgive me?" Miriam said.

"You don't have to apologize—"

"Quit avoiding this, Seth Lambright."

He threw up his hands in surrender. "Yes, I forgive you, a thousand times over, if you'll forgive me for saying it. We understand each other better now. I do not think you are a snob."

"Anymore."

He curled up the corners of his mouth. "Okay, not anymore."

"I heard two women behind that screen door. They talked about my brother and my family the way I used to gossip about your family with..."

Seth's eyes stopped dancing. "Ephraim."

"Jah."

"It doesn't matter."

"I am so ashamed. I thought I felt compassion for you, but in reality, I judged your mother for her illness and decided that your parents were neglectful in rearing their children. I wish I had been a different person back then. I wish I hadn't been so blind to my own faults. I am very sorry for how I behaved."

Seth stared at her for what seemed like an eternity. His solemn expression melted into a cautious smile. "Thank you. That means a great deal to me."

"I want to be a better person, Seth. To love better and to quit casting judgment yet."

"My friend, Doug, says that when something bad happens to someone, it's normal to seek a reason, to tell ourselves that they somehow deserved the bad thing. It helps us to make sense of life. Even the disciples thought that way. When they saw a blind man, they asked Jesus who had sinned to cause the man to be born blind. Do you remember His answer?"

"He said that neither had the man nor his parents sinned but so the works of God could be made manifest."

"Jah. We shouldn't consider our trials a curse from God for

some bad behavior or believe that God does not love us if He lets us suffer. The greatest One of all was despised and rejected by men. He was perfect and sinless, yet He suffered. None of us is greater than He."

"But Ephraim says we are blessed when we follow the Commandments. Doesn't the Bible say that?"

"We are blessed when we try to follow the Commandments. But that doesn't mean unfortunate things won't befall us. Ephraim believes that nothing bad has ever happened to him because of the righteousness of his family. That is what Job's friends thought too, but they were wrong and God chastised them for their unrighteous judgment."

"It wonders me if there is a reason for anything, then."

Seth looked away and fixed his eyes on a lone fence post. "I finally gave up asking why my mamm took her own life. I cannot work out an answer that brings any peace. I must trust in God and lean not to my own understanding. When something bad happens to us, it is easy to become bitter with God if we don't understand why it happened. But the opposite is true also. When good things happen to us, we can be tempted to be proud. We think that maybe God loves us more than someone else. He doesn't. Rotten things happen to people who are minding their own business, doing their best to live as God wants them to."

Like he had in the stable yesterday, Seth gently laid his hand over hers for a moment before quickly pulling it away. The gesture felt like a warm blanket. "I am very sorry. What you heard at that door must have stung."

"Mostly because I've heard those same words come out of my mouth. It was dreadful to come face-to-face with my own weakness."

"I hope you will not let it burden you. Someone like you

should always be smiling." He leaned back on his hands. "How is Yost?"

"He tries to be contrary and angry, but he is hurting badly. You were right about his conscience plaguing him. He won't admit it, but he feels terrible about what he did. Most people try to be understanding, but a few look at him with suspicion or avoid him altogether."

"What does Ephraim think?"

Tears sprang up again. "He hasn't talked to me since the night Yost came home from detention."

Seth furrowed his brow. "He hasn't?"

"He and his brother always sit next to Yost during services, but they sat on a different bench today."

Seth rubbed the whiskers on his chin. "I noticed."

"I feel like the walls are closing in around me. I don't know what to do."

"Would you like to take a walk?"

Miriam immediately saw the advantages of being away from curious eyes. She nodded.

"I'll be right back," Seth said.

He jumped up and ran into the house. When he reappeared, he found Priscilla, who was playing in the yard, and took her by the hand and said something to her. She looked at Miriam and waved. Miriam waved back and tried her best to smile.

Seth came back to the tree, held out his hand, and pulled Miriam to her feet. "The only bad thing about a walk is that you must forsake the shade."

"It is not that hot."

Miriam motioned to Callie, who ran around like a wild man. "Callie, tell Mamm I walked home."

Callie's eyes darted to Seth. "Okay, I will tell her."

"Don't forget."

Miriam and Seth turned and strolled down the lane in the direction of Miriam's house. Summer wildflowers grew along the fence that separated Yoders' pasture from the road. It was a beautiful day for a picnic with not a hint of rain in the sky.

"Leaving your buggy here?" Miriam said.

"Laura will take it home. Ellie is not happy when Laura drives, but she does fine. My dat slept in this morning. Once we finally got ready to come, Ellie insisted that we were going to be late and stayed home because she refused to show up late. I am glad we were late. I got to sit by your brother."

"Denki. That was very kind."

Seth slowed his pace to match Miriam's. "I asked Doug about Yost. He says teenage boys are difficult. Their front lobes aren't connected by the corpus calculus—okay, that is not what he said, but it sounded like French to me. Some boys react to it extra hard."

"Can anything be done to help?"

"Yost could be depressed. Doug wants to meet him." He stopped and looked Miriam in the eyes. "Not many people know about this, but there is a small group that comes to my stable every Tuesday night, if you want to bring Yost. Doug calls it 'group therapy.' We talk about emotional issues people are having, like depression or anxiety. I only ask that you don't talk about who is there or what is discussed."

Miriam folded her arms. Ephraim wouldn't approve. "I don't know if that would be good."

Seth glanced at Miriam. "If you don't feel comfortable, don't give it a second thought. Would Ephraim not like it?"

Miriam kept quiet. That didn't sound like a good reason, even to herself.

He put his hands in his pockets. "Everybody deals with trouble in his own way. Ephraim might not be sure of what to say. If he is afraid of saying the wrong thing, he might stay away." He shrugged his shoulders. "There is a gathering at Wengerds on Wednesday. Talk to him. Maybe he is waiting for you to come to him."

Miriam almost felt like smiling. "I hadn't considered that before, but surely you must be right. Like as not I have been worried over nothing. Susie leaves on Wednesday afternoon for Canada, but perhaps I can come to the gathering after I see her to the bus."

"She doesn't seem happy to be leaving."

"It will be a great adventure. She has never been outside the county before."

Seth put a hand on her arm. "Miriam, look at me. Does she want to go?"

Miriam couldn't meet his eyes, but she couldn't lie to him. "The thought of going makes her ill."

"How long will she be gone?"

"Until January."

"Why is she going, Miriam?"

"I...I thought it best...for us."

Seth pressed his lips into a stiff line and considered her for a moment before his eyes grew wide. "*Oh sis yuscht!* I am beginning to see." He took his hat off and ran his fingers through his hair. "She is going to have a baby, isn't she?"

Perhaps she should have been angry, or mortified, at Seth's declaration, but to her surprise, Miriam felt a profound sense of relief rush over her. More inevitable tears ran down her face. "How did you know?"

"I only just realized it. I remembered that strange encounter at the drugstore, and when I saw Susie today, I thought she didn't look good and hasn't for many weeks—like all the life has drained out of her."

Bitterness filled Miriam's mouth. "Another testament to the wickedness of our family, Ephraim would say."

Seth stopped walking, took her hand, and pulled her to a stop. "Why do you say that? You must never believe it."

"Don't you?"

He studied her face. "You know Susie better than I do. Do you truly believe that your gentle sister is wicked? She is afraid of singing too loudly in church."

"She has committed a grievous sin."

"Jah, I suppose that is true, but I do not believe Susie set out to find wickedness, do you?"

"Nae."

"Perhaps she tried to fulfill her need for love in a forbidden relationship."

Miriam thought of her conversation with Susie.

"I only want to be loved."

"You are loved."

"I am ignored."

The gravel crunched beneath their shoes as they slowly walked down the road. A bird high overhead spread his wings in flight. Seth kicked a pebble near his feet. "She is guilty of letting someone stronger persuade her. She could not have completely understood what she was getting into."

Miriam put her hand to her heart to keep it from swelling out of her chest. "Most men are not as forgiving as you."

"Who am I to judge Susie?"

"Please, keep it a secret. She would be crushed if anyone knew."

"I won't tell a soul."

Silence prevailed between them for a few moments as a lone pickup truck passed them and kicked up a dust cloud. "She is going to deliver the baby and place it with a family in Canada and then come home. No one will ever have to find out."

"Your parents hope to protect her from embarrassment."

"My parents don't know."

Seth stopped walking again. "You haven't told your parents?"

The kindness in his voice brought fresh tears to her eyes. It felt wonderful to receive a little sympathy. "A few weeks ago it seemed like a gute plan, for Susie and for our family. It would have spared us the disgrace...but that doesn't seem to matter anymore. Susie could turn to dust and blow away, she's so unhappy. I want to do what is best, but I don't know what that is anymore."

Seth shook his head. "I can't imagine what you have been going through, and I certainly do not know the right answer for your sister, but can I give you one piece of advice?"

"Please."

"Your parents love Susie more than anyone else does. Talk to them. They will know what to do."

"I am afraid of what they will say."

"They would be heartbroken if they knew their daughters were bearing this burden all by themselves."

Earlier, Miriam had dismissed telling her parents, but when Seth made the suggestion, it seemed like the most sensible idea in the world. A burden shared was a burden lightened. "You are right. It wonders me that I didn't do it sooner."

"It wonders me how you could be so brave with all you've had to bear." He held her gaze with that intense look in his eyes, as if he were trying to see through her skull and read the thoughts in her head.

Miriam's face grew warm, and she put her hand to her forehead under the pretense of wiping her brow. "Did you know what I was trying to pay for at the drugstore?"

"Nae. I told the girl that the Amish are very private people and asked her to show a little compassion. I don't think she knew how to argue with that. I am sorry if you felt uncomfortable."

At the moment, she felt nothing but gratitude. "I was uncomfortable to even be there. If I hadn't still been so mad at you, I would have thanked you a thousand times over."

"I am glad I could help."

Miriam saw a green mailbox with ivy twining around it and realized they had reached her house.

Seth put his hat on his head. "Will you be all right?"

Miriam nodded.

"I feel very bad for Susie. I am sure that the thought of leaving her family is terrifying. And giving up her baby—I cannot imagine the heartache. It is gute she has such a sister as you to help her through this." He gave her a half smile. "I will see you at the gathering on Wednesday night?"

"Jah, I will come."

"Gute. If you will be there, I might be able to convince Laura to attend. She wants your approval on some fabric."

Walking backward, Seth kept his gaze fixed on her until he passed the fence that marked the edge of Bontrager property. Then he ambled down the road with his hands in his pockets.

Miriam took the edge of her apron in one hand and swished it back and forth as she walked to the house. She let her hand glide along the railing of her porch and fingered the pink-and-cream roses on the trellis outside the front door. Burying her face in one of the blooms, she breathed in the scent of strawberry taffy.

Even though nothing had changed, she felt lighter than she had for weeks as she walked into the house.

CHAPTER
THIRTEEN

Susie ran the back of her hand across her nose. "Okay. I am ready."

If Susie's red, puffy eyes didn't alert Mamm and Dat to the fact that Susie had been crying, the uncontrolled sniffling and hiccupping would have given her away immediately. Even though she was terrified of Mamm and Dat's reaction, once Miriam persuaded her, Susie agreed that they should be told everything. The burden of the secret had become unbearable.

After supper, their parents strolled to the bench swing that hung from a sturdy beam jutting out from a wall of the barn. The swing faced west, and they often sat there on a Sunday evening, visiting, while the children played Scrabble or Chinese checkers.

As soon as the little boys were occupied with a game and Susie composed herself enough to go through with it, Miriam and her sister followed their parents outside.

Miriam let Susie lead the way. After all, it was ultimately

her story to tell and her life that would never be the same, no matter what she chose.

The sky glowed orange and pink, and an occasional bird chirped an evening song. If not for the circumstances, it would have been the perfect evening to sit on the grass with Ephraim and her siblings and tell funny stories or read verses from the Bible. Ephraim would never try to steal a kiss, but perhaps on a night like this he would brush his hand over hers and squeeze her fingers affectionately when her brothers weren't watching. He'd never attempted it before, but it was a lovely thought.

Miriam caught up with Susie and grabbed her hand as they approached the swing. They stood in front of their parents, hand in hand, leaning on each other for support.

Dat immediately took his arm from around Mamm's shoulders and raised his eyebrows. "This looks important."

"Susie has something to tell you," Miriam said. She wrapped an arm around her sister, who seemed to wither under Dat's curious eye.

Mamm looked from Miriam to Susie. "What is it, dear? You have been crying. Have you changed your mind about Canada?"

Miriam could feel Susie trembling. She squeezed Susie's hand.

"Something terrible has happened," Susie said—and then her courage gave way and she pulled from Miriam and sobbed into her open hands.

Together, Mamm and Dat stood and wrapped their arms around Miriam and Susie in a four-way hug. "What is it, Susie?" Mamm said. "What is the matter?"

"We need to sit," Miriam said.

They broke the connection and sat side by side on the bench, Susie in between Mamm and Dat with Miriam on the other side of Dat. Mamm and Dat both put an arm around Susie and leaned in until their heads almost touched.

"I can't do it," said Susie between sobs. "Miriam, you must tell."

Miriam saw no other option but the plain, painful truth served quickly and calmly. "Susie is pregnant," she said, her voice unable to mask her own distress.

Mamm and Dat looked at each other, their eyes wide. Their mouths sank into deep frowns.

"How can that be?" Dat said, measuring each word as if it weighed a ton in his mouth.

They sat in shock until Mamm took in her breath sharply. "I should have known. How could I not have recognized it?"

A low, soft growl escaped Dat's throat. "When did this happen? Who is the father?"

Mamm put a hand on his knee.

"It does not matter," Miriam said. "What's done is done."

"It is the only thing that matters." Dat's voice rose with his agitation. "He must do what is right by our daughter."

"She does not want to marry him, Dat. And he does not want to marry her."

"Does not want to marry her? After what he did to my daughter? Is he an Englischer, then?"

Mamm patted his hand. He unclenched his fists and took a deep breath.

"When will the baby come?" Mamm asked.

"December," Susie said in a barely audible whisper.

"We planned for her to go to Canada to have the baby and leave it with a family there."

Pain flashed in Mamm's eyes. "And never tell us?"

"Jah," Miriam said, "but we changed our minds. If Susie were my daughter, I would want to know."

Dat slapped his knee and stood up. "She is my daughter, and I want to know who the father is."

Mamm and Miriam scooted closer to Susie to shield her from Dat's anger, the anger that had never surfaced before Yost's arrest.

"John," Mamm scolded, "hold your temper. We must think what is best for Susie."

"I know what is best for my daughter. There is no argument."

Mamm's voice rose to match Dat's. "I will argue with you if you are wrong."

"Please," Susie said. "Please, stop."

Dat took a step forward and pointed to the ground in front of him as if he had written his words in the dirt and wanted to make sure Susie saw them. "You ask me to stop? Susie, you are in no position to ask anything of your fater. How could you have done this?"

Squaring her shoulders, she stood and motioned for Dat to sit in her place. "Pappa, I will not marry the father. Can you trust me and accept what I say?"

Dat declined Susie's invitation to sit. "I will not trust a child who has sinned in the vilest way."

Miriam had thought that Susie might wither under Dat's serious eye. Instead, in a strong, determined voice that Miriam had never heard before, she said, "I know I have sinned. You cannot imagine how I have suffered for that sin. You don't listen anymore, Dat. You don't listen to Yost, and you don't listen to me."

Dat spun on his heels and strode a few steps away. He stood with his back to them, his hands on his hips. They stared at him while he slowly dropped his hands to his side and bowed his head. Was he praying?

The uncomfortable silence persisted until Dat raised his

head, turned to face them, and softened his expression. He sat next to Mamm and slid his arm around her shoulders. "I am sorry. I will try to listen. I hope you understand my anger. This is a great shock."

"Miriam and I thought it would be best to keep my baby a secret from you. I feared you would stop loving me the way you have stopped loving Yost."

Dat looked as if he had been struck by lightning. His mouth fell open, and he furrowed his brow. "I never for a minute stopped loving Yost." He shook his head slightly. "But no one would ever know it, would they?" He reached out and took Susie's hand. "You have done something very serious, Susie, and you carry a great burden because of it. A great burden with grave consequences. But you must never for one minute believe that I don't love you or that you are a lesser person because of this. We are all sinners and come short of the glory of God, but we are never short of His love."

Susie studied Dat's face, trying to determine whether he meant what he said. What she saw in his eyes must have convinced her. She wept in relief. "I know it would be better if I left Apple Lake, but I dread being away. I think my heart would break."

Dat stood and pulled Susie into his arms and held her while she cried. After a few minutes he reached into his pocket and produced a handkerchief to replace Susie's soaked one.

"If you stay here, there is no hiding the truth and you will live with it forever," he said softly. "Most will look past what happened and show you love, but others will say unkind things about you and probably avoid you. You will feel the sting of their rejection."

Susie dabbed at her face with the handkerchief. "I have thought about this for so long. My head spins with unpleasant choices. This is my sin, and I take responsibility for the consequences. I think I could stand the shame from the community, but my decision affects the entire family, as we have seen with Yost. The Neuenschwanders wouldn't even sit by him at gmay."

Miriam caught her breath, surprised that Susie had even noticed, when she seemed completely wrapped up in her own problems.

Dat massaged his forehead. "Since I have not treated my own son with compassion, how can I expect anyone else to? But, Susie, we would never wish you to go away, no matter the consequences."

"I can endure anything if I am with my family," Susie said, "but I will do anything to make Miriam happy, and Miriam would rather see me go."

Miriam's heart flipped over in her chest. Hiding her own embarrassment had been more important than Susie's feelings, and Susie had sensed it. Miriam felt about six inches tall.

"I want you to do what is best for you," Miriam said.

Susie sat next to Miriam on the swing. "You are so good. I am not worthy to be called your sister. If I go to Canada, you won't have a daily reminder of my sin."

Miriam threw her arms around Susie and clutched her tightly, not to comfort her sister but to draw comfort from her. How could she have been so blind to her own behavior? She had treated Susie with disdain, even if it was only with her negative thoughts.

Ach, how grateful she felt that Seth had chastised her so many weeks ago at the auction. He'd forced her to examine her own heart and find weakness there.

"I have been selfish," Miriam said, thinking of Seth's unconditional concern for someone else's sister. "If you would rather stay, I want you to stay. You are my sister. I will never be ashamed of you."

Susie pulled away and smiled the exultant smile that Miriam hadn't seen for weeks. "I want to stay with my family. I won't be a burden to anyone. I will do all the cooking and the cleaning. You won't regret my decision."

"Don't be silly," Mamm said. "You have a buplie coming. We will take care of you."

Dat patted her arm. "No matter the choice, it is a hard row to hoe, Susie. Do you understand?"

"Jah. I still must decide if I will raise the baby or give it away."

Wrinkles lined Mamm's forehead. "Give away my grandchild? I cannot bear the thought." She studied Susie's face and sat back. "I apologize. This is your decision. We will support you no matter what."

Miriam relaxed her shoulders as the weight of the world fell from them. They still faced another week of house arrest for Yost and a fatherless baby for Susie, but Miriam felt like kicking off her shoes and running through the grass. Love for her family enveloped her as she rejoiced in her lightened burden. She had finally done the right thing, letting go of control and trusting in God and her parents.

Thank you, Seth Lambright, for nudging me in the right direction.

She hugged Susie and practically danced to the house, amazed at how differently she'd felt only an hour ago. But her steps slowed as she walked up the back steps. The community would soon know everything.

So would Ephraim.

Her heart lurched.

Difficult times lay ahead.

CHAPTER
FOURTEEN

Miriam rapped firmly on the Neuenschwanders' front door. Her heart beat wildly at the prospect of being alone with Ephraim but also in dread of how he might react. She scolded herself. Ephraim would be her husband soon. She had nothing to fear from the man who loved her.

It was a bold step, to be sure, but since there had been no sign of Ephraim for over two weeks, Miriam knew she must go to him. Gossip about the baby would grow with Susie's abdomen, and Miriam wanted Ephraim to hear the news from her first. Besides, Seth had said that Ephraim might be waiting for her to come to him. He probably felt the horror of what was happening to her family as keenly as she did.

Light from a propane lantern flooded the porch as Ephraim's brother Freeman opened the door. "Oh, Miriam, it is you," he said.

"I have come to see Ephraim."

"In the barn." Freeman pointed and promptly shut the door.

Miriam stepped back instinctively as her heart slowly sank to her toes. Was Freeman being rude, or had she only imagined it? Ephraim had three older brothers and three younger brothers. None of them seemed to be gifted with exemplary manners.

She trudged across the lane, holding up her dress and picking her way around the mud puddles to the old barn built by Ephraim's grandfather in the forties. The door creaked softly and quickly swung shut as she scooted inside. A single lantern hanging from a rafter lit the space, casting a thousand shadows in every direction.

Ephraim sat on a bench beneath the lantern, sharpening an ax. He didn't look up as he carefully glided the ax along the whetstone.

"Ephraim."

Someone blew out the sunshine in his eyes when he looked up at her. He frowned and then just as suddenly managed a half smile. "Hullo. Haven't seen you for a while."

She ventured a step closer as he laid his ax on the bench and stood up.

"I've been seeing to matters at home, as you suggested."

"I'm glad. At services Yost seemed solemn, as if he's sorry for what he has done. Are you making sure he remembers his guilt and how he has hurt your family?"

"I hope I am treating him as the good Lord would want me to."

"How is his behavior? Do you think he'll mend his ways?"

"Lord willing. The detention center was a horrible place for him. I doubt he will do anything to get himself sent back there."

"I pray every day that he will learn his lesson and repent. It would be a shame if Yost's wickedness kept us apart."

Miriam took another step forward and wrung her hands to

keep them from shaking. "I have bad news, and I wanted you to hear it first before anyone else is told."

A dark cloud hovered over Ephraim's expression. "Go ahead."

"We have discovered...that...Susie is going to have a baby."

Ephraim held his breath for what seemed like five minutes and began pacing in front of the bench. "Oh, Miri, this is very bad."

Miriam willed herself to stay calm even as every muscle in her body tightened up. She reminded herself that her first reaction had been similar. "We were planning for her to go to Canada in two days and deliver the baby there then place it up for adoption. To keep it a secret."

Ephraim charged at her and grasped her upper arms. "Yes, yes, that is gute. No one has to know about this. That is a very smart plan."

"But she has changed her mind. She doesn't want to go, and Mamm and Dat thought it best that she stay here and be with our family."

He scowled. "Well, Miriam, it is her sin, and it is too bad for her if she doesn't like the consequences. Your family must not justify her bad behavior by giving in to her wishes. She has to go. Surely you can see how your whole family will suffer if the secret gets out. You must talk her out of staying."

Miriam felt her panic rise with her pulse. How could she make him see? "I will not ask her to leave her family and place her baby in the hands of strangers if she cannot bear to do it. I would not be that cruel."

Ephraim let go of Miriam and paced more frantically. "Cruel? Is that what you call it? The wages of sin is death. Whether you like it or not, consequences cannot be avoided. Do you know how she will be treated once people learn she is with child? Can you understand what this will do to your family's good name, which is already tarnished? If your parents let her stay in their home, it will be seen as unspoken approval of her sin. If you thought the community's reaction to Yost was harsh, wait until this comes out."

Miriam shook her head. The only harsh reaction she remembered toward Yost was Ephraim's. She wrapped her arms around her waist. Her mouth went dry, and she couldn't speak.

He pinched the bridge of his nose. "When Yost got arrested, I decided to give things a little time. If he straightens up, most people will forgive him and not think less of your family for his mistakes." His voice rose in volume. "But Miriam, people don't forget a baby. It will grow up in the community and be a constant reminder of Susie's sin and your family's dishonor. How can anyone overcome that reputation?" He practically tore his hat off the bench and flung it to the ground.

Miriam jumped back, and they both stared at the hat. He slowly bent over, picked it up, and brushed away a few errant strands of straw. He wouldn't look at her. "What has she told you about the father?"

"She refuses to name him."

He laid his hat back on the bench. All his fury seemed spent. "At least she will not pull someone else down with her."

Miriam slumped her shoulders and sighed. "I hope once he finds out about the baby, he will come forward and do his duty. Lord willing."

Ephraim studied her face. "Miriam, if you love me, please reconsider. You must convince Susie to go away."

The panic rose inside her like boiling water. "I do love you. With all my heart. How could you ever question that? But sending her away would do more harm to Susie than good. She needs to be with us."

He turned away from her and picked up the whetstone.

"Why are you coddling her? I thought you had more sense than to give in to Susie simply because she is unhappy. She must learn that you will not stand for such wickedness."

Miriam didn't understand her own feelings. She and Ephraim used to be of one mind. She never disagreed with him about anything. But this time, Miriam hoped she had judged the situation more wisely. Plain and simple, Ephraim was wrong. Sending Susie away would not be better for anybody.

Except Ephraim.

That realization clung like a cocklebur to her heart, and she felt slightly dizzy. For the first time in her life, she recognized a weakness in Ephraim.

No man was immune to frailty. When they married, she would see many more of his weaknesses, and he would surely find hers. That was all a part of growing in love, learning to cherish one another in spite of the annoyances and disagreements. The quest to lift one another was the task and blessing of marriage.

Miriam didn't think any less of Ephraim. A few short weeks ago, she would have agreed with him. But Seth had given her a wonderful gift—difficult to accept at first but precious all the same.

She motioned to the bench. "Can we sit?"

He shook his head.

She pretended his resistance didn't sting like an angry wasp and forged ahead. "I know what a gute heart you have, Ephraim, and if you knew Susie as I do, you would understand. What people think is not as important as what is best for Susie."

"Going away would be best for Susie. In a few short months, she could erase a mistake that otherwise will follow her the rest of her life."

"If Susie is willing to bear the shame, then I cannot urge her to do otherwise."

"But did she ask if you were willing to bear it? And what about me? Does she even care how I would feel about having a fornicator for a sister-in-law?"

Miriam couldn't keep her voice from shaking with emotion. "You *will* have a sister-in-law who was a fornicator even if we send her away."

"But everyone will know it. And they will look down on me." He blinked rapidly and shook his head. "On us."

"I don't believe that, Ephraim. Our people are forgiving."

"This will follow us forever. It will stain our good names and everything we do."

Seth's words came to Miriam like a gift from heaven. "Job's friends told him to repent. They said that if he was a righteous man he would not have trials. But they were wrong. Our trials are not a curse from God for the bad things we have done. Bad things happen to everyone, and Derr Herr doesn't love us less because of them. And no one in the community will love us less because of Susie's transgression."

"You are wrong. The Bible says the eyes of the Lord are on the righteous. 'He delivered me, because he delighted in me.' Righteous choices bring God's blessings."

"So anything bad that happens to us is because of sin?"

"Just look at Susie." Ephraim hung his head. "There is no use discussing this. I know what I know. I thought you, of all people, would recognize the truth. But if the truth doesn't change your mind, change your mind for me. For your love for me."

Miriam doubted herself for the first time since she'd stepped into the barn. She loved Ephraim so dearly and had always trusted his judgment over her own. He knew the Bible better than she, and his father was a minister like hers. Miriam possessed trivial abilities with the needle and the frying pan. What did she know about sin or repentance or life?

"I...I want to do what is right."

He saw the look in her eyes. "Of course you do." With a smile full of pity, he came to her and gently laid a hand on her shoulder. "Carefully consider what must be done—not to make Susie happy, but to make things right. I know you will do what is best for you and me and Susie in the long run. In years to come, she will thank you."

Miriam looked at her hands. "I will do my best."

Ephraim nodded in satisfaction. "Go. Go talk to her. There is still time to prepare for the bus on Wednesday if you go now."

"Okay," she whispered, not trusting her voice with anything louder.

He gave her one last pat on the shoulder and turned to his bench, where he picked up the ax and resumed his sharpening. Miriam kept her eyes glued to him as she backed out of the barn.

She wanted to make him happy, didn't she? In truth, he did not have the strength she did to withstand the scandal of Susie's pregnancy. Was his claim for sympathy any less valid than Susie's?

Miriam couldn't feel any lower than if she had sunk to the ground and crawled out of the barn. She slowly climbed into the buggy and pointed the horse home, but she'd never felt so much reluctance to actually get there.

She would talk to Susie again. Susie had promised to go if Miriam wanted her to. It would be the work of a minute to convince her. She must consider Ephraim's feelings in all this as well.

Yet the more distance she put between herself and Ephraim's house, the more agitated she became.

She thought of the Lord's treatment of the adulterous woman.

"*Hath no man condemned thee?...Neither do I condemn thee: go, and sin no more.*"

"*And be ye kind to one another, tenderhearted, forgiving one another, even as God for Christ's sake hath forgiven you.*"

Dat seemed to sense her arrival before she even came down the lane. He dashed out of the house as she drove up and opened the buggy door for her. He offered his hand and helped her down.

"I will unhitch. Go inside and eat some apricot pie. Mom bought ice cream."

"You do not need to do my work for me."

"I want to. You never rest, Miriam. Go, give your brother a hug. He will not take one from me."

It would take some time before Yost trusted Dat again.

With heavy heart, Miriam trudged to the house. She actually heard laughter inside. Susie's laughter. How long had it been?

When she came through the back door, Susie jumped up from the table, grinning widely, and gave Miriam a hug. "The pie is so gute, Miriam. The first apricots from our new tree."

"I cannot believe how many apricots grew from that one little tree," Mamm said. "I put up two dozen quarts today while you were at work."

Even Yost sat at the table eating with the family, looking relatively cheerful as he dug into what looked like a quarter of the whole pie.

"Guess who made the pie," said Raymond, with a dab of ice cream on his chin.

"Who?"

Raymond pointed at Susie.

Miriam threw her hands in the air in jubilation. "Susie made the pie? I must have some."

Susie's eyes lit up as if she had fireflies inside. "Sit down and I will bring you a piece. Do you want ice cream?"

Miriam observed Susie closely as she moved around the kitchen serving her family, giving them her gift. She was still pregnant, still guilty of a serious sin, but she acted as if all was right with the world, as if being in the place she loved made her perfectly happy.

Miriam's heart swelled. Susie had hope again.

Did she take her sin lightly? Did she believe that what she had done wasn't so bad? Was Ephraim right? Did she see her being allowed to stay as a sign that her parents approved of what she had done?

Nae, Susie did not excuse or justify herself in any way. How many nights had Miriam heard her weep over what she had done, wishing with all her might to be able to go back and change it? Neither did she seek to hide her sin. The whole world was about to know what she had done, while they would know nothing about the father. Susie didn't have a heart for malice or revenge.

If only Ephraim could see.

She took a bite of pie. "This is surely the most delicious pie I have ever tasted."

Susie blushed. "The secret is in the dough. And Hollow says I am the best pretzel maker in Apple Lake."

Try as she might, Miriam could not justify making Susie miserable, not even to spare Ephraim's feelings. And certainly not to satisfy Ephraim's pride.

Later, Miriam lifted Ephraim's completed Nine-Patch squares from her sewing basket and arranged them on the floor of her room. She organized the squares so the yellow-and-burgundy patches alternated diagonally from left to right and right to left. Ephraim would love the orderly pattern.

After gathering up her blocks, she pinned the squares of each row together. If she had time this weekend, she would begin sewing them together.

Fingering the tan fabric, Miriam thought of Ephraim's tortured face. She wished he would accept her comfort. Like a violent thunderstorm, the trouble that now seemed so big would blow over and Ephraim would rejoice in Susie's happiness. Time would heal all things and bring her and her dearest love closer to their wedding day.

She couldn't wait.

CHAPTER
FIFTEEN

"My legs feel like jelly," Susie said as she stumbled up the steps.

Mamm took a deep breath. "I'm shaking like a leaf."

Miriam, Mamm, and Susie looked like a parade as they marched single file up the steps to Aunt Emma's house for a quilting frolic. Miriam carried her basket of sewing supplies while Mamm followed with a pot of cheeseburger soup for dinner and Susie took up the rear with an apricot pie in each hand.

Miriam's heart felt likely to pound out of her chest. Once they'd made the decision last night that Susie would stay in Apple Lake, they agreed that it would be best to break the news of Susie's pregnancy to the aunts and cousins first and let word spread from there. Susie had not been baptized yet, so she would not be shunned, but they thought it unwise to leave everyone guessing as she grew bigger and rounder. Better to get the bad news out in the open and give the community a chance to adjust before the baby came. Neither of the aunts had loose lips and most of the cousins would be silent, but Ada, cousin Aaron's wife and Bishop Schwartz's daughter, was a notorious gossip. By sundown tomorrow, not one person in the community would be left in the dark.

Dat had agreed to miss work and stay home with Yost, who was still under house arrest. When Susie made her confession to the relatives, Yost's presence would be unwelcome at best.

Aunt Emma threw the door open and let out that little squeal she used whenever she saw one of her relatives. "Bless my soul, it is the Bontragers!" She gave her sister and then the nieces a hug. "I am especially glad Miriam and Susie are come. We need better quilters than me if we are to finish this quilt today. Mary and Kate and Ada are already here. We expect Erla and her girls any time now."

Mary waved from the kitchen, where she fed her baby in his high chair. Kate rushed forward to hug her cousins. "It is so good to see you." Glancing at Ada, who sat on the sofa with her feet propped on a stool, she pulled Miriam close and whispered into her ear. "Nathaniel and I pray for Yost every day. How is he doing?"

Miriam gripped her basket. "It has been hard, but we are through the worst, Lord willing. Yost is not happy, but at the moment, he is compliant. That is something."

Even at four years older, Kate had always been one of Miriam's favorite cousins. Before she'd married Nathaniel, Kate had thought of jumping the fence herself. She'd even gone to music school before, as she told it, Nathaniel made himself completely irresistible and she couldn't tell him no.

When Kate left Apple Lake for college, Ephraim expressed concern for her soul, and Miriam spent many nights praying that Kate would choose baptism and come back home.

"And how are you?" Miriam said. "Still feeling like a newlywed?"

Kate's eyes shone. "Every morning I wake up and think, 'I can't believe I am married to this man.' Good measure, pressed down, shaken together, and running over."

"I have never seen two people as happy as you and Nathaniel."

"Have you kept track of Rebecca and Levi? They look as if they are floating six inches off the ground."

"Is she coming today?"

"Jah, with her mamm, if she can stand to be away from Levi for more than three minutes."

They laughed. Oh, the joy of being so deeply in love!

Aunt Emma and Mary brought the quilt frames from the shed. "Miriam and Ada, will you set it up at two of the corners?"

Ada shifted her weight on the sofa. "My back is giving me mighty trouble, Mamm Weaver."

"Cum, Susie," Aunt Emma said. "Take the end, will you?"

Four of them positioned the stands in four corners of the room and lay the boards across them. Everyone but Ada surrounded the outside of the boards and stretched and tacked the backing onto the frames. Then came the thin batting and the quilt top over that. Keeping a close eye on the center seams, they tacked the quilt top to the frames, readying it for the tiny stitches that were the hallmark of every Amish quilt.

Cousins Rebecca and Linda came through the door just then with their mamm leaning heavily on their arms. Aunt Erla suffered from arthritis that kept her homebound most of the time. It was a good day when she could attend a get-together.

Aunt Emma squealed her greeting as Rebecca and Linda led Aunt Erla to the overstuffed sofa and helped her sit. Rebecca fluffed a pillow to put behind her mother's back while Linda removed Aunt Erla's shoes and got another pillow for her feet.

"Denki, girls. Now go quilt. I will be fine," Aunt Erla encouraged.

Rebecca hugged everyone in sight while Linda made a beeline for Susie. They were the same age, but Susie was about to grow up very fast.

"I must warn everyone; I am a terrible quilter," Rebecca said as Aunt Emma threaded needles.

"You are a fine quilter," Miriam insisted. "You simply don't like to quilt."

Linda picked up a needle. "She will hardly get a stitch in. All she does is moon over her new husband all day long."

Sunbeams flashed in Rebecca's eyes as she smiled. "I have the most handsome husband in the world."

Kate propped her hands on her hips and grinned. "I think not. There is no one Nathaniel's equal."

Ada turned up her nose. "It is vanity to say such things, but as sure as you're born, my Aaron has a finer countenance than either of them."

"There will be no argument about this," Aunt Emma said. "Solomon is the handsomest man alive, and I can prove it."

"And how is that?" Aunt Erla said.

Aunt Emma stretched out her arms and put her fingers together in front of her, pantomiming Uncle Solomon's protruding stomach. "There is more of him to love."

Miriam joined in the laughter, but she couldn't be completely comfortable. There was still the revelation they must make about Susie's baby. The unpleasant truth would surely put a damper on the quilting party.

Aunt Emma glided toward the kitchen. "Before we start, we have an announcement to make. Wait here."

Miriam held her breath. The perfect opportunity for Susie to make an announcement of her own had come.

Aunt Emma returned carrying a small cake frosted in

yellow with a tiny candle burning on the top. She tilted the cake so everyone could see the writing.

"B–A–B–Y," it read in big orange-frosting letters.

"I am going to have a baby in December," Kate blurted out, her face the picture of happiness.

Linda squealed and clapped her hands. Others sighed and cooed and congratulated Kate on her good news.

Miriam glanced at Mamm. Would Susie's revelation spoil this wonderful moment for Kate? Perhaps waiting for a better time would be wise.

Susie made up their minds for them as she promptly burst into tears and fled out the front door.

The room fell into shocked silence. Aunt Emma stared wide-eyed at Mamm. "What is wrong?"

Mamm chased after Susie, leaving Miriam to face the curious eyes alone. She chose to be cowardly. "Will you forgive me? I will be right back." She promptly turned tail and marched through the door.

Mamm stood on the porch, embracing Susie while she moaned her grief. "That is how a baby should be brought into the world—with a cake and candles and a mother and father who love each other. Nobody is going to think my baby is good news."

Mamm smoothed a hand over Susie's kapp. "Let's go home. We can tell them you don't feel well and try this another day."

The heaviness in Miriam's heart grew like a pile of stones. What advice would Seth give her? At this moment, she needed his clear thinking. She imagined his gray eyes gleaming with sympathy for Susie's distress. He would want Miriam to do what was best for Susie.

"What do you want to do, Susie?"

Susie sniffled softly. "What do you think I should do?"

"You decide. It is your secret to tell when you want to tell it."

Susie looked at Miriam as if making a decision were the strangest idea in the world. "I don't know." She pulled a hanky from her apron and mopped her face. "I am afraid this will get harder the longer I put it off, but I don't want to spoil Kate's happy day."

"Her good news is still good," Mamm said.

"How I wish I could go back and change that one foolish decision. Sin brings nothing but misery." She wiped her eyes, blew her nose, and squared her shoulders. "I will tell them."

Mamm and Miriam followed her into the house, where the aunts and cousins waited in silence.

Susie motioned for everyone to sit as she stood behind the sofa and leaned on the back for support. "First of all," she said, "I want to apologize to Kate for ruining her wonderful news. I am very, very happy for you."

Kate rubbed her hand over the quilt. "You haven't ruined anything."

"I am here to ask your forgiveness of my sin." Susie clutched the back of the sofa. "The truth is, I am going to have a baby too."

The silence doubled in volume. No one moved.

"I have made a terrible mistake," Susie said, as her tears reappeared and splashed like rain on the back of the sofa.

"And no husband," Ada murmured, pursing her lips and looking around the room for others to join her in disapproval.

Linda and Rebecca glanced at each other before lowering their gazes to the floor. Kate, with distress evident in her eyes, touched her mother's arm and then covered her mouth with her hand.

Susie forced out her next words through uncontrollable sobbing. "I'm so ashamed."

Aunt Emma shook off her shock like shedding a coat on a hot summer day. "Oh, my poor little girl, come here right now." She jumped from her chair and saved Susie the trouble of taking a step. Enfolding Susie in her arms as only a mother could, she said, "We love you no matter what."

"Thank you," Susie said between sobs.

Soon Kate, Mary, Rebecca, and Linda surrounded their cousin in a five-person hug. Even Aunt Erla, who didn't move from the couch, took Susie's hand and squeezed it as tightly as she could with her gnarled fingers.

Only Ada stayed put with her feet still propped on the stool. She looked as if she had eaten a fat, juicy slug.

Aunt Emma pulled away from Susie and patted her cheek. "What a brave girl you are to share the news. We all want to help you. When is the baby coming?"

"December," Susie said. "Like Kate's. But it will be a blessing when her baby is born."

"Every baby comes into this world by God's grace," Aunt Erla said. "We will rejoice for both."

Ada seemed to explode from the sofa. "I am sorry to have to chastise you, but rejoicing at a time like this is improper. This girl has committed a grave sin. We do not rejoice over wickedness."

Aunt Emma lifted her chin. "We rejoice over a baby, Ada. Susie has already owned up to her sins. I am sure she has suffered through weeks of grief. Am I right, Susie?"

Susie nodded.

Aunt Emma nodded back. "It is time for repair, not condemnation."

"It is time for repentance," Ada said. She grabbed her sewing basket from the table and her bonnet from the hook. "I won't be back."

They stared at her as she huffed and puffed out of the room and slammed the door behind her.

Mary bounced her baby on her hip. "Ada must feel the need to rush home and repent."

Either that or spread the news to at least twelve neighbors by bedtime. Miriam thought of Ephraim and her heart skipped a beat. He would soon hear the news from somebody besides her. There was no stopping Ada now.

Once Ada marched out the door, they seemed to breathe a collective sigh of relief and quickly forgot that she had been there.

"How are you feeling?" Mary asked. "Any morning sickness?"

Susie laid a hand on her stomach. "A little. Ginger pills helped."

Kate took Susie by the arm and led her to Ada's place on the sofa. "What will you do once the baby is born?"

Susie frowned. "I do not know. I want my baby to have a gute home, but right now I cannot face giving it up."

Aunt Erla patted Susie's hand. "You will know what to do when the time is right, Lord willing."

"Lord willing," Susie said.

Mary handed her baby to her mamm. "In the meantime, we have a quilt to make. But if any of you feel like crying, step away from the fabric. I will not stand for tears on my new bedspread."

CHAPTER SIXTEEN

"There she is. Don't stare."

Miriam turned to see who was behind her, but whoever it was had disappeared behind the row of buggies in the lane. She went around to the back of the house.

Miriam had arrived at the Wengerds' alone, on foot. Thick, ancient maples towered above the broad lawn where two volleyball nets stood side by side. Three long tables set with lemonade, cookies, pretzels, and pickles awaited hungry teenagers.

Yost was confined to house arrest for three more days, and with the news of Susie's baby still fresh, Mamm and Dat thought it best that Susie stay home and away from curious eyes tonight. The time for her return would come soon enough. Let the community adjust first.

With some anxiety, Miriam decided to attend the gathering. People were bound to be offended or downright hostile to her, as Susie's sister. But she swallowed her pride and determined that the Bontragers would not live in the shadows. They belonged to the community, and the community should be given a chance to accept them, warts and all.

More than anything else, Miriam knew she must set things right with Ephraim tonight. He deserved to know why events had not gone as he'd hoped. She knew she could make him understand. People were always more important than what they had done. Just as Seth said.

Miriam scanned the milling crowd as she stepped into the backyard. Seth had talked Laura into coming after all. They stood together on the lawn, playing volleyball. Miriam smiled as Seth hit the ball and launched it high into the air. His teammates gasped and squealed as it landed twenty feet behind him, barely missing the snack tables.

"Seth, we know you have muscles. No need to show us how strong you are," Peter Wengerd called.

Both teams laughed.

Seth sprinted to retrieve the ball and then served it over the net as he ran back to his place.

Miriam saw Ephraim in the corner of the yard farthest from her, sitting with a group of boys. High-pitched noises came from their direction as they pulled grass and used the blades as whistles. Miriam wanted to march straight to Ephraim with her explanation, but it wasn't a good idea while he was surrounded by his friends. Surely they could find some time later to be alone.

Hollow and his sister Esther Rose must have been watching for Miriam. They were at her side almost as soon as she set foot in the yard.

"Miriam," Hollow said, "how is Susie?"

Esther gave Miriam a quick hug. "She told us today at the pretzel stand. We are crushed. Crushed. We love Susie like she was our own sister."

"I sent her home," Hollow said. "She was too upset to work once she told us the news."

Miriam studied Hollow's face. She was still not sure that Hollow was not the father of Susie's child. But the sharp angle of his jaw and the shadow in his usually bright eyes spoke of concern for Susie, not of guilt for himself.

"It took courage to tell us like she did," Esther said.

Hollow leaned close. "A certain person told us that she would not be buying pretzels from us so long as Susie worked there."

A pit yawned at the bottom of Miriam's stomach. "Ada Weaver?"

"I ain't saying who. But I am afraid I was unkind. I told her, never mind that, because I wouldn't never sell her another pretzel even if she paid me a thousand dollars. After work, I went to her house and asked for forgiveness."

Tears stung Miriam's eyes. "You are both true friends. The next few months will not be easy. Susie needs all the friends she can get."

Hollow stuffed his hands into his pockets and looked at the ground. "What she did was not right, I know, but she is a sweet girl. Not a wicked bone in her body. I can't help but think that someone took advantage of her gute heart."

"She said she wanted to be loved," Miriam said.

"She should know better than that," Hollow said. "We all love her."

Esther took her brother's elbow. "Maybe we wasn't good at showing it."

They stood in silence for a few moments.

Hollow turned his head and glanced around the backyard. "Do you want to play volleyball?"

"Jah, okay."

Hollow led the way as Miriam walked arm in arm with Esther behind him.

Miriam's cousin, Elmer Weaver, Kate's brother, ran to catch up and gave her a warm embrace. "You okay?"

"Jah."

He backed away from her and continued his path to the snack tables. "Remember, we love your family."

Three of the Wengerd girls—Ruth, Naomi, and Hannah—passed Miriam, carrying trays of pretzels and cookies. They paused to acknowledge her.

"We are praying for Susie and for a healthy baby," Naomi said. "Will you tell her? And Yost too."

Miriam hadn't ventured halfway across the lawn before her progress completely stopped, as neighbors and friends surrounded her with good wishes and assurances of their love for Susie and their family. Miriam had hoped for understanding; she hadn't expected to be smothered with love. Fear of melting into a puddle of grateful tears kept her from uttering a word. Nodding and smiling, she blinked repeatedly to keep her eyes from overflowing.

How could she ever have doubted the goodness of these people?

Because she doubted it in herself.

In the not-so-distant past, news of a girl with child would have set her righteous indignation ablaze. She might not have spread the gossip like Ada Weaver, but she would have talked it over endlessly with Ephraim, and they would have concluded to avoid the sinner and disdain her wicked ways.

Almost every one of her neighbors showed more love than she would have.

Miriam eventually made her way to the volleyball game, where she stood on the opposite side of the net from Seth. He smiled at her with his whole face, his eyes dancing and arms held away from his body, ready to hit the volleyball.

His look sent a thrill of satisfaction down Miriam's spine. She had made a bold decision, and he was proud of her. She wasn't sure why, but Seth's approval meant a great deal to her.

She didn't know how he did it, but his smile reassured her that Susie and Yost would be all right, that her family could weather this storm, and that she would be happy again. She put her hand to her heart to feel the warmth that grew there.

Laura stood next to Seth. She breathed heavily from exertion. "I warn you, Miriam, if you stand right there, even with a net between you, Seth might pop you in the nose with the ball."

"Jah," Seth said. "I have no skill. The balls I hit fly in every which direction."

Miriam crouched and cupped one hand around the other. "I will take my chances."

As it turned out, Seth did not possess false humility. He truly proved a terrible volleyball player. Most of his volleys either hit an unsuspecting teammate in the head or went so far afield that they put everyone in the Wengerds' yard in harm's way.

His final hit hurtled the ball into a leafy maple tree, where it disappeared. Players on both sides of the net erupted in laughter.

"You are getting better," Abner Yutzy said. "At least you didn't hit anybody that time."

Seth grinned, jogged to the tree, and started climbing. "Everybody sit down," he hollered. "This may take a few minutes."

Miriam giggled at Seth's pathetic skills. Ephraim was an excellent volleyball player. There was nothing he wasn't good at.

Thinking of Ephraim made Miriam catch her breath. She must talk to him. Surveying the group of young people, she caught sight of him standing near the house, talking with his brother Freeman and Sarah Schwartz, the bishop's daughter. Ephraim ran his fingers through his hair as he visited, seemingly without a care in the world.

More than a little eager, Miriam practically jogged across the yard. He glanced her way, said something to his companions, and took long strides toward her.

His frown sent ice through her heart as he came at her with his fists clenched, his shoulders and back as rigid as stone.

Miriam's heart thumped against her ribs. He was more upset than she had ever seen him. How could she have expected otherwise? She had expressly gone against his wishes, and his pride had been wounded. She had a lot of explaining to do.

"Is this how you show your love for me?" he said in a hushed tone, glancing around to be sure they were not overheard. "By telling the whole world mere hours after I begged you not to?"

"It would have been wrong to send her away, Ephraim. She feels things so deeply."

"How can I marry someone who puts her own selfish wishes ahead of mine?"

Miriam couldn't quell her twinge of irritation. "Ahead of *your* own selfish wishes?"

He glanced around again and forced a smile through clenched teeth. "I tried to warn you. If you had sent Susie away, there might have been a chance to save your family's reputation. You are low because of Yost, but I could have endured it. I would have endured it because I love you. But now, oh, Miriam, don't you see how Susie's wickedness has ruined our future? I can't marry someone who has been tainted like this."

Miriam tried to wrap her mind around Ephraim's words but felt as if she were in the middle of a nightmare. His lips moved in slow motion and his voice echoed in her head as if he stood very far away.

She heard herself speak. "What are you saying? I don't understand."

"Can I make my feelings any plainer? I will not see you anymore. You are a stranger to me. Sarah is the bishop's daughter. She is more suitable."

Miriam put her hand to her forehead as the ground began to spin.

"We are lucky that we have not been published yet," Ephraim said. "Imagine our embarrassment if we had to call it off after we were engaged. This way will be easier for both of us."

His lips formed a tight line, and without another word, he rejoined Sarah and Freeman, who waited for him.

Miriam watched them go, disbelief her only emotion.

Her breathing became ragged and forced as she wrapped her arms around her stomach and tried not to throw up. Try as she might, she could not subdue the trembling of every muscle in her body. *Somebody, please wake me from this horrible dream.*

A warm hand slid around her wrist. "Miriam."

Who knew that so much compassion could be conveyed in one word?

"Miriam, cum," Seth said, with barely contained composure in his voice. He looked behind him. "Cum, I will take you home."

She thought her shock might suffocate her. "He...he doesn't want me anymore." She turned her head to see if she could catch a glimpse of Ephraim.

"Don't look. He's not looking at you." With a firm arm around her shoulders, Seth led her away from curious eyes. Laura soon joined them, wrapping her arm around Miriam's waist to help prevent Miriam from collapsing into a heap on the grass. Together, brother and sister supported Miriam all the way to the front, where their buggy waited, parked at the side of the lane. She stepped up numbly into the seat with their assistance, and they got in around her.

Seth took the reins, and Laura put her arm around Miriam as a mother might comfort her frightened child.

"What happened, Seth?" said Laura. "I saw you run to her, but I—"

"Not now," Seth replied.

Miriam wanted to protest, to ask them to please stop talking about her as if she weren't there.

But she wasn't there. She stood in the Wengerds' yard, watching the world crumble as Ephraim walked away. She would never be whole again.

They rode the short distance to her house in silence. Seth glanced at Miriam periodically while pretending to concentrate on the road. His breathing came as irregularly as hers did, as if his lungs were too crowded for air.

Seth stopped the buggy in front of the house and slid off the seat. Miriam followed. He took her hand and helped her to the ground.

She couldn't look at him for fear of seeing pity in his eyes. He had witnessed her humiliation and heartbreak, and she could not stand the thought of one more person rejecting her.

"I will help you in," he said.

"Nae, I can do it."

"You are shaken up. Let me help."

"Please, Seth, let me go." Her voice cracked, and as he

reached out a hand, she fled to the safety of the house where no one could see her turn to dust.

CHAPTER
SEVENTEEN

"I want to know everything," Susie said.

Miriam swished her soapy rag around the bowl before handing it to Susie to rinse and dry. They had done dishes together after breakfast ever since she could remember.

Miriam mustered a cheerful tone to her voice. "I already told you. We played volleyball. It was fun."

"Did people talk about me? What did they say? Do they hate me?"

Focusing her gaze out the window and concentrating very hard on the cow grazing in the pasture was the only thing that kept Miriam from dissolving into tears.

Think about the cow. She gives such gute milk. I wonder if Callie gathered the eggs this morning.

"Do they hate me?" repeated Susie.

"Of course they don't hate you. The Wengerd girls are praying for you. Cousin Elmer says he loves you. Hollow and Esther are worried about you. Almost everyone I talked to told me they hope the best for you. They were very kind."

Susie placed her clean stack of bowls in the cupboard. "I didn't mean to hurt anyone. Do you think they know that?"

Miriam dried her hands and squeezed Susie's wrist. She couldn't look her in the eyes for fear that Susie would see something amiss. "They know, Susie, and they love you. It will still be hard. Many won't know what to say to you, but I think things are going to be okay."

Susie threw her arms around Miriam, oblivious to the throbbing heartache below the surface of Miriam's smile.

"I was so nervous when you left for the gathering last night. I didn't want people to treat you bad because of me. Oh, Miriam, I am so relieved."

Miriam resisted the blissful innocence of her sister's embrace and pulled away. "Are you going to work today?"

"Jah. Hollow is picking me up in a few minutes. He says he will not have me walking to work in my condition. I told him that was a silly notion, but he wouldn't listen to any objections."

"Go get ready," Miriam said. "I will wipe the cupboards."

Susie tripped lightly out of the kitchen. The difference in her demeanor from just a few days ago was stark, even astonishing.

Miriam knew with all her heart that they had done the right thing by Susie. But she still felt as if a pile of stones sat on her chest and made it impossible for her heart to keep beating.

She heard a knock at the door.

She didn't think she could bear to face Hollow and his persistent cheerfulness this morning. Miriam slipped out the back door and plopped herself on the steps to wait for Hollow and Susie's exit. Once they left, she would finish up in the kitchen and then spend the day working in the garden, where she could water the dirt with her tears and avoid the curious eyes of her family. Praise Derr Herr she had the day off.

How long would Ephraim's rejection be a secret? If she could keep her family in the dark for another month or even two, Susie may not ever realize that Ephraim's decision had to do with her transgression. There was enough misery to go around without adding that to Susie's burden.

Miriam's every thought and hope revolved around Ephraim. He held all her dreams in his hands, and he had crushed them like fragile flowers.

Miriam caught her breath as a wave of despair engulfed her. She didn't know how to live her life without Ephraim. She leaned back on her hands, tilted her face toward the sky, and got a head start on her crying for the day.

She wasn't aware of Seth's presence until he spoke. "Hullo."

Miriam sat up straight and quickly wiped the tears from her face. "Hi."

He looked like he was in mourning. His eyes appeared black-gray under his half-open lids. The corners of his mouth were turned down, and his forehead furrowed with worry lines. He stood with his shoulders slumped, one hand holding a beribboned shoe box and the other hand stuffed into his pocket.

"Can I sit?" he said.

Still trying to clear away the tears, Miriam sniffed and nodded.

He trudged up the three steps and sat next to her. Resting his arms on his knees, he put the box between them and fixed his eyes on the cow Miriam had been so interested in earlier.

Although she'd thought she wanted to be alone, she somehow found Seth's quiet presence comforting. He knew about everything already. She suddenly didn't feel so isolated.

Miriam didn't know how long they sat there—five

minutes, ten?—but the knots in her neck slowly untied and the urge to cry retreated to the very back corner of her heart.

He didn't offer a useless word of condolence or comfort, simply sat still so she wouldn't have to sit by herself.

"I don't think even my mamm has seen me cry as much as you have," she finally said, embarrassed at the truth of her words.

"It is not your fault if you feel like crying every time you see me. I have that effect on babies and small children too."

"What's in the box?"

Seth picked up the shoe box and handed it to Miriam. His half smile didn't quite reach his eyes. "Priscilla wanted you to have this. She hoped it would make you feel better."

Miriam untied the bright pink ribbon around the box and lifted the lid. Lady Dancing lay inside, wrapped in the Nine-Patch quilt she and Priscilla and Laura had made together.

Miriam's heart almost stopped beating. "I can't take this. This is Priscilla's most precious possession."

"You mean a great deal to Priscilla. I can't think of anyone else she would sacrifice her doll for."

"But you know I can't keep this."

"I was afraid the doll would make you feel worse," Seth said.

"It does."

"Please, keep it. Priscilla was so eager that you have it. Maybe her sacrifice will help you remember how important you are to many, many people, even if there are a few who will never recognize your true worth."

A lump stuck in Miriam's throat. "I will," she said, pulling the doll from the box and cradling it like a real baby.

"Denki." Seth clenched his teeth and turned his eyes to the pasture again. The cow grazed peacefully, oblivious to all the attention it drew this morning.

"Are you angry?" she said.

Seth balled his fists. "He should be ashamed of the way he treated you."

"Please, say nothing against Ephraim. I love him."

Seth flinched and hung his head. "I'm sorry."

She nudged him with her shoulder. "Thank you for caring."

As if she had a stiff wind behind her, Susie came tearing around the corner of the house, with Hollow following. She pulled her mouth into an awkward grimace as her face turned beet red. "Why didn't you tell me you fell ill last night?" Her question seemed more like an accusation.

"I didn't fall ill."

Susie shook her finger at Miriam. "You and Ephraim were talking and then Seth had to carry you to his buggy."

Seth turned to stone beside her, and Hollow shifted his gaze from Miriam to Susie and back again.

"She felt shaky after our volleyball game," Seth volunteered. "I offered to drive her home."

Susie ignored Seth and glared at Miriam. "Why didn't Ephraim drive you home? He is practically your fiancé."

"He wanted to stay longer," Miriam stuttered. Her heart sank. Her secret was about to shatter.

"He was too busy driving Sarah Schwartz home," Susie protested. "Miriam, look at me." She marched up the steps and pulled Miriam to her feet with uncharacteristic firmness. "He called it off between the two of you, didn't he? He doesn't want to marry you now." A sob tore out of Susie's throat. "Because of me." She wrapped her arms around Miriam's neck.

Miriam had no words of comfort to offer. There were none in the whole world that could make their hurt disappear.

"I am sorry," Hollow murmured. "I thought Miriam took sick. Honest. I didn't think—"

"Hush, Hollow," Miriam said as she rubbed her hand up and down Susie's back, "You have no fault in this."

Susie was inconsolable. She groaned from the very depths of her soul. "Don't hate me. Don't hate me, Miriam."

Seth stepped off the porch as if there were no room for him. He and Hollow tried to look invisible. Miriam didn't blame them. They must have felt like intruders.

Susie's distress broke through Miriam's already-weak defenses, and she let the tears flow right along with her sister's. The only thing they had left was their mutual grief.

"I would have gone to Canada," Susie cried. "If you wanted me to go, I would have gone."

Hollow and Seth had disappeared. Miriam pulled Susie down to sit on the steps while keeping an arm around her. She brushed a finger against Susie's chin and compelled her to meet her eyes. "Think about how sad you were to leave us. I couldn't bear to ask you to go."

"But you lost Ephraim because of me. You should not have been the one to make the sacrifice. I am the one who committed the sin, and you are paying for it."

Miriam took a deep breath and found her composure. "We bear one another's burdens. They belong to the entire family. Lord willing, this will work out to our good. 'All things work together for good to them that love God.'"

"But it still hurts," Susie said.

"Worse than anything."

They sat clasped in each other's arms until there were no more tears to shed.

Susie looked around. "Where did they go?"

Miriam sighed. "If they were smart, they hightailed it to Minnesota to get as far away as possible from two blubbering girls."

Susie stood and smoothed her dress and apron. She pulled

a hanky from her sleeve and dabbed her face for any errant tears. "Do you think Hollow gave up and left without me?"

"Let's find out."

They walked arm in arm to the front of the house, where Hollow and Seth stood talking in hushed voices. They turned their heads at the same time.

"Do not be alarmed," Miriam said. "The Bontrager sisters are done bursting into tears for the rest of the day. Or, at least, we promise not to cry for the next hour."

Hollow didn't shed his troubled expression. "Don't worry about coming to work today, Susie. It has been a bad few days for all of us. You need to rest."

Susie lifted her chin and wiped her hand across her moist eyes. "I will be a mother soon, and I am going to stop acting like a baby right now. Let's get to work."

Hollow cracked a smile and motioned to the buggy. "Your ride is waiting."

Susie stomped past him. "And I am perfectly able to walk to work from now on."

"Oh no, you aren't."

They continued to contradict each other until Hollow helped Susie into the buggy, hopped in the other side, and guided the horse down the lane.

Miriam watched them down the road until, out of the corner of her eye, she caught Seth staring at her.

She turned to him. "What?"

"I don't know how I could have been so wrong about you, Miriam Bontrager. I wanted to believe that you were a certain type of person so I could tell myself you were not worth my time. The more I get to know you, the more I am ashamed of myself. You tried to shield your sister from what happened last night to protect her feelings. You are..."

Miriam's breath caught. "What?"

Seth's gaze met hers. "Astonishing."

Miriam felt warmth pulse through her veins. After all the trouble today, the sensation was very pleasant indeed. "The terrible news needn't hurt both of us."

"I've never known someone as kind as you, except for maybe my mother."

"Ach, Seth. I wish I were what you say. I have so many faults yet. As you said, I am a snob."

"Nae, you are not."

Miriam was ready to contradict Seth once again when Yost came out the front door. "Miriam, do you know where my pocketknife is?"

Miriam shook her head. "You are not allowed to have a pocketknife until probation is over."

"That's not true."

"Jah, the officer told me."

Yost scowled. "They won't even let me use a pocketknife to whittle a stick? Who made that stupid rule?"

"I do not know who made it, but you must follow it."

Yost stomped down the steps. "Where did you hide my pocketknife?"

"You will get it back when probation is over."

Seth stepped forward and placed a brotherly hand on Yost's shoulder. "Hello, Yost. How are you doing?"

Miriam knew Yost liked Seth okay, but he was in a surly mood. "How would you be doing if you were forced to sit in the house all day and listen to your little brothers whine and your sisters boss you around?"

"Miriam says you have done really well, even being cooped up."

"I feel like I am going crazy," Yost said.

Seth glanced at Miriam. "I have a group that meets every Tuesday night at my stable—just people who are going through hard times. We get together to talk about our problems and what we can do to solve them. You are invited to come, if you want."

"Oh, that's great," said Yost, shrugging Seth's hand off his shoulder. "Now you think I am crazy too."

"Nae, not at all. We just talk."

"The last thing I need is your pity." Yost bounded up the steps in two long strides, escaped into the house, and slammed the door so hard, it made Miriam jump.

Seth stuffed his hands into his pockets. "I shouldn't have said anything. He's not ready. How could I be so *deerich*? I made things worse."

"They can't get any worse," Miriam said. "It will take time with Yost. He is so angry yet."

"I am sorry I interfered. I really came over today to deliver a message from Laura. She has picked the fabric she wants for her quilt, if you still feel up to helping her with it."

"Of course. I want to help."

"I am sorry about what happened last night. It upset me to see you so distressed."

"I did not thank you properly for taking me away from there. I wouldn't have been able to take a step on my own."

"You are welcome. If there's anything I can do—"

"Will you take me to see the horses?"

"Jah, of course."

Miriam took a deep breath. "But since the wedding is off, maybe neither of them is mine anymore."

"Your dat made a down payment on a horse. He didn't say you must marry to own it. Besides, two years is a long time." He cleared his throat. "Maybe you'll find someone else."

Realization sucked all the wind out of Miriam's lungs. "I won't marry. How could I ever?" With that, she broke her recent promise, covered her face in her hands, and wept.

CHAPTER
EIGHTEEN

Seth watched Miriam as she stood in the middle of the pasture and ran her fingers up and down the colt's long nose. She had her other arm wrapped around the colt's neck while she whispered and cooed at him. "You're such a pretty, pretty boy."

His silky chestnut ear twitched as if he understood every word.

It had been three weeks since Ephraim had made the biggest mistake Seth had ever seen in the history of mistakes by settling for Sarah Schwartz when he could have had Miriam Bontrager. But even though Ephraim had wounded Miriam deeply, Seth couldn't be sad that Ephraim and Miriam were no longer together. Ephraim didn't deserve her.

Funny how he used to think that Ephraim and Miriam were perfectly suited for each other.

She had come to see the foals almost every day after work since then except Sundays. She seemed better today. Or maybe Seth was wishing she seemed better today and his wishes made it so. He might be imagining that there was more color to her cheeks or that the corners of her mouth didn't constantly turn down into a frown.

Not that any of it marred her beauty. She was still as pretty as ever, with her lavender-blue eyes and hair the color of wheat fields in the glow of sunset. Seth could have stared at her all the day long and never grown tired. He felt his face get hot, quickly averted his eyes, and turned off the hose before it filled his boots with water. He mustn't ever let his mind wander in that direction. That kind of foolish daydreaming would only get him into trouble. He tried not to look in her direction as he wound the hose onto the large spool hanging on the wall of his stable.

She came to see the horses. He was just the stable boy.

Before he knew she was coming, she stood by him. He couldn't resist the urge to breathe in her scent. She smelled of vanilla and honey.

"The foals are growing so fast," she said.

"They look forward to your visit every day."

"I think I might choose the colt. He's feisty, and he seems to like me."

"Jah, he does."

Miriam took her canvas bag off a hook on the side of the stable. "I am off to your house to help Laura finish her quilt top."

"She's been working every spare hour on that thing."

"It is going to be beautiful. I didn't know whether the green and pink would go well together, but they complement each other perfectly. I am glad she will have something from home at college."

"Thank you for helping her."

"No thanks necessary. Working on Laura's quilt has helped me take my mind off my own troubles."

Seth gave her a half smile. "I'm glad. I wish there was something more I could do."

Miriam placed a hand on his arm.

He ignored his surging heartbeat.

"You listen to me even when I whine. And you don't scold or tell me what I'm doing wrong. You are a true friend—one of the few I have."

Seth tried not to burst with happiness. "You don't whine."

"Only a true friend would say that."

Seth returned her grin. "Cum, I will walk with you to the road before I leave for my shift at the mill."

Seth pointed to a spot near the main road close to the entrance to his property. "I am going to build a house right there, under the trees."

"When?"

"As soon as I do the last summer cut of alfalfa, I will pour the foundation. There is a man in Madison who can give me a gute price, and Junior Herschberger says his work is quality. But I do not know how big to build it."

"You will want room enough for a family. Even though it would be extra money, in a few years, you will be glad you spent it."

Seth's entire midsection did somersaults when Miriam talked about a family. He couldn't help but think of the joy of having a family with a beautiful wife by his side.

Sunflowers and black-eyed Susans bloomed up against the fence that separated the alfalfa fields from the lane. Some sunflowers stretched almost six feet high. Seth reached up, snipped a large blossom from one of the stems, and handed it to Miriam. Her eyes danced, and she twirled the flower in her hand as they strolled down the path.

"I wish I could spend all day with the horses. They don't have any problems that need fixing," Miriam said.

"Trouble at home?"

Miriam threw back her head and growled. "Ach, Susie frets over what to do with her baby, and Yost can't find a kind word for anybody. I thought that once house arrest ended he would cheer up—that things would go back to the way they were—but he is angrier than ever. What do you think I should do? I'm at my wit's end, and so are Mamm and Dat."

She gave him that look of confidence that Seth always found unnerving. It boggled his mind that she trusted his judgment, when he didn't feel like he knew anything about anything. He kept up a steady pace so she wouldn't guess that his thoughts were a jumble.

Miriam failed to mention the thing that caused her the deepest personal pain, but Ephraim Neuenschwander was probably never far from her mind.

Seth stuffed his hands into his pockets. "You take care of so many other people. I hope you take care of yourself."

She didn't even have to think about that. "I come to see the horses every day when I should be tending to things at home. I'm plenty selfish."

"It doesn't count if you feel guilty about it."

"But I should feel guilty. I ought to spend more time with Yost. I ought to sit with Susie and help her decide what to do."

"Does Yost want you to spend more time with him?"

Miriam breathed out a long sigh. "No."

"It hurts when someone pushes you away. Yost must feel very unlovable."

"When you train a horse, you don't run at him to gain his trust," Miriam said. "I try to hold back, to let him come to me. And I feed him good food. But I'm sure I am doing everything wrong."

"Not likely." Seth caught himself staring, redirected his eyes down the lane, and cleared his throat. Why did her skin have to be so flawless?" "You are doing more good than you know. Like as not, Yost will have a rough time of it yet. Is he still friends with Joe Bieler?"

"Nae. The officer at the detention center said they could not see each other anymore, and Mamm and Dat talked to Joe's parents about it. They all agreed it would be better to keep them apart. Dat keeps Yost closer to home now, although he still spends time with a few boys after work. I hope he finds new friends in the district, although I don't know who would let their son associate with him. It is impossible to force anyone to be friends with him."

"It doesn't mean you love him more if you give yourself an ulcer worrying about him. Anxiety is not the same as love."

Miriam slowed her step. "I suppose I think that if I worry myself to death, I can prove how much I love my family. I wish I were smart like you."

"You are much smarter than me. Some days, I sleep in a barn."

Smiling weakly, Miriam shook her head. "Ach, here I am, whining to you again. Have you grown tired of me yet?"

"I don't think that's possible."

Out of the corner of his eye, Seth saw three boys, two Amish and one Englisch, jump his fence at one end of the pasture and trample his alfalfa as they tromped through the field. His heart sank. He knew exactly who those boys were, and Miriam would be very unhappy if she caught sight of them. Seth didn't mind people taking shortcuts across his land, but when they purposefully leveled his crops on more than one occasion, he knew they were doing more than looking for the shortest distance between two places.

Miriam didn't notice them until she heard their loud laughter as they made their way across Seth's field. She looked up and furrowed her brow. Seth couldn't do anything to divert her attention. The damage had been done. She frowned as recognition registered on her face. "Is that Yost? Who...who is that Englisch boy?"

Seth remained mute and let her draw her own conclusions. Hopefully her assumptions wouldn't be as unpleasant as the truth.

"Yost!" she called, but the boys either didn't hear her or ignored her. She stared after them, her frown deepening as they stomped away. "That is Yost," she murmured, "and Jonas, Mary Shetler's boy." Seth saw the distress grow on her expression as she watched them hop over the far fence and disappear into Millers' orchard.

She stood like a statue, her eyes riveted to the spot where Yost had passed through the trees. "They shouldn't step through the alfalfa like that. They'll damage your crop. Why would they want to damage your crop?"

Without warning, Miriam threw her arms around Seth's neck and dissolved into a flood of tears. Tentatively, he wrapped his hands around her waist, his only thought to comfort her.

Ephraim Neuenschwander and Bishop Schwartz and even Miriam's fater might have considered their touch improper, but when Miriam needed a shoulder so desperately, Seth couldn't bring himself to pull away.

"No bark! Pookie, stop that barking!"

Pookie barked and barked at the door until Laura opened it and shooed the dog back. He gave up the fight when faced with opposition and padded his little feet to the kitchen before Miriam even stepped over the threshold.

Miriam smiled to herself. There were so few certainties in

life, but she could always count on Pookie to bark at her no matter how many times she had been to the Lambright house. She felt honored, actually. Pookie still barked at Seth, and he had been a member of the family longer then Pookie had.

Laura's smile faded as she studied Miriam's face. "Oh, Miriam. If this is a bad day, we can do it another time."

Miriam couldn't do anything about the red, puffy eyes that proclaimed she had been crying, but she forced the corners of her lips to curve up. "Nae, this is a gute time. You leave in a month, and we are so close."

"You've been very kind to help me with this quilt, and I've been selfish," Laura said. "I know how unhappy you are."

Miriam took a deep breath and pushed the pain deeper into her heart. She didn't need a reminder of the shambles that was her miserable life, and she wished Laura didn't think that talking about Ephraim made her feel better.

Because it didn't.

It poured salt into an open, festering wound.

"My mind is carefree when I'm quilting," Miriam said, adding extra lilt to her voice so Laura would believe her sincerity. "*You* are helping me."

That answer satisfied Laura. "Cum, I have a surprise for you."

Ellie appeared in the front hall, tying her black bonnet under her chin. "Miriam, welcome to our home. I am sorry the floors are a mess, but Laura promised to mop later."

Miriam smiled to herself. In all her visits to Lambrights' home, she had never seen so much as a pin out of place. The sofa in the front room was brushed every time, and the propane lamps shone with a spit-shine polish.

The only room that seemed lived-in at all was Laura's. Occasionally untidy but homey and comfortable, it felt like a haven in a sea of order, where Miriam could rest a hand on the table without worrying about leaving a smudge.

Priscilla darted through the back door, slamming it, as she ran into Miriam's arms.

"Priscilla," Ellie scolded. "Go back and show me how to close a door properly."

Miriam lowered Priscilla to the floor. Contritely, Priscilla shuffled to the back door, cracked it open, and closed it carefully and quietly.

"Twenty times," Ellie said. "So that I know you've learned your lesson."

Priscilla pressed her lips together and began opening and closing the door.

Feeling uncomfortable, Miriam stood next to Laura and silently counted to twenty as Scilla did what Ellie asked.

Ellie nodded curtly when she was satisfied. "I am going to my dieter's meeting. The boys are out back. Keep a strict eye on them, Laura. I won't have them tracking dirt onto the rugs."

"I will," Laura said as she shut the door behind Ellie.

Miriam spread her arms wide, an invitation for Priscilla to return to her embrace. Priscilla wrapped her arms around Miriam's neck.

"Do you know why I feel so gute today?" Miriam asked Priscilla.

"Why?"

"Because Lady Dancing sat on my pillow and smiled at me when I woke up."

Scilla burst into a grin and nibbled on her fingernail. "Do you like her?"

Miriam gave Priscilla an extra squeeze. "More than anything. Thank you."

"I told Seth it would make you happy, but he didn't want me to be sad for losing Lady Dancing."

"Do you miss her?" Miriam said.

"I am glad you like her."

"Cum," said Laura. "Let's show Miriam the quilt upstairs." The sisters led Miriam to Laura's attic room, where she had spread the completed quilt top on the bed.

Miriam clapped her hands in genuine delight. "You finished it?"

Priscilla grinned. "Isn't it pretty, Miriam?"

"It's not near as good as if you had helped me," Laura said, "but I wanted to surprise you."

"Of course it is good." Miriam ran her hands over the fabric. They had chosen a simple pattern of squares and rectangles, easy to piece together and easier to quilt. The pink-and-green patches reminded Miriam of a plate of sliced watermelon on a hot summer day. "It turned out so cute. And your corners match nicely."

Laura blushed. "I did a lot of unpicking last night. I wanted it to be good."

"It is wonderful-gute. It will look nice in your college room."

"Do you want to see what Seth got for Laura?" Priscilla said, her little legs already taking her to the stairs.

"What did he get?"

Holding on tightly to the rope, Priscilla stepped down the ladder. "I will bring it."

Miriam loved Priscilla's contagious enthusiasm. She grinned at Laura. "Let's organize a quilting circle for next Tuesday."

Laura's smile sagged. "No one will come. Why would they help a girl like me finish my quilt?"

"That doesn't matter one little bit, and don't you ever believe it does. Leave everything to me. I'll have a dozen ladies here, no doubt about it. You need to buy the batting. Do you still have the dark green for the back?"

"Jah." Laura pulled three boxes of her mother's fabric from under her bed.

The green they had decided on lay at the top of the first box. "You need to sew two pieces together or the back won't be wide enough. I'll show you how."

A deep blue fabric the color of a cold December lake sat underneath Laura's green. "Oh, this would make a beautiful quilt," Miriam said.

"That is the leftover fabric from Seth's favorite blanket. Mamm made it for him when he was born. She would wrap him in it and read him stories. Even when he stopped carrying it around, he slept with it. By the time he was ten, the thing was in tatters. Mamm offered to make him a new one, but he told her he was too old for such things. He never got rid of it, though. He kept it folded at the foot of his bed until Ellie burned it."

"She burned it?"

"Three days after she moved in. Snatched it from his bed and threw it into the cookstove. She said she refused to keep her children in rags. But that one was not her fault. She couldn't have known how important it was to him.

"Seth was twenty years old, but the loss of that blanket really shook him. For over an hour, he stared at the cookstove as if wishing might bring his blanket back. That was the first night he slept in his stable. It was almost like the blanket was the last thing holding him to our family. He told me once that it smelled like lilacs, Mamm's favorite flower, and that he wouldn't have any way to remember her once it was lost."

A heavy sadness for Seth's loss pressed on Miriam's shoulders. She pictured Seth staring into the fire that devoured his blanket and his memories. She felt as if her heart might break.

Miriam unfolded the material and spread it on the bed on top of Laura's. In an instant, she saw a quilt in her head. "Would he think me silly if I made him a quilt with this fabric?"

"Why would he think it silly? He needs a proper covering for that cot he sleeps on at the stable."

"Does he sleep there every night?"

"Nae," Laura said, "only if he gets extra busy. He mostly sleeps here at home so he can keep an eye on Ellie."

"He has been so kind to me. A quilt is a suitable thank-you gift...but maybe not for a man."

"If you make it, he'll love it. Miriam Bontrager's quilts are famous in Apple Lake."

"Now you are talking nonsense."

"You are welcome to any of my mamm's fabric, or do you only want the blue?"

"What else did she have?"

"What colors do you want?"

"Blues and greens, perhaps a yellow. I think I will make a sampler quilt."

Laura opened all three boxes and pulled out fold after fold of fabric. She held up a forest green speckled with small white flowers. "Our kitchen curtains were made out of this."

Miriam took it from Laura and laid it on top of the blue. She thought of the green-and-blue fabric that Ephraim had talked her out of at the store. It would tie these fabrics together perfectly. Her heart beat faster. She so loved matching fabrics for a feast of pattern and color. Now that Ephraim was out of her life, nothing brought her more pleasure.

Laura found three more greens, four blues, a white, and a charcoal gray. Miriam laid them on her pile and let her eyes drink in the possibilities.

"These will make the most wonderful quilt ever," Laura said.

"You are sure he won't think my making a quilt for him is strange?"

"Of course not."

Even if he did, he would not be anything but gracious. Seth had such a kind heart. He would never say anything to hurt her feelings. Miriam felt her face warm. Except that one time when he'd called her a snob, that is. But she would be forever grateful to him for saying what needed to be said. He was a true friend before they were even friends.

Priscilla climbed up the ladder with a bright purple backpack clutched in her hand. "Look what Seth got Laura to carry her books in at college."

Miriam took the sturdy backpack from Priscilla. The pattern of the fabric made it look as if Seth had bought Laura a backpack made of purple snakeskin. The heavy fabric and thick stitching showed its quality, but Miriam couldn't get over how ugly it was.

Laura glanced sheepishly at Miriam. "I'll stand out on campus, that's for sure, but I wouldn't trade it for the world. Seth is so good to me."

Miriam was more worried than ever that Seth would not like her quilt. As the hideous backpack showed, he didn't seem to have any taste at all.

SIGHING, Miriam deposited the bags on her bed and sat down next to them. She had bought five fat quarters and the blue-and-green fabric plus batting and a new rotary cutter blade. She tipped the bags upside down and let her treasures tumble onto the bed.

Would Seth like the colors she picked? Ephraim certainly hadn't. She'd almost gone to the stable this morning to ask Seth's opinion, just to be sure. She desperately wanted him to like the quilt, but she also wanted it to be a surprise. Lord willing, blue and green were his favorite colors. Either those or snakeskin purple.

Miriam decided to frame each quilt block with the dark blue of Seth's childhood blanket and put the new green-and-blue from the fabric store on the back. Even if Seth didn't end up liking it, she could barely contain her enthusiasm. This would be a fine quilt.

She pulled her sewing basket from under the bed and opened it. The blocks for Ephraim's Nine-Patch lay at the top, finished and ready to assemble. She had taken such care with these, the corners expertly matched, the seams ironed smartly. Today, the painful memories did not reduce her to tears. Perhaps she was numb. Or perhaps the sorrow had been with her so long, she had grown accustomed to it.

Miriam nearly tossed the burgundy-and-tan blocks into the trash. She didn't need the reminder every time she opened her sewing basket. Instead, she wrapped them in one of the plastic bags from the fabric store and stuffed them into the very bottom of her basket. Throwing all that hard work away would be wasteful. In a few years, when it didn't hurt so much, she could pull out the blocks and make a quilt for charity.

She pulled graph paper and a pencil from her supplies and began drawing plans for Seth's quilt, hoping he would love it as much as she would. Five-by-six squares would make a quilt big enough to cover his small bed at the stable. She filled in the grid with images of her favorite quilt block designs. Log Cabin, Flying Geese, Bear's Paw, Hole-in-the-Barn-Door...but no Nine-Patch. Ephraim's quilt was a Nine-Patch. She wanted nothing to do with it.

Shading squares with her colored pencils, she was engrossed in her drawing when Susie ambled into the room and sat beside her on the bed.

"Oh, how very pretty," she said as she examined Miriam's sketch.

Miriam looked up and flashed her a smile before returning to her work. "I will make one for the baby next. You can pick the colors."

She didn't expect the shadow that passed across Susie's face. "Unless I give him up. There would be no use in making him a quilt if I don't keep him."

Miriam set aside her notebook and took Susie's face in her hands. "Giving him to a gute family doesn't mean that you love him less. And I will make him a quilt no matter what happens. He will always be your baby, even if he belongs to someone else."

Familiar fear sprouted on Susie's face. "I cannot do it, Miriam. I cannot be strong enough."

Pulling her sister into a tight hug, Miriam responded, "Then keep him. We will love him all the same."

"And people will whisper behind their hands when we pass by. They will treat him differently because he doesn't have a proper father. Their rejection will sting, and he will grow up never being able to fit in, always unhappy."

It was the conversation they knocked about several times a week. It seemed a choice between complete misery and absolute heartache. Miriam hated to see Susie suffer so, would have gladly borne Susie's pain, but Seth had counseled her to let Susie make the decision, no matter how agonizing. Susie must make her own choices and live with the consequences so that she would not blame Miriam for her unhappiness afterward.

Yost swung open the door without knocking. "Mamm says come to supper."

Susie rose from the bed, her shoulders slumped and lifeless. Without a word, she left the room and Yost followed.

"Yost, wait," Miriam said.

Yost popped his head back into the room as a signal that he would be giving Miriam exactly five seconds to say something significant.

"Come in here," she said.

Yost stepped in reluctantly and plopped himself on Susie's bed. Had he always worn that near scowl on his face? "What do you want?"

Mustn't attack, mustn't accuse. She tried to decide how to tiptoe around a crouching wildcat. "I saw you yesterday."

"I saw you yesterday too." He stood up. "I'm going to supper."

"You were walking through Seth Lambright's alfalfa with Jonas Shetler and an Englisch boy."

Color crept up Yost's neck and spread across his cheeks. "We were taking a shortcut. Last time I looked, that's not a crime. Unless Seth Lambright has us arrested for trespassing. He told you some wild story about me and my friends, didn't he?"

Miriam wasn't sure what to do with Yost's sudden anger. She didn't know how to tiptoe any softer. Why had she said anything?

She stood and tried to put her arms around Yost. He backed away as if she were holding a poisonous snake. "Of course not. Seth cares about you, Yost. He would never want to hurt or—"

"He is such a hypocrite, pretending to be nice and religious, all the while going with Reuben Shetler's wife. Jonas's dat won't stand for it no more. Jonas said so."

Miriam caught her breath as indignation smothered her. Had Yost any idea of the seriousness of such an accusation? She stopped with the tiptoeing and put her foot down. "What is this ridiculousness belching out of your mouth, Yost Bontrager? Such stories are pure evil. You will hurt more people than you know with that talk. Shame on you!"

"What? You never seen Seth and Mary together? You never seen her at his stable?"

Miriam tried to keep her expression unchanged. So Seth and Mary had talked together once or twice. That didn't mean anything. Seth would never...

"You think that means anything? I saw you with an Englischer yesterday, Yost. Does that mean you are selling drugs again?"

Yost sneered and actually kicked the door shut. "You always think the worst of me. I don't know why I even try. You all hate me."

Miriam took several deep breaths. The anger ebbed as quickly as it had come. Seth said Yost felt unlovable and consequently pushed people away. She had let him push her away today. How could she have been so reckless as to lose her temper? Any good feelings Yost might have felt for her had vanished. She had lost his trust once again. If only Seth were here. Seth would know the right words to say to make it better.

Not even a butterscotch pie or an apple-pudding cake could soothe Yost's anger.

She immediately backed away from him and laced her fingers together. "I am sorry. My tongue ran ahead of my thoughts. I did not mean it."

Yost's face softened before the scowl masked his features once again. He grabbed the knob and threw open the door. "You should take a good, hard look at Seth before accusing me of wrongdoing. If he knows what's good for him, he will leave Mary Shetler alone."

CHAPTER NINETEEN

As of four weeks ago, Miriam hated Sundays—specifically Sundays when services were held.

Dat put a gentle hand on Miriam's elbow. "It will be all right. The first time will soon be over."

Miriam, Yost, and Susie, plus Mamm and Dat and the three little boys, piled out of their long buggy for gmay at Herschbergers. Yost brought with him a jar of pickles, and Miriam carried two loaves of bread for dinner after service.

Miriam wore her cheery mint-green dress but the bright color could not lift her spirits, which were so low they were scraping the ground. She dreaded the sight of Ephraim Neuenschwander. She hadn't seen him since the fateful gathering at the Wengerds'. At the last gmay, his family had been visiting another district. No such blessing this week. Would she keep her composure when she laid eyes on him? What would she say?

Mamm glanced at Miriam and pressed her lips into a hard line. Ephraim's rejection had taken Mamm and Dat completely by surprise. Mamm's eyes had grown wide and Dat considered riding to Ephraim's house to plead his daughter's case. After sharing many tears, they decided they couldn't do anything but comfort each other and try to forgive Ephraim for his blindness.

Miriam clasped her hands together and trembled as she followed her family down the lane and up to the house.

The first time will soon be over.

As if waiting for her arrival, Ephraim stood on the sidewalk, smiling widely and greeting newcomers. Miriam caught her breath. He was as handsome as ever with that arrogant grin and tousle of unruly yellow hair.

His smile faltered when he saw her, but he pasted it back into place and grabbed her dat's hand as if searching for anything to divert his attention so he didn't have to look at her.

"John, you have come," he said. *Nothing like "I am happy to see you," or "I am glad you and your family are here." That wouldn't be completely truthful, would it?*

Dat shook hands vigorously, probably hoping by sheer willpower to make Ephraim give Miriam his notice. He actually pulled Ephraim in Miriam's direction before he released Ephraim's hand.

Ephraim was obliged to acknowledge Miriam or appear very rude indeed for ignoring her. His eyes flashed with irritation. Miriam knew how little he liked being forced into anything. His reaction made every space in her chest ache.

He tilted his head as if to study her more closely. "You are wearing the peacock dress."

It knocked the wind right out of her.

Then he pretended to see someone very interesting on the other side of the yard and quickly marched away.

Smoothing an imaginary crease in her sleeve, Miriam looked around her to see if anyone had heard. She felt as small as a pill bug and wished she could roll herself into a little ball and hide from curious eyes. She glanced to the corner of the house, where Sarah Schwartz stood sufficiently humble in a navy-blue dress. Even Laura Lambright wore deep purple. Had she herself fallen so far?

Seth seemed to have a special talent for recognizing her distress. He appeared at her side from out of nowhere and gave her a warm smile, though deep concern smoldered in his eyes. "I hope you do not think me improper for saying so, but you look very pretty today."

Miriam merely nodded, knowing that if she tried to speak she would make a fool of herself in front of Ephraim and the entire district.

Seth inclined his head toward the bishop's wife. "Look."

Miriam turned. Barbara Schwartz wore a blue dress the color of the sky at noonday.

Seth held his gaze on Miriam until she looked into his eyes. "That is a beautiful color of dress she has on. Brighter than yours. No one would dare say the bishop's wife wears anything improper."

Miriam took a deep breath, nodded again, and squared her shoulders.

The corners of his lips curved up, and he patted her hand. "Gute. Will you sit by Laura? She needs a friend."

Miriam nodded. She hooked an arm around Susie and led her to stand by Laura.

As she walked away, she realized she hadn't said a word to Seth—not even a word of thanks for talking her heart off the ground. But she knew he had not been offended. He was a true friend.

"Do you think we will have enough food?" Mamm said.

Enough food? Miriam prayed they would not be overflowing with leftovers. She had assured Laura vigorously that everyone would be eager to come to her quilting circle. But as Tuesday approached, Miriam began to have her doubts. She had seen Ada Weaver and her sister, Sarah Schwartz, at the bulk food store and invited them to come and quilt. Ada told Miriam she and Sarah were dreadfully busy this time of year and couldn't possibly spare the time.

Miriam had not expected more of them. But would the others come? Cousins Rebecca and Kate? Mary Shetler and Edna Miller? Would they see the circle as a chance to show charity or to make an unspoken statement about their feelings for Laura? Perhaps people would stay away because Susie would be there.

If the old Miriam had been invited to a quilting circle for Laura Lambright, she would have found a convenient excuse not to be there. After all, Laura had rejected the Ordnung and the church. Miriam would have considered Laura worldly and vain and would have made it a point to have nothing to do with her. Laura was not the sort of person the old Miriam would have wanted her name linked with.

Recognizing the change in her own attitude filled Miriam with astonishment. She was a new person, less judgmental, more accepting. And although she had lost Ephraim because of it, Miriam could not for a minute regret the person she'd left behind. She liked herself better these days.

Mamm and Susie would come, of course. Mamm had assured Miriam that helping Laura Lambright with a quilt was the charitable thing to do. "Seth cares for your foal," she'd said. "It is kind of you to take an interest in his sister."

Ellie would be there, but not to quilt. Quilting wreaked havoc on her fingernails, she had told Miriam.

So with at least five people at the quilting circle, it would not seem completely empty, and perhaps Laura would not recognize that she had been slighted. Miriam prayed hard that morning that, Lord willing, there would be a crowd. She would not for the world want Laura's feelings hurt.

They knocked on the Lambrights' door with Miriam toting a box of needles and tacks, thimbles, and thread. Susie held the plate of cold meats for dinner, and Mamm carried a large bowl of frog-eye salad—enough for twenty people.

As expected, Pookie barked right on cue. Laura threw open the door, her exuberant smile tainted by the uneasiness in her eyes.

They will come, Laura. Don't worry about a thing. Everyone will come. I hope.

From her seat at the kitchen table Ellie scolded Pookie, and the dog stopped mid-bark and ran away. Miriam craned her neck to see if she could catch a glimpse of Seth. No such luck. He had probably removed himself as far as possible from the prospect of a quilting bee.

Laura took the bowl from Mamm. "Thank you for coming. You are so kind."

Priscilla ran from the kitchen to her familiar place in Miriam's arms.

"Priscilla! Don't stomp your feet in the house," Ellie yelled.

Miriam flinched at Ellie's display of temper.

Priscilla tightened her arms around Miriam's neck. "Sorry, Mamm."

"Be more considerate next time."

As if nothing were amiss, Priscilla gave Miriam an enthusiastic kiss on the cheek. "I am so excited. Did you see Laura's quilt?"

Miriam squeezed Priscilla tightly. "Are the frames outside?"

Laura nodded, almost breathless. "Jah, set up like you said. Come through the kitchen."

Ellie, in bright yellow rubber gloves, sat at the table with an old toothbrush in her hand. "We needed one more good scrub before the quilting circle." She glanced at Susie's shoes as she shuffled to the back door. "Will people be walking in and out all day, do you think?"

The corners of Laura's mouth sagged. "Just a few people, Mamm."

Laura had set up her mother's old quilting frames beneath a tall maple in the backyard. Ten folding chairs stood like sentinels in a circle around the frames. Laura's quilt top and bottom and the batting sat patiently on one of the chairs.

"Okay, let's get moving," Mamm said. "The others will be here soon."

The others. Yes, Lord willing.

Miriam and her mamm had set up so many quilts over the years, the process was almost like a dance. They folded the bottom fabric to find the center of each side then laid it facedown on the frames. Scilla raced from person to person, handing out tacks as if she were playing Button, Button. Susie and Laura quickly tacked the centers while Miriam and Mamm lightly tugged the fabric out toward the corners. When the corners were secure, they pressed a few more tacks into each side, pulling gently to stretch the bottom nice and smooth.

The fluffy polyester batting came next. Miriam let Scilla pull it from the package. The little girl giggled when it seemed to grow twice its size once free from the plastic bag. "It's like popcorn," she said. She bounced it in her arms and handed it to Miriam.

Once they unfolded the batting, fitted it to the bottom, and trimmed it, the top went on easily. They again started at the centers, adjusting the corners and securing the clamps a final time. Mamm and Susie oohed and aahed at the beautiful colors and striking pattern. Priscilla danced around the frames, waving her hands in the air and shouting at the top of her lungs, "It is the most beautifulest quilt in the world! Look at me, I am Lady Dancing!"

Laura beamed happily, but Miriam noticed her hands shaking slightly. They were both nervous wrecks.

Mamm pulled a chair up to the quilt and started threading needles. She rested her glasses on the end of her nose and looked over the rims. "How do you want it quilted, Laura? Around the edge of each square? Or we could stitch a star in the middle of each one. That would be cute."

"Oh, my," said Laura, sinking into a chair as if the entire quilt were a lost cause. "I don't know. What shall we do, Miriam?"

"You can do it like my quilt," Scilla said. "It was for Lady Dancing. I stitched around the squares."

"Cum, Priscilla," Susie said, grinning at the little girl's exuberance, "I will show you how to start."

"I know how to start. I made a quilt that I gave to Miriam."

"I know you did," Susie said. "It is on Miriam's bed. Lady Dancing is sleeping under it."

Priscilla smiled. "Jah. I know."

Miriam studied the quilt top. "What would you like, Laura? I thought a line two inches on the inside of the edges would be nice. And simple. But stars would be darling. We would have to draw them in."

"Let's do lines two inches in," Laura said. "I think even I can manage that."

Edna Miller and her sister Naomi came around the side of the house just then. Edna had the spring in her step of a much younger woman, while Naomi plodded stiffly along as if she were marching to her own grave.

Miriam's relief was palpable. If anyone would make the effort to come, it was Edna. Miriam wanted to jump to her feet and throw her arms around the dear woman. She opted for a wide smile. "I am so glad to see you."

"The note on the door said to walk around the house to the back," Edna said.

Naomi fanned herself with a handkerchief. "It is a miserable hike. The rocks are nasty on that side of the house."

Edna planted an affectionate kiss on Laura's cheek. "Look at you. I ain't seen hide nor hair of you for going on three years. You are so grown-up, I hardly recognize you. And Priscilla. You are so tall. How old are you now?"

"Six."

"Six! I had not thought it possible."

"I am helping with the quilt," Priscilla said.

"You are? Then you are more grown-up than I thought. Any girl who can quilt is as smart as a tack."

Naomi headed for the nearest chair.

Edna embraced Miriam. "Oh, my darling girl," she whispered. "I heard what happened with Ephraim. That poor boy can't see past the nose on his own face."

Miriam resisted the urge to cry and let the pain wash through her. "I will be all right."

"I know you will. Broken hearts mend in time, Lord willing. But Ephraim will come to regret it. I am sorry for it. When you feel extra sad, know that I say a prayer for you every day. I hope it will make you feel better." Edna pulled away, patted Miriam's arm, then moved a chair close to the quilt. "Cum, Naomi. Sit here and I will be next to you."

Naomi groaned and made a great show of rising from the seat she had occupied for less than a minute. "Why can't you leave me be, Eddy?"

Edna smiled and winked at Laura. "Naomi is the fastest quilter I know. We'd never finish this quilt today without her."

Naomi sat in her new chair and held out her hand. "Well,

hand me a needle, then. And a good, small thimble. I don't like when it slips off my fingers."

Next, cousins Kate, Linda, and Rebecca came around back with much more enthusiasm than Naomi had. Linda and Rebecca carried two folding chairs each, and Kate balanced a chocolate sheet cake on top of a bowl of potato salad.

"Extra chairs," said Kate. "In case we need them."

The chairs were nice, but Miriam rejoiced over the extra people. Considering how sparse she thought the attendance might be, she could be perfectly content with the size of their little group.

Mary Shetler arrived with Deborah Yoder and Deborah's two married daughters. Laura's smile got wider with each new guest. This was a true quilting circle now.

Seeing Mary, Miriam couldn't help but recall her conversation with Yost when he'd said that something was amiss between Seth and Mary. She had seen Mary at the stable the first day she went to visit the foals, and Mary's presence had not felt quite right then. Miriam shook her head to clear out such dark thoughts. This was exactly why she'd chastised Yost. There was no end to the troubles started by a rumor like that.

Edna had spoken the honest truth. Naomi was a speedy quilter—partly because she refused to carry on a conversation with anyone. Naomi was as sour as a green cherry, but Edna didn't cater to her moods, so no one else did either.

Once Priscilla had a needle threaded, she planted herself next to Naomi and began chatting merrily. She didn't seem troubled by Naomi's sour disposition. Perhaps she knew that Naomi was the only person there who would let her talk without one word of interruption.

Laura threaded her needle for the third time and came close to Miriam. "Denki, Miriam," she said, her smile as wide as the sky. "This is better than my best imagination."

Everyone treated Laura as a dear friend or favorite niece. Miriam breathed easier for Laura's sake, but she watched Deborah Troyer and her daughters make a wide path around Susie and sit as far from her as they could. Miriam felt a momentary prick of pain for Susie, but since everyone else acted so graciously, she thought herself ungrateful to focus on the few unkind ones. A few months ago, she would have behaved precisely the same way. Today, she took pity on those who stumbled on their own pride.

With most of her fears put to rest, Miriam found a spot next to Mamm, picked up a needle, and began to stitch. She worked a needle almost as quickly as Naomi. Before long, Miriam had completed a straight row of tiny stitches. She sat back and heard six or seven conversations going on at once. She always fancied that was why it was called a quilting bee, because talk around the quilt sounded like a buzzing beehive.

Rebecca and Deborah Troyer's oldest daughter, Millie, talked of Rebecca's husband, Levi. "I didn't think he could get more handsome," Rebecca said, "but the beard suits him."

"My dat saw Levi's mamm with Isaac Yutzy, driving down the road in a courting buggy."

Kate perked up her ears at the mention of Isaac Yutzy. "He works for Nathaniel. A very nice man, but a bit old for Levi's mamm. He's going on seventy."

Rebecca kept her eyes on her stitches. "I don't give my opinion to his mamm. She might find older men attractive."

A few of the women giggled.

"No one can speak for anyone else in matters of the heart," said Edna.

Mary Shetler and Mamm leaned their heads together and carried on a hushed conversation. Miriam sat close enough to hear every word if she paid close attention.

"And did you know there is an Englisch boy hanging about with them?" she heard Mary say.

Miriam should have known they were fretting over their sons who had decided to befriend one another. It was not a relationship that either mother celebrated.

Mamm pressed her lips into a thin line. "Jah, Miriam said as much."

"I am all aflutter to know what to do about it. I've got all *die kinner* at home who don't give a moment's peace, and Reuben badgering me that the house ain't clean enough, and me feeling so tired. I can't pay Jonas no attention nor get him to finish his chores. Reuben yells at him until he's blue in the face, but it don't do no good."

Mamm turned her eyes to Miriam, put an arm around her shoulders, and pulled her into the conversation since she was eavesdropping anyway. "Miriam makes Yost goodies, and we try to give him lots of hugs. But sometimes it is like hugging a porcupine."

"Jonas says I am a bad mother, and his fater upholds him. Reuben tells me I cry too much at silly things."

"Of course you are a gute mother. The little ones adore you. Surely Reuben can see that."

"Nae, he is right. I am sorely lacking. I shouldn't have come today, for all the work at home. My floor ain't been mopped for three weeks, and the tomatoes are rotting on the vine. The thought of having to can tomatoes and peaches and corn makes me want to lie down and never get back up. Reuben says we will starve come wintertime because of me, because I won't put up the tomatoes. And Jonas won't heed a word I say. He thinks I am wicked."

"Why would he think a thing like that?" Mamm said.

Miriam squirmed in her chair and buried her doubts. She

had no reason to suspect Seth of any wrongdoing with another man's wife. How dare Yost plant the seed.

When Mary didn't answer, Mamm squeezed Miriam's shoulder at the same time she patted Mary's hand. "Do you have a canner?"

"As Reuben says, it sits idle in my cellar."

"And bottles?"

"Jah, plenty of bottles."

Mamm raised her eyebrows expectantly at Miriam and gave her a slight nod. "Okay, Miriam and I will come tomorrow after she gets home from work and help you can the tomatoes. Does that work for you, Miriam?"

"Jah. I would like to help."

"I have two canners," Mamm said. "That will be enough to keep us hopping."

Mamm didn't spend a lot of time talking about how people could solve their problems. She found something to do about it, rolled up her sleeves, and got to work, usually at the sacrifice of a great deal of time. Canning Mary's tomatoes would not stop Reuben's complaining or inspire Jonas to straighten up, but it would relieve some of Mary's immediate burden.

"I am powerless to do anything about your marriage or your wayward son, but let me come to your house and make spaghetti sauce and ketchup"—that was the kind of thing Mamm did. And when all was said and done, it did make things better in some unexplainable way.

"Oh," Mary said, trying to hide both her eagerness and her embarrassment, "I could not ask you to do that."

"It will be fun. I will make sure Yost comes with us, and you tell Jonas too. Perhaps if we have them in the same room, we can scold them until they beg for mercy."

Mary managed a half smile. "Or until they decide to abandon us altogether."

The quilting progressed in earnest. Soon they were ready to roll the first side, and then the next. Miriam finished another row and stuck her head under the quilt. She loved to see the tiny points of light through the fabric that outlined the patterns on the top. The thread bonded the batting and fabric together, leaving the spaces in between the stitches puffy and raised—truly a three-dimensional work of art.

At this rate, the quilt would be done by dinnertime. They all could eat a good meal and still have time to make it home for afternoon chores.

Miriam threaded another needle. The last time she'd made a quilt for charity, Ephraim came over to the house and played volleyball with her brothers while she quilted. He came running into the house every ten minutes to check on her progress, teasing her that she was not fast enough and prodding her to hurry up so she could join them in volleyball.

Miriam ran her finger over the stitches and caught her breath. That was the first time she'd thought of Ephraim without being overcome with grief. Perhaps because it was a happy memory.

Volleyball in the backyard.

Miriam nearly laughed out loud when she thought of Seth playing volleyball at the Wengerds' gathering. Her brothers would get a big laugh out of Seth's skills. And he would laugh right along with them.

Her heart swelled. For the first time in a long time, she pictured happy days ahead.

Miriam carefully matched her corners and used about twice the pins she usually did to secure the last two panels together. She positioned the fabric under the presser foot and slowly moved her toes and heels up and down, up and down, in a methodical rhythm. The needle bobbed under the edge of her quilt squares and up again, sewing an orderly row of tiny stitches. At the end of the fabric, she doubled back to tack the thread in place, carefully cut the leftover threads, and pulled out all her pins. It was finished.

She unfurled the quilt top like a flag and let it float to her bed. The deep blues and emerald greens made her imagine that she was standing at the edge of a crystal lake, looking at leaves so radiantly green they almost hurt her eyes. To Miriam, green was a healing color. Hopefully Seth would feel the healing power of her gift.

Next week she would put it on the frame and quilt it. For now, she let it rest on her bed. She would think of Seth every time she walked into the room.

That was an uncommonly pleasant thought.

CHAPTER
TWENTY

Carrying a bucket in each hand, Seth came out of the stable as Miriam rode Daisy up the lane. His buckets must have been heavy. Miriam could see the veins and muscles of his forearms bulging with the strain. He wasn't as bulky as Ephraim at the shoulders, but his entire body, even the way he moved, testified of Seth's strength. He stood four or five inches taller than Ephraim and, therefore, towered over most everybody. Where Ephraim was of a thick, solid build, Seth stretched lanky and *lang* and probably didn't have an ounce of fat on his entire body.

Seth caught sight of her and burst into a grin. He put down his buckets and came to her. In earlier days, if she hadn't been concentrating on avoiding him, she would have recognized how handsome he was with his thick, dark eyebrows and hair so black it glistened in the sunlight. When he smiled, he revealed a hint of a dimple that Miriam found delightful.

"You are late today," he said as he took the reins. "I don't think it is safe to ride home in the dark."

Miriam led Daisy to the small trough next to the stable and

then tied her to the post. "I will not stay long. But I really wanted to see the foals. It's been more than two weeks."

Seth gave her a slight smile, put his hands into his pockets, and looked to the pasture. "I started to believe you had forgotten us."

"Forgotten? This is the only place I feel like myself." She patted Daisy's neck. "Besides work at the quilt shop, I have been quilting and canning and canning and quilting." She held out her hands. "My fingers are permanently brownish-red."

Seth took her hands in his and studied her palms. His warm, calloused skin felt comfortably pleasant, like a favorite pair of garden gloves. "I hear you did spaghetti sauce and tomato juice."

"Two days straight. And then we put up corn and peaches. Clingstones, mind you. I've a good mind to chop down that tree myself."

"They have a gute flavor."

"Clingstones are stubborn, but I am not complaining. There is nothing better than a shelf full of bright peaches ready for winter. And while we slice and wash, we can talk the ears right off a man's head."

She didn't mind that he still had hold of her hands, but they couldn't stand like that forever. She fell silent and slowly pulled from his grasp.

With a sheepish twist of his lips, he cleared his throat and lowered his eyes. "Laura couldn't be happier about her quilt. It's packed at the top of her suitcase."

"You wouldn't believe how quickly we finished it. I feared —" Miriam's face grew warm. She'd almost said the wrong thing.

"You were afraid no one would come to help?"

When Miriam didn't answer, Seth nodded vigorously. "Me

too. The Lambrights aren't the most favored family in the district."

"I didn't mean that at all."

"Don't worry. I'm past getting my feelings hurt."

"They could have just as easily stayed away because of Susie."

He searched her face. "Your family is simply going through a rough patch." Then he cast his eyes downward. "The Lambrights are hopeless."

"Don't be ridiculous," Miriam said, but she wasn't quite sure how to contradict him. She regretted every superior thought she'd ever harbored about anybody.

"Joshua and Jacob are mucking out the stable," Seth said. "Will you say hello to them before you go? I think Joshua wants you for his girlfriend."

Miriam laughed. "I'm flattered. Joshua is a very handsome ten-year-old. Does he care that he would have to stand on a milking stool to put his arm around me?"

Seth's gaze riveted Miriam's attention. "I've missed your laugh. I didn't even want to go to work this week for fear you'd come while I was away and I'd miss you."

She knew she was blushing as she stifled a smile and went into the stable. She was grateful that the stable was significantly dimmer than the outside, since her face must surely be glowing bright red. Why did her heart skip a beat and the heat rise to her cheeks when he looked at her like that? She couldn't make sense of it.

"Miriam!" Both of Seth's brothers charged and practically bowled her over where she stood.

"Did you see the new stallion?" Joshua asked. "Seth bought him two days ago. He is pure black with a tiny white patch no bigger than my thumb on his front leg. And he runs so fast you almost can't see him. We feed him the special feed that Seth got."

"He won a race," said Jacob, vying for Miriam's attention.

"I was going to say that," Joshua insisted.

Miriam lifted her eyebrows and nodded in amazement. Joshua never ran out of words.

"Maybe she'd like to see the horse instead of talk about him," Seth said, interrupting Joshua's discourse about the condition of the stallion's teeth.

"I'd love to." She took the boys' hands and let them lead her out of the stable.

They walked to the pasture on the north end of Seth's property where a majestic horse trotted around the perimeter of the fence. His black coat gleamed in the sun, and powerful muscles rippled underneath.

Miriam put her hand over her mouth. "Oh my. He is the most beautiful horse I have ever seen."

Seth didn't disguise his pride. "An investment, for sure, but Lord willing, he will be worth a hundred times his price."

The stallion stopped prancing and looked in their direction, as if he knew they were talking about him. Always prepared, Seth pulled an apple out of his pocket and sliced it into three pieces with his pocketknife. He handed one to each of his brothers and Miriam.

"Horses like apples the best in the world." Joshua stretched his hand between two fence slats. "Jacob, don't curl your fingers like that, or the horse will bite them off."

Jacob pinched his face in irritation. "I know as much as you do."

"Well, you were curling your fingers around the apple. It didn't seem like you knew anything. Horses are very gentle and wouldn't hurt a fly, but you have to know how to behave around them or they could step on you. They don't want to hurt you, but they are so big and don't know any better."

Seth put a finger to his lips. "Hush now, Joshua. More likely, he will come if we stay still."

Joshua and Jacob, with their hands still sticking through the fence, became like statues. Seth winked at Miriam, and she flashed a delighted smile back at him as she caught sight of that dimple.

They watched as the stallion twitched his ears and regarded them with feigned disinterest. He nodded his head twice and took a cautious step toward them. Slowly at first and then with a faster gait, he came to the fence and sniffed both apple slices before gobbling them up. The boys giggled as the horse licked their hands.

"Now you, Miriam," Jacob said.

Miriam stretched out her hand to the stallion, making sure that Joshua saw her perfectly horizontal fingers. When the horse took her offering, she rubbed his nose and cooed. "That's a good baby," she said, closing her eyes and nuzzling the horse with her cheek. "Good boy." The stallion's coarse hair tickled her skin, and Miriam felt his warm breath on the back of her hand.

She stood savoring the sensations before opening her eyes. Jacob and Joshua leaned with their backs against the fence, staring at Seth. Seth stood with his hand pressed against the slat, studying Miriam with those gray eyes as deep as a wintertime lake.

She wished he wouldn't look at her like that. How could a girl keep her head on straight?

The color drained from Seth's face. He looked away, cleared his throat, and promptly knocked Joshua's hat off.

"Hey!" Joshua protested.

Seth picked up the hat and tapped it back on Joshua's head. "Just checking to see if you have any bald spots."

"We was about to feed the horses," Joshua said. "Do you want to help, Miriam? Then we are going to brush them and bed them down for the night."

Seth patted Joshua's shoulder. "Miriam can't stay long. I don't want her riding home in the dark."

"Seth Lambright. I would have words with you."

Startled, Miriam turned to see Reuben Shetler standing behind Seth with his hands on his hips and the shadow of a scowl on his face. Miriam tried to calm her racing heart. None of them had even heard his approach.

Seth pressed his lips into a hard line and furrowed his brow. He and Reuben stood staring at each other for what seemed like an eternity, but it could only have been a few seconds. Jacob sidled close to Miriam and put his hand in hers. She wrapped her fingers protectively around his hand.

Seth pinched the bridge of his nose between his fingers before glancing at his brothers and softening his expression. He nodded and managed a friendly smile at Reuben, which, considering Reuben's hostile demeanor, was a miracle in itself. "Good to see you again, Reuben."

Seth moved forward, and Reuben, untrusting and unsure, took a quick step back. For a moment Miriam thought Seth would try a hug. Instead, he placed both hands on Reuben's shoulders and gave him a firm pat. "Will you come with me while I run the water into the far pasture?"

Miriam felt the sudden urge to clear her throat, as if her collar were too tight and she couldn't quite catch her breath. Yost's accusations, the ones that had seemed so outrageous last week, came back to her.

"Don't tell me you've never seen Seth and Mary Shetler together. Jonas's dat won't stand for it no more."

Seth put a brotherly arm around Reuben, who acted as if he were being embraced by a snake. Looking back at Miriam, Seth silently communicated with her as he walked away.

"Keep an eye out for the boys. They don't need this."

Miriam nodded with a sick feeling in her stomach.

Seth walked to the edge of the small pasture, where the foals played with their mother. He propped his boot on the bottom fence rail and folded his arms. Reuben started in on him. Miriam couldn't hear what he said, but she could hear his voice, loud and angry, and watch as he pointed an accusing finger at Seth and displayed an unattractive scowl.

Jacob, with eyes full of fear, slid his arms around Miriam and held on tightly. "Cum," Miriam said, pretending not to hear the tirade going on a hundred yards away, "Show me how you feed the horses."

Neither boy moved.

"He looks very mad," Joshua said, not turning his eyes from the spot where Seth stood calmly and humbly while Reuben yelled at him.

"Do you think he will hurt Seth?" Jacob asked in a muffled voice, his face hidden beneath the folds of Miriam's apron.

With shaking hands, Miriam pulled Jacob away from her and looked him in the eyes. "Reuben is cross about something, but he would never hurt Seth."

"Jonas Shetler came yesterday with Yost Bontrager and an Englischer," Joshua said, as if he had forgotten that Yost was Miriam's brother.

Jacob released his hold on Miriam and turned to his brother. "Don't tell that. Seth said no telling, like water under a bridge."

Joshua lifted his chin stubbornly. "I can tell Miriam."

Jacob sighed and reattached himself to Miriam's waist. "Seth said don't tell."

Joshua ignored his brother. "Jonas screamed at him and told Seth to keep away from his mamm. Then he slapped the bucket out of Seth's hand and pushed him against the wall."

Miriam felt as if someone had sucked all the air out of the pasture. The emptiness in her lungs almost choked her. "Yost... and...Jonas—they pushed him?"

"Only Jonas pushed. Jacob cried, and they left in a hurry."

"You cried too," Jacob protested.

At that moment, Miriam felt so ashamed of her brother, she thought she might fall to her knees and weep. How could she ever in a million years make things better?

The yelling at the other end of the pasture buzzed in Miriam's head like a wasp. She resisted the urge to clap her hands over her ears. The boys must not know how upset she was.

Jesus said he who is angry with his brother without a cause is in danger of the judgment. What could justify such rage?

Miriam knew what Yost's answer would be. But even with doubt clinging to her, she couldn't bring herself to believe that Seth was such a man. Such immorality was not in his nature.

The yelling subsided briefly. Miriam risked a look in Seth's direction. He spoke now with his eyes fixed on Reuben's face. She didn't hear what he said, but his calm tone should have pacified even the most determined enemy. Yet as soon as Seth paused, Reuben attacked again, unmoved by whatever Seth had said.

The alarm written on the brothers' faces mirrored Miriam's own turmoil, but it also spurred her into action. Taking each of their hands, she said, "Walk with me to the stable."

Such a journey would take them closer to Seth and Reuben, but it couldn't be helped. The stable would provide a sound barrier and a haven where Joshua and Jacob would not have to witness what transpired between Seth and Reuben. As they passed close to the two men, Reuben watched them resentfully and lowered his voice.

Miriam pulled the boys through the squeaky door. All three stood in the cool dampness of the stable and caught their breath.

"I think we should pray," Miriam said.

Breathing heavily, Joshua nodded.

All three knelt on the ground to pray silently. When Miriam got to her knees, she realized how many things she had to pray for. She asked that Reuben's heart be softened, that Seth could forgive Yost, that she could forgive Yost, and that all would be right in the world again, Lord willing.

She heard the door squeak and sensed the space brighten as the orange afternoon sun flooded the stable. She opened her eyes to see Seth silhouetted in the doorway, studying her quietly.

The boys leaped up and raced to their brother. He squeezed them tightly then patted each of their heads. "Denki for taking good care of Miriam."

Seth held out his hand and pulled Miriam to her feet. Pain saturated his face, and his eyes were bits of moonlight in the dead of winter. "I wish you had not been here. You should not have been forced to see that."

She shook her head. "I am not upset." She spoke in a whisper, afraid her voice would give her away if she talked any louder.

He rubbed a thumb against her cheek. "Can you forget it happened or pretend it was a bad dream?"

Miriam couldn't help herself. "Why... What did he want?"

A line appeared between Seth's eyebrows. "Reuben is the best of men. But there are things he refuses to understand—things he chooses to ignore that I will not let him ignore. I make him very angry because of it. But I would never do anything to hurt him or his family. I wish he could understand. I would not for the world have you worry."

Miriam swallowed three times but the lump would not vacate her throat. "What happened with Yost yesterday?"

Seth's eyes grew wide and then narrowed as they darted from Jacob to Joshua. The little boys grew so quiet, it was if they weren't breathing. Seth turned his back on Miriam and rested a hand against the wall. "Yost did nothing."

Miriam knew she shouldn't get angry, but her embarrassment, her shame at her own brother's actions overwhelmed her.

"He spreads ugly gossip about you, he tramples through your fields, he harasses you and your family." She felt she might burst with indignation. "That doesn't sound like 'nothing' to me."

"It *is* nothing, Miriam. Yost is going through a hard time right now. I never should have suggested group therapy. I offended him. He is angry and needs someone to take his anger out on. I am fine. You have enough pain in your life without my adding to it."

Miriam growled and stomped her foot. "*You?* You're adding to my pain? What about Yost? Do you think he bears any responsibility for this?"

Seth came close and took her face in his hands. "Please, Miriam, please. I cannot bear to see you so unhappy."

"Unhappy?" She pulled from him and swiped a hand across her eyes. "I am drowning in it."

Seth was the only person who understood her, who listened and didn't judge. She knew she could tell him anything in her heart and he would still like her. Was Yost purposefully trying to alienate every friend she had?

Who would want to be friends with Miriam Bontrager? If her sister wasn't embarrassing the family, her brother was.

Ephraim was right to stay as far away from her as possible. It was only a matter of time before Seth came to the same conclusion.

The last time she came to Seth's ranch, she had cried like a baby on his shoulder. This time, she determined to fall apart in the privacy of her own home.

She couldn't utter one word without bursting into tears, so she spun on her heels and marched out the far door. She jumped onto Daisy and trotted her down the lane.

"Miriam, come back," she heard Seth call.

Miriam was convinced that she would never show her face at Seth's again.

She wouldn't be coming back.

CHAPTER
TWENTY-ONE

"Good morning!" Martha called.

There were already three tourists waiting outside Martha's quilt shop the next morning when Miriam and Martha arrived. Martha greeted the couple and their teenage son, and before she'd even gotten the door unlocked, she found out they were from California and were here visiting relatives. Martha was a good merchant. She took a keen interest in every one of her customers.

The shoppers filed through the door. Miriam followed and quickly hopped onto the ladder to light the propane lamps hanging about the store. Miriam found the hiss of the lanterns a comforting, pleasant sound, a constant in every Amish home like the Bible, the *Ausbund*, and the family.

Once the lamps were lit, Miriam dusted the counters and swept while Martha gave her customers a guided tour of the shop. Four more people came in the shop. It looked to be a busy morning.

Miriam massaged her temples and tried to focus her thoughts on work instead of her family troubles. When she returned home last night, Yost was not there. She had shut herself in her bedroom under the pretense of working on Seth's quilt so she would not have to face Yost when he did come home. What would she say to him? Or should she say nothing? She knew she could not see him without lashing out. Best to cool off first so she wouldn't say something she regretted later about his disgraceful behavior.

Miriam clenched her teeth. Why did she need to figure out how not to offend Yost, when he made all the trouble? He didn't deserve special treatment. He deserved a good, swift kick in the *hinnerdale*.

"Miriam, will you wrap this quilt for Mrs. Dustin?"

Miriam snapped to attention. Enough of the self-indulgence at work. She went to the counter and Martha carefully handed her the thousand-dollar quilt that used to hang in the front window. Appliquéd with a circle of roses and lilies, it read "I AM THE ROSE OF SHARON."

"It will go great in the guest room," the man said as Martha rang up his purchase and took his credit card. "They'll think they stepped back in time."

Miriam cleaned her hands thoroughly with a wet sanitary wipe before gently enfolding the quilt in crinkly, white tissue paper and placing it in a large gift box perfect for travel.

Her packing job pleased the man. "I like how you handled that quilt. A work of art shouldn't be stuffed in a plastic bag with groceries."

Miriam smiled. "Something this precious requires great care. It will give you years of pleasure, Lord willing."

She came around the counter and handed the man his box. He thanked her, and he and his family walked out the door. Martha squealed quietly and gave Miriam a swift hug. "Open ten minutes and already made a thousand dollars. What a happy day."

The little bell on the door tinkled faintly and Laura, with a red face and moist eyes, hurried into the store. She caught sight of Miriam immediately and came to her, agitated and breathless. "I am sorry to bother you at work," she said, glancing at Martha. "But is there any way you could leave for a few minutes?"

Laura's wild expression sent Miriam's heart racing. Whatever the matter, it wasn't good news. "What's wrong?"

Laura wrung her hands together. "Seth has been hurt."

Miriam's heart almost leaped out of her chest. "What happened? Is he okay?"

Laura grabbed Miriam's hand. "He just got home. I hate to impose like this, but you are so important to Seth. And—and I need your help. I am supposed to leave for school tomorrow, but how can I abandon him like this? Tell me what I should do."

Miriam tried to comfort Laura even as her own panic threatened to eat her up. She squeezed Laura's hand. "It's going to be all right. Everything is going to be gute, Lord willing." She turned to look at Martha.

Martha shooed them out the door. "Go. I will manage here."

The buggy sat just outside the shop. They jumped in and started down the road before Miriam had time to gather her scattered wits.

"How is Seth? Do we need to take him to the hospital?"

"He has been at the hospital all night. Once they put a cast on his arm, he refused to stay longer and the policeman brought him home."

"The police?"

By this time, tears made trails down Laura's cheeks. "Seth won't say a word about what happened. It aggravates me how forgiving he is. He walked home from the stable really late last night, and the policeman told me that a truck driver spotted three boys at the side of the road beating up on him."

Miriam gasped.

"The driver honked his horn and scared the boys away. He didn't get a good look but thought one or two of them were Amish. I can't believe it. No Amish boy would do something like this."

Miriam felt as if she had been thrown from a horse. The world started to spin and she cradled her head in her hands. She knew exactly who those boys were, those boys dressed as Amish.

Never in her life had she found it so difficult to speak. "How badly did they hurt him?"

"He says it's nothing. He is so long-suffering, I hate it. But his arm is broken and there are bruises on his face, and he can't stand up straight. When he got home, I sent him straight to bed. Even Ellie is concerned. She's making him chicken soup. Pookie didn't bark at him once, and Pookie always barks at him. That stupid dog whined and ran off with his tail between his legs." Laura snapped the reins. "Who would do such a thing to Seth? He doesn't have a mean bone in his body."

With her head still in her hands, Miriam squeezed her eyes shut and tried not to cry. Yost had gone beyond anything she ever thought possible. She hadn't believed things could get any worse. As they came closer and closer to the Lambrights' house, Miriam let her screams echo inside her head.

Take me home! Take me home right now!

Knowing what Yost had done, she couldn't bear to look Seth in the eyes again.

How he must hate her!

The buggy seemed to fly down the road, and Miriam's sense of dread deepened with each mile. Once they reached the house, Miriam felt as heavy as a pile of stones.

Laura grabbed Miriam's hand and pulled her across the yard and the fourteen flagstones. They blew through the door, passed Ellie in the kitchen tending to her soup, and went straight to Seth's bedroom, which was set off from the washroom on the main floor and almost as small as his room at the stable.

Miriam thought it wasn't possible for her to feel any worse, but when she saw Seth, an icy hand wrapped itself around her throat and she ceased breathing. He lay on his bed with his eyes closed and work boots still on his feet. His face shone ashen white except for three large purple bruises on his left cheek and jaw, and his left arm rested at his side with a cast up to the armpit.

They tiptoed into the room, but Seth immediately opened his eyes. His gaze flew to Miriam's face, and he pressed his lips into a hard line.

Miriam understood the look. She wanted to crawl into a dark hole.

"Laura," Seth whispered, "the upset multiplies, the more people you bring into it."

Laura plopped her hands on her hips. "Oh, and you don't think news of the attack will be all over the district by dinnertime? Miriam is your friend. I thought she would want to be told first."

He furrowed his brow. "What have you told her?"

"What do you think?"

Seth studied Miriam's face. Even though she thought she could never look him in the eyes again, she returned his gaze and hoped he would recognize the regret she wanted to communicate.

His lip twitched almost imperceptibly, and his eyes darkened to coal.

He knew. He knew that she knew.

His entire face became a looming storm. "Miriam, I am okay. Do not concern yourself about this for one minute. It is nothing," he said with such intensity that he practically growled.

"Don't concern yourself that your brother just broke my arm and put me in the hospital."

Miriam shook her head.

Seth must not have liked what he saw on her face. He shifted painfully on the bed and propped himself up on his good elbow. "Laura, do you think I could speak with Miriam alone?"

Laura twisted her lips and studied both of them suspiciously. "Why?"

"We want to discuss your future," Seth said dryly, before turning his eyes to Miriam and becoming serious again.

"That should take about thirty seconds." Laura glanced at Miriam doubtfully before shutting the door behind her.

Seth fell back onto his pillow like an old man on his deathbed. He closed his eyes momentarily, and Miriam watched pain travel across his face.

She scooted a short stool next to his bed and laid a hand over his arm. She felt him tense beneath her touch and, in dismay, withdrew her hand. Her need for forgiveness ached like hunger deep in the pit of her stomach. "I'm so sorry."

"It wasn't your fault."

"I'm so ashamed."

Concern flashed in his eyes. "This is why I didn't want you to know. I can't stand to see you so upset. It's worse than the physical pain. Yost does not have a cruel heart. He's young and easily influenced by other boys. They wanted to scare me, not hurt me."

Miriam hated facing up to the monster her brother had become. "They broke your arm."

"Nae, I tripped while running away."

That revelation did nothing to diminish her distress. Miriam felt as low as ever. "I promise that no one in my family will bother you again. I'll see to that."

The clouds darkened on his face. "Don't say that, Miriam."

Seth deserved to be free of the Bontragers forever. The thought of never going to his stable again made her want to cry, but for once she would be unselfish. For Seth.

"I'll go now," she said.

"When will you come back?"

"You don't want me to come back."

"Jah, I do." He pinned her with a stare. "More than anything."

"Why? My brother has—"

"You don't know me very well if you think anything that Yost could do would make me reject you. I think I'd die without you. Is that enough motivation to come back?"

Die without you?

His declaration briefly stunned her. "You don't hate me?"

"How could I?"

Relief washed over Miriam like waves on the lakeshore. "I don't deserve your kindness."

"Now you are talking hogwash." The elusive dimple appeared on his face, sending a warm sensation tingling into Miriam's fingers.

Laura opened the door and came into the room.

"What should we do about Laura?" Seth said. "She has this crazy notion to miss first semester and take care of me. You've got to talk her out of that right quick."

"And leave a cripple to care for the horses?" Laura wiped the last of the tears from her eyes. "You are more important than college. You've got to get that house started before it's too cold, and now you won't be able to work at the mill."

"I can walk fine. And the cast comes off in eight weeks." He pointed at her with an intense gaze. "You will not miss college."

"And who will take care of the boys and Scilla? And your horses?"

"Jacob and Joshua can manage things today. I'll be at the stable tomorrow."

"With one arm?" Miriam said.

Seth lifted his good arm and gasped in pain. He tried to hide it by clearing his throat. "One arm is better than none. I'm already feeling better."

Miriam prepared for resistance. "Better? Jah. I'm coming to the stable to help every day."

"You have your own chores and a job. I refuse to be a burden to anyone."

"If I postpone my trip one week," Laura said, "I will only miss freshman orientation and a couple of days of classes. By then you won't be walking around like an old man with arthritis."

Miriam shook her head.

Seth did too. "Absolutely not. If anyone needs orientation, it's a girl who doesn't even know how to drive a car."

"He's right, Laura. You have been waiting for this day for five years. Let me help. At the very least, Seth can sit on a lawn chair at the stable and tell me what to do."

A ghost of a smile flitted across Laura's lips. "You mean, boss you around."

Seth shook his head again. "I can't ask you to—"

"You're not asking," Miriam said. "I'm telling you. I know more about horses than you, and you can't stop me. I can run faster than a one-armed man."

Seth curved his mouth in mock indignation. "More about

horses than me? Now, wait a minute. That's going a bit too far."

If it weren't for the nagging emptiness in Miriam's stomach, Seth's expression might have made her smile. "I'll be by first thing in the morning."

Seth smiled in surrender and shrugged his shoulders. The movement made him catch his breath. When Laura and Miriam leaned toward him in concern, he weakly waved them away. "I'm fine. Feeling better already."

AFTER HANGING her bonnet on the hook, Miriam marched to the kitchen to see if she could help Mamm with supper.

It seemed as if a month had passed instead of just the day. Work had rolled on like a dream Miriam couldn't quite recall. Neither she nor Martha knew the reason for the steady stream of customers, but today had been one of their best days of the year.

Mamm rolled out dough on the counter while Susie and Hollow sat at the table cutting out biscuits and putting them on the baking pan.

Susie looked good today, more lively and cheerful. She grinned and teased Hollow about his pathetic pieces of biscuit dough. "If you pick them up like that, they will fall apart. You'll not have a gute circle."

Hollow laughed and placed his blob of dough on the pan. "They taste the same no matter how they look."

"Tell that to your pretzel customers," Susie said.

Mamm looked at Miriam and winked. "Miriam, my dear, how was work?"

Susie jumped up from her seat and wiped her hands on the

towel tied around her waist. "Did you hear about Seth Lambright? Isn't it terrible?"

Miriam felt her face get hot. "Jah. I went to visit him."

"Visit him? During work?" Mamm asked.

"Martha let me duck out for a few minutes. His face is bruised, and the cast goes up to his shoulder. I didn't see any other injuries, but he can barely move for the soreness."

"I am sorry to think that one of our own cannot even walk on the back roads and be safe," Mamm said.

Susie went to the sink to wash her hands. "It wonders me who would do such a thing. He had no money to steal."

Miriam forced herself to breathe normally, when she wanted to cry out.

"Will he be down for long?" Mamm asked.

"He is in a lot of pain, but he is determined to be at his stable tomorrow, Lord willing."

Mamm pointed her rolling pin at Miriam. "No one would doubt that he is a gute worker. Nothing wrong with that. A man who knows how to work will never see his children go hungry."

"I can go in the evening to help," Hollow said. "Tell him, won't you?"

Miriam smiled faintly. "Oh, Hollow, you are so kind." *Kinder than some of her own family.*

Yost appeared in the kitchen with his shoulders slumped and dark circles under his eyes. He frowned at Miriam, and the lines etched on his face made him seem like an old man with years of sorrow behind him. Miriam had never seen him look so deathly.

Her pulse raced, and the shame inside her exploded. She couldn't bear to look at him, knowing what he had done, knowing the black heart that lived inside her brother.

Without a word, she spun around, stormed out the back

door, and walked across the yard. Before she knew it, she ended up at the swing by the barn.

Plopping herself on the seat, she balled her hands into fists and tried to quell the sense of humiliation and anger that had overtaken her so suddenly. How dare he stand so innocently in the kitchen, expecting to be fed and cared for and loved, when less than twenty-four hours ago he had put another man in the hospital? How could she live in the same house with him—a daily reminder of the violence Seth endured?

That was why her parents must never know what Yost did. The truth would break Mamm's heart, and Dat would never recover from such a blow.

She would stay away from Yost as best as she could until... until what? Until the bruises faded from Seth's face and the cast came off and she could look at her brother without feeling a sick emptiness in her stomach.

The way she felt now, she might be waiting until the end of her days.

CHAPTER
TWENTY-TWO

"I can't believe I let you help me carry this. You can barely walk," Laura said.

Early the next morning before dawn, Seth and Laura carried her monstrous trunk down the stairs together. Seth couldn't manage it with one hand, and Dat was sleeping in. With every step, Seth bit his tongue and fought the urge to groan and collapse into a heap. The pain proved excruciating—worse than yesterday. Every muscle felt as tight as a wire and as stiff as a board. Laura had been right. He walked like an aged man with a serious case of rheumatism.

But Seth wouldn't let Laura see the pain. This was her day, the day she became her own person, and Seth refused to overshadow it. In no case must she worry about her troublesome brother.

Her excitement showed in every movement, the casual curve of her lips, and the sparkle in her eyes. She wore new jeans with a bright red T-shirt that said BADGERS across the front—a present from her friend Britny. She hadn't cut her hair but wore it in a high ponytail. Even up like that, it reached to her waist. Seth suspected that the long locks would be the first thing to go at school.

The longing tugged at him like it always did when he contemplated Laura's absence. She was his sounding board, his best friend. What would he do without her?

If Mamm were alive, Laura wouldn't be leaving. Neither would Seth have to shield his siblings from their stepmother or watch every penny like a miser to help support his family.

The familiar stab of regret. If his mamm were still alive...

Seth and Laura stood together by the side of the road and waited for Laura's ride. Britny's parents were driving them down and helping them move in. A confirmation that Seth couldn't be there for his sister this time. He relied on the kindness of strangers to see her through.

Laura hooked her thumbs in her back pockets and smiled at Seth. Her eyes danced even in the dimness of early sunrise. "Well," she said, "this is it. I'm either going to float off the ground any minute or throw up on your boots."

"Please, no throwing up. I oiled these boots three days ago."

She took his hand. "Are you honestly going to be okay? I am worried sick about you."

He sighed in exasperation. "Give me a hug. And write every once in a while."

She melted into his arms, and without the slightest hint that the pain was torturing him, he squeezed her tightly.

"I'll be home for Christmas break, Lord willing."

"Gute. But I can't promise you the new house will be ready by then."

"I love Ellie's cooking. Christmas won't be so bad."

They heard the front door shut. Dat, with Joshua, Jacob, and Priscilla in tow, stepped across the flagstones.

"Good-bye," said Joshua, giving Laura a brief hug and stepping away for Jacob.

Jacob held on a lot longer than his brother, probably hoping to keep the memories from escaping his eight-year-old brain. Priscilla stepped forward and handed Laura a small piece of waxed paper with a violet pressed between the folds. "It's a bookmark. You'll be doing lots of reading, Seth says."

Laura gathered Priscilla into her arms. "I'll write every week."

"I wish you would stay," Dat said, giving Laura an awkward pat on the head. "But Ellie has talked until she is blue in the face. If she can't convince you, I suppose nothing I say will make any difference."

"Nae, Dat. But it makes me happy to know that you want me to stay." She threw her arms around his neck, and he pulled back in surprise before surrendering and wrapping his arms around his oldest daughter.

Seth smiled and had pity on his fater. Dat loved his children as far as he was able.

Britny and her parents drove up in their big white SUV. Her dad hopped out of the car. "Sorry we're late. Britny has to look perfect, and that means every eyelash must be separated."

"Dad!" growled Britny from the backseat.

"It was my fault," Britny's mom said. "I couldn't find my phone."

Britny's dad hoisted Laura's purple backpack over his shoulder and her smaller suitcase under one arm. Dat and Seth carried the trunk to the back and slipped it beside Britny's suitcases.

Seth gave Laura one last hug and could feel her heart pounding against him. "Be good," he said. "And stick with Britny. She knows what she's doing."

Laura blinked away her tears. She wasn't about to admit weakness to anyone. "Take care of yourself."

His obligations fulfilled, Dat went back into the house. Seth, Priscilla, and the little boys watched the car drive away until the taillights disappeared behind the bend in the road.

SETH PUSHED the stable door open, and the horses stood at silent attention to honor his return while he lit a lantern. It felt as if he'd been gone for a whole year instead of one day. How he was ever going to pitch hay or muck out the stalls or train his horses with one hand was anybody's guess, but none of the horses were missing, the stable was still standing, and he was alive. Put on a scale, his blessings were great indeed.

She materialized just as he thought of his blessings. Like an angel of mercy, she stepped into the stable and gave him a look of concern that pretty near melted his heart.

"How are you this morning?" Miriam said, coming close and brushing her fingers along the bruises on his face. She bit her bottom lip. "You should lie down."

He straightened his shoulders and didn't even flinch at the pain that seared through his rib cage. An inaudible groan escaped his lips. "Would you like to help me get these horses watered and out to pasture?"

She studied his face for a split-second, her lips pressed into a line, and went to hook up the hose.

Miriam helped him put the horses to pasture. Seth didn't think he could handle the stallion with one hand but was a little nervous about letting Miriam do it. He didn't want the spirited horse to hurt her.

He needn't have worried. Miriam handled the stallion like a trained expert. Seth rubbed the whiskers on his chin as he watched her. Maybe she did know more about horses than he did.

The mucking out proved more difficult.

"Let's work together," Miriam said. "One stall at a time." She laid two shovels across the wheelbarrow and pushed it to the first stall.

Seth picked up his shovel. Using one hand, he scooped the manure, but the pain wouldn't allow him to raise the shovel high enough to get the manure into the wheelbarrow. The shovel tipped and his load fell on Miriam's shoes.

His heart sank. Even being with Miriam couldn't lift his spirits today. "Sorry. I am useless."

She shook off her shoes. "Considering you were in the hospital yesterday, it is a miracle you are even standing." She smiled reassuringly. "Do you have a can of WD-40?"

"Jah."

"Those doors could use a squirt or two."

Seth gave her a half smile and surrendered his shovel. He went to his storage shelves and retrieved a can of lubricant.

"Your brothers will be here soon," Miriam said. "And Hollow is coming after work. And my dat can spend the day tomorrow."

Seth knelt down next to the lowest hinge and felt very ungrateful indeed. Miriam Bontrager was watching out for him. What else could he ask for?

He studied her as she cheerfully loaded the wheelbarrow with fresh manure. Ellie wouldn't have come within ten feet of the stuff.

The thought that he once disliked Miriam seemed incomprehensible to him now. If he went a day without seeing her, he felt out of sorts, that things weren't quite right with his life. She was like a bright light in a deep cave. He held his breath. Did she ever think of him that way?

Someone like Miriam could have any man in the world. Why would she even spare a second thought for Seth? His prospects for supporting a wife were questionable. He didn't have a proper home. Most of the time he lived like a farmhand in his stable. He wasn't well-known in the community, having spent so much time with only his horses. His sister had gone off to college, and his mother had taken her own life.

Not a good list of qualities for a girl looking for a husband.

Not by the stretch of anyone's imagination would he ever measure up to Ephraim Neuenschwander, the minister's son.

Seth couldn't ignore the sting this realization gave him.

Nae, more than a sting. A stab right to his gut worse than the pain of breaking his arm.

He wiped a trickle of sweat from his neck. How had he let his emotions run unbridled like this? He was more than halfway to falling in love with Miriam Bontrager.

His heart did a somersault. A lot farther than halfway.

Once he recognized the pain, it seemed to fill every space in his body.

He didn't deserve her. She wouldn't have him anyway. He thought he might turn to ice, kneeling there on the stable floor. Turn to ice and crack into a million pieces.

Shifting away from her, he tried to pretend she wasn't standing fifteen feet away, shoveling out his stalls with those soft hands that sent his heart racing when they brushed his skin. He tried to imagine instead that she had never come into his life and wipe her from his thoughts. It was his only hope of ever feeling normal again.

The door on the opposite side of the stable squeaked open. Reuben and Jonas Shetler appeared at the threshold. Reuben strode through the door while Jonas ventured a single step inside. Seth jumped to his feet as quickly as his sore muscles would allow. He immediately went to Miriam's side. If there was to be trouble, she must not be here.

"Miriam," he said, dismayed at how out of breath he sounded, "you need to get out of here now."

Miriam's eyes reflected an almost irrational terror. She put down her shovel and, to his surprise, took a step to put herself between Seth and the Shetlers. He couldn't believe it. He took her by the shoulder with his good arm and pulled her back, close against his chest. "Go out the far door, Miriam," he whispered. "Go now."

"Not on your life," she whispered back.

Reuben grabbed the sleeve of Jonas's shirt and dragged his son farther into the stable. Jonas hung his head and refused to look at anyone. His eyes were red and moist, and he sniffed quietly.

Reuben looked like a different man than the one who had visited Seth's farm two days ago. Deep lines of fatigue were carved into his forehead and cheeks. His mouth was turned down, and his eyes held none of the fire of their earlier encounter. They glowed dull and lifeless, as if he were too worn out to put up a fight anymore "Seth, may I speak with you?"

Seth nodded. "Miriam will go so we can talk."

"I won't leave you," she stuttered, standing her ground and looking first at Reuben and then at Jonas.

Reuben clenched his teeth and glared at his son. "Do you see what your actions have sown? You are a disgrace." He turned his gaze to Seth—eyes full of sadness. "Mary is in the hospital."

Seth couldn't help it. Anger bubbled up inside him. "What have you done?"

Reuben pressed his fingers to his forehead. "Jonas came home very late on Wednesday night."

Jonas, with his eyes still to the ground, wrapped his arms around his chest and began to cry.

"When Mary heard of your broken arm, she guessed what happened. She locked herself in our room and bawled like when her sister died. She would not let me come to her."

Seth remembered Reuben's stern countenance on Wednesday. He could not blame Mary for shutting her husband out.

"I finally broke the handle and forced my way in. She was lying on the floor and..." Reuben's voice cracked, and he bowed his head in humiliation.

"Miriam doesn't need to hear this," Seth said.

Reuben put his head in his hands. Except for Jonas sniffling softly beside his dat, the silence in the barn was oppressive. Reuben massaged his brow and raised his eyes to Seth's face. "The doctor said she hadn't cut deep enough to bleed to death."

Miriam gasped and covered her mouth with her hand.

Seth growled as his anger and frustration exploded like a pot boiling over on the cookstove. "I tried to tell you. She has been depressed for several months. She needs help. You would not believe me. Why didn't you believe me?"

Reuben pinched the bridge of his nose and closed his eyes. "I did not want to think that my Mary could be like your mother."

He might as well have slapped Seth across the face. Guilt tore through him.

My mother.

If only I had been there...

He felt as if he were falling backward even as he stood still.

Miriam must have sensed his anguish. She reached back and took his hand in hers. Her grip steadied him, and he stopped falling.

"How could I have known?" Reuben said. "I thought she

was lazy, sleeping all hours of the day to avoid caring for die kinner or doing her chores. When she cried, I scolded her. A woman of faith does not want to leave her children. A woman of faith does not wish to die. I thought your group sessions were foolishness. I forbade her from coming back."

"And what do you believe now?" Seth whispered.

Reuben took a deep breath and chewed on Seth's question. "I am reaping the consequences of my stubbornness." His voice cracked and he could say no more.

Jonas lifted his head. "I didn't know she came here for help. Dat was so mad at you. I thought...I thought..."

"We know what you thought," Miriam said, squeezing Seth's hand. Her touch gave him courage and called forth love from deep in his heart. Any resentment he might have felt for Jonas and his fater melted away like snow in the warm sunlight.

He savored the feel of Miriam's skin before releasing her hand and stepping forward to wrap his good arm around Jonas's neck.

"I am sorry, Seth," Jonas said, bursting into a flood of tears. "I am sorry for what we did to you." Jonas's tears soaked Seth's shirt while Seth held on tight. "It is my fault that my mamm did this."

"Nae, nae." *Jonas must not carry the guilt for this.* Seth knew how it felt to bear the crushing weight of remorse. "This is not your fault. Your mamm has been suffering for a long time."

"But if she had not been so upset about my wickedness—"

"It might have happened anyway. She was very, very unhappy."

Reuben's head snapped up and his gaze seared a hole through Seth's chest. Seth hadn't meant to hurt Reuben with such talk, but Reuben might as well face the truth. How many times had he begged Reuben to look past his own pride and see his wife more clearly?

Jonas kept sobbing, as if crying would wash away the burden of guilt. "Scott said that if we scared you, you would leave my mamm alone. I never wanted to break your arm or give you those bruises. We—" He glanced at Miriam. "We got carried away, especially Scott. It all happened so fast, as if I was watching it instead of doing it."

"I care nothing about what you did. It is forgotten between us." Seth pulled away and pinned Jonas with an intense gaze. "Do you understand? It is forgotten."

Jonas merely nodded. He could not answer with the sobs wracking his body.

"I only care that your mamm receives the help she needs so she can get better."

"The doctor has put her in a special place in the hospital," Reuben said. "He wants her to be there for at least three weeks."

"Yes," Seth said. "That is what she needs. Hurting herself was another cry for help."

Reuben rubbed that spot just above his eyebrow again. "Jah. I wouldn't listen to the others."

Seth released his hold on Jonas and approached Reuben. "But now you understand?"

"I do."

"Then that is all that matters."

Reuben nodded, deep in thought. "But where do I go from here?"

"Talk to the doctor first. He will know how to manage the medicine and therapy. When she comes home, she needs to know that you love her and you don't think she is wicked. Try to understand what she is feeling. Right now, she thinks you don't care—that you only see her as the woman who cleans your house and takes care of your children."

"That is not true."

"But that is how you behave." Seth might as well be blunt. Beating around the bush wouldn't do for a man like Reuben Shetler.

An argument flashed in Reuben's eyes before he slumped his shoulders and looked away.

"When Mary gets home, I want you to allow her to come to our group therapy sessions every Tuesday night," Seth said.

"I will come with her."

"Nae. Mary will not speak freely if you are there, and she needs the therapy more than you do."

"My wife should be able to tell me everything."

Seth nodded. "Jah, she should. But you must earn her trust."

Reuben turned his back on Seth and rested his hand against the post. He had been confronted with enough hard truth for one day. Seth would say no more.

The longer he stood there, the more effort it took for Reuben to speak, like a man who hadn't slept well for several days. "When Jonas is not at the mill, he will be here to help until your arm is well. To make up for what he has done."

Seth pursed his lips. "Now that Mary is in the hospital, I think Jonas had best help at home."

"All the same, he will be here. He must make amends where he can. I and my other children will handle the load at home."

Reuben patted Jonas on the shoulder, and they trudged slowly from the stable. The squeaky door declared their departure.

Seth filled his lungs with air. He felt as if he'd held his breath the entire time the Shetlers were here. He turned to Miriam. Her presence surrounded him like a fragrant flower that made the world seem more beautiful. She looked at him with undisguised tenderness in her eyes. The expression made his heart leap in his chest and beat an unfamiliar and wild cadence.

"I could never have been so kind," she said, leaving the stall to be close to him. He loved the way she smelled, even with manure all over her feet. "I've never known anyone to be so little concerned about himself. You are amazing."

He shouldn't let her praise go to his head. She made him feel as if he were floating three feet off the ground. "Nae, do not say such things. I was very concerned for myself on Wednesday while running away. I wish I did not harbor ill feelings toward anyone in the first place."

"But that is why you are amazing. If you never got upset, you would never need to muster the strength to forgive. I admire your strength."

"You would do the same thing."

Miriam's face clouded over. "I wouldn't. I'll never forgive Yost. You are stronger than I can ever be."

"If you keep saying these things, I will start to believe them."

She twitched her lips into a brief smile then grew unusually solemn. "I am sorry what he said about your mother."

Seth looked at the ground. "It didn't mean anything."

"You don't like talking about her, do you?"

Seth swallowed the lump in his throat. "No use dwelling on bad memories."

"But there must be some gute memories too."

Seth walked back to the squeaky door and picked up his can of lubricant. "Gute memories won't bring her back."

WITH THE CHORES DONE, Miriam went to her room to avoid Yost. She had finished sewing Seth's quilt top together last week. Even on her new, slick treadle sewing machine, piecing together the blocks had been several hours' work. She always took great care on her quilts. Now the frames straddled her bed with the half-stitched quilt stretched like a tent across them. Mamm and Susie had both helped with the quilting.

With Seth's quilt, she felt she sewed memories of his mother right into the patterns. When he looked at the Log Cabin square, would he remember reading books with her? Or would the basket pattern bring to mind how much she liked flowers?

After threading the needle, she dove in to her work. Miriam hoped to finish the quilt by next week so Seth could use it on his cot when the weather turned cold.

It surprised her how anxious she was for him to like it. She wanted to bring him as much happiness as he had given her. She caught sight of Priscilla's doll propped against her pillow. Just as the doll reminded Miriam that people cared about her, Seth would have something to comfort him when he thought of his mamm.

"*Gute memories won't bring her back.*"

But just like the quilt, gute memories could warm him on a cold winter's night.

CHAPTER
TWENTY-THREE

"Don't walk into a tornado out there," Martha said as Miriam opened the door.

A stiff wind nudged her backward as she left the shop. With it being mid-September, the crowds at the quilt shop had thinned. As the days grew shorter, she would be working fewer hours until the Christmas rush.

If she had still been promised to Ephraim—she held her breath as sadness passed through her like the wind at the thought—she would have been quite anxious about her loss of income. Ephraim had always been insistent that they have plenty saved before the wedding. But this year, Miriam didn't mind that things in the shop slowed. Less work at the shop meant more time to make quilts—time to finish Seth's and start one for Susie.

She arched her back and sighed. This afternoon she'd sat down to sponge a smudge off one of the quilts and had almost fallen asleep. In addition to chores at home, she now spent late hours at the stable every day. She'd caught Seth staring at her with concern yesterday. She must have looked exhausted. He'd begged her to go home and get some rest. She, of course, had refused. She loved to see the look of exasperation on Seth's face when she was contrary. He would throw up his hand and twist his lips into a grin of surrender.

Ephraim, on the other hand, always thought he knew best and would frown and pout and quote Scripture until he won Miriam over to his way of thinking. Miriam smiled to herself. Ephraim was so adorable when he pouted, sticking out his bottom lip ever so slightly and folding his arms across his chest.

Every day felt like a frolic at Seth's stable. His little brothers were there after school unless Ellie insisted they stay home and do chores. Jonas also came daily. Dat had helped three days last week, and Hollow had been there every night too, sometimes with Susie in tow. In Susie's condition, Hollow insisted that she relax while he worked like a beaver. His was the most valuable help. He knew enough about horses that Seth trusted him to assist with the training.

Yost always had an excuse to stay away, for which Miriam rejoiced. Right or wrong, she couldn't abide the sight of her brother.

She braced herself against the wind and made her way down the street to the small market where most of the Amish shopped. Except for the Sabbath, today was the first day since the attack that Miriam would not be going to the stable. Mamm had a sore throat, and Miriam had promised that she would pick up the groceries and make supper.

The wind slammed the glass door behind her as she scooted into the market. Menno Schrock, the cashier who stood behind the counter, snapped his head up at the noise.

"Sorry," Miriam said. "The wind is stronger than I thought."

Menno nodded. "I don't wonder if I should use a squash as a doorstop, but it might be smashed to bits."

The door slammed shut again as another customer entered the market. Menno took a paper and pen from beneath the counter, quickly scrawled a few words on it, and taped it to the door. It said, MIND THE WIND AND MIND YOUR FINGERS.

"That should do the trick," Menno said.

Miriam only had a few minutes to gather what she needed for chicken pot pies. Susie would fetch her in the buggy at three o'clock, and she didn't want to keep her waiting. Chicken, carrots, and shortening were the only things on her list. Mamm insisted on a well-stocked pantry, and they already had at home most of what she needed. Miriam put an extra can of shortening in her basket. They were completely out.

As she headed down the next aisle to the meats, she came face-to-face with Ephraim and his brother Freeman. All three stopped short as if frozen in place by a sudden Arctic gale. Unembarrassed, Freeman turned away and grabbed a package of sausage. Ephraim studied her intently for a few moments. She couldn't read his expression, but whatever his emotion at seeing her, it was soon replaced with indifference. He gave her a casual wave of his hand, pivoted, and dragged Freeman with him to the opposite side of the market.

Miriam clutched her chest. She did not expect anything more from Ephraim—he had made his sentiments perfectly clear—but the rejection still left her panting for air. How could he go on living his life as if nothing were different? Had he not loved her as deeply as she longed for him?

She picked out a package of chicken without really seeing it. Ephraim saturated her thoughts. She wanted to stomp her feet in frustration. Why? Why did he still have such power over her?

Willing herself to breathe normally, Miriam pictured Seth in her mind with a wise expression on his face.

"You are pretty," he would say. "You are the kindest person I know besides my mother, and everybody likes you," he would say. Then he would twist his lips into that funny grin and add, "Well, most everybody likes you. And Ephraim Neuenschwander really isn't that smart."

She reined in her imagination. Seth would never say that about Ephraim. He never mentioned Ephraim's name at all. If only her thoughts could be as disciplined as Seth's tongue.

Keeping her head low, Miriam hurriedly stuffed a bag with carrots and made a beeline for the checkout counter.

"You making stew?" Menno said as he inspected each carrot to make sure there were no bad spots.

"Pot pies."

"Etta has a gute recipe for potpies. I'll have her send it to you."

Menno's leisurely pace had never bothered Miriam before. He seemed to have a personal stake in every meal anyone made with his groceries. Today she eagerly waited for him to hurry it up before Ephraim came around some corner and she melted into a puddle of embarrassment.

"Etta makes piecrust with lard." He checked the price a second time on the tub of shortening. "She claims it makes them extra flaky."

Miriam nodded and handed him her money, hoping that if she didn't say anything, he wouldn't have anything to say in reply.

To her relief, he counted out her change without additional comment. She catapulted out the door with her groceries, cringing as the wind slammed it behind her.

Mind the wind and mind your fingers.

Susie sat in the buggy in the parking lot. Miriam hopped in. "I'm ready to go," she said breathlessly.

A shadow lingered on Susie's expression. "I saw Ephraim and Freeman."

Miriam fiddled with her bonnet bow. "They did their best to stay away from me."

"They pretended not to see me." Susie stared at the market's door as if they would appear any second.

Even after her unsettling encounter with the Neuenschwanders, Miriam found herself comforting her sister. "Don't worry yourself about it. They mean us no ill will. They are uncomfortable and don't know what to say."

Susie frowned. "Jah, *they* are uncomfortable. They suffer so much."

Miriam had never heard such bitterness from Susie before. The harshness surprised her. Better to change the subject. She would rather not talk about Ephraim or his little brother anyway. "Did you have a gute time at work today?"

"Hollow bought a stool for me. I told him I didn't mind standing, but he wouldn't hear of it."

Miriam glanced at Susie out of the corner of her eye. She was beginning to show a small bump under her dress. Susie had always been pretty in a delicate sort of way. If not for the circumstances, Miriam would have told her that she was even more beautiful now, pregnant. Her skin radiated with a peaches-and-cream glow, and her lips and cheeks looked full and supple. But Miriam had rather not talk about the baby. With Susie already out of sorts, talk of adoption or labor like as not would make her sister despondent.

Hollow was a safe subject. Susie liked talking about Hollow. "Hollow has been so gute to Seth. I don't think he would have been able to manage as well as he has without Hollow's help."

"Oh, Hollow knows so much about horses and everything. I don't think I've met anyone so clever. Yesterday he fixed the propane stove in the pretzel stand without even reading the instructions. Esther Rose says their dat doesn't even check on the pretzel stand much anymore. Hollow has his complete trust."

"He volunteered to help on Seth's farm without so much as a second thought. I am very grateful."

Susie's mood brightened with every word about Hollow. "That's the kind of man Hollow is. He has a gute heart."

As soon as they arrived home, Miriam hurried to the kitchen to make her dough. While it cooled in the icebox, she put the chicken in the skillet with the vegetables and boiled them together. With the skill acquired through constant practice, she soon had two potpies baking in the cookstove with dough hearts dotting the top.

Since Mamm was feeling poorly, Miriam and Susie had received strict orders to stay as far away from her as possible. Especially Susie. No good for her to get sick while carrying a baby. Callie was the designated nurse who took Mamm drinks and food while holding a towel over his nose.

Yost and Dat came through the back door together at suppertime. Dat had an arm around Yost's shoulders and was telling him a funny story. Yost could have added four inches to his height if he'd stood up straight. His eyes were dull and cast downward, and his face would have cracked into a hundred pieces if he had tried to smile.

Miriam turned her back on him and busied herself at the cookstove. She squeezed her eyes shut as she thought of Yost standing over Seth with a raised fist and an ugly sneer to his lips.

Yost's chair squealed as he pulled it away from the table.

Ignoring him, Miriam brought the pies to the table along with fresh corn on the cob and a green Jell-O salad.

Callie dutifully loaded a plate for Mamm to take to her room.

"You are a gute boy, Callie," Miriam said.

The rest of them—Miriam, Yost, Susie, Dat, Raymond, and Isaac—bowed their heads in silent prayer. When Miriam lifted her gaze, Yost was staring at her with unmistakable sorrow in his eyes. She quickly looked away and busied herself by serving up the pot pies.

Dat glanced at Miriam and cleared his throat. "You would have been proud of Yost today, children. We were passing Herschbergers' when Mayne opened her screen door and the wind blew the thing clean off. Yost ran after it, and I helped him repair the hinges. He fixed them real gute. That door won't be running off again without permission. Mayne thanked us three times."

"My hat blew off on the way home from school," Raymond said. "Even when I held tight to it."

"Are you going to the stable tonight, Miriam?" Dat asked.

"Nae. Not tonight."

Dat patted Yost on the shoulder. "Yost says he might come to Seth's with me on Saturday. Some of us are thinking of replacing the rotted wood and painting the outside."

Miriam gazed out the window. "I think there will be plenty of help. Yost need not be bothered."

Yost laid down his fork and stared at Miriam.

"Last weekend there were some Englisch boys up by Cashton making trouble," Dat said. "They spray-painted Ike Weaver's buggy and knocked over a couple of mailboxes. It wonders me if they ain't the boys who attacked Seth."

"Whoever it is, Seth isn't saying a word," Miriam said, making eye contact with Yost.

Realization flickered in Yost's eyes, followed by a look of sheer panic.

At least now he couldn't think he fooled everybody.

Yost shot from his chair, scraping it loudly against the floor once more. "I'm not hungry."

"Of course you are," Dat said. "Sit and eat."

"I'm going to the barn." Yost grabbed his hat from the hook and blew out the door as recklessly as the wind blew in.

Dat frowned and lifted his eyebrows in Miriam's direction as if Yost's outburst were her fault. She tried to ignore the nagging of her conscience and fell silent while she sullenly ate her supper.

Dat took a bite of food and stared at the door as if waiting for Yost to change his mind and come back. When Yost didn't show up, Dat scooted his chair farther under the table and talked on and on about Yost and what a good worker he was and how he had helped in the garden yesterday and how Yost milked the cows better than he did.

Supper sat heavily in Miriam's stomach while she and Susie did the dishes. Susie chattered on about pretzels and Hollow and baby quilts and didn't notice Miriam's reluctance to speak.

After cleaning the kitchen, Miriam ventured outside in the dimming light to take down the last batch of clothes that whipped around furiously on the line. While she folded clothes into her basket, she heard the screen door slam and saw the silhouette of a tall figure on the porch.

With his hands in his pockets, Dat ambled toward her with the casualness usually reserved for a Sunday afternoon stroll. She wasn't fooled. His expression told her that he wanted a serious talk.

"Susie says you saw Ephraim today. Are you okay?"

"Nae," Miriam replied flatly.

"I wish I could make the pain go away."

"So do I."

"Do you blame your brother?"

Miriam doubled her efforts with the laundry. "Ephraim rejected me of his own choice. I do not blame anyone." Her stomach felt hollow. Did she truly believe that?

"Then why do you treat Yost the way you do?"

Her heart sank to her toes. She'd thought no one had noticed. "What do you mean?"

"When he walks into a room, you walk out."

"I eat supper with the family every night."

Dat furrowed his brow. "In complete silence."

Miriam didn't know what to say. There was no way to explain herself, no way to describe the sick, angry feeling she got whenever she looked at Yost.

"I will do better," she said.

Dat nudged her arm and invited her to sit on the back steps. She followed.

"Are you mad at him?" Dat asked, pinning her gaze with his bright blue eyes.

His intensity surprised her. "I—I am not mad." Dat kept staring, not letting her get away with anything. She turned her head to look at the remnants of the sunset. "I am ashamed."

Dat opened his mouth to say something and promptly closed it. He shifted on the step and slowly stroked his beard. This deliberate thoughtfulness was one of Dat's best qualities. He wasn't one to speak without thinking or to upbraid Miriam rashly because of the way she felt.

"We were all hurt by Yost's arrest," he said. "Susie reminded me how badly I had treated him. I have repented sorely for my behavior. But you were not like that. You showed him great love, spending hours in the kitchen cooking rice pudding and baking pies for him. I am proud of how you acted." He took her hand. "What has changed?"

Miriam wanted to unburden her heart, but her secret would only multiply the pain, not lessen it. "I have been upset about what happened to Seth, that's all. I will do better. I promise."

"Yost has been unhappy for a long time. I am only now recognizing how unhappy. He has been worse, much worse, since you started avoiding him. Do you not see it?"

"Are you saying it is my fault?"

Dat shook his head. "Of course not. But for some reason, you are like the rain to his dry pasture. He needs your approval. Without it, he will dry up and wither away. Has your broken heart made you bitter?"

Miriam felt the pressing need to defend herself. "I am not the reason Yost is miserable. His own conscience plagues him."

"All the more reason to show forth an increase in love, bringing him to repentance. He'll only find real happiness when he opens his heart and lets forgiveness flow into him."

Miriam felt like a twisting tornado.

How can I tell you, Dat, that every time I lay eyes on my brother, I see Seth lying in that bed, pale and weak, with bruises on his face and a gray plaster cast wrapped around his purple fingers? Seth—kind, compassionate Seth—didn't deserve that.

Her eyes stung with tears that she blinked away before they betrayed her. She cared deeply about Seth Lambright. And her own brother had done him unspeakable violence. Sometimes she felt as if Seth were her only friend, and if she lost him because of Yost, she wouldn't be able to bear the loneliness. Her brother and sister had alienated the entire community, and the two of them were too wrapped up in their own problems to care about Miriam.

She cleared her throat. "I will do better."

The set of her chin must have convinced Dat that she would say no more. He gave an almost inaudible sigh and stood up. "I know you will, Miriam. For Yost's sake."

He trudged up the steps and into the house as the wind whipped through the trees and moaned a lonely tune.

With her conscience hanging around her neck like an iron yoke, Miriam shoved the rest of the clean laundry into the basket before it blew away. She ducked her head into the wind and ran to the house with her full basket. At the kitchen table, she folded clothes and carted them upstairs to put in drawers.

The wind whistled around the house. It seemed to increase in force with every passing minute. Miriam hoped they weren't in store for a tornado.

Downstairs, the front door slammed shut, probably by the force of the wind, and she heard Dat yelling—not the yelling that accompanied anger, but the-house-is-on-fire kind of yelling.

"Miriam!" Dat called loudly enough for the neighbors to hear him. Was it a tornado after all?

Depositing the piles of clothes on her bed, she ran downstairs. Yost stood in the living room, clutching his bleeding left hand. Miriam caught her breath. "What happened?"

Dat ran from the kitchen with a towel. "The wind slammed his hand in the barn door and pinched it right bad."

Sweat beaded on Yost's forehead, and his face glowed white as a sheet. His breath was ragged and shallow, testifying to his excruciating pain. Miriam rushed to his side and directed him to the sofa before he fell over.

Yost groaned as Dat wrapped the towel lightly around his hand.

"We are going to the doctor. Take care of him while I hitch

the buggy." Dat ran out the front door, and the wind slammed it shut behind him.

Susie appeared from the kitchen, and Callie and Raymond ran down the stairs. "What happened to Yost?" Callie said.

Miriam wrapped her fingers around Yost's arm. "He hurt his hand. Go upstairs and tell Mamm that we are taking him to the doctor."

Her little brothers did as they were told. Susie stood over Miriam and Yost, wringing her hands and fidgeting something terrible.

Yost panted in agony as Miriam lifted the blood-soaked towel from his hand.

His three middle fingernails were purple, and the nail on his pinky finger was completely torn away. All four fingers had gashes on the palm side, and the other side sported deep ridges where the door had pinched him. The skin there was blue but not broken.

"Susie, warm up some water on the stove and bring the first-aid kit."

Susie ran from the room.

Miriam turned to Yost. "If we get some of this blood washed off, we can see how deep the cuts are. Can you stand to soak it?"

Yost stared into her face as a different kind of pain filled his eyes. "Miriam," he whispered, "I'll do anything to make you love me again."

His eyes, his voice, his painful vulnerability were like hammers to Miriam's hard heart. She melted like warm butter. Clutching his good hand, she pulled Yost toward her and kissed him on the cheek.

"I didn't want you to find out," he moaned. "I am so ashamed, Miriam. Please, please, forgive me. I think I'll die if you hate me."

It was impossible to harden herself against such a plea. Yost was her brother, not her enemy, not the evil boy she had made him out to be. Had she been swimming in self-pity for so long that she didn't even recognize it anymore?

"Jonas got so mad at Seth. Scott is Jonas's friend from the mill, and he said he could make it so Seth never bothered Jonas's mamm again. I thought we were just going to scare Seth, and then Scott went wild. He hit him over and over, and Jonas and I didn't do anything but stand there. We didn't mean for it to get that far. Now you know what a coward I am." He held up his bleeding hand. "I deserve this—for what I did to Seth and for what happened with you and Ephraim. I deserve all your silence, but I cannot bear my just desserts."

Miriam put her palm to his cheek. "Hush now. Lean back and rest your head. The pain must be something terrible." She carefully rolled up his sleeve. "I have been pitying myself because of Ephraim. The attack was a perfect excuse to punish you, all of you, and show you how hurt I felt."

Yost clamped his eyes shut and clenched his teeth as she gently tried to straighten his fingers. "I've only cared about myself even as I ruined your life," he said. "I'm sorry about Ephraim."

Miriam twitched the corners of her mouth. "My life is not exactly ruined. I am learning to be happy without Ephraim."

Yost covered his eyes with his hand to try to block out the pain. "He is a fool."

"Do not say such things."

Susie came into the room with a pan of warm water and some towels. "I will go find the bandages."

Miriam tested the water. Lukewarm. "This will sting," she said as she lowered his hand into the pan.

Yost flinched and hissed but he stayed put as she gently

stroked the smudges and blood from his hand. Susie brought the special antibacterial soap and a washrag. Miriam dipped the rag in water and worked her way around his wounds with a circular motion.

"Can you flex your fingers?"

Holding his breath, Yost slowly made a weak fist and then straightened his fingers. "Jah, but it hurts something terrible."

Miriam put light pressure on each finger. "I do not think any of your fingers are broken. The cuts are deep, but I believe we can avoid a doctor visit."

"Gute. I would rather not go."

As if summoned by talk of the doctor, Dat came through the door. "The buggy is ready."

"I do not think he will need a doctor," Miriam said. "The bones are sound."

Dat came to the sofa and watched as Yost made another fist. "Are you sure?"

"They hurt, but I can move okay."

Dat nodded, concern still painted on his face. "I'll go unhitch the buggy."

Susie fetched a needle while Miriam cleaned Yost's hand. She smeared ointment on his cuts and bandaged his palm firmly. With the needle, Miriam lanced each of Yost's fingernails and let the blood drain out. "You will lose all of these," she said, examining the pinky finger, which looked tender indeed. She finished with another gauze pad over the palm and a wrapping around the hand to keep the other bandages from shifting.

She sent Susie off again to find the bottle of painkiller. Yost would need it badly.

He studied her face as she stacked the dirty towels. "I wish I could make it as if it never happened."

"Will you talk to Seth?"

Doubt flickered in Yost's eyes. "Jah. Anything you want."

Miriam smiled sadly. "That will be enough."

Resolve spread over his countenance, and he squared his shoulders. "I'll do whatever I can to make everything right again."

CHAPTER
TWENTY-FOUR

"I deserve this. I deserve whatever happens," Yost said. He covered his eyes and groaned softly.

Miriam parked her buggy down Seth's lane behind three other buggies and a silver car. She could almost hear Yost's heart pounding in time with hers. After securing the reins, she pulled the gift box from the backseat. "It will be alright." Her courage almost failed her. Seth's group therapy sessions were shrouded in mystery. What happened there? How would Seth treat Yost? How would Yost react? The uncertainty rendered her breathless.

With Yost close behind, she practically tiptoed to the stable and cracked the door open. Two tall propane lanterns stood guard over a circle of folding chairs in the space between Seth's sleeping room and the stalls. Horses peeked curiously over their stall doors to see what all the fuss was about. The air echoed softly with the animals' quiet movements in the dimness—the swish of a tail or the rustle of hay or the occasional whinny to get someone's attention. Seth sat next to his

Englisch friend, Doug Matthews, and an Englisch woman. Three Amish women and Jonas Shetler completed the group. Jonas sat with his elbows on his knees and his head bowed, trying to be as unnoticed as possible.

Seth smiled brightly and jumped to his feet when he saw them. "You came."

He reached out and clasped Yost's hand. Both had injured their left hands. They could shake, at least. Seth's expression betrayed nothing of resentment for what Yost had done—only warmth and genuine compassion.

Yost's voice trembled like a leaf in the wind as he recited the speech he had been rehearsing all day. "Seth. I came to apologize. I am wicked and evil, and if I can do anything to mend what I have done, just tell me what."

Seth nodded solemnly. "Denki for saying that. The arm did not hurt as badly as knowing you attacked me. That crushed me. And your sister."

Yost's intense whisper felt like a shout. "I know. I am very ashamed. Even before we came that night, I knew it was wrong. I avoided you because I couldn't bear to own up to my sins."

"Your coming here takes a lot of courage," Seth said as he placed a hand on Yost's shoulder. "You were caught up in emotions and actions you didn't understand, and I forgive you with all my heart."

"What can I do to make it better?"

"I am going to pretend it never happened. You need not believe that you must make restitution. You already have." He motioned to the circle of folding chairs. "I want to help you. Would you consider coming to our therapy sessions every week?"

"Jah. I already promised Miriam."

Seth regarded Miriam with those stunning gray eyes of his. "Then Miriam's wishes are most important. Cum, join us."

Seth nudged Miriam's elbow and led her to an empty seat.

"Denki for your forgiveness. It means so much to Yost."

Seth grinned. "What do you mean? I don't remember the event you are talking about."

Miriam shook her head and smiled to herself.

Seth sat next to her. "Don't be nervous. You don't have to say anything. This is for Yost."

Miriam laid her box behind her chair.

"What is in the box?" Seth said.

"Something for you."

"Me? What is it?"

"Something, hopefully, to make your life easier. Someone should watch out for you now and then."

A slow smile spread across Seth's face. "You want the job?"

Miriam wasn't sure why the heat traveled up her neck, but before she could reply, Doug stood up. "I'd like to welcome you here tonight. Jonas Shetler and Miriam and Yost Bontrager are joining us for the first time." He pointed to the three Amish women. "This is Anna Coblentz, Elizabeth Burkholder, and Deborah Miller."

Elizabeth was in Miriam's district, but she didn't recognize the other two women. They must have come from the district to the north.

Doug motioned to the Englisch woman sitting next to him. "This is my wife, Carrie. She comes with me so everything is proper in the eyes of the community and the bishop." Doug shifted his gaze to Miriam, Yost, and Jonas. "We have a few rules. Everyone here is encouraged to speak freely. That means you may hear some things you don't like about your neighbors or your church. But we do not judge other people's feelings.

Try as we might to control our own feelings sometimes they can't be helped. Secondly, what we say is not to be repeated. Everyone must feel safe to express themselves. Don't attack another person or try to give them advice. Just listen. Does this make sense?"

Miriam didn't plan on saying a word. For those who knew about them, there was some opposition in the community to Seth's group sessions. Seth had told her the bishop gave reluctant approval, mostly because he thought it could do no harm. And if the sessions helped people like Mary Shetler, there must be some good to them.

"I first want to tell you that I have seen Mary Shetler several times since she has been in the hospital."

Anna Coblenz wrung a white hanky in her hand. Jonas sank his head lower and didn't so much as glance at anybody.

"Mary feels terrible guilt. She needs to know that we love her and that she still has favor in the eyes of God."

Anna's voice didn't carry much farther than her lips, and Miriam almost missed her question. "But how can that be? How can any of us be right with God if we have such thoughts? 'Thou shalt not kill.' Everyone says that Seth's mamm is gone to hell."

Miriam knew Anna had no intention of being cruel, but Seth's face turned pale all the same. She flashed him a look of concern, and he gave her a reassuring half smile. No doubt his mother's situation had been discussed many times in group therapy.

Doug sat down. "If your friend got cancer, Anna, would you say it was her fault if she died?"

"Nae," came the whispered reply.

"We have talked about this before," Doug said. "Depression is an illness as real as cancer. If it is ignored or untreated, it can make a person feel hopeless and dark, as if there is no way out of a horrible nightmare. They might think the only relief from the incredible pain is to take their own life."

A single tear made its way down Anna's cheek. "Don't let that happen to me."

Doug put his elbows on his knees and leaned closer to Anna. "Are you taking the medication?"

"Jah."

"And Aden accepts it?"

"He thinks it is foolishness, but he is willing to pay for it."

"You are doing so many things to help yourself get better, Anna. Group therapy is not optimal, but it is a very good thing you come. And remember, 'God hath not given us the spirit of fear; but of power, and of love, and of a sound mind.'"

Once Doug finished his update on Mary's condition, he invited others to share what they would. Deborah talked of her mother with Alzheimer's, who was increasingly abusive. Elizabeth was constantly anxious for her children—afraid that something bad would happen to them if she were not with them.

In the stable amid the hay dust and the pungent smell of horses seemed a fitting setting for such a meeting. The Plain Folk would have felt out of place in a sterile clinic with blinding fluorescent lights and metallic industrial tables. They might not have been willing to come.

Jonas ventured a comment at the end of the session. "I want to know what to do for my mamm."

Doug leaned his elbows on his knees and laced his fingers together. "You may not understand how your mother feels, but don't dismiss her feelings as foolishness. Let her talk to you, and don't judge her. Remember, feelings are powerful things. How much do you help her with chores around the house?"

Jonas shifted in his seat. "Not much."

"When you let her do all the work in the home, you send her the message that whatever you do is more important than her work and her health. Wash the dishes and do the laundry. Not only will you ease her burden, but you will put yourself in her place and appreciate her work more."

Jonas pursed his lips and fell deep into his own thoughts.

Yost didn't say a word the entire session, but his willingness to attend was encouraging.

Anna, Elizabeth, and Deborah left quickly once the session ended. Jonas followed close behind. He and Yost didn't even look at each other as he left. Their friendship persisted as a reminder of the terrible thing they had done to Seth. And who would want to be reminded of that?

While Doug and Seth sat conversing quietly with each other, Miriam retrieved her box and took it to Seth.

He gave her a cautious grin as he examined the box. "Aha. Something to make my life easier. Is it a new arm?"

Miriam shook her head quickly and folded her arms so Seth wouldn't see how her hands were shaking.

Oh, how she wanted him to like it!

He untied the twine and lifted the lid. Miriam had folded the quilt so the Log Cabin patch would face up when Seth opened the box.

His lips parted and his eyes grew wide. He smoothed his hands over the fabric. "I used to have a blanket...."

He stood and lifted the quilt from the box. Doug and Carrie each took a corner and held it up so Seth could see the entire thing.

"Wow," Doug said. "That is really something."

Carrie rubbed her thumb along the binding. "Did you make this? It is fabulous. Absolutely fabulous."

Miriam watched Seth's face. His eyes darted across the quilt.

A heavy weight pressed on her chest as if someone had tightened a clamp around it. She'd made a horrible mistake. Of course the quilt would stir up painful memories. Better that she should have let them be. Looking at Seth's expression, Miriam wanted to snatch the quilt away and pretend she had never given it to him. Terrible, terrible idea.

Seth took a corner of the quilt and put it up to his nose. Then he closed his eyes and buried his face in the fabric. His shoulders rose and fell with every breath he took.

Gathering the quilt in his arms, he sat down and held it close to his chest. "I thought I'd lost it," he whispered. He looked at Miriam, his eyes shining with deep emotion. "I thought I'd lost it forever."

"I'm sorry, Seth," Miriam said, almost too heavy to speak. "I hoped it would make you happy. I wouldn't ever—"

Seth reached out and grabbed Miriam's hand. "Miriam," he whispered hoarsely. Keeping his eyes on her face, he squeezed her fingers. "It is the most wonderful thing I have ever seen."

"You like it?"

"There are..." He breathed deeply. "There are no words," he said. "How did you know? Mamm made a dress and my blanket out of the same blue material." He ran his fingers along the bear claw block. "She died in that dress."

Miriam caught her breath. Laura hadn't told her. Maybe Seth was the only one who remembered.

A sob parted his lips as he clutched the quilt and disintegrated in a torrent of tears. "I knew it was a bad day for her. I never should have gone to work. She died alone while Priscilla screamed in her crib." The sobs came from deep in his throat. "I should have been there. I could have saved her life. Dat didn't understand. No one understood but me. I should have been there." He wept until Miriam thought her own heart would break.

She pictured Seth as a little boy in the comfort of his mamm's embrace, wrapped up in the quilt she'd made especially for him. She saw the devoted son watching his mamm descend into the darkness of her own mind and feeling powerless to do anything about it. She saw a confused and desolate young man as they laid his mother in a grave.

Miriam knelt next to Seth and put a hand on his arm. "Hush, hush," she said, as if comforting a small child. "She loved you with every part of her soul. You were seventeen years old, Seth. She was sick. You didn't fail her. Don't ever believe in a million years that you failed her."

Seth let out a deep, gut-wrenching sigh and buried his face in his hands.

They sat quietly as Seth cried himself out and then tried to regain his composure. He repeatedly swiped the back of his hand over his eyes until Carrie found a tissue in her purse so he could mop his face. "Denki, Miriam. You have given hours to this for me. I have something to remember my mamm by again."

"You do not think it is too fancy?"

"Proud people have fancy things. This is not a fancy thing. This is a beautiful piece of your heart, made to give me comfort."

His warmth seemed to permeate the very air. Miriam put a hand to her cheek and felt the glow of heat. When he looked at her like that, she felt shy and energetic and excited all at the same time. She couldn't have felt more cozy sitting by her cookstove and drinking hot cocoa on a cold winter's evening.

"I will never forget your kindness," Seth said.

"And I will never forget yours." She pulled Yost close to her. "For both of us."

"We had better get on home," Yost said.

Doug took his wife's hand. "Me too."

Miriam felt disappointment descend like fog. She didn't want to leave, not when Seth smiled at her like that and her heart was like to burst with happiness. How long had it been since she felt so much like herself, so right with the world around her?

Seth folded the quilt over his good arm and stood. "Seems almost too special to use."

"You will need something to keep you warm in the winter," Miriam said. "It is more special if you use it. What value does something have if it sits on a shelf?"

"Then I will use it every day." Seth wiped a leftover tear from his eye. "To remind me of precious relationships and abundant blessings."

He winked at Miriam and set her heart fluttering.

"OH, Seth, smell the lilacs. Cut me some blooms, and we will fill the house with their sweet scent."

While a million memories flooded his mind, Seth watched as Miriam put her arm around Yost and left the stable.

He closed his eyes and saw his mother's hands kneading bread dough in the morning before breakfast. She had worker's hands with long, thin fingers and veins that stood out in relief. He loved to trace those veins with his fingertips and make a map of them from her wrists to her knuckles.

He heard his mother's voice, reading him stories about bear hunting and horses. And Bible stories. He could have listened to her tell the story of Noah every day. No matter how many times she told it, tears pooled in her eyes when she lamented how many people died in the flood. "If only they had listened, Seth. If only they had heard God speaking to them."

She smelled like roses and clover. In the evenings, he would wrap up in his blanket and cuddle next to her. She played with his ears while she read.

Seth buried his face in Miriam's quilt and wept; for how long, he couldn't guess. The ache of losing his mamm would never go away. He didn't want it to. The hurt helped him remember the love.

Miriam had done this. Miriam had helped him remember the love.

If none but God was perfect, then Miriam came very close. She was so pretty, Seth sometimes felt like he had to force his hands behind his back to keep from stroking her silky skin. And when she stood close, Seth couldn't avoid taking in her scent with every breath. She smelled like an apple orchard right before harvesttime...or sometimes like a honey-cinnamon pumpkin pie.

As he sat stroking his quilt, he knew. This struggle against his own feelings was futile. No one could ever love someone as much as he loved Miriam. How could he possibly banish her from his thoughts when she came to the stable almost every day, distilling her way into his heart like sunlight through the slats of a barn?

The time they spent together had only intensified his feelings for her until she filled up every corner of his being. She was in and through every thought he had, every word he spoke, every breath he breathed.

But how far could he take his love? Would she ever be able to forget Ephraim and marry someone as lowly as Seth Lambright?

Pain kicked him in the gut.

He didn't dare hope.

The blue fabric of his childhood blanket caught his eye, and he traced his finger around a square of green and yellow triangles. Miriam had given him this quilt. She'd spent hours making it, and her eyes glowed with an inner fire when she handed it to him.

Gathering the quilt in his arms, he clutched it to his chest as if trying to squeeze every last bit of hope from it. The propane lanterns hissed as he sat holding onto it like a lifeline.

CHAPTER
TWENTY-FIVE

Miriam glanced out the window while she sliced bread for supper. Callie set the table while Mamm tended the pork chops. "We must make two extra loaves tomorrow for gmay," Mamm said. "The district is growing so big. With those two new families from Lancaster, we will have almost two hundred people at service."

By the middle of October, the thermometer had taken a journey south. The vibrant rust-and-yellow leaves dazzled Miriam's eyes on bright afternoons when the waning sun cast its golden glow over the trees. Soon there would be mountains of leaves piled on the roads and in the pastures that would provide rich compost for spring planting.

As she often did lately, Miriam thought of Seth and his eagerness to prepare the fields for winter—with one arm.

Miriam arranged the bread slices on a plate. "There is talk of splitting the district," she responded.

"Jah, we will see. The Lord's will be done. It would be nice to feed a smaller group each time instead of cramming people into every nook and cranny of the house."

MIRIAM'S QUILT

Miriam set the bread on the table along with a pat of freshly churned butter and a bottle of homemade raspberry jam. "Seth gets his cast off tomorrow."

Last week a big cement truck had lumbered up his lane and a crew of men poured the foundation for his new house. She and Seth had both prayed that the weather would be clear so the men would be able to do their work. This week, with his cast freshly removed, Seth and several of the men from the district, along with a crew of construction workers, would start framing the outer walls.

"Gute," Mamm said. "The poor boy has been long enough without his arm. I know he will be glad to have it back. But I am guessing that you will spend as much time at the stable as ever."

"Of course," Miriam said. "I love the horses, and Seth doesn't mind me there. We have fun together. He made me laugh so hard one time, I snorted—and that made him laugh harder."

Mamm turned her face from Miriam and gazed out the window. "He is a gute boy. Such a hard worker. And tall and handsome. Your dat says he can hold his own in a Bible discussion too. You know how Dat respects a scholar."

"Oh, yes. He is so quiet that I used to assume he would be dull and hard to talk to. But when you get to know him, he talks plenty. Did you know he almost died three times as a child? The good Lord watched out for him."

Susie practically skipped into the kitchen. Her eyes sparkled with excitement, and a flattering blush spread across her cheeks. "Mamm, will you come to the living room?"

She left Mamm standing there without waiting for an answer.

Mamm took the chops off the cookstove. "Dinner will get cold."

Susie reappeared. "And you, too, Miriam. I want you to come too."

Miriam followed Mamm into the living room. Dat sat on the sofa, while Hollow and Susie stood in front of him as if he were conducting an interview. Dat glanced at Mamm doubtfully before she settled onto the sofa. Miriam sat next to Mamm.

To Miriam's surprise, Hollow took Susie's hand, right in front of her parents. What was he thinking?

His face glowed bright red and sweat beaded on his forehead like dewdrops on the grass.

"What is it, Hollow?" Dat asked, clearly uncomfortable with a young man holding his daughter's hand.

Hollow cleared his throat. "John, I love your daughter, and I am come to ask permission to marry her."

Dat's jaw dropped to the floor. He and Mamm looked at each other in astonishment. Miriam covered her mouth with her hand. Could such a perfect solution be possible?

Hollow said no more. Embarrassment or terror rendered him mute.

Susie, on the other hand, beamed and started talking a mile a minute. "This is the answer to my prayer, Dat. I was heartbroken about giving the baby away, but I didn't want him to grow up without a fater either. Hollow will be a gute fater, and he has a fine job to support the family. The baby can grow up in a normal home. In a few years, no one will remember how he came into the world."

Dat stood so he could meet Hollow eye-to-eye. He folded his arms across his chest, and his expression grew stern. "I must be told the truth. Are you the father of this child?"

Hollow returned Dat's serious gaze and shook his head slowly. "Nae, I am not. Only Susie knows who is. If she wants to tell me, I'll listen. Otherwise, it is her secret."

"But people will assume that you are the father. They will talk."

Hollow squared his shoulders. "Let them talk. I am not afraid of what man can do."

"So you want to be a fater to my Susie's baby."

"Jah. Every baby deserves a gute home. And every mother deserves a husband. Susie especially."

"There must be more of a reason than the baby to join together," Dat said. "The baby will not be enough to make you happy."

Hollow put a protective arm around Susie. "I have loved Susie ever since she came to work for us three years ago. She was young yet; I didn't need to rush her. But now seems like a good time for it. I would not have her suffer, and I can give her protection from cruel tongues by giving her my name. I would do anything for Susie."

Miriam wanted to leap from the sofa and embrace this gute man for his willingness to raise another man's child for Susie's sake. What more could they hope for?

Dat stuck out his hand. Hollow took it enthusiastically and they shook. "You have permission to marry my daughter."

Susie squealed and threw her arms around Dat. "Oh, thank you, thank you."

Miriam and Mamm leaped to their feet and took their turns hugging Susie.

The best possible conclusion to all their months of heartache.

Mamm wiped away tears that were immediately replaced by fresh ones. "I have prayed with all my heart for this day. Blessed be the name of the Lord. I couldn't ask for a better son-in-law."

"And I could not ask for a better wife," Hollow said.

Miriam's heart swelled in her breast. Susie had her greatest desire—a man who truly adored her.

Miriam refolded a quilt and hung it back on the metal arm. A customer had wanted to see it and then decided not to buy. It was almost time to close. When done with her work at the quilt shop, Miriam would go to the market. With Thanksgiving less than a month away, the store was running a special on frozen turkeys. Mamm wanted her to buy eight whole turkeys. Four turkeys would be cooked for the wedding dinner. The day after the wedding, Mamm and Miriam would can the meat from the other four.

It was decided that the wedding should take place as soon as possible. Susie and Hollow would need to be settled before the baby came, and November began wedding season in Apple Lake. If everyone pitched in with the preparations, they could be married the second week of the month, five weeks before the baby was due to arrive. The bishop agreed to give Susie special baptism instruction classes, which usually took nine weeks, in three weeks' time. Everything proceeded in the best interest of the baby. The bishop, often so rigid and stern, could bend when someone's very soul hung in the balance. He was strict, but he was a gute man.

Preparations for the wedding had begun in earnest. It would be small and modest, but Mamm still wanted Susie to remember it as a wonderful day. Because of all the preparations, Miriam spent less time at Seth's stable than she would have liked, but with his cast gone, at least he could do more of the work himself.

Susie and Hollow would live in the dawdi house attached to the Bontragers' house. The houses shared a wall, with a private entrance at the side of the big house—a wonderful-gute arrangement for a couple starting out. Miriam had once thought that she and Ephraim might live there the first years of their marriage.

Miriam glanced at the clock on the wall. She could lock the quilt shop entrance in four minutes.

She saw him before he saw her. Ephraim sauntered through the door and gazed around the spacious shop. Miriam had always found his strong profile and confident air attractive. Her heart pounded, and she clenched her teeth. Why could she not root this powerful emotion from her breast?

Miriam hurriedly fluffed the quilt and headed to the back of the store, where Ephraim would never see her behind the rows of quilts. She knew he wanted to avoid an encounter as much as she did.

"Miriam."

Miriam doubled her pace. Why in the world would Ephraim call her back?

Suddenly, he stood right next to her between two rows of baby quilts. "Miriam, we need to talk."

She somehow found the courage to meet his eyes. None of the affection they used to hold remained, but she recognized the pity. The expression was like a bee sting right to the heart.

He pitied her? As she had once pitied Seth? The thought made her ill.

"Ephraim," she managed to choke out before falling silent. If he wanted to talk, let him talk. She couldn't find any words.

"Miriam, I know what you are trying to do. I understand how you feel. We are both hurting, but this is no way to resolve things."

"What—what are you talking about?"

"Someday I hope Yost will prove himself to be a gute boy, to repent and be baptized, but even if he were the most righteous boy in the district, I would not hear him. You must understand, Miriam. I am asking you to leave me be."

Miriam found her voice through her shock. "What have we done to deserve scolding?"

"You know very well that Yost has been to our house three times in the last month."

"Nae, I did not know that."

"He asked me to take you back, to give you another chance." He rubbed the whiskers on his chin. "Nothing good can come of it, Miriam. It will only bring more heartache. Please tell him to stop coming. I am tired of hearing it."

Miriam caught her breath even as her heart swelled with affection for her brother. Yost had gone to Ephraim, no doubt to try to make amends for his past mistakes. She should have been embarrassed, mortified by such a revelation, but she felt nothing but profound gratitude for Yost. He truly walked taller every day.

Her smile surprised him. "This isn't funny."

Miriam looked at the hard line of Ephraim's mouth and remembered the times it curved into a smile. She thought of what Ephraim's pride had done to him. Seth had told her that any man would be doubly blessed to have her as a wife. He had been teasing her, of course, but for the first time, she saw the truth of his words—saw her own value in the eyes of God. The feeling didn't feel like pride. It felt like an overdue acknowledgment of her true self who lived to give glory to the Lord.

Ephraim might pity her, but she pitied him all the more.

She would have made him very happy. Seth would say Ephraim had no idea what he had thrown away.

She sighed. Ephraim was every bit as valuable and loved of God as she was. How could she bear him ill will?

She reached out to touch his arm, but he backed away from her. "I am sorry if Yost made you feel uncomfortable. He is trying to make amends in the only way he knows how. He is a gute boy with a gute heart."

"That has always been your problem with Yost. You do not see him for what he really is."

Miriam couldn't keep a sad smile from her face. "We will not trouble you again. May the good Lord be with you."

She turned her back on him and left Ephraim standing there with only his pride.

TWO WEEKS BEFORE THANKSGIVING, Susie and Hollow were married in a small ceremony that took place in the Bontragers' front room. Miriam's older brothers, Marvin and David, were there from Ohio with their wives and children along with the rest of Miriam's siblings. Aunts Emma and Erla attended with their families as well as a half dozen district members. Ephraim did not show up, but his dat came with the bishop.

There would be no coupling-up or singing or extra meal, but Miriam thought Susie and Hollow looked every bit the pair deeply in love. "A truly lovely couple. They will be very happy, Lord willing," she overheard a guest say.

The bishop performed the ceremony in High German and they sang three hymns before Mamm served a hearty dinner of turkey and celery stuffing. Mamm had cooked two turkeys in her stove and Aunt Emma and cousin Kate had each cooked one and brought them.

Except for Laura, Seth and his entire family attended. They rarely saw Seth's dat at anything. Once the service ended, Seth jumped up to help put together tables out of benches.

Miriam watched him from the other side of the room, and when he noticed her looking, he grinned. He pointed to his newly healed arm and flexed his muscles.

Miriam laughed at the silly expression on his face. He had grown progressively more animated and cheerful since they'd first talked at the auction last spring. Miriam was glad. She hated to see him unhappy.

Once the tables were ready, he practically raced to her side. She set paper plates and cups on the tables while Callie and Raymond folded plastic forks and knives into napkins.

"It's been nine days since I have seen you," he said. "You are prettier than I remember."

Miriam stifled a smile and kept her eyes trained on her plates. "Ach, quit your teasing. If you're not careful, I'll start to believe what you say."

"It is wonderful-gute for Susie. I think she and Hollow will be as happy as any married couple can be."

"Jah, and now the healing with the community can begin. Last week at gmay, two people told me what a gute fater I have. He has always been gute, and not only because Susie is married."

"The community knows the value of your family." He took the cups from her hand and began placing them beside each plate. "What's for dinner? The smell from the kitchen is delicious."

"Turkey with celery stuffing. And tart cranberry salad. Susie made it herself. When I marry, I want to make—"

Miriam closed her mouth.

"When I marry?"

Since Ephraim, she hadn't even considered it a possibility. She furrowed her brow in confusion.

Seth glued his gaze to the stack of cups in his hand. "Have you changed your mind about that?"

"I—I don't know."

He must have sensed her confusion, because he tried to lighten her mood. "Well, if you have changed your mind, keep it to yourself, or you will have a score of young men at your doorstep."

"Stop your teasing this minute, Seth Lambright, or you'll get no cranberry salad."

Seth threw up his hands. "I am serious. Ignore my advice at your own peril."

Miriam couldn't contain her delight after dinner when Jacob and Joshua each took one of her hands and pulled her to sit next to them on the sofa. Priscilla soon followed and deftly maneuvered herself between Joshua and Miriam.

"I can't wait for Thanksgiving," Joshua said, leaning towards Miriam so Priscilla didn't get the notion to divert Miriam's attention. "Do you know what is my favorite pie? Pumpkin with whipped cream on top. But cherry is sweeter, unless you get a stone and then Seth says you could break a tooth. I only got a stone once but I found it with my tongue before I chewed on it. I hope Ellie lets me have two pieces."

Seth lingered near the sofa, leafing through Dat's Bible without reading it. It was probably just Miriam's imagination, but he seemed to gravitate closer and closer until Jacob grabbed Seth's hand and pulled him to sit down.

As soon as Seth was settled, Jacob popped from his place next to Miriam and nudged Seth's knee. "Scoot over, Seth. Sit next to Miriam. She's pretty."

Seth turned one shade darker, grinned sheepishly at Miriam, and slid next to her without protest.

Her heart danced with pleasure at the look in Seth's eyes. His arm nudged against hers, and she was acutely aware of the tingling sensation his touch produced.

"My new quilt is nice and warm," he said, when Joshua stopped talking to take a breath. "Thank you again. I am so grateful."

"I owe the greater share of thanks, knowing how happy it makes you."

"And Teacher says we will make paper turkeys next week for Thanksgiving decorations," Joshua said.

Miriam put her arm around Priscilla while she concentrated on Joshua's story, which ended only with his visit. Her gaze was turned to Joshua, but she still felt Seth beside her, solid and immovable. She could have gladly spent the rest of the day at his side—not even making conversation or paying particular attention, but just feeling his presence, like springtime in the air or the smell of freshly baked bread throughout the house.

CHAPTER
TWENTY-SIX

"There are three ministers who will be living within the boundaries of the new district," Bishop Moses Schwartz said. He stood in front of the congregation, holding three hymnals wrapped with rubber bands, his air more solemn than usual. It wasn't every day that a district divided and a new bishop was chosen. Miriam had never seen a new bishop ordained in her lifetime.

Wedged tightly between JoAnn Kiem and Millie Troyer, Miriam could barely breathe for the tension in the air. Yoders' house was crammed with what Miriam thought surely must be every person in the entire district. It was certainly high time to be divided, even though such a division proved bittersweet. Lifelong friends would be separated. Families that had worshipped together for decades would be split from each other. It was not as if they would never see each other again, but it was certainly easier to maintain friendships with the people you worshipped with on the Sabbath.

The only family that seemed to be missing was the Neuenschwanders. Ephraim's family was visiting relatives in

Missouri. They wouldn't return for another week, the Monday after Thanksgiving.

The bishop raised the three hymnals. "These three men will draw lots for the new bishop. Whoever's book has the proverb in it will be the new bishop by the Lord's will."

Everyone sat perfectly still. The new bishop would dictate the rules for the district. A bishop might decide to allow certain things that a former bishop had not. That was why their district had indoor plumbing when many of the Wisconsin districts didn't. There had been a case of typhoid fever in the district right before Bishop Schwartz was ordained. Due to the sickness and concerns over sanitation, he had decided to allow indoor plumbing.

A new bishop might also decide to forbid certain practices that he thought pulled the People closer to the world. Miriam thought of her horse. Some districts in Cashton didn't allow girls to ride horses.

Miriam closed her eyes and said a prayer for the Lord to choose a merciful man. So much depended on the bishop.

An equally troubling worry was the fact that her dat was one of the ministers who would draw lots.

Bishop Schwartz called the three ministers up. "Sol Gingerich—"

Miriam put her hand to her heart. A gute man, but stern and grave like the bishop.

"Noah Kanagy, and John Bontrager."

Miriam's stomach did a flip.

Please, dear Heavenly Father, not my dat.

Millie, her expression overflowing with sympathy, put her arm around Miriam to steady her. Miriam grabbed Millie's hand as she studied her fater's face. All the color drained from his cheeks as he stood and slowly walked to the front of the room. It must have been the longest walk of his life.

Some men desired the honor of being the bishop as confirmation of God's favor, but those men were few. Most hoped they would not be burdened with such a weighty responsibility. Dat would never seek for the calling. But as a baptized member of the church, he had made a commitment that if the lot ever fell to him, he would willingly serve.

Dat stood between Noah and Sol, eyes cast down, with an arm around each of them. Noah clasped his hands in front of him, while Sol shifted nervously from one foot to the next.

Seth caught Miriam's eye and nodded slightly. Why did that small gesture give her so much comfort?

Silence echoed through the house. Even the little ones seemed to sense that something significant was about to happen.

As the three men turned to face him, the bishop placed the three hymnals on the table.

Each man picked up the book directly in front of him and in turn handed it to the bishop. The bishop thumbed through Sol's book first. No proverb hidden within its pages. The bishop picked up Dat's book next.

Miriam squeezed Millie's hand until she was sure she had cut off her circulation. Miriam didn't know what to do with all the suspense. She kept her gaze riveted to Dat's book and whispered, "Lord willing, Lord willing," over and over again.

The bishop found what he looked for and raised his eyes to the congregation. "The Lord God has chosen our brother John Bontrager."

Miriam would never forget the look of shock on her fater's face.

~

DAT SAT in the dimness of the barn next to Daisy's stall, stroking Daisy's nose and quietly humming a hymn.

"It's dark," Miriam said. She took a match from the shelf and lit the kerosene lantern that hung on the post above Dat's head.

She'd known where he would be. When something particularly heavy weighed on Dat's mind, she could find him out feeding or brushing the horses. Since it was the Sabbath, he would probably be sitting on that wobbly milking stool talking to Old Jack or Daisy about his day. He talked to the horses the way she did. They were very good listeners who gave just the right amount of scolding when she needed it. When Old Jack lifted his head and twitched his ears, he was saying, "Stop feeling sorry for yourself." And when Daisy tapped Miriam with her nose, she assured her that everything would turn out all right in the end.

Dat gave her a tired smile. "Old Jack is trying to sleep. He likes it dark."

Miriam scooted onto the cement ledge that enclosed one side of Daisy's stall. "Are you nervous? About being bishop."

Dat folded his arms and bowed his head. "I know why the Lord called me."

"You do?"

"Because I have been begging Him very hard all week not to call me, and He did it to punish my stubbornness."

"You will make a fine bishop, Dat."

"Nae, I know nothing. What do I do when someone comes to me with a problem? How will I help them?"

"You have a son who was once in jail and a daughter with child before marriage. You have known deep suffering."

Dat rubbed his chin. "But that is what does not make sense to me. The bishop should be a fater of obedient children. If I had been a gute fater, my children would not have traveled so far astray."

"The more I think about it, the more I see that no family in the community is untouched by trouble. The Bielers struggle with a wayward son just like us. Several families have the burden of special children. Vernon Mishler's parents must care for him night and day. Four old people passed on this year as well as Lizzie Glick in childbirth and the two Schmucker children in that car accident. God makes His rain fall on the righteous and the wicked."

"Why would the Lord want one such as me?"

"You have been a wonderful fater. I have barely heard a cross word come out of your mouth. It has taken me a long time to learn, but Seth says the Lord doesn't judge us by other people's choices—only what we do with our own lives."

"Seth is a gute boy and wise. What if I had been the bishop when his mamm died? I would not have known how to help him."

"He came through it a better person."

"That is the kind of tragedy that terrifies me." With his elbows on his knees, Dat covered his face with his hands and began to weep. "Lord," he whispered, "make me equal to my burden."

CHAPTER
TWENTY-SEVEN

Seth sat atop his mare, Patches, while Miriam rode the chestnut, Bitty. The crisp air landed on Seth's skin like an invigorating shower. The horses needed exercise, and even though the end of November got colder all the time, he tried to ride the horses frequently to keep them fit. Miriam often accompanied him because "it makes sense to exercise two at once." No complaints from Seth. If he had his way, Miriam would be by his side every day.

He glanced in her direction and watched her prod her horse into a canter down the road with a look of pure joy on her face. A million hours wouldn't be long enough to drink in her silky-smooth skin or the freckles that dotted her nose. And her lips? He had to concentrate very hard not to stare at them when she talked. Her beauty took his breath away.

Seth nudged his horse forward to keep up with Miriam's while those feelings he constantly tried to bottle came spilling out, saturating his whole being with longing.

He loved her. He'd long ago admitted to himself that it was useless to fight the overpowering feeling.

If he told her how he felt, would she run screaming for safety? The thought of losing her company made him feel ill. But if she never knew his deepest feelings, she might never open herself to the possibility that she could be with someone besides Ephraim.

They slowed to a walk as they approached his lane.

"Did you have a gute Thanksgiving?" Miriam said.

Seth tried to appear unaffected by the thoughts spiraling in his head. "Jah. Ellie is a wonderful-gute cook. Her brother Thomas came with his family."

"I ate until I thought I would burst."

"Ellie tells us how much we each get to eat...but I did sneak an extra piece of pumpkin pie when Ellie's back was turned."

Miriam grinned. "Did you get away with it?"

"She thought my dat took it, so she didn't complain."

"We had pumpkin and cherry pie. My dat needed to counsel a family and missed the entire meal, but he got three pieces of pie."

"Will he be gone often, do you think?"

"He has only been bishop for a week, but I have never seen him so busy. I hope it will get easier."

Seth pulled his knit hat tighter over his ears. "He is a gute man to sacrifice so much of himself for the district. I do not envy him."

They turned up Seth's lane and rode past the stand of trees. "The house looks gute," Miriam said. She guided her horse in the direction of Seth's small house.

"The outside is finished, which is something I wanted to do before bad weather hit. The crew I hired worked fast with the men from the district. They framed the inside too. Next week there will be a Sheetrocking frolic for the inside. Then I can work on painting and laying the floor when I have spare time."

Miriam dismounted, tied the reins to the railing, and walked up the stairs to Seth's covered porch. Seth followed her.

"This is a gute spot. The trees are big. You will be cool in the summer." She rested her gloved hands on the railing.

"I want to move my brothers and Scilla in before Christmas."

"To live with you? Why?"

Seth did not want to speak ill of anyone. "I think they would be happier." He trained his eyes on the trees. "I will not watch their childhoods stolen. I am determined to see them grow up in a happy home with people who care about them."

A soft glow filled Miriam's eyes as she looked at him. "I wish I were more like you. You are so gute."

"There is none good but God."

She pressed her lips into a resigned smile. "As you wish."

An irrational resolve pounced on Seth as he stood there gazing at Miriam. A voice inside his head screamed at him to keep his mouth shut, but his heart would not let him back down. He coughed weakly. "Miriam, I want to tell you something, but I would never want to make you feel uncomfortable or unhappy."

"Okay," Miriam said slowly, studying his face. Then the corners of her mouth turned up. "You are not going to tell me I am a snob, are you?"

Seth would have laughed if he had not been so terrified. He dared to move closer and take her hand in his. She did look surprised, raising her eyebrows and staring at his hand, but she didn't pull away. That was something, at least—enough to encourage him to move forward with his reckless plan.

"Miriam," he began. His throat seemed to swell shut. "I would never want you to feel uncomfortable..." He'd already said that. Why did he have to be so awkward? If he were Ephraim, he would already be holding her in his arms and whispering sweet phrases into her ear. "I think...you are so dear...I think I love you." He wanted to say, "I know I love you," but "think" was less threatening, and if she wanted to, she could discourage him without feeling like she'd ripped out his heart—even though that's exactly what would happen.

A cautious smile bloomed on her face. "You do?"

She didn't seem upset or resistant. His heart pounded faster, if that were possible.

Seth's thoughts whirled with a hundred reasons to drop the conversation, a thousand cautions to heed, and a million words he wanted to say.

He did not know what he would have said next, because they were interrupted by the sight of a buggy turning up his lane. Miriam pulled her hand from his as the occupant of the buggy pulled alongside their horses and the last person in the world Seth wanted to see climbed out.

Miriam caught her breath and turned to stone. Seth wanted to grab her hand and run far away, but he was as paralyzed as Miriam was at the sight of Ephraim Neuenschwander.

Ephraim didn't look at all himself. Dark circles rimmed his dull eyes, and a day's growth of whiskers darkened his features. He looked...repentant, ready to make a confession. Seth stopped breathing. He didn't like it. Didn't like it one bit.

"They said you were here," Ephraim said, ignoring Seth completely.

Miriam, tense and rigid, simply stared at him. Seth wanted to wrap her in his arms. Since Ephraim's rejection, Seth knew firsthand that her encounters with Ephraim had been short and painful. Seth had witnessed the behavior at gmay. He followed Miriam's lead and stared at Ephraim, trying not to despise him, trying not to let his tongue take hold of his restraint.

"Can I talk to you? Alone?" Ephraim said.

Miriam shook her head. "What do you want?"

He glanced at Seth. "Miriam." Ephraim hesitated as his voice cracked before every emotion seemed to spill out of his mouth. "When I think of how I gave up on you, the way it hurt you, I can't stand it." He swished his fingers through his hair. "I want you to come back to me. I want to be together again."

Seth stared at Ephraim in astonishment. He had never seen him so penitent. On the surface, so sincere.

Seth studied Miriam's face. Her mouth twisted in confusion as she trained her eyes on her former intended, the man she had always loved. The man she would always love.

"I don't understand," she mumbled.

"A day hasn't gone by that I don't regret losing you. Even on the night of the gathering when I was so angry, leaving you there like that was the hardest thing I ever did. I wanted to do the right thing in regards to Susie and Yost, but more and more I see that your family problems don't mean a thing compared to how much I need you. Please, Miriam. Give me another chance."

Miriam's eyes darted from Seth to Ephraim; doubt and distress were written all over her face. A bottomless pit opened up in Seth's gut. He felt her slipping away as plainly as if they were at the top of an icy hill and she lost her footing and tumbled over the edge.

"Seth," she said, pleading with her eyes, "Seth, I don't know what to do."

Even with his heart melting into a pathetic puddle at her feet, Seth knew he had to do the noble thing, the thing that would bring Miriam the least amount of suffering. Of course she wanted Ephraim. With her loving spirit, she certainly would have forgiven Ephraim his trespasses long ago. What was there left to keep them apart? Who wouldn't choose Ephraim over Seth Lambright any day? But she had to believe he would be okay or she would be ripped to shreds with remorse.

"Go with him," he said, unable to disguise the shaking in his voice. "This is what you have always wanted."

"I think so," she said, doubt running circles around her face.

Ephraim seemed surprised at Miriam's hesitation. He looked at Seth and furrowed his brow. "Miriam, don't we at least owe it to each other to see what will come of this? We used to be everything to each other. I want to have that again, don't you?"

Miriam looked at Seth, tears sparkling in her brilliant lavender-blue eyes. "Seth, I think...I think he is right. For good or ill, our relationship deserves a second chance."

By biting his tongue, Seth kept a sob from escaping his lips and attempted a carefree smile that he was sure fooled no one. "Our friendship should not stop you from being with the man you truly love. Go," he said, even giving her a little nudge to display his sincerity. "Go with him. I will take the horses back to the stable."

Miriam took the three stairs as if she were going to her own execution. He hadn't been convincing enough. She felt sorry for him. That was the only thing he didn't want from Miriam— her pity.

Why had he ever thought it was a good idea to share his true feelings? They meant nothing now but something to laugh with Ephraim about.

No, no, he must not let bitterness take root. Miriam would never turn his love into a joke.

Would she?

Ephraim slid open the door and Miriam climbed in. She leaned forward to look at Seth through the glassless window as the buggy rolled down the lane. Seth listened to the *clip-clop* of hooves as the buggy reached the paved road and watched as his best reason for living rolled out of sight.

He relaxed his grip on the railing and unclenched his teeth. He'd bitten his tongue so hard, he had actually drawn blood.

Seth lifted the collar of his coat around his neck to block out the chill that suddenly surrounded him. He tromped down the porch steps of his shell of a house and grabbed the reins of both horses.

"Come on, girls. Let's get out of the cold."

Patches puffed a warm breath of air into his face and nodded wisely. She seemed to understand that everything had changed.

The world had gone dark.

Who would have thought a heart could break twice in the same lifetime?

CHAPTER
TWENTY-EIGHT

Miriam trained her eyes on Seth as Ephraim drove away. His face betrayed nothing as he stood all alone on the porch of his empty house.

"I think I love you."

His declaration had taken her by surprise, certainly, but when he said those words, the sun rose and a rainbow appeared in her sky.

She didn't want to cry in front of Ephraim, but the tears flowed unbidden. Seth had told her he loved her, and she had rejected his gift. He tried bravely to cover it up, but she knew every line of his face, saw every subtle emotion. He was worse than hurt. He was devastated.

"Go, go with him. Be with the man you truly love."

Ephraim saw the tears. "Miri, what is the matter?"

A feeble sob escaped her lips. "I don't know. After all this time of being without you, it feels strange—"

"You thought we'd never be married, and you wonder if I really mean what I say now." Ephraim went so far as to stop the buggy and pin her with an earnest gaze. "I promise you, Miri, we will never be separated again."

"The things you said about Yost and Susie—"

"Will never be mentioned between us. Can you forget all our old disagreements?"

Miriam swam in confusion. Had she made the right decision? Ephraim was the only boy she had ever loved for as long as she could remember. Even Seth said as much. Surely God had put them together. But if being with Ephraim was the Lord's will, why did she feel so miserable?

Maybe the thought of Seth, all alone in that cold stable, brushing his horses in silence, troubled her. Maybe her concern for his feelings overshadowed her joy at being with Ephraim again.

The good Lord would heal all things. In time Seth would find another girl to love.

Miriam didn't expect the pang in her heart. Did she want him to find another girl to love?

Ephraim furrowed his brow. "Are you okay, Miri?"

"I don't know."

"You've got to believe me, Miriam. I thought about you the whole time I was visiting relatives. My family got back from Missouri only an hour ago. We heard your dat was the new bishop, and I went straight to your house to see how you were doing. I didn't even unpack. Your mamm told me I could find you here. I rushed over, not wanting to spend a minute more of my life without you."

Miriam stared at him in puzzlement. Could this really be happening? "What about Sarah Schwartz?"

Ephraim didn't miss a beat. "There is only one girl for me, Miri. You haven't been off my mind since I saw you in the quilt shop. You looked so pretty, like the day I laid eyes on you when you were in the first grade. Do you remember how we found that cat at recess and fed it pieces of our lunch?"

"Until Teacher caught us and sent a note to your dat." Miriam quit frowning. "You chased me around the playground every day and tried to pull my hair."

"That is a sign of affection, you know. For an eight-year-old boy." He flashed that blinding smile. "That affection has only grown stronger. We understand each other. Always have. Even when I broke things off with you, deep in my heart I knew we would end up together. You must have felt it too."

Maybe that explained why she could never truly get over his loss, why the very sight of him made her heart pound like a set of drums.

"When I heard that your fater was the new bishop, I knew I had misjudged your family. I regretted judging you so quickly."

As Ephraim turned onto Blossom Lane, Miriam realized where they were going. His gaze darted to her face. "My mamm wanted me to bring you for supper."

"Mamm is expecting me at home."

"Don't worry. My little brothers went over to tell them that you would be eating with us."

Already? How did Ephraim know before he left home that she would choose to come with him?

Miriam took a deep breath to calm herself. A visit to Ephraim's house this soon made her uncomfortable. She hadn't been there since early summer. What had they been saying about her in her absence?

"Mamm scolded me for breaking up with you." Ephraim pitched his voice an octave higher. " 'That is the finest girl in the district, Ephraim Neuenschwander. Mark my words. You will regret it.' And she was right. She threatened to never feed me again if I didn't bring you over today." Ephraim's cheerfulness grew the closer they got to his house. He winked at her. "I didn't want to starve. Do you remember last year when I had a stomachache and didn't eat anything all day?"

"Jah, you had a green tint to your face just before you fainted."

"Denki for at least trying to catch me."

Miriam cracked a grin. "I tried, but you went down so fast."

Ephraim rubbed his chin. "Still have the scar."

"I like it. It makes you look rugged."

"Only until I grow a beard."

Ephraim's white clapboard house stood on a narrow rise of ground close to the road. The Neuenschwanders' porch traveled all the way around the house, making it perfect for foot races with the grandchildren. Smoke rose from both chimneys, and three bare peach trees hunched over the front yard.

Ephraim's mamm exploded out the door before he even parked the buggy. She ran to Miriam and gave her a solid hug. "I have a bone to pick with you. We ain't seen you since June. Why have you been a stranger?"

Miriam hid her astonishment. Why had she been a stranger? Did his mamm want to dredge through the past or pretend it hadn't happened?

Pretend it hadn't happened. She waved her hand in dismissal. "No matter. You are here with Ephraim now. All things are as they should be. Cum in. We are having *yummasetti*, Ephraim's favorite."

Miriam sat at her regular place at Neuenschwanders' table. Everything felt familiar, as if she'd never left. The awkwardness of the situation could not let her relax, but Ephraim's family acted as if nothing were out of the ordinary. Ephraim had three younger brothers and three older brothers. The three older had families of their own, but the four boys left at home made an enormous racket. Ephraim's mom brought a long wooden spoon to the dinner table to give her boys a whack if they ever forgot their manners. The boys weren't afraid of the spoon. It was more of a joke than anything else, but they did try harder to behave if they felt the wrath of the spoon.

After the silent prayer, Ephraim sat close to Miriam and didn't stop smiling. Freeman, Ephraim's brother closest in age, sat on the other side of Miriam. She had never really adored Freeman. He acted too big for his britches and loved being the center of attention in any room he entered.

"I am glad you and Ephraim are back together," Freeman said, shoving a large spoonful of yummasetti into his mouth. "You are like two souls sharing one heart."

Miriam wanted to roll her eyes. Where had she heard that before? Probably some honeyed words that Ephraim used to feed her. Ephraim used flattery to make her laugh. Seth's compliments, on the other hand, made her blush. Sometimes she thought Seth spent his days thinking of nice things to say to her. He was seldom without three or four compliments. The thought gave rise to a smile. Seth would examine her expression, decide it was safe to proceed, and express his admiration of her face or her intelligence or her sense of humor. Miriam found it quite charming.

Thinking of Seth, she felt the weight of the world pull her to the floor.

"I think I love you."

After supper Miriam and Ephraim's mamm finished up the dishes, and then the entire family played an energetic game of Scrabble. Miriam and Ephraim were partners, and he soon had her laughing at all the nonsense words he crafted out of the seven letters in their pile.

"N–U–P–E–N–S–I," he said, showing Miriam his new word. "And what does it mean?"

"It means we have some gute vowels."

Miriam remembered why she liked Ephraim so much. He knew how to make her laugh. "Jah, we do."

"Actually, a nupensi is a tiny hair in your nose. When it gets irritated, you sneeze."

"If you use that word, your dat will insist on the dictionary."

"I don't think he would dare. I am the best speller in the family."

Miriam giggled. "Jah, I can see that."

Once the game ended and Ephraim and Miriam lost miserably, Ephraim took Miriam home. Miriam could imagine the surprise Mamm must have felt when Ephraim had shown up at their door in search of her. What would she say?

Ephraim walked her to the door but, true to form, never laid a hand on her. "Can I take you to the gathering tomorrow night?"

Facing the suddenness of being thrown back into Ephraim's life, Miriam hesitated. What would people think?

Nae, she wasn't concerned with what they would think. Everyone loved Ephraim. But the thought of seeing Seth there filled her with a sense of dread. She couldn't bear to face the pain in his eyes. She couldn't bear to be reminded of her own pain.

Her own pain?

Didn't she have what she truly wanted?

"I don't know. I am finishing a quilt for Susie."

Ephraim lifted his eyebrows. "No excuses, Miri. I have lost too much time with you already. I will pick you up at six." He quickly turned and walked away. That was how he avoided an argument.

Miriam slipped through the door, deep in thought. This was what she wanted. Ephraim's apology testified to his change of heart. She had loved him forever. In time, they would be comfortable and easy like before.

Mamm's voice came from the kitchen. "Is that you, Miriam?"

Miriam lit a kerosene lamp in the front room and draped herself on the sofa.

Mamm bustled into the room with all the concern of a mother hen. Susie and Hollow crept in from the kitchen with Yost close behind.

"Ephraim came over, and I sent him to Seth's," Mamm said. "What happened?"

"Ephraim wants to get back together."

Yost cracked a smile. He had never told Miriam of his visits to Ephraim. He probably felt responsible for their reunion. Maybe he was. Let him think whatever he wanted as long as it made him happy.

Susie gasped and sat next to Miriam on the sofa. She frowned and folded her arms. "I am glad my sin did not keep you apart in the end." She didn't look glad at all. She stood up as quickly as she had sat and began pacing the floor. "You and Ephraim back together—this is good news."

Susie's lack of enthusiasm was evident, and it seemed to mirror Mamm's. Mamm creased her forehead as her lips turned down and a look of alarm burned in her eyes. "What did Seth say?"

"He told me to go with Ephraim. That it was what I have always wanted."

"Is it?"

Miriam brushed her hand across her eyes. "Seth always gives good advice."

Susie and Hollow exchanged a look of concern.

Mamm clucked her tongue. "Oh, poor boy."

The heaviness pressed on Miriam with greater force.

"What else can I do? Ephraim broke up with me. I wanted to be together. He has made many mistakes, but I owe it to both of us to give him another chance. He is giving me one."

"Jah, I suppose he is," Mamm said.

Why did Miriam feel like she had to defend herself? "Ephraim is a gute boy from a gute family. He is the minister's son. What more could you want?"

"What more could *you* want?" came Mamm's muted reply.

The question was left unanswered.

Miriam rode Daisy down the lane as she had done countless times since she met Seth, glad this time for the sweatpants underneath her dress and the long johns underneath her sweatpants. The snow-covered path felt like an old friend, beckoning her to spend some time. She took Daisy slowly. Daisy showed her age more than ever, and snow was never easy for the horses to walk through.

A full week had gone by before Miriam found the courage to visit the foals.

How could she face him, knowing how he must despise her?

With Ephraim's renewed and full attention, it had taken no time at all for Miriam to return to the good graces of the entire community. At Ephraim's insistence, they had attended three gatherings last week in three different districts so Ephraim could "make up for lost time." Deacon Kiem's wife from the old district had baked Miriam a cake, and Ada Weaver even invited her to a quilting bee. Miriam should have felt honored. Ada was very selective about who she chose for her quilting circles.

Miriam needn't have feared that Seth would be to one of the gatherings. Just as Ephraim had once disappeared from her life, Seth was now nowhere to be seen. She had spied his brothers walking home from school one day, but the wind whipped up and they didn't hear her calling to them.

Tying Daisy's reins to the hook, Miriam remembered the first time she came to Seth's stable—the first and last time she had knocked on the door. But today she felt more like an intruder than a friend. She knocked softly, and when she got no response, she rapped louder. Still no movement from inside.

She cracked open the door and peeked inside. "Seth?"

Moving farther into the stable, she looked over each stall. No one here but her and the horses. On the cot in the tiny alcove where her quilt used to be was a thin white sheet, as if he didn't care whether he froze to death. The sight of his cot stripped of the quilt hit her like a snowball to the back of the head. She knew exactly why it was missing.

Averting her eyes, she walked to the large stall where her two foals stood with their mother. Well, they weren't both hers, but she still hadn't chosen the one she wanted.

They were taller now, although their legs still seemed out of proportion to their bodies. She held out her hand, and the colt, which she had named Diamond for the patch on his face, came to her immediately. He nudged his nose into her hand, looking for a treat.

"Sorry, Diamond. I didn't bring raisins or anything," she cooed. Seth had always supplied her with plenty of apples. She'd never thought to bring her own.

Light flooded the space as Seth came in carrying a hose and a shovel.

"Hello," she said. Her voice sounded timid, even to herself.

He stopped short when he caught sight of her and sucked in his breath. His expression went hard, hiding any and all emotion behind those cold, gray eyes. "It's a chilly day to be out riding."

"My coat is warm." Miriam wished she knew how to make everything better. All the things she had planned to say to him flew out of her head, leaving her with thousands of painful emotions and no words. They stared at each other until she found the courage to speak.

"Seth—"

He turned from her and rested his shovel against the wall. "I must go fix the shaft on the windmill. There are apples in the storage closet if you want one."

She didn't want to be let off so easily. "Seth, wait."

He gripped the coil of hose in his hand and slapped it against his thigh. "Best I get out there before dark."

"I want to say I'm sorry. I don't understand how things got so twisted and confusing, but Ephraim and I have been together for so long, it seemed to be the right decision."

He looked away and stood as still as a statue. "Don't be sorry. Your feelings cannot be helped."

"I never wanted you to be hurt."

Was it resentment or regret she saw flash in his eyes? "You don't have to feel sorry for me. I will get along fine. Now that my arm is healed, I don't need your help." He forced a warped smile that made him look more wretched than ever. "You have been a gute friend. Denki."

Miriam didn't know what else to say. His "thank you" suggested a desire to end the conversation, but the hollow feeling in the pit of her stomach told her that nothing in the least had been settled between them. She searched for something, anything, to keep him talking, to keep him close to her until she could find the perfect words to repair the damage. "Yost said the therapy session was gute last week. I am sorry I missed it. I will be with him next time."

He snapped his head around to look at her. "Nae. He can come by himself."

"Oh."

"Yost is almost a grown man. He can do therapy without his sister."

"Oh, I see." Miriam swallowed hard as her throat swelled up. "How do you think he is doing?"

"I must go fix the windmill."

"Do you think Yost is better these past few weeks?"

Seth let out a long breath as if in surrender. He met her eyes, and she caught a glimpse of his very soul. She saw raw, bitter pain that knocked her backward with breathless shock.

He slumped his shoulders and kneaded his brow with his thumb and forefinger. "Miriam, I don't want you to come here anymore."

His declaration struck her mute.

"The foals are weaned. I will give the rest of the money from your dat to Matthew Eicher. He will do a gute job training your horse."

Miriam felt so low, she could have fit under the crack in the door. "I don't want Matthew Eicher to train my horse."

He raised his chin and looked away from her. "All the same, I'll not do it."

Her tears were so close to the surface, Miriam did not dare speak.

Seeing him standing there, chin high, muscles tense, Miriam chastised herself. How could she even compare her pain to Seth's? She had a beautiful foal, a loving family, and the man she had always wanted. Her life was good. It was pure selfishness to feel sorry for herself because Seth Lambright did not want to be her friend anymore.

"Which of the foals do you want?" he said.

Miriam took several deep breaths. "I'll take the filly."

Seth would get more money for the colt when he sold it. It was the only thing she could give him.

Puzzlement flitted across his features, and then he nodded. "I will make the arrangements with Matthew tomorrow." He went to his sleeping room and brought out a thick wool blanket. "Put this over your legs on the ride home. It is mighty cold."

She took it from his hands, and he raced out the door before she had a chance to say thank you.

He was gone. Gone for good.

CHAPTER
TWENTY-NINE

The morning light shone grayish purple, as if someone had spread a gauzy black curtain over the sun. Clouds rolled lazily from the west, promising snow, but maybe not until later afternoon. Sunlight peeked through the gloom to the east, but Seth paid it no heed. As far as he was concerned, there was no sun in the sky and he'd be a fool to hope for it.

Nathaniel King helped him carry in the last of the Sheetrock from the warehouse truck. Twenty-three men stood inside the house, ready to hang it. It was a gute day to be out of the cold. As gute a day as any for a Sheetrock frolic. Even his dat had come to help the neighbors finish Seth's house.

The front door opened to a hallway with a sitting room on the left, situated so that at a future date, he could knock out the side wall and expand the room for gmay. In the hall to the right climbed a set of stairs leading up to the bedrooms. Down the hall stood the kitchen, the biggest room in the house. Seth's mamm had always told him the kitchen was the heart of the home, and he wanted his home to have a big heart. A roomy back porch opened up behind the kitchen and washroom, where someone could sit in the shade and look at the pastures and stable beyond. Seth used to spend hours with Mamm on his own back porch, shelling peas or shucking corn after harvest. The memories did not warm his heart today, but he kept hold of them in hopes of better times.

Up the stairs, Seth had framed four bedrooms. He wanted ample room for his siblings—the house would be full before it was even finished.

Two of the men, Enos Glick and Sol Gingerich, Sheetrocked houses for a living. They supervised everyone else in how to hang it most efficiently. Saws and hammers created continuous noise as men worked on both floors at once. Seth picked up a battery-operated drill and went to work in the kitchen. Benjamin Yoder and Ike Weaver measured and scored the drywall while Seth and Nathaniel King hung it. Seth's muscles ached and his lungs burned as he pushed himself hard enough to force the painful memories out of his head. He would rather think about his throbbing shoulder and sore arms than his broken heart.

It didn't help when John and Yost Bontrager showed up. John had passed on enough of his look to his daughter to bring Miriam quickly to mind as soon as Seth saw him.

Seth heard three or four people call out. "Bishop!" Oh, yes. John was the bishop now—the reason why Seth had lost Miriam. He had no doubt about Ephraim's motives. Miriam was worthy of Ephraim Neuenschwander again, and Seth was unworthy of her. He caught his breath and faced the truth. He had always been unworthy of her.

John marched into the kitchen with Yost close behind. "Sorry we are late. We had to drop Miriam somewhere this morning."

Yost shook his head and grinned. "At Ephraim's. She's always with Ephraim."

Seth puzzled why this information should give him such a crippling stab of pain right to the chest. He already knew how Miriam spent her time. Why did he let it bother him?

John's face turned slightly pink, and he pushed Yost toward the hall. "Go upstairs and start there."

Yost studied Seth, who tried to make his expression as cheerful as possible. Where John's color deepened, Yost blanched as he gazed at Seth and realization caught up with him. "Oh." He slumped his shoulders. "Okay."

They turned away. "I'm sorry, Dat," Yost said as they disappeared down the newly Sheetrocked hall. "I should have known."

Seth let the feeling wash over him, drown him. He had a small sense of what his mother must have felt when she lost the will to go on living. But he would not give in to it. Priscilla and the boys needed him. He would find the strength for them, even if he didn't have the heart for himself.

Sol came into the kitchen. "They are mudding and taping upstairs already. We will send out a call for two more nights this week. If you can sand in between our coming, we can paint on Saturday."

Seth let that piece of news cheer him up. "Denki. I appreciate all the help."

"I wouldn't have a roof on my barn if not for my gute neighbors. It is a blessing to be a fellow citizen in Christ."

Seth heard the patter of small feet in his hall. Jacob and Joshua ran into the kitchen, and Seth had just enough time to deposit his screws and drill before they leaped into his arms.

"It looks wonderful-gute," Joshua said. "Like a real house."

Jacob held onto Seth as if he were afraid to let go. "Ellie is coming in. Can we stay here for supper?"

"A letter came today," Joshua said. He pulled it from his pocket and handed it to Seth. The second one this week from Laura.

"Go look upstairs at the bedrooms," Seth said. "It wonders me what room you would choose if you could choose one."

His brothers raced away so quickly, it was almost as if they were never there.

Seth took off his gloves and opened Laura's letter.

By the time you get this letter I will be on a bus to Apple Lake, so you can't talk me out of it. Don't worry, I'm not coming home for good. But both Joshua and Jacob have written and say you are looking miserable. You tried to cover it up in your letter, but I know how you must be feeling. That girl wouldn't know a good thing if it bit her in her superior little hinnerdale. See you soon.

Laura

SETH WADDED UP the letter and stuffed it in his pocket. He wished Laura wouldn't bother. She couldn't afford to miss school or take a bus home, and any mention of Miriam only made things worse. Much worse.

Ellie entered the kitchen with Priscilla. Priscilla looked around the room wide-eyed. "Oh, it looks like a real house now. What color are you going to paint the walls? Mandy has wallpaper with flowers in her kitchen. Will you do wallpaper, Seth?"

Seth patted Scilla on the head and pulled her close. Her presence made him feel like he might be able to breathe for a few minutes.

It was the first time Ellie had been on the property for months. She hadn't even seen the outer walls go up.

"Small," she said as she turned her nose in the air and examined his kitchen. "But there is only one of you. I suppose it will do."

Seth pointed to the basket Priscilla had hung on her arm. "What is in the basket?"

"Banana bread," Ellie said. "Your dat rushed through breakfast because he didn't want to be late for your little frolic. You shouldn't have made it seem so important. He needs a hearty breakfast or his blood sugar crashes. A more thoughtful boy would have let his fater finish his food."

Seth counted his blessings that he hadn't really spoken with Ellie for weeks. He spent all his time with his horses if he wasn't working at the mill. When he did sleep at home, he came in late at night when everyone else was abed. It was easier for him to be away from Ellie, but it troubled him how hard his absence was on the children. Three weeks ago Joshua sported an angry welt on his neck where Ellie had slapped him.

Could his siblings live in a house with bare walls and unfinished floors? He regarded Ellie's hard mouth and piercing eyes. Could they live in a house without affection and kindness?

"Ellie, could we go to the back porch and have a talk?"

She immediately became hostile. Narrowing her eyes, she pressed her mouth into that inflexible line. "It is cold out there."

"Priscilla, take the basket to Dat. We will be right back." Seth motioned in the direction of the back door, making sure Ellie knew he wouldn't take no for an answer.

Ellie led the way, taking small ladylike steps. When Seth shut the door behind them, she turned on her heels to face him. "They told you, didn't they? Probably came to your stable begging for food."

Seth had no idea what she was talking about, but he didn't

interrupt. He would let her dig her own grave. Folding his arms, he pinned her with a stern eye.

Ellie braced her hands on her hips. "Did they also tell you how they tracked mud and snow all over my floor after I spent two hours polishing it? It was a shameful mess. I told those boys that if they wouldn't walk with care in my kitchen, then they couldn't come in at all."

It took all the self-control Seth could muster not to explode with outrage. He pressed his lips together to keep his anger from escaping. Only when he was certain he could control his raw emotions did he speak. "How long was it before you let them eat?"

"What happens between a mother and her children is private. They know better than to tattle to you."

"How long, Ellie?"

"All day. They needed to appreciate how long I spent polishing the floor."

Seth thought he might be sick with fury.

One day last week the boys hadn't come to the stable. They were prisoners, starving in their own home. Seth wanted to growl in frustration for not being there.

He turned from Ellie and leaned against the wall for support. His forced breath was ragged and halting as he thought with horror about what she had done. Was it time for persuasion? Or blackmail? Would Ellie let him have the children if he threatened to tell the police?

"The boys told me nothing. It is irritating how loud a guilty conscience screams, isn't it?"

"You're lying to protect them. How else would you have known?"

"You just told me."

Ellie opened her mouth then clapped it shut as she recognized her mistake. Scowling, she grabbed the doorknob, but Seth pressed his hand against the door so she couldn't open it.

"What do you want?"

Just in time, Seth decided the wiser course of action to be persuasion. If Ellie were backed into a corner, she would refuse to give Seth anything. "I do not aim to chastise you. Die kinner are careless, and you must do what you feel is right." Seth almost choked on his words, but Ellie's expression softened a bit. "You and Dat are barely married, and you have to care for three children. I know it must be hard."

"Not a day goes by that I don't have a headache."

"I want you and Dat to have some time alone, like all newlyweds should. Why could the children not live with me? Then you could have your privacy. You deserve it."

Ellie folded her arms and glared at him suspiciously. "Why would you want them?"

"You and Dat should get more of a chance alone. And I am at the stable so much that I never get to see my brothers and sister. I miss them."

"What about money? I am saving up for a cruise. How much would you want us to give you?"

"Nothing. I will be able to buy enough groceries with the extra money from the horses."

A light turned on in Ellie's eyes, but she proceeded cautiously. "This is a nice big house. The kitchen is almost as big as mine."

"I will bring a stove in once the floor is laid so we will be plenty warm. They could move in next week. Then you and Dat could spend Christmas alone together."

Generosity saturated Ellie's smile. "But you all must come for Christmas dinner. I will make a special Christmas dinner."

And that was that. Seth didn't need to say a word to Dat. Ellie would talk him into it by suppertime.

He opened the door and let Ellie into the house. If he didn't ache so badly for Miriam, he might almost feel relieved.

CHAPTER
THIRTY

Ephraim sat next to Miriam as she hand-stitched the binding on Susie's baby quilt by the light of a lantern. "What do you think about getting married next November?" he said.

Miriam looked up from her sewing as a dull ache settled into her stomach. Ephraim wanted to move so fast. Next November was too soon.

She stuck a pin in the cushion bracelet around her wrist. Six months ago she would have jumped at the chance to move her wedding up a year. Now, something didn't feel right.

She gave him a half smile. "Two years from now. I haven't worked for most of the winter. Surely you can see the wisdom in waiting until we both have more saved up. Bishop Schwartz would approve of that plan."

"There are other ways to get money. You could make quilts to sell."

"Jah, of course."

"What about the foal at Matthew Eicher's? Your dat

bought her as a wedding present. I am sure he wouldn't care if we sold it."

"That is not funny, Ephraim."

He took the quilt from her hands and laid it next to him on the sofa. Then he raised his eyebrows and willed her to make eye contact. "I am not joking. You know how I feel about this. Girls riding horses should not be allowed."

Miriam furrowed her brow. "Both Bishop Schwartz and my dat say it is okay."

"But many districts in other areas do not. Besides, when we marry, you will be too busy with kinner and such to ride. And we will get more money for it if we sell it now."

"I could not think of selling it."

Ephraim stuck out his bottom lip. " 'For of this sort are they which creep into houses, and lead captive silly women.' "

"You are irresistible when you pout," Miriam said. "But this time you will not get your way. And I have both bishops on my side."

"It is discouraging to think that anytime my wife wants to win an argument, she can invoke the name of the bishop who will always take her side."

"Discouraging for you." Miriam giggled. She reached over Ephraim and picked up her sewing.

Susie's quilt was a Cornerstone design made from navy and deep purple squares. Once she completed the binding, Miriam would finish Ephraim's quilt. Overjoyed that she hadn't thrown the squares away, she planned on putting it together this week and next, in time to give it to him for his birthday, December sixteenth.

She thought of Seth's quilt and wondered what had become of it. The familiar twinge of sadness pricked her heart. She had thought that with time her sorrow over Seth would lessen, but the pain seemed to intensify every time she thought of him. Was he eating well? Freezing to death in his stable? How many days before he moved into his unfinished house? At least then he would be warmer than when sleeping in his stable.

Ephraim studied her expression and his lips formed a rigid line. "You're thinking of him again, aren't you?"

"Who?"

"The horse boy. You had that look the day I got you from his farm."

"He was a gute friend to me when I had no other friends. I have not been as gute a friend."

"When we broke up, like as not you latched on to the first person who was nice to you. If you and I had been together, you wouldn't have been friends with him. You need not search elsewhere to find love." He put a hand to his heart. "All you need is right here."

Ach, the breeze blew bitter-cold today. Miriam had bundled up in her heavy black coat with a long wool scarf covering her head and tucked in at the chin, but gloves were no gute when hanging laundry. They got wet and froze solid and made it impossible to maneuver the clothespins. With stiff fingers, she worked as quickly as possible to get the rest of the wash hung. In the winter, it didn't really dry. It froze. Then they would bring it into the house and thaw it out before folding it.

With the last shirt secured on the line, Miriam picked up her basket and made a beeline for the back door, hoping she didn't have to venture out for the rest of the day.

Susie stood at the cookstove tending a pot of soup. She spent most of her day at the main house, especially if Hollow was at work. Her time was close at hand. Yesterday Mamm had declared that the baby had dropped and would be coming any day now. Susie thought she still had at least two weeks.

"Oh," Susie said as Miriam blew through the door. "She just left. I didn't know where you were."

"Who just left?"

"Laura Lambright. She is back from school for a few days. She left a package for you, and I gave her the doll. You could probably still catch her. She walked out less than a minute before you came in."

Miriam deposited her basket on the table and ran out the front door. It took her a moment to realize that the young woman walking down the lane was Laura. She wore a lime-green coat, blue jeans, and midcalf lace-up boots. Her jeans were tucked into her boots, and she looked quite sophisticated.

"Laura! Wait."

Laura turned around. Her black hair fell around her face and brushed her shoulders. In her arms, she carried the doll that Priscilla had given Miriam.

Miriam cut through the snow. "Laura, it is so gute to see you. Do you have time to come in and sit?"

Laura didn't reply. She looked like a schoolteacher who had lost patience with a scholar. Miriam's uneasiness grew. She had been unsure of Laura when they first met, but they had grown to care for each other a great deal. Now an invisible ten-foot wall stood between them.

Miriam glanced at the doll cradled in the crook of Laura's elbow. "Does Priscilla want her doll back?"

"It is very special to Scilla. Someone who doesn't care about it shouldn't think she has a right to have it."

Miriam tried to ignore the hurt that grew inside her, as well as the nagging feeling that she deserved every word. "I do care about it. Priscilla gave it to me when I was very low. Her sacrifice was the sign of a true friend."

"She gave it to you after Ephraim embarrassed you that night at the gathering. So you don't really need it anymore."

"I—I guess not."

"I brought your quilt back. Seth doesn't need it anymore."

Miriam felt dizzy. "He gave it back?"

Bitterness tinged Laura's words. "He doesn't even know I took it. It was stuffed in the top of his closet at home. He doesn't need to be reminded of you every time he sees it. You've hurt him enough, don't you think?"

Mutinous tears stung Miriam's eyes. "How is he?"

"Seth does not want your pity."

Miriam remembered one of the first conversations she and Seth had. *"I hope I am past my own pity, but I cannot abide yours."*

Laura pursed her lips, closed her eyes, and took a deep breath. "Tell me something. Why did you push yourself into our lives like that? Were we the only ones who were nice to you after Yost's arrest? Or were we a charity project? Did you want Seth to feel blessed that you paid attention to him?"

"Nae, you are my friends. My true friends."

Laura laughed, but there was no happiness in it. "This is why, before you, Seth hadn't so much as looked at a girl since Mamm's death. He thinks people will always disappoint him. And you have proved him right. I haven't ever seen him this bad, even when Mamm died. He won't eat, he won't sleep, and he doesn't put two words together to save his life. He spends hours at the stable trying to work himself to death."

Miriam wanted to apologize, to express concern, to be Laura's friend, but she didn't know how to do it without being accused of pity. "I'm sorry," was all she could say.

"The last thing Seth needs is for you to feel sorry for him. Go have a perfect life with your perfect boyfriend. It's exactly what you deserve." With the doll still firmly in her arm, she turned her back on Miriam and trudged away in the deep snow.

Miriam's legs felt like rubber as she silently mourned the death of another friendship.

Laura was wrong. Miriam didn't feel sorry for Seth. She felt sorry for herself.

"I will be back to get you after group therapy," Yost said. He stopped the buggy in front of Ephraim's house. "Will that give you enough time yet?"

"Plenty. We are eating supper and having cake." Miriam anxiously fingered the corners of the box in her lap.

"He will like it, Miriam," Yost said. "Your quilts are famous."

"Ach, not famous." She fluffed the bow on top for the tenth time. "I am afraid he will think it is too fancy."

"Seth...Seth loved his quilt."

"He gave it back."

Yost turned pale. "Miriam, I think I have made a terrible mistake."

Miriam narrowed her eyes and prepared herself for whatever Yost had to confess. "What happened?"

"I visited Ephraim and asked him to give you another chance. Three times. I thought it was the right thing."

"It is all right. Ephraim told me."

"I hoped being back together with Ephraim would make you happy, but it hasn't. You act as if the sun will never shine again."

The hollow space in Miriam's chest grew bigger. "Things with Ephraim will get better. They are new yet. So much has changed since the summer. I think I seem sad because—"

"Because Seth loves you."

"Did he tell you that?"

"Anyone can see it plain enough."

Miriam rubbed her forehead. "I miss him. He is the only person who ever seemed interested in what I had to say."

Yost waved a hand dismissively. "I've been to group therapy. You can pay someone to listen to you."

"You are right. It is selfish to think of him like that. I like being with him, and he liked being with me. He was my friend."

"Maybe you love him."

Miriam couldn't focus on Yost hard enough to make sense of that comment. Right now she was working on loving Ephraim. It wouldn't be fair to him to think on another boy. Even Seth. With no idea how to respond to her brother, she jumped out of the buggy.

"I don't want you to pay for my mistake for the rest of your life," Yost said.

"You have done nothing wrong. I am grateful that you cared enough about me to try with Ephraim. It must have been humiliating."

"It was."

Miriam blew her brother a kiss and trudged up the path to Ephraim's house with a nagging feeling that Ephraim wasn't going to like her quilt. She'd chosen the yellow and burgundy to brighten up the drab tan, but somewhere deep in her heart, she harbored a bit of spite that day for his rejection of the fabric she wanted to buy. If he didn't appreciate the quilt, it would be her own fault.

Ephraim threw open the door before she even knocked. "Presents! More presents." He took the box from Miriam and laid it on the table next to his plate.

"Welcome," Ephraim's mamm called while pulling a pan of

hot rolls from the cookstove. "We are almost ready for supper, if these boys would wash up."

"Gute day?" Miriam said to Ephraim.

"Mamm made me German apple pancakes for breakfast, and Dat gave me some cash." He leaned close to Miriam's ear. "A hundred dollars to add to our wedding savings." He winked and smiled.

Knowing what Ephraim expected of her, Miriam smiled back.

"I want to take him camping for his birthday," Freeman said.

Ephraim shook his head. "Winter camping? No, thank you. Too cold."

"Nae," Freeman said. "There is a wonderful-gute spot at Baker's Lake. A place where the boulders almost form a cave. It is sheltered and nobody can find it unless they know exactly where it is."

Ephraim glanced at Miriam. "It doesn't matter where it is. You are not right in the head to think that sounds fun in the winter."

Ephraim's mamm placed the steaming rolls on the table. "Wash up, or you'll get no pudding."

She must have spent all day cooking. In addition to fresh rolls, there were candied yams, corn, pork chops, pickled cucumbers, and pudding in individual bowls with whipped cream on top.

At supper, the four boys were loud and obnoxious, but no one got the wooden spoon. Nothing would be allowed to dampen the mood of the festive evening.

Before he started in on the pudding, Freeman said, "Open your present, Ephraim. I want to see what Miriam got you."

Miriam's heart beat faster. Ephraim's dat was more conservative than Ephraim was. Would any of the family like it?

MIRIAM'S QUILT

Ephraim scooted his chair from the table and reached under his seat, where he had deposited Miriam's gift. Miriam ignored the breathless feeling that came over her.

"For me?" Ephraim teased as he lifted the quilt from the box.

"Hold it up," his mamm said.

Ephraim spread the quilt and held it high so his family could look at it. She had designed each Nine-Patch either burgundy-and-tan or yellow-and-tan. The patterned squares alternated with the plain tan that Miriam thought gave it a simple charm.

"That is quite an eyeful," Ephraim's dat said.

"A Nine-Patch. How pretty." His mamm grabbed one corner and examined the stitching. "Look at how she stitched the squares. A small heart in the middle of each one."

Ephraim shaped his lips into a funny little twist. "Men don't notice things like that, Mamm. But I like the tan. I picked it out myself, you know."

Miriam's throat sank to her toes. Ephraim's tempered enthusiasm was obvious.

"It has the perfect country look to it," his mamm said. "That is the kind of quilt that tourists are looking for. Very typical Amish. And skillfully stitched, Miriam."

Ephraim studied his mamm's face, and Miriam could see the wheels in his head turning. He folded the quilt in his lap and ran his fingers over the stitches. In a matter of seconds, he seemed to like it better. "It must have taken you hours."

"Susie helped me with the quilting even though her time is almost at hand."

Ephraim cleared his throat. "Thank you. This is a fine birthday gift. Now I am doubly curious to see what you will bring me for Christmas."

Since it was Ephraim's birthday, he got to pick the after-supper game. Miriam hated his favorite game, "Life on the Farm," but she feigned enthusiasm. Besides, Yost would be here soon and save her from having to play a whole game that could last for hours. She glanced out the window as they sat down to play in hopes that simply watching for him would inspire Yost to hurry up.

Miriam slid onto the sofa, confused at her own discontent. Why were her emotions so jumbled? Six months ago she would have willingly played any game Ephraim wanted just for the chance to sit next to him and gaze into his handsome face. She had jealously spent every moment she could with him and rearranged her life to fit his. How could feelings that deep ever die?

They couldn't. Surely she wasn't that shallow.

So why was the thought of spending more time in this house unappealing to her?

Miriam rolled the dice.

"How many cattle do you want to buy, Miri?" Ephraim said.

"Oh, um, how much money do I have?"

"We just started, silly. You have ten thousand dollars and no cattle."

Too much noise here. How could she reason through such questions when Freeman bragged about how many girls liked him and Ephraim's dat insisted that they pay attention to the game?

She wondered what Seth's opinion would be. Although he would never in a million years believe it, he was very smart. He had an exceptional understanding of human nature and why people did what they did. He'd be able to tell her what went on inside her own head.

The urge to cry took Miriam by surprise. Seth would never share his wisdom with her again.

Ephraim drew a card for her. "Miri, one of your cows just got shot by a hunter. At this rate, you'll never get to sixty cows."

Miriam smiled weakly, trying to pretend she was having the time of her life.

Freeman held out his hand. "I just passed the barn. Give me a milk check."

Two hours later, Miriam had never longed so badly for a telephone. Had Yost's group therapy session gone that late? Her only hope for deliverance was that Freeman would win two more cows and the game would mercifully end. Ephraim laughed when she went broke paying taxes, but she merely laid down her money and fell back into the sofa.

He furrowed his brow. "You feeling okay? You're not one to get upset when you lose."

"I suppose I am tired. It is almost ten."

"I thought Yost was coming to pick you up."

"He's very late. Maybe he forgot."

Ephraim counted his money. "I think I can beat Freeman with two more times around the board. Let us finish and I'll take you home."

Her unhappiness made Miriam feel sleepy. She did not want to figure out why she was unhappy. She wanted to go home. She couldn't even rest her head on Ephraim's shoulder or tuck herself under his arm while he finished the game. Touching was strictly forbidden. She rested her head on the plump arm of the sofa and nodded off to sleep.

It seemed like three seconds later that Ephraim shook her. "Wake up. Yost is here."

"What time is it?"

Ephraim grinned sheepishly. "After eleven. The game went longer than I expected. But I retired first. Yost says your sister had her baby."

Miriam sat up with a start. "She did? Boy or girl? Is everything okay?"

"I don't know. Yost is waiting in the buggy."

Miriam grabbed her scarf from the chair and hooked up her coat. "Will you come tomorrow to see the baby?"

Ephraim rubbed the late-night whiskers on his chin. "We have a big shipment coming in."

"Come after work."

"I can't make it tomorrow."

Miriam was in too much of a hurry to make sense of him. If he didn't want to see Susie's baby, she would have to argue with him about it later.

CHAPTER
THIRTY-ONE

"Four hours," Mamm said, cuddling her new granddaughter in her arms. "Four hours of labor is short for your sixth child. Unheard of for the first. What a blessing."

Miriam reached out and stroked the fuzz on top of the baby's head. There wasn't much, but what hair she had glowed the color of Miriam's, light, golden brown. Mamm had wrapped her in a receiving blanket with her arms pinned tightly to her side, just the way babies liked it. Little Rose Lynn's eyes were closed and her pink rosebud lips twitched slightly as if she were in the middle of a pleasant dream. Miriam marveled at a newborn's ability to sleep. This baby wouldn't have been awakened by a crack of thunder directly over the house.

The local midwife, Miriam King, their cousin Kate's mother-in-law, had delivered Rose Lynn right there in the dawdi house at nine thirty last night. Yost had been sent to fetch the midwife and hadn't picked up Miriam from Ephraim's until the baby came.

Susie lay on her pillow as if her head were too heavy to lift. She shifted uncomfortably in bed and rested her forearm over her eyes. "Miriam King says next time I must send for her at the first labor pain or she might not get here in time. She said my time was very easy for a first one. Oh, Mamm, if that was easy, I hope I never know what hard is. I thought I would die."

Mamm handed Rose Lynn to Miriam and pulled the covers tight around Susie's shoulders. "Cum, we will care for the baby and let you sleep."

They tiptoed into the little sitting room of the dawdi house outside Susie's bedroom and shut the door. Hollow stood at the sink washing dishes. The baby seemed to draw him like a magnet. He wiped his hands and stood at Miriam's side instantly, caressing the baby's cheek with the back of his finger.

"She is so beautiful. Like her mother."

Mamm gave Rose Lynn a kiss and went to the front door. "I must see to that mountain of laundry from last night. Let me know if you need help with the baby."

Miriam turned the baby from the cold air as Mamm opened the outside door. Once Mamm shut the door, Miriam sat on the sofa with the baby cuddled tightly in her arms.

Hollow sat next to her and placed the quilt Miriam had made for them over the already-bundled baby. "I didn't think I could ever love anyone the way I love this baby."

"She is a precious gift from heaven, to be sure."

"I want you to know it makes no difference to me that I am not the man who got Susie with child. I will be the true father. A true father loves the child's mother. And I love Susie with all my heart."

"I can't imagine the boy who did this loved her at all, but he must have convinced her he did."

Hollow watched Miriam's face before looking away. "She told me it happened in a cave."

"A cave?"

"At Baker's Lake. They met there secretly several times before the boy, whoever he was, convinced her that he loved her and talked her into it. I haven't even told Susie this, but I went to Baker's Lake and found the place and filled it with rocks. Seven wheelbarrows full." Hollow stood and turned his gaze out the window. "I am still grieved about what happened to my Susie. But I am trying hard to forgive the man who did it. I want you to know that I am trying very hard."

So am I, thought Miriam.

Someone knocked softly on the door, and Hollow opened it. Seth Lambright stood on the threshold as tall and handsome as ever. Miriam thought her heart would dance out of her chest and skip down the lane.

Hollow threw out his arms and pulled Seth in for a bone-crushing hug. Seth laughed, actually laughed, before he and Hollow let go of each other.

"I came to see the new dat," Seth said before catching sight of Miriam. His guard immediately went up upon spotting her, and his face lost all hint of happiness. "I am sorry to bother you."

His reaction pained her, but sitting with Rose Lynn in her arms, she had nowhere to hide. She kept her moist gaze firmly glued to the baby.

With halting steps, Seth came to her. He held two brown gift bags, one tied with a pink ribbon. He handed the pink one to Hollow before sitting next to Miriam and cooing at the baby. "She is beautiful. What did you name her?"

"Rose Lynn," Hollow said. "Seven pounds, three ounces."

Miriam found her voice, low and scratchy. "Would you like to hold her? Or are you uncomfortable?"

Seth put down his bag and held out his arms. "I took care of Scilla every day."

When his mother died.

Seth was seventeen years old when Priscilla became his baby, his responsibility. That was one of the things she treasured about him. He had a heart for the children.

As she gently passed the baby to Seth, her hands brushed across his arms. She suddenly became very aware of his warmth, his strength. As she expected, he cradled Rose Lynn in his arms as naturally as any seasoned mother.

Miriam studied his face. His eyes filled with unmistakable tenderness as he stroked Rose Lynn's cheek. Loosening the blanket, he nudged one of her tiny arms out of the folds. He placed his pinky in her hand, and she immediately wrapped her fingers around it.

"I love how every part is perfectly formed," he said to Hollow. "There is nothing more beautiful than a baby." He inclined his head to the bag. "Open it."

Hollow sat down on the coffee table in front of the sofa. "You needn't have brought a gift."

"Priscilla and I have been looking forward to this baby for a long time."

Hollow reached into the bag and pulled out a baby blanket almost an exact duplicate of the one Miriam and Priscilla had made for Priscilla's doll, except that this one measured larger and had four Nine-Patch squares instead of one.

"Priscilla sewed it together on the machine and I helped her stitch it."

Miriam's heart melted. The corners didn't match up, the fabric puckered in several places, and the stitches were impossibly wide, but Priscilla and Seth must have worked very hard. It was a labor of love that couldn't have been more beautiful if the best quilter from Holmes County, Ohio, had made it.

"It's wonderful," Miriam said.

Seth kept his eyes turned to Hollow.

"Denki," Hollow said. "Susie will be thrilled. Send Priscilla our gratitude. Better yet, bring her to see the baby and she can help us wrap her in it."

With the baby comfortably sleeping in his arms, Seth settled deeper into the sofa, and Hollow asked him about his horses. Miriam didn't really listen. She trained her eyes on Seth, sitting so close and yet so distant. His ebony hair fell carelessly over his ears and made a sharp contrast with his stormy gray eyes. The muscles of his neck and shoulders continued down his arms, attesting to his quiet strength. No harm would come to the baby while his powerful arms enfolded her like that.

Miriam heard only the low hum of their voices as the emptiness in her heart grew to fill her entire soul. The emptiness gave way to a longing so powerful she almost couldn't bear it.

A longing for what?

For home and family? For a new baby to call her own? Or a longing for the love that used to fill her life?

The confusion twisted her around until she couldn't see straight.

Did she long for Ephraim? Or Seth? She couldn't begin to understand her own heart, but when she pictured her own baby in her mind, she saw Seth holding him instead of Ephraim.

She sprung to her feet. "I should see to Susie."

Hollow studied Miriam's face. Unease darkened his features. "I will go. Give me the baby. I will lay her in the cradle by her mother. She is exhausted, too, from all this excitement."

Seth handed over the baby and Hollow went into Susie's room and abandoned both of them.

Seth picked up the other bag and looked doubtfully at Miriam. "I came to see you today as well. But don't worry. I hope it will be the last time I pester you."

"Don't say that."

"I came to apologize for Laura." He reached out a hand as if to touch her, thought better of it, and let it fall to his side. "I would never for the world want your feelings hurt. She brought the doll home and confessed the whole story. I am very, very sorry."

"I deserved it."

Seth's intense gaze pierced through her skull. "Nae, you did not. You cannot change the feelings in your heart anymore than I can. Her unkindness to you was in defense of me, and even though her anger was wrong, I love her for wanting to protect my feelings."

"Me too. She is a gute sister."

He reached his hand into the bag and pulled out Priscilla's doll. "Will you take this back? Priscilla cried when she thought you didn't want it anymore."

Miriam all but burst with gratitude. "I didn't want Laura to take it, but she was so determined."

"She gave in when she saw how upset Priscilla became. Priscilla thought you rejected her when you rejected her gift, especially since she sacrificed so much to give it to you."

"But I didn't give it back."

"I know. Priscilla understands."

Miriam took Priscilla's doll and the blanket that went with it. She pressed it to her heart. "Thank you for bringing it back even though you didn't want to come."

The sadness sank deeper into his eyes. "Nae, I did not."

Miriam lowered her head and studied the floorboards. His words stung to her very bones.

Seth stepped far away from her. They could have been on

separate sides of the ocean. "I must go now. My family will pray for the baby that she will be healthy and strong, Lord willing. And Susie too."

Miriam nodded and tried to clear the lump from her throat. She found her voice to ask the question that had been gnawing at her ever since Seth stepped into the house. "Do you—do you want the quilt back?"

He gripped the doorknob, and Miriam could see the muscles in his arm tense as if he were fighting himself. "No." He didn't look at her as he stepped out into the cold, leaving the door open behind him as he walked away.

She had to get away from the house before someone heard her. Without a coat, she raced to the swing by the barn, slumped into the snow-covered seat, and bawled like a wounded calf.

You rejected Priscilla when you rejected her gift.

He didn't want the quilt back. The quilt she had made out of his mother's fabric. The quilt that made him weep with unspoken memories. The quilt he said he would use every day to remind him of precious relationships and his blessed life.

He didn't want it back.

It was the cruelest rejection of all.

CHAPTER
THIRTY-TWO

One week before Christmas. Miriam had the afternoon shift at work. She took the bus, and thankfully it dropped her right on the shop's corner. It was a cold day. If she had to walk more than a few hundred feet, she thought her face might freeze off before she got there.

Miriam did a double take as she passed the window of the quilt shop. Martha had rearranged the display. The quilt Miriam had made for Ephraim hung from the very top and spread the length of the front case! Either that or one that looked just like it. She pressed her face against the glass and winced when the icy surface touched her skin. Each square of the burgundy-and-yellow Nine-Patch had a small heart stitched in the center of it. She looked at the name card sitting next to the quilt.

Made by Apple Lake's Own Miriam Bontrager. $400.

Breathless and flustered, Miriam ran into the store and let the door slam behind her. "Martha, how did you get my quilt?"

"What do you mean?"

Miriam pointed her finger at the display. "A quilt I made is hanging in the front window. Where did it come from?"

Martha raised an eyebrow. "Ephraim said you wanted to sell it. He came in last night at closing time. Doesn't it look charming? I'll have no trouble selling that one."

Miriam thought she might explode with indignation. Ephraim wanted to sell his birthday present?

The bell tinkled as she nudged the shop door open again. "Martha, can you spare me for ten minutes?"

"Jah, but don't freeze out there."

Miriam bolted down the sidewalk in the direction of Neuenschwanders' warehouse. Her shoes filled with snow, but she didn't even notice the cold. She stomped into the office without saying hello to Amanda, the secretary, and raced past the front counter into the stuffy warehouse that smelled of wet cardboard and freshly cut pine.

"Ephraim!" she yelled, not even bothering to look for him. If he knew what was good for him, he would come to her. "Ephraim Neuenschwander, come here this minute."

Freeman stuck his head around the corner of one of the aisles and then disappeared.

"Don't try to hide from me. I see two pairs of feet."

Ephraim stepped into view with his hands in his pockets and a mischievous grin on his face. "I wasn't trying to hide. Just wondering what wild woman was screaming at me."

Miriam was in no mood for his good mood. "Ephraim Neuenschwander, why is your birthday present for sale at Martha's quilt shop?" Her frustration caught up with her, and she unwillingly burst into tears.

"Now, hold on there. Nothing to cry about. She gave me three hundred dollars for it. Doesn't that make you happy?"

"If you reject my gift, you reject me," she said, not knowing why those particular words sprang to mind.

Ephraim growled. "Don't be ridiculous. Freeman, get out of here and quit listening to our conversation."

Freeman, with that arrogant smirk, came out of hiding and headed to the front office.

"Sit here on this box," Ephraim said, pulling up a crate and dusting it with his hand. "You are a gute quilt maker. The quilt is very pretty, even Mamm said so, but you knew I did not want a fancy quilt."

Miriam wiped her eyes. Jah, she knew.

"Can't you see that I am being practical? It will never be used in our home, the home of the bishop's daughter and the minister's son, and if we can get some money for it, then it is truly a wonderful gift."

"The value of the gift is not in the money you can get for it."

"Nae, the value in a gift is how it will benefit the recipient. And that quilt benefits both of us. Three hundred dollars buys a lot of wood for a house."

"I suppose it does," Miriam said, sniffling away the last of her tears.

"Did you really give me that quilt?" he said. "Because if it is mine, then I should do what I want with it."

"Yes, of course. I freely gave it to you."

"Why?"

"Because it was your birthday."

"Then, if you love me, you'll understand why I did this. I want our hearts to be knit together as one, of one mind and one flesh. I did this for us." He handed her a tissue from his pocket. "Now, dry your eyes and walk out of here with your head held high. I do not want Amanda to think we had a fight. That's my good girl."

Miriam sloshed out of the warehouse in her soaking-wet shoes. The walk back to the shop was miserable. She shook violently by the time she walked through the door. Martha insisted she take off her stockings and sit in the back by the stove to warm her feet.

Ephraim said the bishop's daughter would never use such a quilt in her home. Was he right? He was so persuasive when she was with him, but when she had time alone to think, she began to doubt everything. How many other things would Ephraim think she must give up because she was the bishop's daughter and he the minister's son?

She craned her neck to look at her quilt hanging in the front window. Martha had arranged it very nicely, and Miriam had no energy left to be angry with Ephraim. The quilt was his to do with what he wanted, and now they had an extra three hundred dollars because of it. He had done a very sensible thing.

The growing emptiness in her chest threatened to cut off her air.

Ephraim had done a very sensible thing.

"I LOVE MY NEW ROOM," Joshua said, as he jumped up and down on his mattress.

Seth and the boys made up their beds by the light of the small kerosene lantern. Although bedtime was two hours ago, the boys bounced on their beds and danced around their new bedroom as if they had just woken up from ten good hours of sleep. Priscilla had conked out over an hour ago in her room, tucked into her own bed with the covers pulled tightly against her chin in the way that she liked them.

"Help me get the sheets on," Seth said, "so you can go to sleep. It has been a long day."

Although he had been a recipient of it all his life, Seth

marveled at the kindness of his neighbors. Nathaniel King had helped him salvage some old barn wood, and twelve men gave Seth a hand with laying, staining, and sealing the floor. It would last many long winters in his new house.

Then this morning, several men from the district appeared at his dat's house with wagons and buggies and loaded up beds and boxes to transport them to Seth's new house. Once the men unloaded everything, they had set up beds, brought in the new stove, and even chopped firewood. Seth found it impossible to express enough gratitude.

Jacob sat on his bed, his legs dangling off the side. "Can we eat in the new kitchen tomorrow?"

"Jah, but we don't have a table yet, so we will have to eat on the floor."

"Can we help with the horses?"

"After school."

"When will Laura be here?" Jacob asked.

Seth shook out the sheet and let it float to the bed. "Joshua, tuck in your side. Laura must work on Christmas Eve. She will be home on Christmas Day, and then she can stay with us for almost two weeks."

They piled three blankets on each bed. Nights were mighty cold, and Seth hadn't had time to put coverings on the windows yet. Once the beds were made, Seth and his two little brothers fell across the bed and lay by each other, propping their chins on their elbows.

Jacob patted Seth's hand. "Can we have pancakes tomorrow? Do you know how to make pancakes?"

"He used to make them every day after Mamm died," Joshua said.

Jacob cupped his hand over his mouth and whispered, "Can I eat as many as I want?"

"You can eat until you are so full, Joshua will have to roll you to school."

Jacob screamed in delight.

"Shhh," said Seth. "Don't wake Scilla."

Joshua rolled over on his back. "Seth, are you glad we are living here now?"

"More than you can imagine."

"You don't seem glad. How come you don't smile ever?"

Joshua nodded wisely. "It's because of Miriam. Laura says she is a snob. What is a snob?"

Seth sighed. If he could manage to not hear Miriam's name ever again, he might have a chance of getting over her. If he lived in another district or never saw another quilt, he could probably go for hours at a time not thinking about her.

"Can I tell you a secret?" Seth said.

"Okay."

"I love Miriam more than I love horses."

"I knew that," Joshua said. "It's not hard to tell."

Seth put his arm around his brother. "When I hear her name, it makes me sad because I remember how much I love her."

To Jacob, the solution seemed obvious. "Why don't you marry her?"

"She wants to marry someone else."

Joshua, it seemed, knew everything. "Ephraim Neuenschwander, Laura says."

"So, you see, it makes me sad."

"But are you going to feel better?" Jacob patted Seth's cheek.

"It would help me more than anything if you didn't ever say her name or talk about her."

"Even Priscilla? Priscilla talks about her all the time."

"Even Priscilla. If you did that, I might be able to forget her and stop loving her."

Joshua sat up and shook his head. "I don't think you will ever stop loving her."

"Why not?"

"Because she is pretty and nice and when you talk about her, you get a look in your eyes that says, 'I love her, I love her, I love her.' You should talk to Miriam and say, 'I'm nicer than Ephraim and I have more horses. Choose me.' "

"But she wouldn't. Ephraim is handsome, and she has liked him for a long time. He would win."

"Laura says you are handsome."

Seth tried to smile so the anxiety would disappear from Joshua's eyes. "Not as handsome as either of you. I bet the girls chase you on the playground at school."

Jacob giggled. "Mandy Herschberger tries to kiss him."

"She does not," Joshua protested.

For a moment, Seth wished he were back in school where some cute little girl might find him worthy to chase around the playground. In third grade a broken heart could be mended with a bowl of ice cream and a game of kick-the-can with friends. As a grown-up, things were not so easily put to rights. With all this talk of Miriam, Seth despaired of ever feeling whole again.

"Hello, Miriam." Alvin Eicher stabbed his pitchfork into a bale of hay and waved to her from his perch above. Alvin, a sturdy young man of twenty-six, had a new wife and a baby on the way. "Didn't expect to see you."

Miriam stamped the snow off her boots and let her eyes adjust to the light. She led Daisy to an empty stall, filled the small trough with water, and swung the door shut. Two of Matthew's grandsons pitched hay above her. The hay dust danced in the air and caught the light streaming through a window in the loft, and Miriam found the rhythmic swish and plop of the hay oddly comforting.

Matthew Eicher's place was double the size of Seth's farm. Matthew had recently expanded his stables, and they were painted a muted shade of country red. Miriam had been there three times to see her foal. With the baby and Ephraim and Christmas preparations, it had been a feat to manage even that many visits. But being with her horse seemed to be the only time Miriam didn't feel that hard knot right behind her eyes, as if she were concentrating too hard on something that eluded her.

But even then, being with the filly wasn't the same as it used to be. She missed the colt's boundless energy and the way the two foals played together in the pasture. Matthew was old, a great-grandfather seven times over. Two sons and four grandsons helped with his horses and small herd of cattle. Matthew welcomed Miriam anytime to see her filly but was absent or busy when she came to visit. Too much work to do to pay heed to a young woman who loved horses. Miriam never felt so alone as when she went to see her horse at Matthew Eicher's stables. No matter how busy Seth was, he had always taken a minute to tell her a story about what the horses had done that day or teach her about the care of the animals. He loved the horses more than she did, and she found his enthusiasm infectious.

It wasn't the same. It would never be the same.

The day turned out, as usual, frigid and humid. Wisconsin in the winter had one type of weather.

"I know it is Christmas Eve," she said to Alvin. "But I might not get back here until Second Christmas."

Alvin propped his hat farther up on his head and scratched his temple. "But it wonders me why are you here when your filly ain't."

Miriam raised an eyebrow. "Where else would she be?"

"Dawdi sold her to an Englischer yesterday."

Alvin must have been mistaken. "Sold her? Why would he sell my horse?"

"I'm sure he mentioned you wanting her sold. Did you not?"

"No, I never told him such a thing."

"Now, that don't seem right, do it?" Alvin fingered the beard at his chin. "I do believe Ephraim Neuenschwander stopped by last week with your message for Dawdi. Was he mistaken?"

Ephraim sold her horse?

But he knew! He knew how important riding was to her. He knew that if she couldn't ride, she'd wither up like a houseplant that never got watered.

How could he have done such a thing? And without even telling her?

Miriam forced herself to breathe. She knew why.

He'd suggested selling the horse once and had met too much resistance. So he decided to count on being forgiven. It had worked with the quilt. She had given him no reason to believe it wouldn't work with the filly.

Ephraim had sold her horse.

Of course he had. She should only have been surprised that it had taken him so long.

Stunned, Miriam waved her hand in Alvin's direction and mumbled something incoherent. Alvin must have been satisfied with her response, because he picked up his pitchfork and went back to work.

Miriam stumbled to a renegade hay bale next to one of the

stalls, sat down, and surrendered to the truth. Ever since she'd gotten back together with Ephraim, there wasn't a day when she hadn't felt angry, hurt, or confused. Now she simply felt numb, exhausted by the struggle within herself and too weary to do anything about it.

She thought of her filly and of her burgundy-and-tan Nine-Patch quilt. She thought of Ephraim's boyish grin and playful laugh. All were lost to her.

Since she'd turned ten years old, her life had revolved around Ephraim. That was why, when he'd rejected her, she felt as cold and hollow as an empty silo in January. She hadn't really known herself separate from him.

Today she did.

In a flash of insight, she saw so clearly that the truth almost blinded her. She had been in love with the idea of marrying the minister's son, the handsomest, most desirable young man in the district, rather than actually being in love with Ephraim himself. Why had she not realized long before now?

Just in time, she saw how Ephraim used his piety as a way to get what he wanted. She had relied on his superior knowledge of the Bible and the Ordnung when they made a decision or had a disagreement. Searching her memories over the years, Miriam could only remember a handful of times they had disagreed. Ephraim, without fail, got his way. She always let him have his way.

She wanted to fall to her knees right there in the stable and thank the good Lord for what she once thought were her darkest days after Ephraim rejected her. His absence had given her a chance to understand herself, to be Miriam Bontrager instead of Ephraim Neuenschwander's intended.

It had taken humble, gentle Seth to teach her a better way. Miriam raised a hand to her heart. The thought of him stole her breath. She hadn't appreciated what he had done for her. He always asked her opinion, didn't force his wishes on her, never told her what to do.... And when he disagreed with her, he told her, with plain honesty and complete trust. His confidence gave birth to faith in herself and the ability to hear her own voice instead of being Ephraim's echo.

Sitting on her bale of hay, staring at the empty stall where her filly used to be, Miriam pictured a future without Ephraim. The prospect frightened her momentarily before her pulse danced with breathless excitement.

She didn't need Ephraim. She didn't want Ephraim. The feeling intensified with every beat of her heart.

Unable to remain still, Miriam jumped up from the hay bale. She had to tell him, to finally set herself free. Would he even care? Of course he would care. How would he increase his income without selling off all her worldly possessions?

Miriam let those unworthy thoughts die a welcome death. Shame on her for letting bitterness ooze into her heart. Ephraim only did what he did because he didn't know better, and she had indulged him.

Ephraim would be hurt, but she hoped he would come to see that they were not meant for each other. She could never make him happy, and he would make her miserable.

Miriam led Daisy out of the stable. The old horse would probably appreciate the warmth of a trot on a cold day. She loosened her hold on the reins and let Daisy go as fast as she wanted. Even an old horse needed to feel the wind through her mane occasionally.

It was almost dinnertime. Ephraim would be at the warehouse, loading pallets and helping customers with last-minute Christmas needs. She turned Daisy toward Apple Lake.

Neuenschwanders' warehouse stood on the outskirts of the two-street town. They dealt mostly with wood and building supplies along with some plumbing fixtures specifically for the Amish. Miriam remembered the last time she went there and the way Ephraim regarded her as if she were a five-year-old throwing a tantrum. She shook her head. How had she been so blind to Ephraim's treatment of her?

Today she strode through the door, her anticipation mingled with raw dismay at having to face him. She wanted to be charitable but feared her anger would conquer her better impulses.

Please, dear Heavenly Father, she prayed, *help me show love.*

Amanda sat at her desk, which consisted of a smooth countertop propped on top of two sturdy shipping boxes.

Miriam walked toward the warehouse door. "Is Ephraim here?"

"Jah, in the back."

Miriam strolled into the warehouse, surprised at her own calm. Was it the calm before or after the storm? She followed the boisterous voices until she found Freeman and Ephraim in the middle of one of the aisles, opening boxes. They both looked up as she came into view.

Freeman took one look at her face and showed all his teeth when he smiled. "Oh, you are in trouble now, brother."

Ephraim didn't seem so sure of himself. His smile didn't quite reach his eyes as he spoke. "How is my favorite girl in the world?"

"Can we talk?" she said.

If it were possible, Freeman's smile grew wider. "I told you she'd be mad."

Miriam found it irritating that Freeman knew more about her life than she did, but she let the annoyance slide off her like mud off a greased pig.

"Is there somewhere we can speak privately?"

The corner of Ephraim's lip turned down in exasperation. "Freeman, go."

"Is there somewhere else? I'd rather not have what I say echo for three blocks."

"Okay," Ephraim said with long, drawn-out syllables. He motioned to a small office at the back of the building. As they walked he studied her face, as if trying to guess what she thought and how mad she really was.

The office window framed a lovely scene outside with the snow piled in flowing drifts and a wood fence that stood guard at Weavers' orchards. The bare trees, piled precariously with new snow, pointed to the sky as if bidding Miriam to look up and not be afraid.

Cardboard boxes lined one wall of the office and a long table stood on the other end, leaving enough room for Ephraim and Miriam to stand but little else. Miriam backed up to the window and put three or four feet between her and her onetime intended.

As soon as Ephraim shut the door, he held up his hands in mock surrender. "I guess you found out about the filly."

She felt a hitch in her breathing as the pain of loss finally caught up to her. "Why would you sell her when you know how much she means to me?"

He actually had the nerve to grin. "It's easier to ask for forgiveness than for permission?"

She pressed her lips together and stared at him.

Ephraim rolled his eyes and gave her the look of exasperation he thought she deserved. "One of us had to be practical. My wife won't be galloping all over Apple Lake on horseback. You're the bishop's daughter, for goodness' sake. Besides, you won't have time for such vanity when we marry." Her expression must have told him he wasn't gaining ground. "It will make you feel better when you find out how much I sold her for."

"I don't care about the money."

"It will buy a lot of wood for a new house." He huffed a sigh as if they were finished discussing the subject. "There is a piece of land a few hundred yards from Dat's that we can build a house on. It could be finished before we marry. Isn't that wonderful?"

She hadn't wanted the anger to broil inside her as it did. Taking several deep breaths, she willed her internal temperature to cool down. She turned and looked out the window and concentrated on the delicate snowflakes drifting to the ground. When she turned back to him, her calm exterior at least resembled what went on inside her. "Ephraim, I don't want to marry you anymore."

He threw up his hands and scowled at her. "Don't overreact, Miri. I shouldn't have to persuade you. In time, you will see that what I did was best for our family. I am the head of the home and the wife must submit to her husband, not question him. Do you believe in the Bible, or don't you?"

Her self-control almost snapped, but she thought of Seth and his even, mild temper. "Thankfully, I am not your wife." She wrapped her arms around her waist. "And I never will be."

"Now you are being childish."

"I mean what I say. I'll not marry you."

Maybe it was because of the set of her mouth or the way the light reflected her eyes, but he finally seemed to grasp that she was in earnest. His eyes narrowed as he regarded her with utter disbelief. "After all I have done for you? You have a no-gute brother and a wicked sister. Your family is the gossip of the entire community, and I still took you back. Is this what you call gratitude?"

"I am grateful to you, Ephraim. I'm grateful that when you

sold my horse, I finally came to my senses and recognized the truth."

"The truth? What—what are you talking about?"

"I do not love you."

That declaration knocked him speechless. Miriam stepped toward the door, and Ephraim actually reached out and grabbed her hand. He had never done that before. That proved enough to stop her in her tracks.

"Don't leave me. I love you."

She pulled her hand away. "Because my dat is bishop. My family might be wicked, but you still love the idea of marrying the bishop's daughter. I am sick to think that it took me so long to realize."

"You think I can overlook your sister's wickedness simply because your dat is bishop?" He paced to the window and back, three steps each way, and his voice rose with every word he uttered. "She cheapened herself in a cave, Miriam. I couldn't be more disgusted. You think I am willing to put up with that girl for a sister-in-law merely because your dat is bishop?"

Like nothing she had ever felt before, rage swirled inside her like a swarm of yellow jackets. How could she have ever loved this man?

"You'll not insult my sister. Susie is gute and kind and—"

She couldn't have been more stunned if a freight train had plowed into her. Narrowing her eyes, she stared at Ephraim in astonishment. "How did you know about the cave?"

His eyes grew wide, and he backed away from her as if she were on fire.

A distant memory nagged at Miriam. Susie's tearful voice rang in her ears. *"He said we were two souls who shared one heart."*

Freeman had spoken those words to her not four weeks ago. *"You and Ephraim are like two souls sharing one heart."*

She looked at Ephraim in horror while she held onto the

edge of the table behind her for support. "Freeman," she whispered.

Alarm leaped into Ephraim's eyes.

The ugly truth rushed her senses like an icy Arctic wind. The relationship between her and Ephraim had brought Susie and Freeman together often. Miriam had thought nothing of it because Freeman treated every girl the same—as if she were blessed that he even paid her any heed. Susie should have seen through his brag. Miriam's stomach sank to her toes. She hadn't seen through Ephraim. How could she expect more from guileless Susie?

A thousand memories stampeded at once. The look between Freeman and Ephraim when Freeman mentioned the cave at Baker's Lake. Susie's dismay at seeing Freeman that day at the market. Ephraim's relief that no one knew the father of Susie's baby.

"At least she will not pull someone else down with her," he had said.

She thought she might choke with an invisible hand at her throat. "You knew."

He lifted his chin defiantly and shook his head, glaring at her as if she were his worst enemy.

Words could not express her contempt, but that didn't stop her from trying. "You hypocrite. You cowardly, lying hypocrite." Miriam knew such accusations were horrible and unChristlike, but she spit them out of her mouth like acrid poison.

Ephraim's nostrils flared and his face turned bright red. "I protected my brother. Freeman is sorry for it, but Susie bears the responsibility—for her willingness, for tempting him. Girls are the guardians of their own virtue."

To keep herself from slapping him hard across the face, Miriam clutched the table behind her until her fingers screamed in pain. She had never felt the scorching heat of rage before, and it frightened her. Fire could so easily burn out of control and consume everything.

"Why did you not make him do his duty and marry her?"

Ephraim wiped a hand across his mouth. "She is responsible for her own fall."

Miriam growled in frustration. How could he lie to himself like this?

She closed her eyes and, by sheer force of will, pictured Susie and Hollow in her mind. She saw Hollow clasping Susie's hand when he told their dat he wanted to marry her. She saw them on their wedding day, so young, so hopeful. She saw Hollow lovingly wrap a blanket around Freeman's daughter to protect her from the cold.

Miriam quietly stepped to the window and rested her flushed face against the cold glass. It would have been worse, much worse, if Freeman had been forced to marry Susie. Miriam would not in a million years wish for her dear sister to be shackled to him for life. Susie would have been irredeemably unhappy. The fire in Miriam's heart cooled to glowing embers. 'All things work together for good to them that love God.' All these months, Miriam had been praying for the fater to step forward for Susie's sake, when Gotte had another, better plan in mind.

Miriam rejoiced that someone far wiser than she ran the universe.

After a few moments of suspenseful silence, she met Ephraim's eyes and regarded him with compassion. He hadn't known how else to protect his brother and his family's name. His reputation was more important to him than even Miriam was. She felt sorry for him.

He looked like a boy who'd been caught smoking in the barn. "You won't tell? No good would come of it for us."

"Or Susie."

He let a sigh of relief escape his lips and moved close to her. "It is better this way."

She nodded, relaxing her expression into a mournful smile.

"I don't love you just because you're the bishop's daughter," he murmured.

Be that as it may, she knew she couldn't love him, any more than Seth could love Ellie's dog, Pookie.

"May the gute Lord be with you," she said, sticking out her hand to shake with Ephraim.

He kept his arms to his side, fists clenched with white knuckles. She lowered her hand, gave him a parting look, and walked out of the office. Her footsteps echoed off the high ceiling as she trudged through the warehouse. Freeman leaned against the front counter visiting with Amanda. He flashed a happy-go-lucky grin as she passed him. "See you tomorrow."

For a moment, indignation simmered in her heart, but she pushed it down and let it keep. Susie was happy now. In time, they both would be able to forgive him and learn to pity a boy who would not bridle his passions.

She lifted the corners of her lips slightly. "Nae, you won't. Good-bye, Freeman."

When she crossed the threshold onto the street, relief soaked her like a spring downpour. After years of planning on Ephraim, after years of believing she loved him, to finally let him go was the most liberating feeling she'd ever known. She exhaled every bad feeling lodged in her heart. The breath turned into a sigh. The sigh became a shout from deep in her soul. Her voice rang through the crisp air and soared to the sky as she threw out her hands and twirled in the empty snow-covered street. Daisy twitched her ears and nodded in Miriam's direction.

Miriam held the reins and ran her hand along Daisy's neck.

The filly was lost to her, and Daisy was old. What would she do when she could not ride Daisy anymore? Did Seth still own the colt?

Without warning, thoughts of Seth rushed into the empty place in her heart and almost knocked her over. She felt as if she were falling from a tall building as her stomach rose to her throat and then her new, bright world crashed at her feet.

How could she have been so blind?

As sure as the sun would peek over the trees on a bright summer morning, she loved Seth Lambright. Why had she not noticed the way he crept into her thoughts and set up a permanent camp in her heart? A thrill of anticipation traveled up her spine. She loved him!

She loved his expression when he was deep in thought, mulling over her problems as if they were his own, gifting her with wisdom and solace. She cherished his rare smile and the way he guarded his heart from grief. She saw the boy—frightened, vulnerable, determined—who had grown into a man who wanted to fix everybody and everything, to make the whole world happy and just and right. And full of love.

Her struggles with Ephraim had torn her heart from its true home. Could she ever hope to return?

"I think I love you."

He'd tried to tell her.

He loved her once. Had he given up on her?

The oppressive sadness returned as abruptly as it had left her.

Seth had sent the filly to Matthew Eicher's stables so he wouldn't be forced to see Miriam. Even when they were together, he might as well have been a stranger. He didn't even want to be her friend.

Laura had returned his quilt without his knowledge, but in the end, he didn't want it back.

If you reject the gift, you reject the giver.

Standing next to Daisy, Miriam leaned her forehead against the saddle. She had lost what she really wanted in pursuit of an illusion. An hour ago, she believed she couldn't feel any lower. Now she had fallen into a hole so deep there was no light at the bottom.

Tears trickled down her face. She willed herself to restrain them, to keep them in check while she stood in the middle of the street where anyone could see her. Ephraim would scold her for her pathetic childishness. Seth would put an arm around her and take her home.

At the memory of Seth's kindness, the rebellious tears would not be suppressed. Her body shook with emotion as a raspy sob broke from her throat. Once her defenses were breached, she couldn't stop the grief. Standing with her head on Daisy's saddle, she released gut-splitting, jaw-aching sobs into the air. The sky swallowed them up and did not answer back.

CHAPTER
THIRTY-THREE

Miriam turned the buggy up Seth's lane. The sky glowed brilliant blue. Not the icy blue when winter tightened its grip on the trees and air, but a bright azure usually reserved for a rare day in June. The stable and pastures spread before her, covered with deep, blindingly white snow. Drifts crowded around the fence posts and sparkled in the rising sun like a meadow of diamonds.

Miriam had awakened early this morning, even before Mamm, to bake two full pans of the cinnamon rolls she had let rise overnight. With the rolls in the cookstove, she hitched up the buggy so it would be ready as soon as the rolls were. She wanted them to be hot when she delivered them. Nothing pleased the senses like the smell of a hot cinnamon roll drizzled with cream cheese frosting and dripping with butter and cinnamon.

She needed every advantage she could get.

Mamm had appeared in the kitchen as Miriam pulled the sweet rolls from the stove.

"The thought!" she had exclaimed. "Leaving your family on

Christmas morning. What about the family? What about breakfast?"

"I must do this, Mamm. I can't live another day with this pressing on me. I can't breathe for the sorrow."

Mamm had given her a firm embrace. "Then, go. Go. No one should live without love." She squeezed tighter. "May the gute Lord go with you."

Miriam pulled the reins and set the brake on the buggy. Smoke curled from the chimney of Seth's cozy clapboard house. A grin fought through her distress. He had even hung a wreath on the door. For a no-nonsense man like Seth, it was an uncharacteristically festive touch.

With her heart pounding wildly, Miriam found it well nigh impossible to breathe. She panted her way to his door with an overflowing basket in one hand and a gift box in the other. The box, wrapped in brown paper and tied with a cherry red ribbon, carried all her hopes. If Seth did not want it, she would be crushed.

A stampede ensued inside as soon as she knocked on the door. Nothing excited a child like a visitor.

Still in their nightclothes, Priscilla, Joshua, and Jacob stood in the hallway and stared at Miriam with wide eyes and open mouths. Joshua slid his hand into Priscilla's.

Miriam didn't expect the tears that sprang to her eyes. "I have missed you all so much."

She heard his voice from the kitchen. The low richness sent a tingle of anticipation down her spine.

"Who is it?"

Joshua shifted his weight and frowned uncomfortably. "I am not supposed to say it," he called back.

"Invite them in so they don't freeze on our doorstep."

Joshua looked at Miriam as if he didn't quite know what to do. "Do you want to come in?"

Miriam nodded and stepped into the long hallway, closing the door behind her. The wooden floors glowed a warm, caramel brown. She looked into the sitting room and down the hallway. Completely bare. No furniture or rugs of any kind.

"Nice to have a visitor on Christmas morning," Seth said as he appeared from the kitchen, a towel draped in his hands. He froze to solid ice when he saw her, his slate gaze riveted to hers. "Miriam."

How could a voice hold both hope and despair at the same time?

At the sight of Seth, so handsome he put Ephraim Neuenschwander to shame, her heart doubled its efforts and pounded violently against her chest. She was sure the echo could be heard throughout the empty house.

"I—I brought presents," she said as everyone stared at her with the intensity of a cat stalking a mouse.

A breathless second passed before Jacob sidled close and slipped his arms around her waist. She steadied her box and basket while giving Jacob an awkward pat with her arms full.

"I knew you would come back," Jacob said. "I told Seth, but he didn't believe me. What is in the basket? It smells good."

Miriam knelt down, placed the box on the floor, and pulled the cloth away from the cinnamon rolls.

Jacob sat close to the basket and breathed in. A smile of delight spread over his face. "Can we have one?"

Joshua, his manner still guarded, put a hand on Jacob's shoulder. "Seth is making us pancakes and bacon."

Seth broke his silence but didn't move from his spot at the edge of the kitchen. "Like as not, they taste better than what I'm making."

Joshua pursed his lips, making him look much older than his ten years. "We should eat Seth's breakfast."

Miriam ignored the twinge of pain that Joshua had not

meant to deliver. Another rejected gift. It didn't bode well for her visit.

A lump lodged in her throat and made it difficult to speak. "These rolls can be eaten anytime you want. I wouldn't want to ruin the special Christmas breakfast you have planned." She reached into the basket for four small packages. "I brought something for each of you, if you like. But I thought Laura would be here."

Seth had grown roots where he stood. "She comes in later today."

Miriam handed the first box to Jacob, who seemed the only person unsuspicious of her presence. "This is for you."

Jacob's face lit up before he turned to Seth. Seth gave him a curt nod, permission enough to open the present. Jacob lifted the lid of the box to reveal the shiny silver whistle she had picked out at the market. Jacob gasped with excitement. "Denki, Miriam. I always wanted a whistle so Seth and Joshua can hear me when I am out in the pasture."

"Only blow it outside," she said. "And not in Joshua's ear."

He grinned and nodded enthusiastically.

Miriam held up a crinkly package and willed Priscilla to come to her. Scilla cracked a smile and extended her hand. Miriam nervously bit her lip as Scilla opened her present. Had she remembered that Seth said he would give Scilla a new doll for Christmas?

"Oooh," said Priscilla as she let the paper fall to the ground. She held the miniature quilt up to the light of the window.

Miriam hadn't had time to design a complicated pattern, just a single pinwheel in the center, tied instead of quilted. Pink and white twirled nicely together on the top.

"Pink is my favorite color," Scilla said.

"Lady Dancing loves her quilt. I thought you might want one for your doll."

Priscilla's face fell. "I don't have a doll."

Miriam glanced at Seth. He melted long enough to give her a wink.

"Come summertime, I can make a doll out of a hollyhock," Priscilla said.

"Gute, then this quilt will be ready for her."

Miriam picked up Joshua's box. He stood with his arms folded, surveying his siblings' gifts. Did he think that if he showed any openness to Miriam, it would be an affront to Seth?

"I would be honored if you would accept this," she said.

He hesitated and then took the present from her hand. He tore the paper casually, as if he couldn't care less what was inside. From his box, he pulled out a smaller wooden box rounded at the top and covered with netting.

"It's a bug catcher," Miriam said, in case he had trouble guessing. "You can put bugs in here and watch them. My brother used to fill his with fireflies."

The corners of Joshua's lips curled up. "Denki. I like bugs."

"I know," Miriam said.

Jacob pointed to the box. "Is that big present for Seth?"

Miriam's pulse, which had slowed to a gallop, raced away from her at the very mention of Seth's name. She picked up the box and stood. "Jah, it is."

He hadn't taken his gaze from her face since he'd come into the hall. Her eyes met his, and she recognized a mixture of confusion and resignation. He came toward her slowly, the towel wadded in his fist like a lifeline.

"You didn't need to bring me a present."

She held it out to him. "It is something to make your life easier."

The first time she had given him the quilt, she had made

him smile when she said that. This time he drew back in alarm, as if perfectly remembering that entire exchange.

He whipped the towel over his shoulder and took the box as if she were giving him poison. After untying the bow, he handed the lid to Joshua. He looked into the box and the hard line of his mouth told her everything she didn't want to know. "Miriam...I—I am sorry, but I told you not to give this back."

Why did she feel so empty when a million pieces of her shattered heart filled her chest? The tears stung her eyes, but neither Seth nor his siblings would see her cry. She would spare herself the humiliation.

"I hoped you might want it," she said, unable to speak above a whisper.

She recognized the concern in his eyes. Always so noble, always trying to make things easy for her. "It's not a matter of wanting, Miriam. I can never have what I truly want."

Her shattered heart made a tiny flutter.

"What do you truly want?"

He took a deep breath and bowed his head in surrender. "You know perfectly well what I want, Miriam Bontrager. This quilt is a reminder of my loss. I am sorry to make you unhappy, but I don't want to be tortured with what might have been." He motioned to Jacob's whistle and Priscilla's new quilt. "These gifts, these gestures only hurt my family. It is unfair to make us grow fond of you, only to lose you."

Compared to the despair of moments ago, renewed hope almost stole her breath. Surely Seth could see her heart hammering on her rib cage in an attempt to get out of her chest.

Priscilla, Joshua, and Jacob stood like statues, staring at their brother and Miriam. If Seth's distress had not been so great and her feelings so tender, the children's expressions would have made her smile. They were witnesses to the unveiling of her heart.

"Will you do me a favor, Seth? It is an enormous favor, but since we are such close friends, I hope—"

His eyes turned stormy. "You have not been listening. I cannot help you."

"You have not heard my favor."

"It does not matter."

She laid a gentle hand over his work-calloused fingers still wrapped around the quilt box. "Will you marry me?"

If she had blown a puff of air at him, it would have knocked him over. Surprise leaped into his eyes, followed closely by a warm glow brighter than the snow outside.

"What does Ephraim think about that?" he murmured, never letting his gaze stray from her face.

"He sees that I am in love with someone who is not him."

One side of his mouth twitched in amusement. "I can live with that."

Unable to resist his deliciously snug embrace, she took the quilt box from him and handed it to Joshua. Then she threw her arms around him and planted a kiss right on his mouth. He jerked backward in surprise before coming to his senses, or losing them, wrapping his arms firmly around her waist and kissing her with so much warmth, she thought she might melt.

Jacob's squeal was so shrill, the dogs within a hundred miles would have been able to hear him.

The kiss didn't last near long enough, but long enough indeed to make Miriam's legs turn to jelly and her pulse set a new speed record.

Seth pulled away from her and took a step back. His breath was shallow and ragged as he steadied himself with the stair railing. "Oh sis yuscht! Do you know how long I've wanted to do that?" The unrestrained joy in his face caused her thumping heart to skip six beats.

With the children's attention still riveted, she tucked herself into his arms again. "I have been so blind and foolish and insensitive. Please forgive me for causing you pain."

He squeezed her tightly. She could feel his heart keeping pace with hers. "Hold your horses. You tell me your faults and think I will jump at the chance to marry you? Shouldn't you hide your bad qualities until after the wedding?"

"You already know my bad qualities. You even point them out to me on occasion."

Seth winced. "You had to bring that up, didn't you?"

She never, ever wanted to let go of him. "Will you please quit stalling and tell me you'll marry me?"

"Maybe I am not looking to marry. I have three children to raise."

Miriam let her mouth fall open in mock indignation. "I proposed in front of your brothers and sister. The least you can do is say yes for all my trouble."

Priscilla looked genuinely worried at Seth's teasing resistance.

Jacob clasped his hands together and jumped up and down. "Seth," he whined, "you have to marry her. You love her more than horses, remember?"

With an enchanting smile, Seth nodded to Jacob and nudged Miriam away to arm's length. Keeping hold of her upper arms, he said, "The man must do the asking."

Laughter bubbled up from deep inside her. "I have waited and waited for you to find the courage."

Seth raised an eyebrow and a playful growl came from his throat.

Miriam pretended to ignore his protest. "I decided that if you were so timid, I must do the asking myself."

His eyes danced. "You will be happy to know that I have found my courage."

Miriam's heart swelled to fill the universe as Seth got down on one knee and clung to both of her hands.

"Miriam, I love you with every part of my being. My life means nothing without you. I will be the happiest man in the world if you agree to marry me."

Miriam looked up to the ceiling as if considering his question.

"Say yes," Priscilla whispered, her sweet face turned eagerly to Miriam.

She wouldn't have believed that such happiness was possible if she hadn't been living it at this very moment. "I love you, Seth. And I will marry you."

The boys and Priscilla screamed in elation and bounced up and down the hall and hugged each other while Seth rose to his feet and slid his arms around Miriam.

"But remember, I asked first," she said.

His lips were within an inch of hers. "I'll never forget." He found her mouth and kissed her until she couldn't remember which way was up. She had to peek to make sure they weren't floating off the ground.

They were called back to reality by Joshua, who cleared his throat when their kiss had gone on long enough. Seth pulled his face away but kept a firm hold on her. Gute thing. She thought she might topple over.

Joshua folded his arms and looked at Miriam and Seth as if they were two misbehaving children. "What is going on here?"

Seth planted a swift, decisive, blissful kiss on her lips. "Would you like to stay for breakfast, Mrs. Lambright?"

"Jah, I would."

Jacob and Joshua took her hands and led her into the kitchen, bare except for the neatly arranged cupboards, smooth countertops, and a wood cookstove resting on a short platform made of stone.

"We sit on the floor," Seth said. "I am afraid there is not one chair in my entire house."

Although his floors were bare, Seth's cupboards were well stocked. He gave her a silly grin when she pulled three bottles of ginger from the spice rack. "No one is going hungry in this house," he said.

Seth made honey-wheat pancakes stuffed with walnuts while Miriam tended the bacon and whipped up a batch of creamy cinnamon syrup. Joshua squeezed orange juice, and Scilla and Jacob swept the floor and kept the stove stocked with wood. The two younger ones spread a sturdy blanket in the middle of the floor and finished it with a lovely set of mismatched plates and forks. They sang Christmas songs while they worked, and Miriam marveled at Seth's deep bass voice that sounded like butter sliding down a stack of hotcakes.

They sang "Silent Night" as Seth flipped the last stack of pancakes onto the tray and carried it to the blanket where his family waited. The song, melodic and simple, echoed through the hall, filling the empty house with the spirit of Christmas. Sitting cross-legged on the floor, they took hands and bowed in silent grace.

Miriam sat next to the man she loved, with her hand in his. Even if she never ceased praying, she could not begin to thank the Lord for guiding her to her new family and showing her the way to overflowing happiness.

The Lord is good. Blessed be the name of the Lord.

DEAR READERS

If you loved *Miriam's Quilt*, could you help spread the word about it? Reviews on **Amazon, Goodreads,** and **Bookbub** not only help us authors but help other readers find us and our books. And please, tell your friends if you liked my book. Word of mouth is invaluable!

For updates on new releases, giveaways, and my other books, please sign up for my email newsletter at JenniferBeckstrand.com. You'll get a free book just for signing up! Be sure to join my Facebook group where I do an interview every other

DEAR READERS

Wednesday night with a sweet or inspirational romance fiction author. You might just discover a new favorite book.

Also be sure to stop by my Facebook page and check out all the news and posts there. I have a great group of readers, and we have a lot of fun!

Thank you for being such amazing readers and fans. I wouldn't be where I am without you!

Jennifer Beckstrand

ABOUT THE AUTHOR

Jennifer Beckstrand is the USA Today and #1 Amazon bestselling romance author of *The Matchmakers of Huckleberry Hill* series, *The Honeybee Sisters* series, *The Petersheim Brothers* series, and *The Amish Quiltmaker* series for Kensington Books. *Huckleberry Summer* and *Home on Huckleberry Hill* were both nominated for the RITA® Award from Romance Writers of America.

Her sweet romantic Western series, *Cowboys of the Butterfly Ranch*, features feisty heroines and tough-as-nails cowboys sprinkled with Jennifer's trademark humor and happy endings. *Dandelion Meadows* is her new, sweet small-town romance, set in a little town in Idaho filled with quirky characters and fresh mountain air.

Miriam's Quilt is the third Amish romance Jennifer ever

wrote, and she is so excited to return to Apple Lake for this new edition of her book.

Jennifer has written thirty-eight Amish romances, three sweet romantic Westerns, two sweet contemporaries, and the nonfiction book, *Big Ideas*. Jennifer is a member of ACFW and is represented by Nicole Resciniti of the Seymour Agency.

She and her husband have been married forty years, and she has six children and eleven adorable grandchildren, whom she spoils rotten.

ALSO BY JENNIFER BECKSTRAND

Cowboys of the Butterfly Ranch

Rachel and Riley

Maggie and Max

Jessie and James

Anson and Abigail (coming soon)

Dandelion Meadows

Dandelion Meadows

Dandelion Meadows Christmas Kisses (part of *Six Kisses for Christmas*)

Larkspur Ranch (coming 2025)

Apple Lake Amish

Kate's Song

Rebecca's Rose

Miriam's Quilt

The Matchmakers of Huckleberry Hill

Huckleberry Hill

Huckleberry Summer

Huckleberry Christmas

Huckleberry Spring

Huckleberry Harvest

Huckleberry Hearts

Return to Huckleberry Hill
Courtship on Huckleberry Hill
Home on Huckleberry Hill
First Christmas on Huckleberry Hill
Second Chances on Huckleberry Hill
Happily Ever After on Huckleberry Hill

The Honeybee Sisters

Book 1: *Sweet as Honey*
Book 2: *A Bee In Her Bonnet*
Book 3: *Like a Bee to Honey*
The Honeybee Sisters Cookbook

-

The Petersheim Brothers

Book 1: *Andrew*
Book 2: *Abraham*
Book 3: *His Amish Sweetheart*

The Amish Quiltmaker

The Amish Quiltmaker's Unexpected Baby
The Amish Quiltmaker's Unruly In-law
The Amish Quiltmaker's Unconventional Niece
The Amish Quiltmaker's Unlikely Match
The Amish Quiltmaker's Uninvited Guest
The Amish Quiltmaker's Unattached Neighbor (2025)

Novellas

A Perfect Amish Christmas (A Huckleberry Hill Romance) in *An Amish Christmas Quilt*

The Christmas Bakery on Huckleberry Hill (A Huckleberry Hill Romance) in *The Amish Christmas Kitchen*

The Reluctant Groom (A Huckleberry Hill Romance) in *Amish Brides*

A Honeybee Christmas (A Honeybee Sisters Romance) in *The Amish Christmas Candle*

Sealed with a Kiss (A Huckleberry Hill Romance) in *The Amish Christmas Letters*

A Peanut Butter Christmas (A Petersheim Brothers Romance) in *Amish Christmas Miracles*

Huckleberry Hill Secret Santa (A Huckleberry Hill Romance) in *More Amish Christmas Miracles*

Ivy's New Beginning (An Amish Quiltmaker Romance) in *Amish Spring Romance*

Peanut Butter Christmas Cookies (A Petersheim Brothers Romance) in *Amish Christmas Cookie Tour*

Nonfiction

Big Ideas

To download a free ebook copy of *Dandelion Meadows Christmas Kisses*, visit JenniferBeckstrand.com.

If you loved *Kate's Song*, could you help spread the word about it? Reviews on **Amazon**, **Goodreads**, and **Bookbub** not only help us authors but help other readers find our books. And please, tell your friends if you liked my book. Word of mouth is invaluable!

SNEAK PEEK!

Turn the page for a sneak peek of
Jennifer's sweet contemporary romance series,

Available in ebook and paperback!

SNEAK PEEK!

Can he get rid of his unwelcome housemate before he falls in love with her?

The last thing Emma Dustin wants is to come crawling back to Dandelion Meadows with her tail between her legs, but a misunderstanding at her financial planning firm has left her without a job and without another option.

Uncle Harvey, may he rest in peace, left Emma his house, and there is nowhere else for her to go. Despite her humiliation at coming home unemployed, Emma is determined to fulfill Uncle Harvey's last wish, even though she isn't quite sure what it is. Is it possible for Emma to make a life in Dandelion Meadows? And will the mayor put her in charge of Sandpaper Awareness Week?

One-time cowboy and full-time geologist Matt Matthews is not the bad guy, even if Emma Dustin thinks he is. He's only trying to restore his father's money, the money that Emma's uncle Harvey cheated his father out of. Harvey must have had some remorse because he left Matt the house in his will, but Emma Dustin has the nerve to show up and claim the house is hers.

Well, possession is nine-tenths of the law, and Matt isn't about to move out. Unfortunately, neither is Emma. Emma is cute and irresistibly feisty, but she's in Matt's way, and he'll do whatever it takes to get her out of his house and away from Dandelion Meadows. Can he get rid of his unwelcome housemate before he falls in love with her?

DANDELION MEADOWS
CHAPTER 1

Emma squinted in the early morning light and for a second, couldn't remember where she was. She raised her head just enough to get a good look at her surroundings. They were pink.

She sighed and fell back onto her pillow, which sort of swallowed her head. No surprise since the pillow was upwards of forty years old. She'd used it as a teenager whenever she'd stayed here at Uncle Harvey and Aunt Gwen's house. This pillow probably consisted mostly of dust mites, but Aunt Gwen had never been able to bring herself to throw anything away.

Pulling the covers over her head, she breathed in the oddly comforting musty smell of old sheets. How long had it been since Uncle Harvey had washed them? It had been six years since Emma last stayed in this room. When Emma left, Uncle Harvey had no doubt laundered the sheets, put them back on the bed, and closed up the room. The sheets had likely been untouched on that bed for the better half of a decade.

Emma cringed. They definitely smelled like old people, but everything in this house smelled like old people, so it was only to be expected.

She sat up, shivered slightly, and pulled the covers around her chin. Only a crazy person would voluntarily come to Idaho in January when the wind was so cold it made your teeth freeze if you smiled too wide. But it couldn't be helped. Emma had nowhere else to go. Dandelion Meadows, Idaho was her second-to-last hope. Her last hope was moving in with her parents, but there was no way in a million years she was going to stay in a retirement community in Gilbert, Arizona, even if they did have free non-alcoholic beverages and Sit-and-Be-Fit classes every weekday.

Emma hugged her knees to her chin and gazed around her old room. It looked like it hadn't been touched since she'd last been here. The blush-pink chest of drawers was plastered with pictures of Zac Efron, Orlando Bloom, and the Jonas Brothers, stuck there for all eternity courtesy of Aunt Gwen and a bottle of Mod Podge. The High School Musical curtains matched the High School Musical quilt Aunt Gwen had helped Emma tie when she was thirteen years old. Emma had long since grown out of the décor, but it warmed her heart that Aunt Gwen had been willing to sew High School Musical curtains just to make her niece feel at home.

Emma couldn't stay in bed all day, but the thought of getting out from under her delectably warm—though smelly—covers gave her goose pimples.

Might as well bite the bullet. She'd have to get up sometime.

Emma threw off the covers and ran for her suitcase sitting on the floor against the wall. Shivering violently, she pulled out a ratty pair of sweatpants and an old fleece sweatshirt that her mom used to wear at curling matches. It was about three sizes too big but nice and warm, and Emma wasn't in a position to be picky. She pressed her lips together hopefully and opened the sliding closet door that doubled as a full-length mirror. She squealed in delight. Her old bunny slippers were still in their spot on the shoe rack. Hallelujah! Frostbite would not claim her toes today.

Emma made her High School Musical bed then went to the bathroom, brushed her teeth, and quickly fashioned her hair into a messy bun. There were about five thousand things she needed to do today, not the least of which was to call her parents and try to explain why she was in Dandelion Meadows. They weren't going to be happy. They'd want to catch the first plane out of Gilbert to Idaho. She'd have to put her foot down about any thought of rescuing their daughter. Emma was twenty-seven years old. If she couldn't solve her own problems, she didn't deserve that expensive MBA she'd just earned. Besides, Mom and Dad were frantically preparing for a curling bonspiel coming up next weekend. Emma wouldn't hear of their missing it just to come to Idaho.

Emma grabbed her phone from the nightstand and padded quickly down the stairs. She didn't get any service upstairs, but on the main floor, she had five bars. Go figure. Hopefully, this wasn't going to be a long-term stay, but if it was, she might have to move downstairs to the master bedroom for the sake of her phone.

As soon as she stepped off the last stair, her phone dinged. Seventeen times. Holy cow! She should have gotten up an hour ago. Who knew what updates from work she had missed? Maybe they wanted her to come back. Maybe they'd decided to fire her. Maybe the SEC, the FBI, and the FTC were all searching for her. *Emma Dustin, wanted fugitive, holes up in a run-down shack in Dandelion Meadows, Idaho.* It would make a great headline but a pretty boring read. The only organization that might be looking for Emma was the AARP, but only because they wanted to recruit her parents.

An exceptionally loud creak came from the family room,

and then it sounded like a door closing. This house creaked like an old man's knees and it was as drafty as a tent, but Emma had never known doors to spontaneously close themselves.

Suddenly, a tall man wearing flannel, denim, and a sinister baseball cap came around the corner with a tape measure and a notebook in his hand. He stopped short at the sight of her, and surprise popped all over his face. Emma's heart flipped over, and she lost the ability to breathe. Forgetting that the front door was right behind her and her cellphone was still glued to her hand, Emma lunged at the side table in the front hall and grabbed a handful of thimbles from Aunt Gwen's thimble collection. "Get out!" she yelled, screaming at the top of her lungs and launching thimbles in the robber's direction. "Get out of my house!"

If you can't run away, scare your attacker out of his wits. Make yourself big and loud and menacing. That's what her self-defense coach had taught her. Or maybe that was her Wilderness Ranger leader. She should have paid more attention during the bear lesson. Or maybe she should have gone to Wilderness Ranger meetings more than once in her whole life.

"Ow!" the intruder said, when one of Aunt Gwen's thimbles hit him squarely in the chest. "Stop that!" He dropped the tape measure and held his notebook in front of his face like a shield.

Emma threw all the thimbles she had. Most of them pinged off his notebook, but one of them hit the robber in the thigh, and another ricocheted off the brim of his hat. She'd always had a good aim. He took off his hat and quickly examined it. What kind of robber was that attached to the Denver Broncos?

When she ran out of ammunition, she snatched more thimbles from the table. Aunt Gwen had an extensive collection. "I said get out!" Emma launched another thimble.

The intruder raised his hat like a surrender flag, lowered his notebook, and took two steps back. "Hold on. I'm not going to hurt you."

It was a tactical error on his part. She wound up, threw hard, and beaned him in the head just above his hairline. He gasped in surprise as a trickle of blood crawled down his forehead.

"Emma!" he yelled. "Will you stop for a second?"

He knew her name?

Of course he did. In a town the size of Dandelion Meadows, everybody knew everybody. Even the robbers.

She was just about to let another thimble fly, when the robber grimaced and revealed a very attractive dimple on his cheek.

Oh, crap.

The robber *had* looked kind of familiar. Now that she got a good look, he was very familiar, even though she hadn't seen him for like ten years. Matt Matthews didn't seem like the kind of guy to choose a life of crime. She raised her fist menacingly, as if she was going to launch another thimble any second. "Matt Matthews, I don't know what you think you're doing here, but get out before I give you a matching scar on the other side of your head."

Matt's mouth fell open. "You gave me a scar?"

"I'm calling the police," Emma hissed.

"You could have put out my eye!"

Emma showed Matt the thimbles in her fist. "If you don't want to spend the night in jail, you'd better get out of my house."

Glaring at Emma, Matt set his wounded hat on the side table, pulled a handkerchief out of his pocket, and wiped the blood from his forehead. "It's my house, and *I'm* calling the police."

Emma was faster with her phone because Matt had to fish his out of his back pocket, but then she hesitated because she wasn't sure what number to call. If she dialed 911, would she get connected to a dispatcher in Dallas? Did Dandelion Meadows even have 911 service? If they didn't, she was toast, because she couldn't remember the number for the local sheriff's office.

She took a chance and dialed 911 while she clutched the remainder of the thimbles in her hand and scowled at Matt, just so he wouldn't get any ideas while she was on the phone.

"911. What is your emergency?"

"Are you in Dallas?" Emma said.

"I beg your pardon?"

"My phone has a Dallas area code. Did this call connect to someone in Dallas?"

"No, ma'am. Your call's location is connected to the nearest cell tower. What is your emergency?"

"Oh, that's good to know," Emma said. "I've always wondered how that 911 thing works. I'm glad I'm not talking to someone in Dallas."

Matt glanced up from his phone and smirked. Emma stood up straighter and smoothed a piece of hair from of her face. It had been a legitimate question, and she wasn't going to let Matt the Robber make her feel stupid about it.

"Ma'am, do you have an emergency?" How dare the dispatcher get testy? Weren't they supposed to be trained on how to be patient with distraught callers?

"Yes. Yes. I do have an emergency." She gave Matt a smirk of her own. He wouldn't be so cocky when the sheriff carted him off to jail. "A man broke into my house, and he won't leave."

"He's still there?"

"Yes. I told you, he won't leave. Will you have someone come and arrest him?"

Matt's scowl got deeper as he simultaneously listened to her conversation and talked quietly to someone on his phone. Maybe he'd skipped the police and dialed his attorney. Good. He was going to need one.

"Do you feel that you're in danger, ma'am?" the dispatcher said.

Emma narrowed her eyes and gave Matt the once-over. The blood oozing from his forehead made him look a little intimidating, but he didn't have that crazed look in his eye like those criminals on TV. In fact, his eyes were brown and broody, like a misunderstood hero in a Jane Austen novel. *And* he was wearing a blue flannel shirt. Nothing said "nice boring guy" like flannel.

"Ma'am?" The dispatcher really needed that patience training.

Emma took a step backward. "I'm not in danger, and I still have a whole handful of thimbles if I need them."

"What is your location?" Emma was sort of disappointed the dispatcher didn't want to know about the thimbles. She had successfully fended off an attack with Aunt Gwen's thimble collection. It would make a great story for a self-defense class.

Matt finished his phone call, put his phone back in his pocket, and folded his arms across his wide chest that ten yards of flannel couldn't hide. "Need some help?"

Emma tried for a glare harsh enough to peel the paint off Uncle Harvey's picket fence, but then she remembered that most of the paint had peeled off the fence already. What right did Matt Matthews have to be so smug? He was wearing flannel, for goodness sake.

"Ma'am? Can you hear me? What is the address?"

An address? "Umm. I'm not sure."

"Can you describe your surroundings? Do you know what city you're in? Do you see any street signs?"

Emma would have looked out the front window, but she didn't want to turn her back on Matt, and the only thing across the road from Uncle Harvey's house was Old Man Kyle's pasture. "I never really knew the address," she said. "All I had to do was tell my ride to drop me off at Harvey Dustin's place and everybody knew where it was. I sent his letters to a P.O. box."

"Ma'am, I want to help you, but I can't unless you help me."

"I know it's on the west side of Dandelion Meadows. It's Harvey Dustin's old house. There used to be a dirt road, but it's been paved sometime in the last six years, and it's blue."

"The road?"

"No, the house." This dispatcher definitely needed more training. Who ever heard of a blue road? "If you're at the Pioneer Hair Museum, you turn north on that main street then drive about three miles, turn left at the big red barn, and go for another two miles or so. You can't miss the blue house."

Matt cocked an eyebrow. "Would you like me to talk to her?"

Emma turned slightly away and pretended not to hear him. Some people just couldn't take the hint that this was a private conversation. She jumped when there was a loud knock on the door behind her. After giving Matt a dark look, she opened the door to a very welcome sight.

Sheriff Hobson stood on her porch with a much younger deputy in tow. The sheriff, who everybody called Hob, had to be at least seventy years old, and he smiled at Emma as if he'd come to pay a social call.

"Ma'am?" The dispatcher was getting testy again.

Emma couldn't be annoyed with the dispatcher. She'd gotten the police here a lot faster than Emma would have expected. "Thank you so much," Emma said into the phone. "That was really quick. Even with my bad directions."

"The police are there?"

"Yes," Emma said. "Thank you so much." She hung up the phone, swung the door wide open, and did her best to point at Matt with her hand full of thimbles. "Come in, sheriff, and arrest this man."

Sheriff Hob's smile got even wider. "Well, bless my soul. If it isn't Emma Dustin."

Emma wasn't really in the mood for pleasantries, but Hob had been one of Uncle Harvey's closest friends. She couldn't just brush off one of the people who had spoken at Uncle Harvey's funeral. "It's good to see you again, Hob."

"You're all grown up," Hob said, stepping into the house. He gave Emma a warm handshake, the two-handed kind that told people you really cared about them. "I'm really sorry about your uncle. He was my favorite fishing buddy."

"Thank you," Emma said. "I miss him terribly."

Hob caught sight of Matt and reached out to shake his hand too. Emma thought it was a little inappropriate to be shaking the hand of an intruder, but maybe Hob was trying to catch Matt off guard so he could cuff him. "Matt Matthews. Making any money on that mine yet?"

Matt grinned. "Enough to pay the bills." He glanced at Emma and back to Hob. "Thanks for coming."

Warmth traveled up Emma's face and clear to the roots of her hair. It wasn't her 911 call that had summoned the sheriff. It was Matt. Being the outlaw that he was, he probably had Hob's number memorized.

Oh, how she hated to be outmaneuvered by someone who wore flannel.